Most Delicious of Privileges

By

Thomas E. Lane

John Randolph, congressman from Roanoke, Virginia (1773-1833), was the first chairman of the House Ways and Means committee. Randolph was an opponent of the Federalists ... a dyspeptic man, sometimes insane, yet one of early America's most controversial spokesmen. Opposing the power of the Federal Government to establish a national bank, he was prescient in warning Congress against,

"That most delicious of privileges – spending other people's money."

In 1982 Congressman Fernand St. Germain, Democrat, Rhode Island, and Senator Jake Garn, Republican, Utah championed an Act of Congress deregulating Savings and Loan banks; granting S&L banks new freedoms in gathering and deploying money.

CHAPTER ONE

In Hyde Park, the assassin completed his prelude. He settled into the wooden bench painted slippery enamel olive; adopting a straight-back posture. His right palm stroked the transmitter cloaked in his coat pocket. On the grey asphalt path a mother braked the black pram she pushed and cooed to her unseen infant beneath the carriage's awning. Giggles bubbled from below a layer of blankets protecting against the chill of London in May.

Jonathan Blair dismissed the mother, his senses funneled into his art. His awareness did not journey beyond tangible reality. Like a quarterback in the Super Bowl he eliminated the distraction of the crowd. Bleating horns from English autos battled to escape Grosvenor Square's round-about. Horse manure that blended into the turf from nearby riders cantering on Rotten Row vanished from his smell. Late afternoon images dissolved into black and white scenes overlaid in bluish-brown hues. He squeezed the send button on the transmitter. That instant the northwest corner of the Hotel Europa's third floor erupted.

Thursday, May 23

"Two bottles of Perrier, two bottles of Coca Cola and," The starched linen jacket worn by the room service waiter at the Hotel Europa had fewer wrinkles than new stationery. He inventoried their expensive beverages, ". . . one especially nice bottle of Moet Chandon." Old manners were ingrained in the twenty-six year old Londoner. He backed away two steps from the Champaign buried neck-deep in chipped ice.

"May I open the beverages for you?" He asked.

"No. We'll handle that," Julie Weidener said.

"If you would sign for me, Madame?" Gold epaulets on the stiff shoulders of his white jacket matched the polished buttons. In the waiter's mind Elton John sang *Philadelphia Freedom*. Yanks were generous tippers. Upside-down he visually recorded the five pound tip.

"Thank you," Julie Weidener, a bank examiner for the Federal Deposit Insurance Corporation, said. She returned the bill to the discreet room-service waiter.

He smiled with a slight bow. His chiseled Mediterranean jaw accented by the Nehru collar on the fresh uniform.

"You are welcome, Madame. Have a good stay in London." Softly, the waiter shut the door as he departed suite 326. He checked his watch, less than an hour until quitting time. *Maybe I'll have a couple of pints at the Antelope tonight.* He mentally spent his tip.

Julie, on assignment in London, freed the champagne from its vault. She rubbed the back of her hand against the French Champagne's dewy green glass, "Let's wrap up our plan to storm the bank tomorrow morning," she said.

The FDIC woman's mood danced to an upbeat tempo. This was her first trip to Europe, an assignment scheduled sooner than she had expected. Two hours of sleep earlier in the afternoon erased jet lag from her seven-hour, cross-Atlantic flight. Thin, dark, stenciled brows meant to be professional, stressed eyes that twinkled. Julie jutted her butt leftward, rested her fist on the accented hip and spiked her right leg stiffly forward. She dropped her chin allowing her chestnut hair to free-fall around her cheeks.

Raising her emerald eyes, she feigned a proper English accent, "This Champagne merits our tribute before the chill flees."

C-4 boomed, peeling off the door-frame inside suite 326. Stunned, wobbling but on their feet, five dazed FDIC regulators searched, their sense of hearing ravaged. Blood leaked from shattered inner ears of the three men closest to the concealed bomb. Their hands slapped against their temples in futile defense. The blast smacked Julie as she posed off-balance. Her arms wheeled in a windmill motion, groping for escape. Her scream wasted amongst the deaf terror. Odor of burnt wood fouled the air during the immeasurable one-second interlude before the second detonation.

Between the solid, eight-floor Hotel Europa, a grimy stone hotel built in the Dickensian-era, and the bench where the assassin sat in Hyde Park, traffic spun around London's most conspicuous intersection, Grosvenor Square. The concrete walls of the Hotel Europa contained the first blast.

Waiting down the hall on the third floor of the Hotel Europa, the room service waiter's raised eyes gauged the floor-by-floor descent of the elevator when a trumpeting gust of displaced air slammed him face-first into the closed steel doors. His empty tray guillotined into his stomach, ramming air from his lungs. Manners deserted him.

"Bloody 'ell!" he rasped.

Two chimes announcing the elevator's third floor arrival went unnoticed.

The five people in suite 326, where the bombardment began, labored as bank examiners for the Federal Deposit Insurance Corporation. Four men and one woman; the woman's previous assignment was team leader on the examination of the Hamilton S&L in Dallas, Texas. Julie had directed the FDIC's controversial agency-crossover examination of the Hamilton; an experiment spawned by the US Treasury. Treasury asked the FDIC, the agency that regulates banks, to take an inside look at the Texas S&L.

This FDIC team had landed at Heathrow Airport that morning, unannounced, to examine the London branch of the third largest American bank. Their directive was to ensure that the Europe bank office employed the sound financial procedures prescribed by domestic U.S. banking statute.

Little European cars spit from the eighteenth-century round-about into Knightsbridge Street. Across the four-lane traffic from the Hotel Europa, inside the ten-foot gate on the southeast corner of Hyde Park, the death play at the Europa could be studied without risk of injury. The assassin sat on the wood-and-wrought-iron bench; a post usually occupied by unhurried visitors for people-watching.

Jonathan Blair sat motionless; he controlled the exact moment, his material was in place. He would critique the tragedy, inception to completion. Jonathan did not appraise death's consequences. Pain to those pinched in death's vise did not anguish him. Damage to property mattered not. Property could be replaced. That bystanders might die elicited no penitence within the assassin. Death releases pain. He harbored no compassion for his victims. He surrendered to the paroxysmal intensity of the assassinator; comparable to the primeval turmoil in one accelerating towards orgasm; physically hungering for release.

Inside the suite at the Hotel Europa, implanted in a hollow carved behind the soft-wood door frame, the pliable putty stretched twelve inches. An electrical detonator plugged into the soft compound. Control wires from the detonator ran down to the carpet. Molding obscured the wire. Halfway across the suite the thin detonation cable merged with three similar sets of wiring; each spliced inside a sham circuit junction box. That morning the false junction box had been painted the same chestnut color of the wall; a low-frequency radio receiver was housed within.

The assassin's radio command from Hyde Park authorized four blasts. Electricity bolted from the bogus junction box, blitzing toward four distinct bombs. A Time Delay Integrated Circuit, an electronic interrupting device, halted three electric commands.

The three TDIC chips interrupting the electricity were well-qualified. Their accuracy tolerance calibrated to a one one-thousandth of a second ... a millisecond. These Time Delay Integrated Circuits tested to *military spec reliability* – the chips worked the first time, every time. Uncle Sam pays a premium for *military spec* electronics.

Each TDIC chip, the size of a fingernail, snuggled against the plastic explosive it would arouse. Each chip would perpetrate one act; a short delay in the electric current. There would be no second act for the three TDIC chips. Each chip controlling the timing of the blast performed as a kamikaze.

Traffic lights are programmed the same way; simple and very precise.

Regaining her balance the FDIC woman twisted away from the initial explosion, her arms shaping a halo to shield her head. Numb she searched the foul, smoky hotel suite seeking escape. Instinct drove her towards the floor-to-ceiling bay window across the room. Half-conscious, she stumbled forward.

A pound of C-4, the second charge, compressed to the thickness of a full envelope lay buried under the leaf-green carpet. Julie accelerated to a gallop toward the window. Unknowingly she stepped over the second bomb. The TDIC chip impeding detonation of the second bomb had delayed the electric current for one second, it released the electricity.

The second boom exploded in a direct line between the hotel room door and bay window. Twice the amount of C-4 than the first bomb, the explosion shredded the thick green carpet five feet behind Julie.

Down the hallway, gasping for breath, the room service waiter spun himself against the still-closed elevator. His eyes scoured the hotel's corridor, demanding an explanation. A single strobe flamed out of suite 326, prophesying the second deafening roar. The elevator doors slowly parted. He spun as shock waves thumped him. The involuntarily wedged backwards into the elevator.

"Bloody, fucking 'ell!" he shouted.

The second blast detonated three paces behind Julie Weidener, the savage power thumped her on the back, kicking the oxygen out of her lungs. Her head cracked backwards, she surged forward. Julie heard her neck snap. She crossed the eight remaining feet to the bay window in less than one half second. As the window raced towards her, she tried to raise her hands; her arm muscles refused. Julie slammed into the dense glass at the pace of an Olympic sprinter.

From Hyde Park the assassin, Jonathan Blair, focused on the Hotel Europa's third floor. He scrutinized the high alcove, expecting one person to reach the bay window, but not knowing who. When the woman battered against the glass, every muscle below his waist clutched.

Pinned against the unyielding two-inch-thick plate glass of the bay window, Julie Weidener gulped, her face broken. Consciousness was slipping away.

Death lay concealed behind the FDIC woman, hidden in the middle drawer of the DuPont Winterthur desk. That morning the sofa had been re-arranged, the back of the sofa fronting the desk. Natural light flooded through the bay window, accenting the hand-crafted walnut surface of the desk.

If someone could have pried open the desk's single drawer, they may have been unnerved by two pounds of Eastern Europe's most feared

Most Delicious of Privileges 7

export; Semtex. This Czech explosive obliterated with twenty times the potency of C-4. Semtex, the preferred killing commodity of terrorists.

The third TDIC chip had blocked the electricity pulsating towards the desk drawer. The electricity, arrested for two seconds, was maliciously pardoned by the chip and released.

Her reflexive leg muscles trussed Julie's body upright, face mashed against the bay window. Behind her the drawer in the Winterthur desk ignited. The sofa, acting as a backboard, reflected power, power that tore the clothing off Julie's back. Skin on Julie's back melted, but she recognized no pain.

The room-service waiter thumped off the back wall inside the elevator, lost his balance and crash-landed on his butt. Scrambling to his knees, he crawled towards asylum behind the protected right forward corner of the elevator. Cowering in the small nook under the floor indicator panel, he stretched his arm upward and hammered the close-door symbol. Rushing air from the Semtex blast tore around the elevator door, slamming him against the side wall. Shock waves rattled the elevator's almost-closed doors. Confused, the deadman switch re-opened the doors.

"Bloody, goddam, fucking 'ell!"

Expanding gaseous heat tore into the concave glass window inside the hotel room. Plate glass, five feet from the Czech Semtex, could deny the energy for only an instant. Slicing shards of the window pane erupted outward. Ballistic glass slivers sprayed to the edge of Grosvenor Square. Julie, the FDIC bank examiner, rocketed outward from the third floor.

Outside the Hotel Europa two pounds of C-4, wrapped in tape, waited beneath the exterior concrete window ledge of the room. After a four second delay, electric current streaked in liberation from the last TDIC chip. C-4 exploded as Julie Weidener's descending body passed the Hotel Europa's second floor. The concluding blast called Grosvenor Square bystanders to attention. The FDIC woman crash-landed on the grounds of the hotel with a nauseating thud.

Every eye in Grosvenor Square locked on the dramatic finale at the Hotel Europa. The rush hour commuters stood hypnotized. Public execution draws a macabre audience

Reverberation from the final blast ricocheted off neo-Georgian concrete buildings enclosing the Grosvenor Square. Over long seconds the roar diminished. London witnesses reported one explosion.

Assassination is a calculated risk; the assassin's calculations had been correct. Jonathan Blair descended from his spell in a somatic block. Expunged, Jonathan drank in the park's air, his head bent towards his knees. His gaze fell to Hyde Park's lawn; he took in the lush green of the spring grass. Stench from decomposing horse manure along Rotten Row pinched his nostrils.

The terrified mother yanked the once-giggling baby from his pram. The assassin heard the mother cry, "It's all right, baby. It's all right."

Shielding the infant at her breast she patted the pale blue cotton blanket, her back shielding the child from the Hotel Europa.

As Jonathan's pulse retreated, sweat trickled off the ridge of his nose. He trailed the single falling droplet, sliced in two by an erect blade of fresh-cut grass. Mowed grass's sweet scent drifted into his senses. Murmurs rose from the pedestrian crowd. Julie Weidener's touch-down ended his commission. The Hotel Europa remained standing.

The taxi stand at Hyde Park Corner is London's busiest during the afternoon rush hour. The traffic jam in Grosvenor Square dammed the black, FOR-HIRE cars to a profitless standstill.

London's cabbies are trained observers. To obtain a taxi permit each applicant must pass the geography test on London. Eighteen months of riding a bicycle through the confusing city is the typical preparation. Known as *DOING THE DUTY*, only those able to memorize particulars win the right to pilot a black London cab. London streets change names block-by-block, the Thames serpentines, and the round-abouts spin traffic in six separate directions, observation is requisite to achieving a taxi permit.

Thirty-seven taxi drivers were locked at Hyde Park Corner for two hours. London police rarely interrogate such accurate observers. After talking to each cabbie, they had no leads.

The assassin slowly rebooted. Wind rustled the leaves. Jonathan Blair rose from the stone-hard bench without using the black, glossy arm rails. Spectators digesting this bizarre entertainment, created a multitudinous anonymity. He left Hyde Park unnoticed.

Tonight he would satisfy himself with the pleasures of Cecille.

CHAPTER TWO

"The testimony as I see it is basically that Charles Keating of Lincoln Savings used a federally insured S&L to operate a carefully planned looting and he had the umbrella of political protection to keep you at bay. Does that pretty well summarize it?"

> Rep Toby Roth; R-Wisconsin to a group of regulators and bank examiners
> at a House Banking Committee hearing
> October 31, 1989

Thursday, May 23, The Hamilton Savings and Loan, Dallas

In Texas, nicknames for Yankee immigrants come as part of the compensation package. Phil Kamerov had been hired by the Hamilton Savings and Loan two months earlier. Kamerov discouraged his Texas tag, "the Pill". His disavowal cemented the label on the Texas tongues of his peers. Slow talking Hamilton S&L staffers drawl the silly name into a two syllable *Pee-ul*.

Pee-ul Kamerov chaired the S&L's Workout Committee, the committee that tries to cure bad loans. Hamilton S&L didn't have a committee, only Pee-ul.

Phil Kamerov's job was to install structure into the Hamilton S&L's runaway lending; his unwanted moniker depicted his status amongst Hamilton lenders.

Most Delicious of Privileges

Creation of his one-man Workout committee had been recommended four months ago, after a scathing examination by Federal Home Loan Bank examination. Thirty-two percent of Hamilton's real estate loans had been classified; ranked as dogs. The Workout guy's job is to nurture these bad loans back to acceptable.

Two weeks ago the Federal Deposit Insurance Corporation, the national bank regulatory agency, a department of the US Treasury, arrived, unannounced, at the S&L to critique the Hamilton. Never before had Treasury stepped into the affairs of a Savings and Loan bank, S&L's fell under the jurisdiction of the Federal Home Bank – and their insurer the Federal Savings and Loan Insurance Corporation; the FSLIC, fondly referred to as FIZLICK in the industry.

The FDIC exam team, headed by Julie Weidener, spent five days interrogating the S&L people; then presented their summary to the Hamilton CEO and his Executive management. *The S&L's procedures, staff and assets were a calamity.* Their final report would be delivered to FDIC headquarters in Washington DC. The S&L was told to anticipate restrictions on their operations.

The Workout guy could not have been more isolated; as the Hamilton sheriff, tasked with bringing law and order to the loan malpractice at the Hamilton S&L, his nickname, Pee-ul, was inevitable.

A 50% pay raise prostituted the 38-year old away from a mundane job at a bank in North Oaks, Minnesota. Compared to this Dallas S&L, the Minnesota bank didn't have problems. Phil the Pill yearned for the Scandinavian simplicity of those Minnesotans.

Phil the Pill stretched his under-exercised upper body three-quarters of the way across the desk of the Hamilton Senior Vice President's cluttered desk. Sitting behind the desk, Randy Peterson's lower jaw hung, dragged down by the weight of his double chin.

"Your entire department is a fucking mess," the Pill said to Randy Peterson.

The Pill had walked into Peterson's office without an appointment. His eyes magnified behind thick lenses, Phil repeated, "A fucking mess."

Randy Peterson, Hamilton's SVP, tasked with creating earning assets and loans, thought this was a piss poor way for the new Workout guy to nurture a working relationship.

"Calm goddam down, what the hell did you discover this time, Pee-ul," Randy accented his Texas drawl to pronounce Phil's despised nickname.

CHAPTER THREE

Friday, May 24, Washington, D.C.

The CEO of the Hamilton S&L slammed the receiver down, "Sonofabitch."

Ken Thompson sat alone in his private office. He pressed backwards into the leather of his $700 executive chair. The CEO's left foot slid open the bottom right drawer of the mahogany desk; he elevated both feet onto the front wall of the extended drawer.

"Fuckin' regulators, " Thompson mumbled.

His desktop had been swept clean of less threatening issues. Federal regulators had no right to harass his Dallas S&L. Ken Thompson's caller identified who, at the US Treasury, was spearheading the persecution of his S&L, The Hamilton in Dallas.

The CEO of the Hamilton S&L blocked out other thoughts. *Distressed*, the term the regulators used to frame the Hamilton, according to his source. The last, late afternoon phone call consuming his thought. He eliminated alternatives one at a time. Ken Thompson needed to buy time to keep his empire, the Hamilton Group, from crumbling under the weight of the regulators assault on his Savings & Loan bank. He eliminated choices one-by-one, until a single solution emerged. Few could deliberate the action the Hamilton CEO weighed; fewer yet could authorize the execution. He dialed the telephone number from memory.

"Senator Anderson's office," the female voice said.

"Ken Thompson here for Senator Anderson," he said to the senator's secretary.

"I am sorry. Senator Anderson is on the floor, Mr. Thompson," said the long-time assistant to the senior Senator from Texas, "Can I help you?"

Her stiff response annoyed Hamilton's CEO.

"Peggy, tell Jimbo I need his ear right away. Priority number one. I'm in D.C." There was no need to reintroduce Peggy to the code the Senator would require to access Ken Thompson's private phone.

"Oh, Mr. Thompson. I didn't recognize your voice." Peggy's tone warmed. "I'll put the message in his hand when he walks through my door," Peggy promised.

Ken Thompson knew she would keep her promise. She was protecting her territory.

"Anything else?" she asked.

"No, just that." Then the S&L CEO remembered. "Peggy," Thompson called through the telephone before the secretary could replace the receiver, ". . . pencil in a departure time of 5:30 pm for the senator on our July 3 trip to Nassau. We're flyin' out of Washington National."

"Consider it in his appointment book, Mr. Thompson." Peggy loved the gift Thompson bestowed upon her each Christmas. Last year the envelope he dropped off on Christmas Eve announced that her second oldest daughter had received a scholarship at Princeton that would pay all expenses for her junior year. The Thompson Foundation endowed with purpose.

CHAPTER FOUR

The Savoy, London

Their private dinner at the Savoy Grill Room on London's Strand was well past its mid-point. Oak paneling, a century dark, framed the dining room. The Savoy's harpist interfered in the exchange of gossip. Cecille's left hand relaxed on his right arm, communicating. Jonathan Blair devoured her, as he might consume a tragedy. He assumed his infatuation was similar to the love people solicited from each other. Only Cecille freed him to climb to this sensual pinnacle.

"You're right," she said, verifying his last observation. I shouldn't let my emotions get in the way of my goals. From this moment on I will be more objective when my theater associates offer constructive criticism."

"Not too aloof, Cecille," he said. "And don't take my opinion too literally. Exposing your emotions may be your most appealing feature."

While his own synthetic emotions could be compartmentalized upon demand, he was intrigued that he could see inside Cecille so easily.

"In business affairs," the assassin continued, "sometimes it's necessary to keep your emotions below the surface. They interfere with objectivity. You must evaluate and control your inner self."

Jonathan Blair had first encountered Cecille in Munich, two years ago. The blue-hued basement club where Cecille danced would have been called a cabaret forty years ago in post-war Germany. Cecille was the fourth performer that evening, the headliner. She executed an athletic, high class strip tease, a dance that vindicated nudity while musically disrobing. After Cecille's first performance Jonathan invited her to join him at his table.

Jonathan Blair's avocation had brought him to Germany that evening. His assignment had been dispatched: an outspoken Bavarian politician who had railed against his party's mainstream. Germany's Christian Democrats battled for economic reconciliation with Soviet eastern bloc countries. That was the official line. However, loyal Christian Democrats listened, and were swayed, by the rebel Munich politician's blunt rhetoric. He shouted to ever-larger crowds that the money the aristocracy at the Wilhelmstrasse had earmarked for repentant Soviet satellite states would be better invested attempting re-unification of the two Germany's. While hurrahs from the German throngs raked-up, flickering black and white memories of the 1930's flashed-back. Christian Democrat leaders feared such Germanic patriotism would result in an economic backlash from the west. Earlier that night the troublesome Bavarian had been silenced. Manacled to his bed frame, the polemic Christian Democrat burned to death in his Munich apartment.

There was no spoken invitation when Cecille re-joined the assassin after her second act that night. She returned to his table with the comfort of an old lover. They discussed her desire to act in the London theater. Germany's seamy club scene was, she felt, a step towards her goal. Although most novice actresses treated the fading cabaret scene as an anachronism, Cecille viewed it as a rite of passage. He didn't leave Cecille's club until closing.

The next morning, as he'd promised, Jonathan arranged for her London apartment. His financial contacts in the City of London introduced Cecille to the shakers of SOHO theater. She would have to accomplish her stage credits on her own. But her living costs would be minimal.

Notes from the harp drifted in a melodic cloud through the Savoy's dining room. Cecille's laughter ascended just high enough to break through, giving the other diners an excuse to glance in her direction. She locked back into the assassin's gaze.

"You tuck your feelings away, then you uncover them selectively. You invest money. Have you ever invested in a feeling?" Her probe adopted parental tone, "Buy Disney World stock because kids laugh at Mickey Mouse."

"You mean let my feelings all hang out?" Jonathan wondered how deep one would have to bore to liberate his own dark emotions, "The answer is no."

"You're difficult to inspect, yet easy to anticipate. I want to see your feminine side. Even men have it; intuitive, irrational behavior."

"I must protect my macho image," the assassin deflected her appraisal.

"You are sensual, not passionate. Passion is a feminine emotion, " she said.

Their table seated four people; they sat on adjacent sides, occupying only half the table. Her intimacy challenged his defense. Cecille beguiled his stolid, internal ramparts. Their relationship had changed. In recent weeks her absence stung him. When separated from Cecille, discipline sometimes lapsed and his thoughts drifted back to her.

Dangerous, he perused. Dangerous, given his peculiar avocation. Deadly, if he did not arrest this unproductive sentiment. Together, tonight in London, this dinner, he knew, was as close to fulfillment as he could come; as close as he wanted to be.

"I want to learn to conceal my inner self and I want to explore yours," she mused. "Take me away for a month. Teach me."

"Your new play starts next week, or we'd leave tonight." He delegated the impossibility of the request to her.

"Too practical, Jonathan. Too practical and too masculine an answer." Silence.

Her face was a chronicle of the Caribbean. Cecille's jaw had been bequeathed by a Spanish ancestor, five generations past, who never knew he had conceived an illegitimate son in Hispaniola in 1831. Dark skin from her African progenitors had been bleached to a Mediterranean ebony hue by the European rogues who sired through Cecille's lineage. The continental profile of her nose was a genetic gift a Frenchman carnally deposited with Cecille's 16 year-old great grandmother in 1871, thirty meters outside a tavern on the island of Martinique. Great Grand-Mere Vauclain never regretted the night.

Her great, great grandfather, a Haitian storyteller, followed the black general Toussaint L'Ouverture to an honorable, but early, death. He gifted the magic of his eyes that now sparkled within Cecille.

The blend of Euro-African lines in her face sidetracked Savoy Grill diners from their own important conversation. The island lilt of her speech intrigued the eavesdropper. Her voodoo eyes consumed nonchalant daydreamers caught within her gaze. .

The pale Natalie Acatrini dress accented Cecille. Cecille's arms and neck were exposed. A narrow inch of flesh on each shoulder concealed by slim straps of the creamy gown. When she stood, the hem of this dress settled three inches above her knees. The neckline cleaved in a delta plunge, disclosing the knoll of each breast.

"You make me feel guilty," Cecille let her words drag across the table to Jonathan. "And to transfer my guilt, I want to scold you."

Cecille's touched the jeweled Jean Schlumberger Caribbean fish with the gold head and ruby body pinned above her left breast. Emerald fish scales sparkled from the pendant. A lone strand of plain ivory pearls sheathed her neck.

"Explain. I don't follow your thoughts," the assassin said.

"You sweep into London unannounced . . . then you disappear. You've discouraged my calls. No one has ever made me feel so, so sure, and I'm left feeling guilty. What did I do? You are not married; maybe not to another woman? But you are married to something, Jonathan," Cecille's question was spoken as an accusation.

"There are commitments," the assassin looked directly into her eyes.

Cecille's skin color verged on Hispanic, her cheeks the smooth, subtle ginger of an autumn leaf. Cecille's right hand released the shimmering gemstone Tiffany fish, her voice softened, "You've told me that. And this time you've only been away from London for two weeks. But, when you are gone, even for two weeks, you leave a void."

Cecille's Safari fragrance teased Jonathan's senses.

"Pazienza, as the Italians say, " he said. "Patience. Even if it is not me. You'll find your fulfillment. You have too much to fail."

"You are wrong if you think others will be my happiness. The men who ask me out are amusing, just boys. They are still learning to be men. I don't have the patience, the pazienza as you called it, for an apprentice."

The assassin let his eyes fall to Cecille's strappy sandals, the color of wet sand, a tone darker than her dress. "Perhaps you are too demanding."

"Perhaps, I am," She stopped then looked up, "You live in the present. I want your future."

"What do you want?" he asked.

"I need to be included in the play. Your play. I don't need to be the headliner. Just a part. I want to sense the audience. I want your attention."

She waited for his response; he didn't answer.

"Have you ever felt that way?" Cecille asked. Her lips were the deep oak tint of an aged single malt scotch, a Naomi Sims' shade that enhanced her dark skin. She pouted.

She tried to reach Jonathan's soul . . . and he couldn't tell her.

Squiring a three-tier dessert cart within two feet of their table, the waiter interrupted, "For after?"

Escoffier, once the preeminent chef of Savoy Grill Room, created his famous peach dish for the London actress Nellie Melba in 1892. Jonathan refused the desert attendant. Refusing the final course was their tradition.

At the coat check the matronly grey-haired attendant accepted the claim check and repaired within the depths of her six-by-eight-foot public closet to retrieve their coats. Without looking at the ticket the plodding woman returned, handing Jonathan his black Burberry trench.

The attendant stroked Cecille's coat. In a thick Yorkshire accent she asked, "That material is so fine, so sheer, darling. What is it?"

Cecille smiled at the older woman. "Microfiber, Sanyo uses it."

A full octave bounce in the coat lady's English lilt betrayed her enthusiasm for the fabric, "Ooh, I like it. So smooth, so light."

Cecille extended her arm to receive the supple Carol Cohen designed raincoat. Cartier sunglasses with rosewood frames created a halo atop Cecille's Asian-black hair. She excused herself for the privacy of the Ladies loo.

The assassin stood closer to the Ladies room exit than one might have expected. Cecille exited seven minutes later with her autumn colored wrap tied in front. Her ink-colored hair cascading over the raised coat collar. They walked through the Savoy's main lobby, exiting through double doors leading to the Victoria Embankment.

In the circular entrance the doorman was outfitted in a dove-gray coat with silver buttons, white gloves, a white silk ascot and a top hat reminiscent of the decapitator in an early James bond movie. His right hand beckoned to the black Morris cab in waiting; already creeping forward. The TAXI sign on the steel roof had been extinguished all evening. Before the cab halted, the Savoy valet caught the left rear door handle. Jonathan and Cecille walked into the cab's expansive rear seating cabin. The doorman's professional eyes trained twenty degrees to Jonathan's left, focusing on nothing . . . perfect to observe, better for disregarding. An expected ten pound Bank of England note relocated skillfully into his cloth palm.

She always looks different leaving the restaurant, the Savoy's coordinator of auto traffic thought to himself.

CHAPTER FIVE

"What do you mean the Enders' new Phoenix office building isn't a separate deal?" Pete Morris, VP of Real Estate Lending at the Hamilton S&L, contested his accuser, the bank examiner from the Dallas Federal Home Loan Bank. Morris, seated at the head of the table in the Hamilton conference room, scoured the other four men in the conference room, all S&L examiners, for reprieve. None offered forgiveness.

"Are you tellin' me the Phoenix deal," Pete Morris said, "should be lumped together with all the other Endres Brothers' loans we've done here in Dallas . . . like one big loan? That would put way over the Hamilton's legal lending limit!"

Pete Morris laughed, like sick people laugh at their own predicament; the other four men in the conference room didn't.

Turning away from Pete Morris, the young FHLB bank examiner exclaimed, "Do you believe this?" The rookie regulator stomped past his senior manager on the examination team. He ricocheted his focus from ceiling-to-floor.

Quiet throughout, the senior examiner rested his butt on the edge of the conference table. Senior Federal Home Loan Bank examiner, Bobby Scamehorn, had been quiet, content to listen and assess, so far. His concerns ran deeper than this specific violation of Federal Savings & Loan

Insurance Corporation regulations, serious though this was. *FIZLICK*, the insurer of S&L deposits, was in turmoil over recent exam summaries arriving from Texas.

Scamehorn stood and asked, "Is it your policy Pete, or the Hamilton's, that the entity Endres Phoenix, Inc., with no assets and owned 100% by Endres Development, was deemed a brand new, unrelated, borrowing customer? Unrelated to the $35,000,000 the Hamilton S&L has already, loaned to Endres Development's secured by Texas real estate?"

Managers at Hamilton S&L weren't purposely fraudulent; they were under-trained.

Pete Morris justified his approach to the examiners. Then maybe they would get off his goddam back. "It's just good business for the Hamilton S&L, and a nice deal for our customer. Phoenix is separate collateral. Hell, even the name of the Phoenix deal is different. And these guys are investment buddies of our CEO, Ken Thompson."

Pete Morris, Hamilton VP, let his unique interpretation of S&L regs sink in with the unappreciative regulators.

CHAPTER SIX

<u>Sunday afternoon, May, St. Croix, U.S.V.I.</u>

Brendan Donahue plunged, his feet waved skyward. Brendan's hands groped forward as he hit the sea. His breathing reflexively ceased, Brendan's lungs protested to his brain, breathing had to wait.

His eyesight blurred. Motion from below vaulted towards him, so quickly that it streaked his vision. Time, Brendan needed more time. He thrust his arm forward. The coarse shell scraped the flesh of his palm. His inner cardiac command to breathe sounded.

He boomeranged, rebounding twelve feet straight up.

He splashed through the surface of the Caribbean Sea. In a briny pose, he raised the shimmying lobster over his head. Brendan Donahue sucked for oxygen.

His audience on the forty-three foot sailing yacht was Melissa Wilson, his shipmate for the past week. At thirty-one, she was thirteen years his junior.

He spit his words, "Dinner." A rattle by the lobster implied it understood.

He called, "Menu complete, two lobsters captured."

Melissa swung the fish net over the port rail. He dunked the langouste, the Caribbean cousin to the lobster, in the mesh.

Brendan Donahue torpedoed into the shallow blue ocean, surfacing on his back. With a swish of his feet, he hovered in the buoyant, salty water. His pulse throttled back. His mind had almost blocked out financial day-dreaming for the last six months.

Melissa potted the langouste in a bucket of cold seawater and returned to the yacht's cockpit. Shaded by the Bimini awning, she watched Brendan body-rafting in the Caribbean Sea.

Deep breath had replenished his oxygen deficiency. Brendan Donahue, forty-four, launched a nautical glide towards the stern of his Beneteau sailboat. He hooked his elbows over the swim deck, hanging there almost a minute. With an uncomplicated roll he swung onto the platform, an easy six-inch hoist from the sea. His lower legs dangled in the eighty-four degree water. Without sighting the flight path, he flipped his mask and snorkel from the sea-level swim deck to Melissa in the cockpit. After eleven months of his self-prescribed West Indies sabbatical, Brendan Donahue had exorcised his addiction; the pursuit of money.

Tropical afternoons presented a limited choice; siesta or solitude. Brendan chose solitude.

Protected inside the reef, the current swung the Beneteau sailboat from the anchor line. The bow trained north. Brendan Donahue scoped Teague Bay, a mile to the south, as he rested on the stern swim platform.

His mind shifted into auto-pilot. Exiting salt seas when Caribbean conditions are ideal is a passage from embryonic comfort to perfect warmth. Evaporating sea cooled Brendan's skin while the Caribbean sun delivered deep-heat. Ascending from a twelve-foot free dive releases the same pressure as soaring 12,000 feet into the sky; a giddy trip.

The 86 degree ambient temperature felt cool as the breeze puffed to twelve knots. Angling at a four P.M. slope, the sun's threat had tapered.

"Four-o-clock, time for tea," Melissa said, she lowered a sweating green bottle of Heineken beer over the stern, "If I'm to prepare tonight's feast, the harbor soon beckons."

He had been in the islands for almost a year. His long-ago immersion in Wall Street, banks and the deal, seemed like another life. He had stopped referring to specific time of day during the third week of this West Indies passage. Ephemeral recollections of fourteen-hour days workdays occasionally bloomed in his thoughts.

"Time to hoist anchor," Brendan said. Lack of remaining daylight limited his Edenistic interlude. Christiansted's harbor lay an hour west. Navigating into the harbor through the coral was challenging in the afternoon, almost impossible after sunset.

Melissa hadn't been able to shed her watch in the six days she had been on board. Brendan had never observed a one-weeker in the islands who could abandon his need to measure the day by the waypoints of time.

"Are you coming up here, or shall I join you down there?" Melissa asked.

Her voice contained more than a trace of sensuality. Brendan's eyes rose first, then his head tilted backwards. Melissa stretched her body thirty degrees over the stern by tethering her left hand to the yacht's back stay. She had adopted seaside French dressing tradition: no top. Her skin had bronzed to a mulatto hue.

He handed Melissa the swim fins and climbed the aft steps into the yacht's cockpit.

Fifteen minutes passed as they stowed the remains from lunch, warmed the diesel engine, and rode the anchor. He motored the Beneteau through the western cut in the reef at three knots, leaving Buck Island astern, and pointing towards Christiansted's harbor.

Melissa raised Brendan's spirits to a level unmatched since his wife had died five years ago. For five years he wouldn't accept the void, wouldn't think about losing her. He tried to fill her absence with the duties of his profession. Sailing the Caribbean had been Brendan's retreat; Melissa was assisting in his resurrection.

"Dinner on board," Melissa said, "Afterwards we'll catch a taxi to the Buccaneer for steel drums?"

CHAPTER SEVEN

Sunday evening, May 26, London

Grey dominated the black in the cabby's thick hair, testifying to John Procter's fifty-one years. He had been their taxi driver in-waiting at every dinner Jonathan Blair shared with Cecille in London during the past two years. Proctor eased his black cab into the Savoy's turnaround. Cabby Procter was a self-educated, English historian specializing in London scandals since 1700. He could weave every major pub, bridge or hotel in central London inside slanderous intrigue. This fare disheartened him. Jonathan Blair insisted on silence . . . and privacy, so the cabby held his tongue.

He never violated Mr. Blair's rules; eyes on the road, take forty-five minutes to reach their destination. Cabby Procter silently scolded his apathetic passengers.

Why, I could bewitch them with a dozen scandals from this very hotel, he thought.

Jonathan supported Cecille with his left hand as she stepped into the spacious back portion of the cab. Leaning forward to the window on the driver's far left, he knocked. Proctor opened the glass without turning his head.

"Hampstead Heath, John. Forty-five minutes would be perfect," the assassin said.

The cabby mapped a forty-five-minute route to the parkland on London's northwest perimeter. He pressed the switch that raised the black privacy panel isolating the back half of his cab. Installing this option had cost him one-hundred-twenty quid. Or rather, it had cost his passenger that amount. Proctor motored his cab out the drive of the Savoy, circumnavigated the Charing Cross round-about, spinning out of the traffic in a northwest circuit that would skirt the lights of Piccadilly Circus.

Jonathan Blair slithered forward to the jump seat in the cab. As the cabby slowed for pedestrian traffic at Trafalgar Square, Cecille leaned forward. She cinched the assassin's belt, hard. When the buckle loosened, she slapped it free through the loops of his trousers.

"Dessert?" she asked.

Cecille shrugged the Sanyo microfiber coat from her shoulders; she had removed her clothing in the Savoy Grill's ladies' room. Flickering, low density, rays illuminated through the side windows capturing still frames of her breasts. Cecille reached forward. She pulled Jonathan's left foot to the edge of the leather; she untied his shoe, stripped his sock. Her hands guided the ball of his naked foot. She used the ball of his foot, in short circular rhythms.

Four waving fingers from her right hand solicited the assassin's right foot. He set it upon her knee. Cecille stripped his shoe and sock. Jonathan's right foot became another tool for Cecille. She matted the ball of his foot against her, increasing pressure with her hand, conveying her need.

She leaned toward Jonathan's jump seat. Cecille unzipped, then peeled Jonathan's trousers in a singular motion. Her hands rappelled upwards, unbinding each successive button of his shirt.

Cecille arched her body backwards, forcing the rear leather seat of the cab to contour to her upper back. Her legs elevated. She grooved her Achilles around Jonathan's taut waist. He executed a massage grip on the underside of her calves and began digging up the back of her leg. A smile emerged from Cecille as she employed her right index and middle fingers for pleasure. Jonathan compressed, then repaired her lower leg muscle.

His fingers then travelled across Cecille's knee, arriving on the topside of her thigh. She demanded deep ministration. Jonathan's five fingers dug into each of Cecille's thighs. He bowed toward her, working slow and deep, stimulating skin and nudging muscle.

Cecille self-massaged her craving in rhythm. Her eyes squeezed shut as Jonathan's hands orbited to the underside of her thigh. His digging fingers plowed deeper.

"Aahh," Cecille uttered with almost surprise as her fingers explored deeper. Her murmurs, soft and continued, disclosed that her rhythm kindled her own eroticism. Her sounds hardened Jonathan.

Cecille's knees rose in unison, allowing Jonathan to probe the rim of her sphincter. She challenged the leverage contributed by Jonathan's to pleasure herself.

Jonathan slanted closer to caress Cecille's buttocks. The back of the taxi was sweetened with a concupiscent scent. She fisted Jonathan's cock with her free left hand as she exploded. Cecille lay still for thirty seconds. Her skin cooled against the leather seat as her body heat diminished; she slid to the floor of the cab. On her knees she moved into him; her tongue snaked the tip of his cock. The assassin could control his own appetite for only seconds.

CHAPTER EIGHT

Summer 1980, the Carter Administration:

"That's all?" asked the Republican Senator from Texas.

Senator Alan Cranston, the Democrat from California, restated the concession to the other two men in the room. "That's all. The big five California S&L's withdraw their objection to the Fed's phasing out Reg Q interest rate ceiling. Let the S&L's pay whatever interest they want on new deposits."

Cranston's fellow congressman from Texas grinned as his head agitated in obliging wonderment. "This is a twist. The condition they request has never appeared in any of our draft bills."

The third member of the late night quorum, the Chairman of the House Banking Committee, summarized, "What your California Savings & Loans are asking for, to the best of my knowledge, has never even come up in staff briefings. If no one here opposes Senator Cranston's condition, I recommend we include it and take this bill to committee."

The Texas Senator's head wagged slightly in disbelief that negotiation had evolved into accord so harmoniously. He said, "You're probably right. The Fed will certainly endorse this."

Most Delicious of Privileges 31

The House Banking Chairman added, "Volker is adamant that interest rates float according to free market influence. That's what is needed to arrest this goddam inflation. And if Paul Volker underwrites this bill, it's a done deal."

Senator Cranston reiterated, "This is a major concession for the S&L's to endorse abolition of their interest rate advantage, they will give up the quarter point advantage they enjoy over commercial banks."

The Texas Senator said, "Carter is demanding deregulation before November. The White House is pissed off no bill emerged from last September's conference. This agreement will shoot through committee. Hell, it'll be law before election day."

The House Banking Committee Chairman rationalized, "This bridges the House and Senate bills. The proviso Senator Cranston presents on behalf of his Savings & Loans is clear. What do you say, Jim?"

Senator Jim Anderson, Republican, Texas, required confirmation of the concession one final time, "Alan, your S&L's agree to drop opposition to congress phasing-out their preferential interest rate, and in return the government will raise the limit on S&L deposit insurance from $40,000 to $100,000?"

"That is their only condition," Alan Cranston said. The California Senator rested his folded hands on the table in front of him.

The House Banking Chair extended his hands, palm up, toward his Texas colleague, indicating consensus was nigh. The Texas Senator felt to summarize again, "I don't see a problem. Hell, then everybody's equal. Plus deposit insurance pays for itself."

Twelve months of negotiation closed with a smile for the House Banking Chairman. These three politicians had no further need to patronize each other.

"Alan, you've done it," the Texas senator paused, "However, I don't understand their request to increase deposit insurance from $40,000 to $100,000?"

Senator Alan Cranston pushed away from the conference table while asking, "Don't understand what?"

"What will the S&L's do with the extra money?"

CHAPTER NINE

<u>Dawn, Dallas, Texas</u>

Janis Lang whistled *"NEVER ON SUNDAY"* to steady her nerves. She knots the paisley scarf, pinching her forehead. Janis flips the car visor down. Her dowdy face reflects from the small mirror, *it's too hot,* she thinks, *and this scarf makes no fashion statement in May.* If Janis Lang, head teller at the Hamilton S&L, doesn't steal the money by Friday, the state of Texas will beat her to it. Then the money is a goner.

Yesterday, after closing out her tellers in the Hamilton main office, Janis Lang sped to the Post Office; parking in the five minute zone. The Hamilton's head teller twirled the knobs on the rented Post Office box. Inside, three new cards, requested only last week. Janis Lang grabbed the cards and skipped to her car with two minutes to spare.

Janis loved her job as head teller at the Hamilton Savings & Loan Bank. She was forty-one years old; a spinster in the jargon of past generations. Nobody ever seemed to notice Janis. Once upon a time Janis would have given anything to be noticed. How long ago was that? Now that the money was here, she discovered plain is anonymous and anonymity could be beautiful. And at forty-one she would take the money, screw being noticed.

Janis double checks her face, in the visor mirror of her 1982 Bonneville. Her risk of being detected will be the moment she stands in front of the Hamilton camera recording withdrawals. She draws the leading edge of the scarf over her forehead, stuffs gauze up her nose, flaring her nostrils. Not another car in the lot. Time check; 6:45 A.M. Dark glasses are wedged onto her nose reflecting the slanted sun.

Let the cameras roll, she says to herself.

The Hamilton's head teller draws the three weapons from her purse and holsters each in the right-hand pocket of the man's trench coat she wears. She exits her car, skips the short distance to the door of the Hamilton S&L kiosk, enters, and stabs the plastic card into the motionless teller.

"Stick up," she whispers. The automated teller is mute. Automated tellers usually are.

Janis grabs the easy money the teller coughs up, withdraws the automated teller card, then jabs a second card into the automated teller; stealing another $200. She completes the third withdrawal as efficiently as the two previous acts.

Dormant accounts she thinks. *Money that doesn't belong to anybody.*

CHAPTER TEN

Brendan held the Beneteau on west heading, a half mile off shore. The pink concrete walls of the Buccaneer Hotel rose from a hilltop off the port side of the yacht. Bougainvillea cloaked the west entrance to the hotel's outdoor veranda. The Buccaneer hosted the hottest "jump up" on St. Croix.

Melissa broke the silence, "I should call my office and check in." She slipped a tee shirt over her mahogany breasts. She hesitated, "How did you turn off?"

"The sea's magic faculty," Brendan explained. "When you step on board and cast off the lines, the real world stays on the pier."

"I don't know," Melissa offered. "Usually my inner voice delivers guilt messages."

Brendan said, "It wasn't that I wanted more. I just wasn't sure if what I had was going to keep me interested."

Melissa looked through him, "I understand, I think," she said, "My life in New York fulfills all the hopes I harbored five years ago. How do I know if I require a personal tune-up?"

"Might not, he said, "Maybe you simply need to re-affirm your commitment to the same goals."

"You've made this trip, huh?" asked Melissa.

He took a deep breath. "Sorry, too philosophical. Yeah, I did. And it's too easy for me to push my own revelations onto an attentive ear."

"You've got me started on something," she said, "Maybe I can learn what my own inner voices are trying to say."

He had only been able to understand his own inner journey in recent months.

"You could live to regret that invitation, Brendan said, "Discussing my mental journey of the last year helps me clarify where I'm going. Let's discuss you."

"No, go on." She said. "I want to understand Brendan Donahue's philosophy. You've calmed since I saw you six months ago in St. Maarten."

"I had reached my targets, business goals," Brendan started, ". . . and I wasn't excited anymore. I was content with life, not excited. And I couldn't identify any new mountains to climb."

He continued, "My self-prescription was the wind pushing my boat through the tropics. Answers come easier behind the wheel in the Caribbean Sea than from the 45th floor of an office on Broad Street ."

"What did you discover?" she asked.

"Nothing until I let go. Just surrendered," he said.

"How did you know?"

"That inner voice emerged, suggesting I skip role call at the office. Initially, I thought it a childish impulse. It wasn't. It was an adult question. Part one of the reformation of Brendan Donahue."

"Go on, professor," Melissa requested.

"My mother used to tell me to develop a foundation of good habits," Brendan explained. "Then as an adult this voice appears *junk the habits you've come to rely on. They are a burden. Clear your mind. And when you're cleansed, we'll sit down and analyze the situation.* "

Melissa looked past Brendan's eyes, "Have you cleansed, are you ready to go back?"

He smiled.

The tailing wind played with her blond hair. She smiled. "It's a bitch to be successful, but not excited. I don't think I can dodge what's coming. Well, with lobster and white wine maybe you can assist me in probing my secret voices tonight?"

"Get ready to make the harbor, wench," Brendan said. "We're within thirty minutes. If the anchor duty isn't handled with precision, you'll be subject to a lashing below decks. This isn't a pleasure cruise."

She checked the anchor lines on the bow for readiness. Pressing the ball of her foot, she tested the windless on the foredeck. A low-pitched electric whir confirmed her back-up on anchor duty functioned properly. She stutter-stepped down the gangway, promenaded across the cockpit bench and nestled behind Brendan as he stood at the wheel. Melissa retrieved the #2 tanning oil from the port-side stowage cabinet. The Coconut butter scent of the tanning oil jumped free.

Melissa's own juices began to flow. She would wait. Someone had to guide the boat. Melissa's left hand poured the light oil into the cup of her right hand. The viscous liquid pooled in her palm.

"Close your eyes, Captain," she instructed.

Her hand slipped down the front of the lycra shorts Brendan wore.

He logged a heading that he could navigate with closed eyes. Brendan altered course ten degrees off-shore, favoring the open sea of the St. Thomas passage, assuring the yacht wouldn't end up on a reef. Entrance to the harbor lay three miles off. Under sail, the boat plowed through the water at six nautical miles each hour. His eyes shut, allowing his other four senses to record the pleasure of the moment.

Melissa angled her fist sideways and streamed the oil onto the tip of Brendan's erection. She touched the tip of his penis, delicately. She drained the last of the lubricant onto him and massaged, expanding the ointment's coverage by hand. By the time red buoy number two passed on the starboard side of the bow, Brendan was complete.

CHAPTER ELEVEN

Late evening, Sunday, May 26, London

John Proctor guided his black taxi past The Spaniards Inn, into Hampstead Heath; forty-seven minutes after he motored out of the Savoy's circular entrance. The taxi turned onto Winnington Road, a deserted secondary street. Several hundred feet from the nearest night lighting he braked to a stop on the vacant lane in an area designated NO PARKING.

Proctor didn't hear his cab's rear door unlatch. A slight bounce tipped him that they exited from the back seat. Proctor expected the quick rap on his window.

"John, signal us in thirty minutes," the assassin said.

"Will do, sir." The cabby extinguished the vehicle's lights.

Cecille and Jonathan walked up the cool heights, neither speaking; they veered from the smooth, worn footpath. Late evening dew moistened the moor's long grass.

They climbed the treeless hill, three hundred fifty feet above London town. From the four-hundred-foot height at the crest of the hill, central London twinkled to the south. The city's anonymous street lamps camouflaged the Savoy they had left an hour ago. London winked from the lights below.

"At the Savoy tonight," Cecille said, "you told me I would find my fulfillment. I need something very specific."

"Can I help?" the assassin asked.

She spoke with a stone voice. "I need information to correct . . . to avenge my past."

"I don't envision vengeance wearing well on you, Cecille," Jonathan said.

"There is an incident, from more than twenty years ago. For so many years, it has dominated me. I have never told anyone of this . . . this," her words tailed away.

"I don't judge you on your past," Jonathan interrupted.

She raised her right hand, signaling him to stop and let her finish. Cecille's eyes focused on the grass of the heath.

"You may yet judge me. Let me finish," she said.

They stopped walking.

The shadows within the Hampstead Heath parkland curtained them. Jonathan stepped in front of Cecille and turned to face her. He spoke without touching Cecille.

"If you wish for your secret to be kept, I keep secrets well," the assassin said.

Wind brushed Jonathan's eyes. The breeze carried Cecille's Safari perfume blended with taxi leather and sex.

Cecille said, "If I reveal myself to you, maybe you'll allow me to reach into you?"

"Tell me," he instructed.

"There is my sister," she said.

Jonathan observed that Cecille shed no tears.

"After midnight my mother pulled us from our bed," Cecille said, "jerked us from our sleep. The old car made it to the Pico Turquino harbor. In the back of our old Desoto my mother made us lie on the floor. She hid us by covering my sister and me with blankets. Mama loaded us on a filthy old fishing trawler. She cried while she hugged us; told us to stay in the stinking bunk room of the wooden boat until the captain said we had arrived. We cried and said no. Mama didn't explain, she left. I went to the bow of the boat and watched as Mama threw the line from the dock herself. *Vayanse, ninas,* she shouted. The boat left. Mama stood on the dock. I waved from the back of the boat as long as I could see her."

Jonathan said nothing.

Cecille continued, "It was 1964. Cuba. The captain, a nineteen-year-old boy was paid one hundred dollars to sail us to Jamaica. My father, I discovered later, had been betrayed by his brother."

Jonathan listened, without touching her.

Cecille resumed. "My uncle Ramon, a Generalista for Castro, had betrayed his own brother, my father, as a sympathizer to the United States. My father's crime was his belief in open government. Papa promoted change in Cuba. He didn't support Battista. Papa loved Cuba, yet opposed socialism. The military tolerated my father's opinions for four years after Castro overthrew Battista. By 1964 people like Papa were in danger. Your botched American invasion at Bahia de Cochinos antagonized Castro. Castro went mad to eliminate subversives. Two hours after my sister and I departed Cuba's shore, Castro's agents executed my parents. Mama and Papa were shot in the head. The government claimed no knowledge."

"I'm sorry." Jonathan could not touch her, he concentrated.

"Don't be sorry for me. I live. This hole in my life will never be filled. I don't grieve for myself. I grieve for my young parents who were betrayed."

He waited.

Cecille added, "And my sister."

They walked down the moor's slope, "Why do you grieve for your sister?"

Cecille looked away. "The porco capitano of that filthy boat raped me. Beat me when I refused him. Beat me until I couldn't defend myself. Two hundred miles to Jamaica, twenty hours. I was thirteen when I went to hell. As we approached Jamaica, off the harbor of Lucea, he threw me into the sea. He kept going in his fishing boat. I thought I would die, but I swam the five hundred meters to shore. Two hours later he sent my sister ashore in a fisherman's rowboat. My twelve-year-old sister. She died from his beating three days later in the Lucea hospital."

Jonathan registered each detail yet didn't speak.

Cecille thought of Jonathan's last comment.

"I need to know where my uncle Ramon lives, where he works, who his mistress is, where he dines, what time he gets out of bed. Every habit the man has. The bastard betrayed my family. This information, can you get it for me?"

Twin head-lamps flashed twice; cabby Proctor signaled that another thirty minutes had expired on his meter. As Cecille and Jonathan walked to the hired car the distance between their worlds lessened. He had always denied compassion within his life. Yet, during their final steps on Hampstead Heath he experienced constant, speechless connection with this woman.

Jonathan filed Cecille's request in his mind.

CHAPTER TWELVE

Monday, May 27, Dallas, The Hamilton S&L

Randy Peterson, the heavy-set Hamilton SVP sat, taking all-day flak from the examiners.

"We been discussin' Endres Brothers' loans for five hours, guys. It's 1:30." The Hamilton Senior Vice President checked his watch, "What say you let us buy you lunch?"

Peterson patted his belly for physical confirmation he was down a couple pounds since sun-up. The Hamilton S&L SVP of Real Estate loans directed his hospitality offer to the three Federal Home Loan Bank examiners grilling his VP, Pete Morris, "We've got a great little spot, Herman's Cellar, two blocks from here."

Pete Morris, Hamilton's loan officer on the Endres Brothers accounts that were under scrutiny, had been taking fifth-degree interrogation. Randy understood clearly that his anticipated promotion was in jeopardy. His belly sagged with every question Morris answered.

Bobby Scamehorn, head of the team examining the Hamilton Savings and Loan Bank for the Dallas FHLB, spoke, "OK, bring a copy of all loan commitments Hamilton has to the Endres Brothers' with you." Federal

Home Loan examiners had set up house inside the Hamilton. They could continue as well at the restaurant as they could inside the S&L.

"Sure thing." Morris scraped up three sheets of paper and hopped out the conference room door. He fled the Hamilton in less than thirty seconds, walking alone to the restaurant.

"Let's ride," Peterson suggested to the three examiners.

Peterson led the enemy out the revolving door into the one-hundred-two-degree heat of Dallas in early summer. His left hand gestured at his white Buick Park Avenue. The two junior FHLB examiners climbed into the rear seat.

"Pete seems jumpy. It's hard to get his focus," The senior examiner commented.

"Pete loves doing the deal," Randy said, "He'd like to be marketing new deals twenty-four hours a day."

"His documentation is a little loose," The examiner said.

Randy, still hoping a positive exam would result in his promotion, said, "I've worked with Pete on record-keeping, but you guys need to reinforce my efforts."

The two junior examiners in the back seat exchanged a quixotic eye-to-eye communique. Peterson pulled into the restaurant parking lot before the car's air conditioning could lower the temperature inside the car by ten degrees.

Bulky Randy Peterson was quickly spotted by the hostess as he entered the front door, despite tailing the three bank examiners.

"Pete's in the corner, Randy. I'll be with you in a jiff," she said.

Randy led the examiners expertly to the table occupied by Pete Morris.

"You got out of the bank fast." Randy complimented his subordinate. Pete Morris disguised the rum and coke he drank by omitting the lime.

"Yeah, the walk felt good," Pete Morris replied. "And you guys didn't need a fifth person heating the car."

Lunch came and went, they refused dessert. The senior examiner returned to his topic of the day, "Pete, I finally think we all understand FSLIC determination of one legal borrower. The Hamilton cannot lend more than $6 million to one customer. The Endres Brothers are one borrowing entity. Have you prepared the complete tally of the Hamilton's total commitments to the Endres Brothers we asked for yesterday?"

"I've got the totals. I wasn't one hundred percent clear on the personal loans, you know, the cars, boats those small things we do as a convenience for the brothers."

"Pete, every loan. Every dollar the Hamilton has loaned to the Endres, regardless of use, has to be included." The senior examiner was twenty-nine-years old and already worn-out by his career choice.

Pete Morris wanted to get his response right. The recent tone of examiners forewarned of personal disaster for his career.

"Before I give you a bottom, bottom line - am I to include the unused portion of their credit lines?"

"Absolutely, Pete." Senior examiner Bobby Scamehorn said. "All potential liability to the Endres Brothers on the table. I have to know if you've promised these guys a toaster."

"Well, I don't see how the unused part of a credit line is any different from an customer accommodation letter. But, here is . . ."

"What the FUCK is a customer accommodation letter?" Scamehorn's voice boomed louder syllable-by-syllable, suspending conversation at nearby tables

"Letters we write on behalf of new customers when they are lining up land to buy. We guarantee the money will be there to close the deal. Best marketing tool we have and we collect a 2% fee," Pete explained."

"I haven't seen any figures on ACCOMODATION letters," The examiner was spitting.

"Don't approve them til' the money is due," said Pete Morris.

Randy Peterson lost control and farted.

CHAPTER THIRTEEN

Sunday, May 26, Christiansted harbor, 6 P.M.

Brendan Donahue stroked his eight-foot dinghy through Christiansted's harbor. Late afternoon shadows rippled on the seaport waters.

Melissa had begged off his trip ashore to retrieve a Sunday *Miami Herald*, favoring a nap on the Beneteau. At anchor, inside St. Croix's protective reef, the cadence of the sea anesthetized her; she slept within seconds.

Brendan landed his one-piece plastic boat against the wharf's concrete steps at the foot of King Street. The shore-side embankment demanded a four foot jump. Gripping the painter, he guided the dinghy one hundred feet west along the pier . . . deserted, as always on a Sunday afternoon.

He cleated the dinghy outside the garden entrance to the King Christian Hotel.

"Ay, Ay, Brendan," Daryl hollered from behind the terrace bar. The barman stood thirty feet distant, inside the hotel's garden terrace, "How's my mon a dee sea?"

Most Delicious of Privileges 47

"Thirsty for news of the world and thirstier for a cold beer," Brendan replied, "There is a dinghy-watching assignment available, Daryl. High visibility, no pay, no benefits," Brendan pinched a final knot on the cleat.

"No problem, mon," accepted Daryl, "How long you be gone?"

"Ten minutes, max. Chill a greeny and reserve a bar stool for me," Brendan said.

Daryl buried the green Heineken beer bottle deep in the chipped ice, halfway up his forearm. Brendan disappeared up King Street.

Every Sunday, at 2 PM, the *Miami Herald* was supposed to arrive at Gustav's News Stand on Queen Street. Islanders needing a journalistic fix formed a loose interpretation of a line out Gustav's door, into Queen Street by 1:45 P.M. Some Sundays the paper missed the first flight of the day from Miami into St. Croix; the second and last flight of the day from Miami to this remote Virgin Island meant the Sunday paper arrived at 6 P.M.

For expat news junkies, the occasional four-hour delay of their paper induces inconsolable depression. Since the February Fiasco, as the eight-page daily St. Croix news rag christened the event, Sunday literary addicts don't return to their homes to await the incoming second flight. They stay in town, checking twice hourly on Sunday newspapers that are in transit. They pass the delay at Christiansted's downtown watering holes.

On the Sunday of the Fiasco, three months past, Gustav's pick-up boys didn't see the newspapers being off-loaded from the Eastern Airlines 727. Handlers dumped the papers in the corner of the Ries Warehouse at Alexander Hamilton Airport.

Gustav repeated the same instructions to the boys, his nephews by his sister, every Sunday. If the papers didn't arrive on the first flight, call him immediately. The Sunday newspaper crowd gets surly by 2:15 P.M.

The boys called Uncle Gustav at 1:50 P.M. telling him the Miami papers had missed the first flight.

The warehouseman at Ries noticed the newspapers hadn't been picked up at 2:20 P.M. He found Gustav's nephews at the airport bar at 2:30 P.M., sampling their best trash-talk on an eighteen-year-old Puerto Rican goddess with a body sculpted by Satan's own hand.

The old warehouseman said to the nephews, "Newspapers be ready, boys. Uncle Gustav not goin' be hoppy you late. Tey inside the warehouse now."

Gustav's young relatives sped that Sunday's Caribbean edition to Uncle's news stand. They never called Uncle Gustav to announce there had been a snafu. Gustav received delivery just before 3 PM; thirty minutes after the *Windward*, disembarked 290 passengers in Christiansted, a harbor that rarely hosted cruise ships, for a two-hour walk-about. Vacationers aboard the cruise ship had not read a newspaper in five days.

When newspaper-in-waiting locals returned for their pick-up, the terrible news struck with the suddenness of an island rain storm. The Sunday newspapers had arrived on the first flight. Tourists from the ship had bought every Miami *Herald*. The *Windward* had embarked; in the distance the ship's four sails cast a farewell salute.

This led Gustav to implement a policy he had resisted for thirty years; the Sunday *Miami Herald* could be reserved for five bucks. Gone was Gustav's first-come, first-serve policy; his guarantee of unbiased service. Gustav had no use for the abuse, or for his sister's sons.

Brendan stepped into the small shop on Queen street. Gustav handed him the Sunday Caribbean edition; priced at $1.00 in Miami. He folded the paper under his arm, gave Gustav $5.00.

"Next week again?" The newsstand proprietor confirmed.

"Sure, Gustav," Brendan said.

Brendan sauntered down Queen Street toward the solitude of the seaside bar at the King Christian Hotel. Twenty paces short of his intended garden bar on the wharf, Brendan froze.

The photo of the gaping hole in the third floor corner of the Europa Hotel dominated the front page. The headline read; *AMERICAN BANK EXAMINERS KILLED IN LONDON BLAST.*

Brendan Donahue commandeered the one public phone at the King Christian Hotel.

Jack Richardson, Managing Director of the Federal Deposit Insurance Corporation, lacked the energy to close his eyes. He had averaged only two hours of sleep each night for the past three days. His unlisted home telephone number on his nightstand began to ring. On the sixth ring he wedged the receiver between his pillow and his right ear.

"Hello," the FDIC man said.

"Jack, what the hell happened in London?" Brendan said.

"Brendan, I've had every agency in the western hemisphere looking for you. Where are you?"

"St. Croix," Brendan shouted through the overseas cable, "I just read about the London explosion in the paper."

"We've got a problem. The muck runs deep," Richardson slurred, "I need help on this one. Get to my DC office tomorrow?" The head of the FDIC's tone suggested that Brendan's Caribbean odyssey had ended.

CHAPTER FOURTEEN

Italy's phone system adopted the temperament of its people. Occasionally it went "in sciopero," on strike, without notice. Clicking connections sounded like track changes on the local run from Roma to Milano. The Hamilton CEO's call took two minutes to connect.

"Pronto," answered a faraway voice, "Stanley Investments."

"Your Managing Director please. Tell him Ken Thompson is calling from the United States."

The voice in Milano shifted to English, "Yes, sir."

The call from the Hamilton CEO was forwarded to the managing director of the Stanley Investments promptly. Ken Thompson's colleague from his college days at Southern Methodist had prospered. The Managing Director of Stanley Investments Italian office, Jonathan Blair, the assassin, was a charter West Texas investor with the Hamilton CEO. Their first deal, the Midland Westridge #3 oil well, had blossomed into a personal portfolio for Jonathan Blair valued at $7,000,000. Since the early 1980's the assassin had lived in Europe, marshalling the Wall Street investment firm through Common Market opportunities, where a business renaissance and relaxed taxation had developed into a hot growth market.

Most Delicious of Privileges   51

"Ken, are you calling to tell me about a dividend check you're sending," Jonathan Blair said, "or do I have to ante up for a new investment you've put together?"

"Neither, partner. When are you coming home for some barbecue and reintroduction to the American way of life?" Ken Thompson asked.

"Not for a while. Pasta Carbonara and Barbaresco wine agrees with me," the assassin said, "I may never touch barbecue again."

"Treasonous talk for a Dallas boy, Jonathan," offered the CEO. "I need your counsel on a current deal. Can you call me later?"

When the code word COUNSEL was spoken, informalities of the conversation concluded. Thompson's mention of CURRENT meant return contact would take place that evening, through the CEO's private line at his Georgetown townhouse.

The assassin noted the current time and recorded the scheduled hour for his return call in his mind: 10:15 PM in the United States Eastern Time Zone.

In his office in Milan, Italy, the managing director of Stanley Investments replaced the telephone receiver. Jonathan Blair had returned from London late this morning. He his outer limbs started to tingle. When his old partner, Ken Thompson, sought *counsel* on an investment, the coming action ignited anticipation.

"Signorina Carfante," the assassin said to his secretary, "There is a minor crisis. I must leave at once and will not return until tomorrow morning. Take all my calls."

"A domani matina. Ciao, Signor Blair." She bade him farewell.

* * *

"Mr. Johnstone's office," answered Becky Riley, the COO's secretary.

"Becky, get me my chief operating officer, pronto," barked Ken Thompson.

"Yes, Mr. Thompson." The Hamilton CEO paid his managers to solve operating problems. When a problem kept reappearing, Ken Thompson concluded that the manager had become the problem.

Becky pushed down on the hold button.

"The boss," she said to Billy Johnstone, the Hamilton COO, "And he's not calm," she understated.

Her finger released the S&L owner from hold status. Becky Riley passed her unwanted telephone receiver to Billy Johnstone.

"Johnstone," opened the Hamilton COO.

"God dammit, Billy, your job is to get these fed regulators through the front door of my bank and back out again, giddy-up fashion," The CEO told Billy Johnstone.

William Joseph Johnstone understood giddy-up. Billy's forefathers had arrived in East Texas, galloping lickety split out of the Louisiana swamps during the Sam Houston era. Lawmen from three states, pursuing retribution, chased the first Texas Johnstones. In 1837, Texas looked like an escape from their problems. If not, they would gallop on into Mexico.

It was an ignominious family whose fortunes wouldn't soon turn. Quite a few of Billy's great and great-great uncles had ended life as Texas tree ornaments dangling in the prairie breeze. Cattle rustlers, pillagers, and horse thieves.

CHAPTER FIFTEEN

<u>Monday afternoon, May 27, The Hamilton S&L, Dallas</u>

"What do you mean the loans disappeared since your last examination?" Pee-ul asked the S&L examiner. "Loans don't walk away!" He twisted the Federal Home Loan Bank Board examiner's last question.

"The loans are gone," the S&L examiner said, "Where did they go? You're the Workout guy."

"The loans are gone!" the Workout guy restated.

"And the files are gone, too," the examiner said. "Every loan in the South Dallas Loan group that we classified, every loan that was ninety days delinquent, is gone. Disappeared, Pee-ul." The examiner adopted the Pill's Texas name. "POOF! Seems unlikely that every shit loan was miraculously repaid since we were here four months ago."

Phil the Pill Kamerov was incredulous. "Every classified loan?"

"Every fuckin' bad loan in the South Dallas Group, Pee-ul," the examiner said. "You're the Workout guy, Where did they go?"

"I don't know. I'm the new guy." The Hamilton Workout guy bought a little time.

"Get back to me before noon, Pee-ul. I gotta write up a first draft of our review on Hamilton's South Dallas portfolio."

Phil Kamerov sketched an invisible circle with his right index finger. *Eighty-five million dollars in delinquent loans disappear off the books,* he thought. *That had to be initiated from the top.*

The Workout guy dialed.

"Mr. Johnstone's office," answered Becky Riley, secretary to the Hamilton COO.

"This is Phil Kamerov, Becky. I need to talk to Mr. Johnstone. It's important."

"Hold on a second," she said.

Billy Johnstone, Chief Operating Officer of the Hamilton Savings & Loan, responded ten seconds later. "Hi, Pee-ul, how you doin' satisfyin' those examiners?"

"I'm trying, Billy, but I keep getting surprises. The FHLB examiner looking at our South Dallas loans was just here. Seems $85 million of bad loans have vanished. He doesn't believe all eighty-five million dollars has been repaid. Where did they go?"

"We sold the South Dallas delinquent loans to Sunbelt Savings," Billy Johnstone replied.

"Did Hamilton get one hundred cents on the dollar?" The Hamilton Workout guy asked.

"Yep. Do the examiners need any more information?" the COO said.

"Aahhh. I don't know. Did the Hamilton get cash for the sale?" The Pill asked. *This is too easy. Sell bad loans for cash without being forced to eat* a discount.

"Sort of cash. It was a non-discounted deal." Billy Johnstone, Hamilton's Chief Operating Officer, said.

The Workout guy was skeptical, "They can't find the files, Billy!"

"All records were part of the sale," the COO said,

Phil asked, "Can Sunbelt put those loans back to us?"

"Informal understanding, Pee-ul. Nothing in writing," Billy Johnstone said, "Pee-ul, if the examiners get pushy for details on the South Dallas loans, defer their questions to me. I don't want you trippin' over old problems. Understood?"

The Workout guy said "If you have a buy-back agreement with Sunbelt, the deal should be accounted for as a potential liability . . . just like, just like," Phil could hardly say the words, ". . . just like those fucking Customer Accommodation Letters."

<u>The Hamilton S&L, Dallas</u>

Working at her desk, she glanced up. Randy Peterson, Senior Vice President, smiled at her from forty feet. Becky Riley rebounded the heavy-set SVP's blessing with a caster-oil grimace. Becky was secretary to the Hamilton S&L's COO, Billy Johnstone. Billy ran the S&L, the CEO, Ken Thompson, was rarely-seen.

Randy's grin-leer was etched.

Pompous piece of pork, Becky thought. Her boss, the COO, gave him his nickname; Randy-Randy.

Becky had overheard the Federal Home Loan Bank examiners verbal assessment of Randy, "Incompetent and looking for a shortcut to the next promotion." They hit Randy-Randy's nail on the head

Randy Peterson, in charge of the Hamilton S&L's lending, passed Becky's desk with the stride of an odds-on favorite in a stakes race. The stout SVP barged towards Billy Johnstone's office.

"He's expecting me, Beck," Randy said.

God, her tits look like an invitation, Peterson speculated, *if she wasn't an employee of the Hamilton . . . .*

Fat asshole, thought Becky.

Inside, Randy shut the door and unweighted into the chair facing Hamilton's COO.

"The fund we set up with money from the DFW land sale is almost tapped," Randy said. "I need more money, or our delinquent loan numbers are gonna jump."

"Gone. Already? $36,000,000 is gone?" The Hamilton S&L sold the property five months ago, creating a slush fund to pay the delinquent interest on behalf of struggling borrowers at the S&L.

"A lot of our customers are having trouble paying interest. Texas is getting a triple whammy, Billy. Bad enough that West Texas Intermediate has sunk to ten bucks a barrel, this drought is killin' the grain crop. Every rancher in Texas is slaughtering his beef." Randy Peterson, fat SVP, had justification enough. "We'll work through this, Billy, meantime, our customers got to ride through the downturn in Dallas real estate."

Only Randy Peterson and the COO controlled the slush fund. They referred to it as the *Interest Reserve*.

"Double-R, do our customers understand that the money we lend them to pay their delinquent interest is a temporary," Billy Johnstone paused, "… a temporary arrangement?"

Randy did not approve of the nickname his Chief Operating Officer of the Hamilton S&L had bestowed; Randy-Randy; shortened to the brand *Double-R*.

"They understand,' Randy said. "The money has got to be paid back within two years. And I told them they can only borrow money to pay past due interest. No new money."

"You're following the accountant's advice?" The Chief Operating guy said.

"Just like Arthur Young advised," Said the SVP for Real Estate Lending, "Don't collateralize the loan for interest with the same property securing the initial loan."

"Make sure, Randy," Billy said. "That the Feds don't discover our interest reserve fund, be difficult to explain how $36 mill appeared from nowhere."

"Examiners haven't asked me question one on the DFW property we sold. Besides the sixty acres you sold was legitimate," the SVP said.

The COO continued, "Yeah, except it cost five mil and I've promised that the Hamilton will re-purchase the property thirty months from now. No $36 million in the fund and the Hamilton is fucked."

Randy-Randy resettled his two-hundred-and-forty-three pounds around the chair's small berth, "Billy, our original loans are all backed by real good real estate. Some customers are just having tough times paying interest."

"Their problem, we sold the airport property for $41,000,000. Now I've got a $36,000,000 gain floating on the books in a fucking slush fund to cover delinquent interest. I get a little nervous, Randy."

"I'll take care of everything," the SVP said.

"The examiners discover facts on our DFW land sale before the buy-back," Billy said, "it's gonna lead them right to our interest reserve. We'll be front page news."

"No problem. I approve every loan; absolutely no collateral," Randy-Randy said, "Examiners can't link our advances to the original loans. New loan is a separate deal. Everybody wins, I just need a few more dollars to tide us over."

"How much?" the COO asked.

The SVP, Real Estate, lowered the amount, he could ask for more later, "Thirty million."

"Let me work on it." Billy dismissed Randy-Randy with a wave.

Tuesday evening, May 29, Dallas

Heather slid the key into the driver's side door lock of her white Mercedes convertible on her second attempt. She shouldn't have requested the second Chardonnay on the plane, but the wine relaxed her. A pop announced the unlocking of both doors. While the well-lit Dallas airport parking lot is a security triumph, Heather Montgomery, twenty-eight year old Vice President of the Hamilton S&L, entered her car with controlled haste. Heather didn't consider her boyish-cut brunette hair and athletic body an asset in the DFW airport lot.

Twenty-two months ago the Hamilton S&L extended their geographical market from a radius of twenty-five miles from Dallas to a radius of one thousand miles. The Endres brothers began construction of office complexes in Houston, Austin, Albuquerque and Phoenix.

Last week, Heather had agreed to traipse throughout cowboy loan-land as an in-house spy, her ticket out of her personal quagmire.

Back in Dallas after three days performing a special inspection, Heather navigated the roadway from memory. At the direction of the Hamilton S&L's Workout guy, she had investigated the four out-of-town real estate projects of the S&L's largest client, the Endres Brothers – investment partners of the Hamilton CEO. The Hamilton SVP of Real Estate, Randy Peterson, wasn't informed of her inspection.

Jesus, fat Randy will fry over this, Heather thought.

Before making the phone call, Heather escaped on a mental holiday; island sand bleached white, turquoise sea, eighty-six degrees. Heather inhaled the salt scent and rolled naked through the sand, alone, no man required.

Heather released the cellular car telephone. *One month. One month I will give him, then I am out of this place.* She placed the phone speaker-down on her lap, hit the recall code and tapped the SEND button transmitting her call to Washington DC.

I'm not going to be alone, not this time, she said to herself.

"Yes," the man answered.

"It's Heather. I just got back from the real estate inspection on the Hamilton CEO's investment buddies, " Heather waited.

"Go on," the man responsible for insuring money deposited in the banks of America said.

"Well, it's a mess, and probably illegal. Between leaving Dallas three days ago and arriving in Phoenix yesterday, the Hamilton loan to the Endres brothers increased by $8,000,000 to $32,000,000. No new money was deposited to the Endres accounts. The loan simply increased. I called Pete Morris, the Hamilton lender, for an explanation. He muttered something about deal flow. The $32,000,000 the S&L has advanced represents 85% of the cost to complete the four projects."

"Where did the $8 million go?"

"That was my riddle: Maybe they took it out the front door in cash," Heather said.

The FDIC man said, "Someone got the $8,000,000."

"The Endres got it. It took me an extra day, but I found the money. I had accounting run deposit histories. The money was deposited to the Endres account March 13, almost three months ago."

Confused, the man asked, "How are the books balanced?"

"Someone else has to figure it out. The four offices should be ninety-five percent complete based on the money already advanced; construction is thirty percent complete, maybe thirty percent."

"What do the contractor completion statements indicate?" asked the Managing Director of the Federal Deposit Insurance Corporation.

"There are no completion statements." Heather let him absorb the impact. "There is a third problem." Heather arrived at the carport at her Dallas apartment, she maneuvered the Mercedes into her reserved space.

"Leases are not as reported. The Endres confirmed to the S&L that the offices under construction are seventy-five percent leased. I was able to substantiate only eight percent of the space being leased . . . and those tenants are in jeopardy because the completion date is behind schedule."

"Did they lose the other tenants?" Jack Richardson, FDIC Managing Director asked.

Heather speculated, "My guess is the leases were falsified."

"Did the Hamilton client realize you were conducting an inspection?" he asked.

"In Austin, then Houston, I was alone. By the time I got to Phoenix, Leonard Endres was waiting, " Heather responded.

"How did he behave?" His question seemed an afterthought.

"Endres got rude, I felt threatened," she answered.

"The situation has become ugly," he said.

Heather had rehearsed her next words. "I'm not the right person. This isn't my bag." Her rehearsal began to break down. "Undercover in a Texas S&L, I want out."

"Heather, stay calm," the head of the FDIC instructed. "You can come out of this wealthy and acclaimed. Keep me posted. Report this to the Hamilton's Workout committee. If you are uncomfortable, I will arrange security for you.

Goodnight," He hung up.

Prick, she thought. Heather pushed the end button.

Heather hoisted her suitcase. Aroma of cut grass lingered. The lawn sprinkler misted at the far end of the apartment complex. She unlocked her mailbox.

Heather segregated the occupant-mail for deposit in the trash. The handwriting on the envelope from her friend in D.C. caught her eye. They had chatted in Dallas three weeks ago, analyzing the chance of women succeeding in the financial world. They found a confidante in each other. Heather had discussed her concerns with executive management at the Hamilton Savings & Loan.

Heather bent down, retrieving four days of the Dallas Morning News, delivered to her door step. Heather opened the envelope addressed in cursive. She read as she passed into the kitchen. Her left hand released the junk mail into the trash, followed by the four newspapers.

Dear Heather:

Thanks for your hospitality while I was in Dallas. Your concerns about the Hamilton are real. The situation has been reviewed here. I return to Dallas in three weeks.

I look forward to our next chat. The Hamilton Gentlemen's Club needs a business lesson. Probably won't see you for a while so you'll have to carry on the battle alone - at least in Dallas.

I'm senior examiner on the team for our next Europe examination. Don't know where I'm headed. The FDIC won't let us know where we're going until the morning of the day we depart. Don't want information leaking ahead of the exam. I'll write from there.

See you soon,

Julie

Heather smiled. Julie was having fun somewhere in Europe. Heather dropped the remaining mail on her kitchen table and re-tracked through the kitchen to retrieve her abandoned luggage. From the trash can the Sunday Dallas Morning News had settled face up.

AMERICAN BANK EXAMINERS KILLED IN LONDON BLAST.

The photo informed Heather before she reached for the four-day-old paper.

CHAPTER SIXTEEN

<u>Monday, May 27, St. Croix, U.S. Virgin Islands</u>

Alexander Hamilton Airport, one half mile inland from St. Croix' southeastern Atlantic shore, is sited on an uncommon, flat two-mile strip on the American Virgin Island. The seven thousand foot landing strip is the only Virgin Island airport with enough runway to land a jumbo jet.

The arrival of a jumbo jet in St. Croix is always a Cruzan happening. Tourists, supplemented by in-flight rum punches, file down the aircraft's rear roll-out steps into the terminal; reload on the tarmac thirty minutes later into commuter aircraft to be deposited in Tortola, Virgin Gorda, or St. John.

The pace at the airport is calypso slow. Travelers leaving the island have to cover one hundred yards from the taxi drop to the boarding area by way of the open air check-in counter. It consumes a full hour.

Brendan Donahue read his boarding pass; he would arrive at Washington National at 2:15 P.M. The American Airlines grounds crew prepped their Boeing 727 for turn-around to Miami.

Brendan's boat-mate Melissa was taking leave from St. Croix on the same flight as Brendan. Over the low jet din, she asked her departing sailor, "Is this your return to the real world?"

He angled his head with a barely noticeable tilt.

Melissa asked, "Why does Jack want you in Washington?"

"Probably because we trust each other. There certainly is enough talent in D.C."

"How did the FDIC find you?" she asked.

"I was a banker in Detroit, and I got bored making loans to tool and die shops. Same customers, same problems. The FDIC, the Federal Deposit Insurance Company made me an offer I couldn't refuse, the chance to become a bank examiner."

"Sounds dull," she said,

Brendan shrugged in front of his simple explanation. "They borrowed Uncle Sam's successful pitch; join the government, see the world. It worked."

"What did you see?"

"Midwest towns. Got bored again," he said.

Brendan reminisced; leaving FDIC to get his master's degree in business choked Brendan financially. His second tour of the University of Michigan had a fringe benefit; he met his wife. When Citibank made him the fantasy offer to enter their fast-track executive program, Brendan's career came to life. The money he didn't earn while in grad school was recouped in eighteen months, and with the dough came Citibank power.

A slim Puerto Rican woman dressed in the blue tropical uniform of American Airlines stepped to the front of the passengers, "We are now boarding, follow me as I escort you to the aircraft."

They climbed the aircraft's self-contained steps, entering from the rear of the Boeing 727. The jet engine whine justified the cessation of their conversation.

Banking left and climbing, the aircraft strained for a heading of ninety degrees north. Brendan stretched forward in his seat to look out the right porthole window. Twelve thousand feet below the light blue, dark blue, coral barrier a half a mile off the Atlantic side collared Christiansted's harbor. He hoped Daryl could tend his bar duties at the King Christian Hotel as well mind his yacht; abandoned in the harbor.

"When will you get back here?" Melissa read his thoughts.

"I don't know. I was just thinking that Daryl had an open-end, boat-sitting job."

Brendan's right hand slid under his left arm and clutched Melissa. He drew her closer. His Caribbean pilgrimage was over.

May, The Hamilton S&L

Randy Peterson trusted his boss would find a way to replenish the delinquent interest reserve fund. Christ, he had to, or Hamilton's fucking delinquent loans would be uncontrollable. Peterson pushed the elevator button for his fourth floor office. His mind calculated the shortfall that would remain even after his boss funded his thirty-million-dollar request. Billy Johnstone was the slickest problem solver Randy Peterson had ever seen.

The elevator clutched to a stop. Still alone, Randy Peterson inhaled his gut before publicly exiting from the parting doors.

Approaching his office, Randy's secretary's left palm waved high in the air in pretense of disguising the pointing motion created with her right index finger. She lipped the information to Randy: "EXAMINERS."

Randy performed a quick mental calming exercise prior to entering his office. His stomach involuntarily sagged.

"Hi," Randy said.

This glum examiner standing in Randy's office had never presented himself before now. Must be new. Peterson speculated if they were hired for glumness or was glum taught? He couldn't have been more than twenty-five years old.

Be cordial, Randy thought.

The blond-haired Federal Home Loan Bank agent rose from the visitor's chair facing Peterson's desk.

"Randy Peterson?" the Federal Home Loan Bank man asked.

"Yes, what do you guys need today?" Randy strode around his desk to the power position, remembering the instructions of Billy Johnstone: be polite and if the examiners ask a question you're not sure you want to answer, stall. The Treasury gestapo held his military mood.

"I just received a fax from the Bank Board in Washington. They would like to review the receipt for your watch." The Federal rep couldn't have been more blunt. "Do you have proof of purchase with you?"

Peterson turned his wrist to look at his Rolex. Each hour was represented by a diamond. The gold band suddenly weighed heavy on his left wrist.

"Washington wants the receipt?" Randy said. *Where in the fuck am I going to get a receipt for this thing?* he thought.

He thrust his left arm forward, "You want a receipt for this?"

"If that's the Rolex, yes, sir," the FHLB examiner said.

"I thought you were here to do a bank audit. You can't ask me for a receipt for personal possessions."

"I have been instructed by ORPOS - that's our Office of Regulatory Policy, Oversight and Supervision - to ask for the receipt. If you are unwilling to furnish written documentation of purchase, I'm to advise you that you are not required to provide the receipt. However, if our examination results in initiation of criminal inquiry by the Attorney General's office, the AG's office does have the power to compel discovery. If we exonerated you now, further questions on your watch would be unnecessary."

CHAPTER SEVENTEEN

<u>Detroit, Michigan, two years earlier</u>

As Heather Montgomery approached graduation at Northwestern with a Master's of Business from the Kellogg School of Business, recruiters identified her as a blue chip corporate prospect, a positive number on the Affirmative Action Reports and she was bright. Five-feet-six, brunette, blue eyed, Heather down-played her appeal.

She received offers from four New York banks, two California banks, four east coast investment houses, and three management consulting firms. The blue-blood financier recruiters promised her a VP slot after a fast track exposure to their financial subculture. Citibank, Chase Manhattan, Banker's Trust, and Manny Hanny all got in Heather's line. Chase's offer had the most sex appeal. Chase's Exec training in New York City followed by six months at their European headquarters; Woolgate House in the City of London.

Heather chose based on perceived love. She selected the National Bank of Detroit.

She traded Fifth Avenue for Woodward Avenue; Wall Street for Greek Town; Broadway for a play to be named later. Her fiancé-to-be, a budding accountant, was serving Ford Motor at the glass house, Ford's headquarters located in Dearborn. He expected to remain at Ford headquarters for two more years.

Heather met Jim just before starting Grad school; at an outdoor Beach Boys oldies concert in northern Michigan. Since then she and Jim had not been together for more than four consecutive days. Intrigue evolved into relationship, catalyzed by long distance phone calls and short sleep-overs. Heather took residency at Jim's Dearborn condominium five hours after driving off Northwestern's Evanston campus as a mint-new MBA graduate. Official announcement of engagement to loved ones and friends would come later.

Heather's commute from Jim's condo required fifty minutes to reach her desk at National Bank of Detroit in downtown Detroit. Ten minutes the opposite direction from Jim's condo, Detroit Metropolitan airport serviced southeast Michigan. By their sixth month of cohabitation the condo's number one benefit was proximity to Detroit Metro airport. Heather was assigned to NBD's west coast corporate accounts, travelling twice a week.

The fog should have warned him, aircraft are grounded when visibility is limited to ten feet. Maybe Jim hadn't looked out the window that morning.

Heather returned to their condo from Detroit Metro at 7 A.M. that Monday. She arrived home two days ahead of schedule, and only 90 minutes after having departed the condo that same morning.

Heather drove through the grey mist, parking outside their condo parking in dank silence. The fog's density, thicker than she had ever remembered, filtered the morning's sounds. The slam of her car door shutting was diluted to a whisper. The clatter of her footsteps soaked into the fog as she walked to her front door. Inside, she slipped her sweating shoes off.

During the past two months, career demands had slowed Heather and Jim's sexual life to a crawl. This morning's canceled flight provided an unanticipated four-hour vacation. During her drive back home from the airport Heather concocted a seduction to rejuvenate passion. Heather, anticipating her lover's surprise, stripped her blue linen suit off and laid it on the couch. She tip-toed towards their bedroom. At the door she froze, then back-stepped one half-stride. Her place in bed had been filled. This wasn't possible. Heather stretched her head around the bedroom door frame, exposing only her eyes.

She watched.

Her place in bed with Jim had been filled by her boss at NBD, Vice President Peter Quist. Heather squinted in a futile exercise to correct the picture.

Heather couldn't move her eyes away from the bedroom door. Her head wouldn't turn. Her eyes would not shut.

The boys didn't see Heather. They never stopped.

Peter Quist, kneeling upright, cued his partner, massaging the back of Jim's head. Quist thrust deeper. In the doorway to her own bedroom, Heather's gut started to spasm.

Heather's visceral choking must have sounded like a fire alarm going off. Removing his mouth from the object of his affections, Jim's head jerked up.

"Heather! My God! Heather."

Her once-to-be fiancé's features pinched, his facial muscles screwed down. He spat as he spidered off their bed and stood up.

Heather stared at Jim's sexual arousal. He was hard.

Jim's head twitched in short, staccato negatives. His arms shook of their own volition. He gathered his clothing from the floor with a single tense sweep and must have dressed as he walked through the living room. The opening suction and closing vacuum of the front door signaled his leaving the apartment.

Peter Quist could not gain control of himself, kneeling on her bed he tripped into sementic orgasm. Heather retched her disapproval. Quist's output flowed throughout his lover's exit . . . he lost all dignity. On his knees he made a mess of the bed. When his orgasmic flow played out, his eyes refused to acknowledge Heather. Scrambling to the side of her bed, Quist stood. His head shivering, his eyes cast down, never speaking, he passed close enough to Heather as he left that she could smell the musk watered down by sweat. Heather heard the front door of the condo slam.

Heather moved three steps towards her bed.

Short of the queen size bed, she crumbled to the floor in a pulpy collapse. Her back mashed against the corner of the mattress. Heather Montgomery cried tears of self-pity.

Her thoughts raced, going nowhere, "Bastards." There was no one to hear her.

Her lover and her boss. God, she didn't know anger could be so real.

"How could they?"

She looked at the bed. Her tears ran out.

Heather dragged through the next two days in her office, then informed NBD her doctor had diagnosed her as "emotionally exhausted" and instructed her to take a leave of three weeks.

She had endured two weeks of the hiatus at her parents' cottage on Crystal Lake in northwest Michigan. May is a remote month on northern lakes. She would not go back to Detroit, to that bank or to the queer bastard she had thought was marriage material. She called Chase Manhattan in New York City to see if their offer remained open after a year on the shelf.

"Chase Manhattan, Mr. McGinnis' office" The receptionist confirmed Heather's call had arrived at its intended destination.

"Mr. McGinnis, please. Tell him it's Heather Montgomery calling. He may remember me from Northwestern University last year." Heather reintroduced herself.

Heather held for fifteen seconds.

"Heather Montgomery! How are you? I'm pleased you're calling," said Chase's best recruiter. He searched his memory to recall the bank Heather had chosen over his Chase Manhattan. His internal computer retrieved the data. "Have you been appointed senior vice president at NBD yet?"

"Not yet, Tim, but things are going well. I've had the chance to work with a couple of your guys on the K-Mart euro-currency financing. They're not bad." *Damn,* she corrected herself, *don't use negatives Heather. Stop. Think. Be positive. We're negotiating in the corporate world.* Heather inhaled in two liters of fresh oxygen.

"How do our guys come off when they are in the Midwest?" McGinnis checked.

Heather recalled the pompous New Yorker financiers. Their obligatory small talk praised the modest room rates at Detroit's Ponchartrain Hotel.

Heather sacrificed truth. "They're good. The Chase bankers incorporated our people into the discussions. Didn't treat us like bumpkins. We ended with a deal the K-Mart finance people sold to the execs in Troy."

McGinnis received a call like this at least once a week. He led the discussion, "We wanted you for Chase Manhattan?"

Heather knew the game; her hand would have to be played first. Her verbal re-application had to be flattering to McGinnis and Chase.

"I am considering Chase now," she said. "You may remember that my decision to go to Detroit was influenced by my other half."

McGinnis confirmed. "I do. That's a recruiting battle I can never win."

"Well, the marriage isn't going to happen. And while I like NBD and the people, my first choice would have been Chase." She stopped.

"Hmm," mused McGinnis, "Heather I want you here." He personalized his pitch to the resurrected recruit. "The timing unfortunately isn't right. Both the International and Real Estate people have a freeze on all new hires for sixty days. "

Heather considered the bad news for a moment and tossed a bone, "If there is a temporary project that will get my foot in your door, I'll consider."

"I'll check around, give me your number." McGinnis kept their mutual future alive.

Shit, she thought as the phone was returned to its cradle. *Last fucking decision I ever make for love. Love me, follow me. I'll live by that motto.*

Tim McGinnis, Senior Vice President in charge of the Chase Manhattan Exec recruiting, recalled Heather. That young woman had potential. He always enjoyed having a lost prospect recant "I made a mistake."

Too bad the Chase had the sixty-day hold on new hires; *Heather is good material, smart, has been slam dunked.*

The Chase Senior Vice President dismissed the idea of a temporary assignment for Heather Montgomery. He dialed his old college roomie, the Managing Director of the Federal Deposit Insurance Corporation.

"Jack, you wanted to recruit one of our hot shots for an FDIC assignment?" The Chase SVP said.

"Tim, you told me you couldn't, outsource was the word you used, outsource Chase talent. Don't call me with one of your malcontents. I need someone qualified, very qualified," Jack Richardson, Managing Direct of the FDIC, said from his Washington, DC office.

"Jack," the Chase SVP said, "run your wish list of qualifications by me again."

The FDIC man spoke, "Real smart, not East Coast, versed and skilled in banking, willing to relocate, has an edge; someone who trusted too much."

The Chase SVP replied, "Here's your contact . . ."

* * *

"Your offer is attractive," Heather said, "The opportunity here appears outstanding."

"Is that an acceptance?" countered Randy-Randy Peterson. He wanted a hard yes before Heather left town.

"Leaving the Midwest, for Dallas is a major commitment for me. I'd like time to consider." The FDIC man in Washington DC had instructed Heather that her position at the Hamilton S&L had to run through the channels; first the Executive recruiter, next the interview with the S&L, then Heather's acceptance. The Texas S&L examiners, The Dallas Federal Home Loan Bank office, had recommended in their previous exam that the Hamilton S&L needed staff with demonstrated banking skills. In recent days the Texas examiners had barraged Randy Peterson with questions on recruiting progress.

Randy Peterson didn't want to interview one more potential recruit. How could he direct the commercial loan department of the Hamilton if he spent seventy-five percent of his fucking time on personnel? She seemed close to a yes.

Randy shoveled a fork-and-a-half of roast beef into his mouth and spoke while chewing, "Leaving our offer to you open is not in the Hamilton's best interest. We want you, Heather." He emphasized the *you*. The Hamilton SVP of Commercial Lending paused to compose his ensuing words.

"There is one personal issue back home I must conclude," Heather said. "When would you like my decision?"

Peterson decided to extend the standard three-day decision period to one week. "How does one week sound?"

"I will weigh the move to Dallas and the Hamilton S&L very carefully," Heather said, "It has to be the right move. Based on the considerations you've shown, I am beginning to feel very comfortable."

* * *

Heather rested both hands on her desk. From her desk on the third-floor of the National Bank of Detroit; she screened the four elevator doors depositing staffers beginning their day. Heather had an unobstructed line of sight; Peter Quist arrived at eight A.M.

Heather had advised NBD the previous day that her physician cleared her to return to work. She spent the rest of the day with her attorney.

Peter Quist stepped from the elevator; he saw Heather immediately. She stood and walked across the bank corridor.

Peter Quist had not yet formulated a plan to iron out this unfortunate matter. Heather wasn't due back for six more days

Bitch, he thought. Quist scanned his Rolex verifying that he hadn't squandered six days.

Heather smiled as she approached, "Hi, Pete."

Quist rasped, "Heather let's talk." Quist stepped around her, heading in the direction of his private office. He assumed, as her superior, she would walk in unison with him down the hallway.

Fifteen paces down the hall he stalked along alone. Quist retraced in a pout, "Let's go!" He commanded in a coarse whisper.

"Why," Heather asked just loud enough to reach those nearby, "Do you have something you want to say to me, Peter?"

"We have to talk . . .to discuss . . .I need to, to," Quist unconsciously stepped closer to Heather, "to iron out," He sluiced his words; chattering sottovoce, each phrase unrelated to the previous.

Heather etched a Mona Lisa smile, "I can't understand you. It sounds like you've got something in your mouth."

Quist groped, "Let's talk about an understanding."

Heather sneered, "We'll talk, you fucking bugger. We'll talk at 10:15 this morning in Hunter's office."

Charles T. Hunter, II, was the Chairman of the Board at National Bank of Detroit. Renowned throughout Detroit and the Midwest as a banker's banker, Hunter had served NBD as president, then chairman, for twenty-three years. His corporate and humanitarian interests included directorships of eighteen organizations. Charles T. Hunter, II, represented blue blood aristocracy in Detroit.

Charles T. Hunter, II, acted with authority, spoke with authority, and demanded decorum from his NBD staff. His world did not allow for sexual misconduct.

"We have an appointment. You, me, the head of Human Resources, and Mr. Hunter." Peter Quist didn't believe her. The brows over his brown eyes arched, and his lips shifted a couple of millimeters.

"Bull . . . " Quist started.

"Let me give you the agenda," Heather preempted. "Sexuality."

"Stick it, Heather. There is no meeting." Quist's effort at macho came off poorly. He required an unequivocal means to eliminate this bitch.

"Wrong, sperm dancer," Heather said, "There is a meeting, but you don't get the podium. Here's a copy of the memo I faxed to the Executive Vice President of Human Resources yesterday."

Heather handed Peter a stapled document. He stripped the bound letter size papers from her hand. The memo was addressed to Charles T. Hunter, II. Copies had been sent to three other people including himself.

"Oh, yeah, one other one thing," Heather continued, "My attorney is attending the meeting also. She knows how you spent the morning at my place three weeks ago. No one else knows other than you, me and your receptacle. You remember him. I used to live in his condo, share his bed?" Muscles in her diaphragm lurched.

Quist couldn't believe what he read. Heather's five page report detailed three attempts by Quist to coerce Heather into sex. Each unwanted sexual aggression by Quist had occurred when he had requested Heather to work late at NBD headquarters. Heather pin-pointed exact locations of Quist's contrived sexual maneuvers in NBD's Detroit corporate office.

Her memo outlined how, during the first two incidents, he insinuated promotion in return for Heather satisfying his physical desires. Graphic, alleged Quist quotations highlighted his second fabricated attempt. Heather's accusation portrayed Quist as a horny young capitalist.

The indicting crunch came with the third, and final, incident. It read;

Most Delicious of Privileges

Peter Quist scheduled a 7:00 A.M. meeting. When I arrived at his NBD office, he said we were to meet the head of Credit at 7:10 A.M. in the Credit Department in the inner conference room on National Bank of Detroit's sixth floor. When Mr. Quist and I arrived at the conference room, no one else was there. From behind me Peter Quist scooped his hand on my breasts. He threatened to ruin my career at NBD, if I continued to play games with him. He pinned me against the credit files, squeezing my neck. When I screamed, he punched me. I was in a trance, understanding , but unable to fight.. Quist was exposed and forcing himself in me. He ripped my skirt, ripped my underwear and he forced himself.

"This is horse shit. What kind of slut are you?" he asked.

"Heterosexual." She responded. "Make a choice. Keep your mouth shut at the meeting or stand up and announce to the Detroit business community the truth, that it wasn't me, it was my boyfriend you were humping. Detroit would love to have their own homosexual banker."

"You cunt. This is your word against mine," Quist said.

"Yes. And if you open your mouth to deny a word at the meeting, I'm leaving. First stop is the Wayne County prosecuting attorney to charge you with rape. Second stop is the Detroit *News*. The papers will love this story. My attorney says they'll keep my name out of the story to protect me. At the trial, when you're under oath we are going to question your sexual habits.

First witness, my former roommate," she said. "I bet we find more like him. I'm sure NBD's Chairman will personally oversee the paperwork for your next promotion, just to show that NBD supports you regardless of your sexual preference. See you at 10:15, stud."

As the meeting began Peter asked for a brief private conversation with Heather's attorney. In the corridor of the National Bank of Detroit he issued his warning.

"These charges are false," Quist said, "You have no evidence. I'll counter. You and your client, Ms. Montgomery, are going to lose. I am going to deny these charges and submit to a lie detector test to prove my innocence. Then I am going to take every dollar the two of you ever thought of having."

"Anything else?" asked Heather's attorney.

"Yes. I want you to walk back into that office, tell everyone present this is a tragic error. Apologize to me, offer to make restitution and confirm your mistake in writing to Mr. Hunter within twenty-four hours. Maybe, just maybe, I'll forget that I can own you." Quist turned and strode into the office where his NBD superiors waited.

Heather's attorney entered the room and presented to the Chairman and Human Resources director of NBD the details of the rape by NBD Vice President Peter Quist against Heather Montgomery. No one took notes. They agreed this conversation would be conducted in confidence. The attorney concluded that Heather's moral beliefs dictated she lodge formal charges against Mr. Quist, despite severe misgivings about potential reprisals by the OLD BOY network in the Detroit financial community, as Heather Montgomery attempted to pursue her banking career. However, Heather had respect for NBD and knew the resulting publicity of the rape charge would malign the institution.

"That's why we requested a private meeting, to sort out the implications of Heather's impending actions," the attorney said, "Would NBD care to review and respond prior to our formal complaint being filed with the city prosecutors?"

The bank's Chairman replied, "Yes."

Quist had been requested by the head of Human Resources to remain silent while Heather's attorney presented the accusation. Quist believing he would absolve himself, understood, this day was not a career highlight. After eleven years at NBD, he had worked into a position of trust. On his signature, he could approve $5,000,000. Peter Quist relocated his stare from the female attorney to Heather. The bitch would be sorry.

Quist exploded, "This is trash. I have never had sex with her." He pointed at Heather, then truthfully revealed, "I have no physical interest. This is a lie."

NBD's Human Resources exec asked, "Do you have any corroborating facts; confidants, photos of bruising."

Quist's mind had vaulted ahead to his rebuttal. Alarms clattered in his head. Heather's eyes returned to meet those of Peter Quist again and confirmed the unspoken disclosure.

"Any internal decision by the bank will require supportive evidence," NBD's Human Resources exec said, "Do you have proof of Ms. Montgomery's charge against Mr. Quist?"

"Yes, we do. Just after the rape, Heather was admitted to Henry Ford Hospital. She underwent full physical examinations. A sample of the semen was recovered, analyzed, and is being stored." Heather's attorney paused. "Are you familiar with DNA fingerprinting?"

"No," NBD's Human Resources exec said, "What is it?"

Heather's attorney explained for the NBD executives, "DNA is a genetic profile. It can be as singular as a signature and can establish identity with far more reliability than conventional blood-typing. In fact, unequivocal reliability."

"How does this involve Mr. Quist?" asked NBD's HR exec

"DNA can be extracted from traces of semen. You may have read about a murder-rape in England solved by DNA fingerprinting last year. The technique was developed by Dr. Alec Jeffreys."

"Can Henry Ford do this, this DNA test?"

"No. They can prepare the samples. There is a company in England, Cellmark Diagnostics that commercially does DNA fingerprinting. The Henry Ford people will verify Cellmark's analysis. Mr. Quist's blood sample can be compared to DNA in the semen; this will determine his absolute guilt or innocence. If the sperm sample is not his, he would be exonerated."

The NBD HR exec asked, "Would you agree, Mr. Quist?"

"Uh, what?" Quist said.

The Human Resource guy clarified, "Would you agree to a DNA genetic verification?"

"I am not sure. I mean I'm not sure what this means," Quist stuttered. "I . . .can we discuss this privately?"

Heather's attorney added, "The test will be requested and the results, of course, would be available to Mr. Quist and his counsel as a matter of discovery prior to the trial on rape charges."

Quist's head slumped. *The fucking bitch. She stole it . . . his sperm.* The date of the slanderous rape charge was the same morning Heather had returned from the airport to the condo. She retrieved his cum from her bed and took it to the goddam hospital. Would she have even put his semen inside herself to make this more realistic? *Jesus Christ Almighty!* The goddam bitch had his genes on ice down at Henry Ford. If he fought her story, his sexual preference would be front page news, and he was going to be convicted of rape.

Heather and her attorney excused themselves and left the executive office on the top floor of the square, chalk-white building.

* * *

Heather motored out of Detroit wealthier by thirty-five thousand dollars, courtesy of National Bank of Detroit's severance. Her attorney told Heather the settlement offer could be substantially enriched if she had patience. She didn't. Heather wanted out; quick. She headed southwest, towards Dallas; west on I-94 steering her almost-new 1985 white Mercedes 450SL, top down. The German machine added a little mystique to the girl.

CHAPTER EIGHTEEN

"I think we hit a home run."
Ronald Reagan, President, United States of America
October 1982, at the signing ceremony for the Garn-St.Germain Depository
Institutions Act; the Act that deregulated Savings & Loans Associations.

By 1987 losses at Texas S&Ls comprised more than one-half of all S&L losses nationwide; of the 20 largest losses, 14 were Texas S&L's. Texas economy was in recession: crude oil prices had fallen 50%, office vacancy soared over 30%, and real estate prices collapsed.
The Government Accounting Office in declaring FSLIC insolvent by $3.8 billion.

A new loan should require incubation before bursting forth as a disaster. Texas Savings and Loan Associations condensed the timeline.

The Federal Deposit Insurance Corporation grades risky loans using a *CLASSIFIED* ranking. Bad loans are assigned repayment probability. Texas S&L's in the 1980's nurtured a bumper crop of classified loans.

Capital must be reserved when a loan is classified. When capital is reserved, the lender's capacity to originate new loans is constrained; restricting profits.

In 1987, the Federal Deposit Insurance Corporation insured 97% of all banks in the United States.

The Federal Savings and Loan Insurance Corporation, *FIZLICK* as the agency was nicknamed, was the S&L industry's analog to the FDIC. Except the FSLIC, a/k/a *FIZLICK*, did not employ and did not control, the regulators examining Savings and Loan's. S&L examiners worked for regional Federal Home Loan Banks, governing organizations owned by the S&L's.

Until December 1985, S&L examiners didn't classify bad loans, did not critique management, did not recommend corrective action.

S&L examinations were random, no regular schedule mandated. After President Ronald Reagan signed the Garn-St.Germain deregulation Act, S&L's were required to file a self-generated critique to the Federal Home Loan Bank on how things were going. This partisan report was due every month, until 1984.

In 1984 David Stockman, Director of the Office of Management and Budget, asked S&L's to stop sending the monthly reports to the Federal Home Loan Bank.

Too much paperwork. Quarterly would be fine.

Washington, D.C., National Airport

Automatic doors parted. Brendan Donahue egressed the aging airport built along the south shore of the dirty Potomac River into eighty four degree Virginia heat. Traffic congestion in the roundabout departing Washington National Airport suggested Congress was in session. A solitary dispatcher on the sidewalk under the TAXI sign whistled; at his screech another cab approached. On the curb, he cajoled the throng to form a line as he assigned the colorful taxis. Brendan stood ninth, four minutes later the dispatcher processed him into a yellow Checker cab destined for Washington, D.C.

The fifty-ish black driver swiveled on a wooden bead seat mat. "Where to today?" He threw the metal flag to the right.

"FDIC headquarters. You know where that is?" Brendan asked.

"Uh, yeah. Midtown, right?" Overweight cheeks wrinkled, betraying his unfamiliarity with the unsung government agency.

"550 Seventeenth Street," Brendan said.

The cabby's face smoothed. Brendan caught the reflection in the rear view mirror. The taxi driver squeezed between a rented Ciera and a Toyota Camry driven by a squat, silver-haired woman who had drifted a little right. The cabby created a third lane in a roadway marked for two lanes. The old lady scowled; the cabby answered with a Louis Armstrong smile.

"Got ya, chief. Fifteen minutes," the cabby said.

Brendan stopped second guessing the gist of his impending meeting with Jack Richardson, his old comrade, now Chairman of the FDIC. He absorbed the Washington monuments as the cab crossed 14th street Bridge.

The cabby deposited Brendan at 550. Exhaust clouded the warm, humid river town air.

Brendan Donahue climbed four quick concrete steps. In the cool lobby of the Federal Deposit Insurance Corporation he approached the security man in the blue uniform for directions. Two ancient elevators were around a granite corner, fifty feet from the security guard; Brendan tapped the button for the sixth floor.

Richardson's outer office was comfortable for having been constructed back in 1951. Jack, hearing his secretary welcome Brendan, stepped from his office.

"Brendan Donahue, you are a welcome sight." Richardson ignored a conventional handshake, instead wrapping his longtime friend in a bear hug. Richardson's fifty-six-year-old secretary had never seen her boss act in such a familiar manner.

Brendan jibed, "And Richardson, you're keeping in shape." Brendan's index finger poked Jack Richardson's thirty-seven-inch waist.

Jack pried ten minutes of condensed tales from Brendan's year of wandering the Caribbean leewards. Richardson exchanged details of his divorce, status of his daughter, and health problems that forced his mother into assisted living.

Their recent histories were up-to-date twenty minutes later. Jack Richardson rose from his government-issue desk, walked to his door and instructed his secretary, "No calls for the next hour." He shut the door, isolating the two men.

"Brendan, have you been keeping up on the mess in our Savings and Loan industry?" asked the head of the Federal Deposit Insurance Corporation.

"Not really," Brendan said. "News in the islands arrives in summary form. In the U.S. Virgins the *Miami Herald* provides a bit more depth. S&L problems are page six blurbs with more innuendo than fact."

"That's because the facts would strangle the S&L industry. Congress gave the S&L's the power to harvest money when they enacted Garn-St. Germain Bill in 1982. Now, the worst of the bunch have become the twentieth century version of the James gang."

"What's the problem?" Brendan asked.

"Real Estate developers have been buying S&L banks. The new owners are lending the bank's money to themselves and their buddies; money deposited because WE THE PEOPLE insure the deposits. So much money has already been siphoned off that the *FIZLICK* can't pay off insured depositors. *FIZLICK* has concluded their only option is stall, and hope future earnings will rebuild the bank's capital."

"Will it work?"

The Chairman of the FDIC exhaled stale air, "Not a chance in hell. In 1984 Stockman's Office of Budget Management mandated reducing the number of FSLIC examiners. Then Ed Gray, the Fed Bank Board chairman, assigned S&L examiners to the district Fed Home Loan Banks."

Brendan said, "Unless things have changed while I have been sailing, the boards of the regional Fed Home Loan banks control the S&L's in each district."

"Still the same, my boy," said the FDIC head.

"So the S&L examiners work for the owners of the S&L banks they examine?"

"Exactly," Richardson said. "and the twelve Fed Home Loan districts have eighty-nine billion dollars, that's billion, in long-term bonds outstanding. Loans collateralized by real estate loans issued by the member S&L's."

Richardson stopped pacing in front of the easel supporting fresh white chart paper, he continued, "So, they don't want to squeeze member banks too hard or they'll launch a bank run on themselves."

"I'm on sabbatical, remember?" Brendan said.

Richardson ceased sociable chit-chat. "Brendan," he said. "I need help. I need someone from outside the S&L industry, untainted by the sins of the recent past and unprejudiced by complicity in the decisions since 1982."

Jack Richardson rose and walked around his desk. He used the front edge of the desk as a lean-to. "You're booked at the Mayfair. We have dinner reservations at the Tabard Inn at eight."

Richardson dropped a stack of papers clipped together on Brendan's lap; the top page read CONFIDENTIAL, *Secretary of the Treasury, United States of America*.

"Sabbatical over. Time to abandon ship, Brendan, rejoin the real world. Here's the condensed version. Brace yourself, Bridget."

CHAPTER NINETEEN

Phil the Pill, Chair of the Workout Committee, received the kind of welcome a leper might expect in a massage parlor. Phil couldn't recall anyone in lending initiating a conversation with him during the past month.

"I'm just pointing, not judging," the accounting clerk said. The in-house accounting clerk didn't even have a title, the cheapest of garnishes. "Here's the ledger on all non-loan assets. It would be real tough to find."

Phil the Pill eyes crawled over his bifocal's rims, "Real tough to find what?"

The clerk said, "The money those elitists at Arthur Young, our overpaid accountants, try to bury."

Phil Kamerov said, "Well, I'm not outside, think of me as your personal safety valve."

"Mr. Kamerov . . . may I call you Phil?"

"May as well call me Pee-ul. Everybody else does." He was about to locate the hemorrhage

* * *

"Whatta ya mean we are going to a special meeting of the fucking Workout Committee?"

A second consecutive day trapped inside the S&L had the appeal of the flu to Pete Morris. He needed to get out on the street . . . with his customers. Morris couldn't add loans to his portfolio sitting through useless Bad Loan Meeting.

Pete Morris said, "Bad enough, Randy, you lasso me into Loan Meetings every Wednesday. And now, Pee-ul's fucking Workout Committee is going to meet? How does a Workout committee generate profit?"

Randy Peterson huffed down the corridor with his VP in step.

"Pee-ul called the goddam meeting. I assume, since you're invited, one of your deals is a few documents short of fucking perfect."

"Double-R, tell Pee-ul to fuck off," Morris said.

"I would, but Billy Johnstone says Pee-ul gets all Hamilton information so that we, " Peterson's chubby hands were propelling out of sync, "that's you and me, don't have to screw with the examiners."

"So," said Morris.

Randy justified to his subordinate, "So, Pete, we report. We play. But, Pee-ul better have a reason or I'm going to be in Johnstone's office in fifteen minutes,"

"Hah!" Pete Morris tossed his head, ceiling-ward. "So we march off to a bullshit Workout meeting. No loan, no files, because we don't know if there's a problem yet?" Pete's voice diminished to a mumble as the two men approached The Pill's office.

Morris concluded. "Fucking waste of time."

Peterson, as head of the Hamilton loan department, stereotypically preceded his underling into the office.

"Have a seat," offered Pee-ul Kamerov.

The two Hamilton lenders dumbly inspected each other, then examined the room for participants, as Phil commenced his Workout committee meeting.

The Pill handed each of his visitors a single sheet of paper with one customer name typed in the center of the page.

"The following documents are in default on item one," The Pill raised his eyes above the bifocals riding down his nose.

Morris stared down at the single name and thought, *No agenda. What's the deal?*

Morris said, "Pee-ul, are you going to buy us a cup of coffee or are you totally wasting our time?"

Phil Kamerov answered as calm as cold soup. "No, Pete, no coffee. This is a special Workout Committee meeting. Item one is review of the documentation missing on the Plano Mall loan."

Randy-Randy stepped in, "Plano Mall? Pee-ul you've got your responsibilities scrambled. Our Loan Committee, and Pee-ul, let me remind you that you are not a voting member of the Loan Committee, will be considering Plano Mall within the coming month. Pete here will bring that proposed deal into the Loan Committee for approval when his analysis is completed. Until, and unless, we actually have a loan, I don't want and I'm not gonna tolerate your interference."

Phil Kamerov held Randy's glare for two full seconds, then redirected his focus downward to his limited agenda and resumed. "The Plano Mall loan distresses me." The Pill continued as though Randy had not spoken.

Randy sprang from his chair. "Pee-ul, let me make myself clear," Randy's voice rose with each word. "FUCK OFF, WE HAVEN'T EVEN MADE THE LOAN."

The Pill looked up from his notes at the quiet VP. "Pete, do you have all the promissory notes, guarantees and security agreements signed on the Plano Mall loan?"

Randy Peterson's two-hundred-forty-three pounds surged out of his chair. Standing, he shouted. "Fuck you, Pee-ul. I'm going to see Billy Johnstone on this. You are out of fucking bounds."

The Pill spoke his next words without malice. Peterson, three steps gone, almost overlooked their implication.

"Randy, I just came from Billy Johnstone's office."

Peterson's paused.

The Pill said, "When you see Mr. Johnstone he'll be familiar with the Plano Mall loan. Preliminaries will be unnecessary."

The bravado Pete Morris exhibited had gone latent.

Phil Kamerov recommenced, "The reason I convened a Workout Committee Meeting, Randy, is that your department has a loan to Plano Mall; a five million dollar loan."

The Pill turned a letter sized page of beige construction paper upside down, so that it faced Pete Morris, "The money was advanced two weeks ago at the instructions of your Mr. Morris."

"What the fuck," the pitch of Randy's voice ebbed on each syllable, "is he talking about?" The Hamilton SVP rotated his head. Pete Morris' personal world began to wobble.

"Pete," The Pill said, "You authorized $5,000,000 be deposited to the Plano Mall account on May 15. No minutes approving the loan. No signed loan note. No signed guarantees. No lien waivers. No sworn statement. No security agreement exists. No title insurance. No deed recorded - no goddam deed that shows the bank's interest. Just $5 million parked in Paulopnos' account."

Randy Peterson followed The Pill's tale with difficulty. Randy said, "No loan to Plano Mall has been put on the books."

"That's right, Randy," Phil said, "But, there is an entry on the bank general ledger debiting the overnight suspense account for five million Hamilton dollars."

"How can that be?" asked Randy.

The Pill explained the accounting chicanery, "When the head teller accepts a memo from your loan office authorizing a deposit, then balances the transaction by parking the entry in the account the bank uses to balance overnight interbank transactions."

"Shit!" Randy Peterson snapped, "Pete, did you advance the fucking five million?" Peterson formed an ad hoc partnership with Pee-ul.

Morris, apprehended for violating bank procedure for the fourth time within the last month, didn't understand. When did all the rules change?

"I haven't actually made the loan, it's just an advance," Pete Morris said, "Until I get the approvals. Hell, we don't even begin charging interest until I actually get all the paperwork signed!"

Phil Kamerov put his head between his hands.

Randy-Randy said, "What do you mean we don't charge them interest? How did you fund five mill without me seeing it on the daily loan report?" Morris shrugged the fifth amendment.

Randy turned to The Pill, "How did you discover this?"

"It's not a loan," Phil explained. "It's money floating on the bank accounting records without a home yet. Beginning last month I had accounting provide daily reports on all credits to customer liability accounts. Five million grabbed my attention."

Pete Morris understood Pee-ul's explanation very well. He had monumental legwork to accomplish once this meeting broke. *All next week will be consumed by detail paperwork,* he thought.

Phil continued, "I can hardly wait to get to the bank each morning to read the report."

Pete Morris tilted his head right. His mind changed channels to an inner place, a private existence.

Peterson said, "What are you telling me, Pee-ul?"

"Ask your officer, Peter Morris."

Randy's focus shifted to the mute Pete Morris.

"What's the problem?" Morris launched a justification. "Look, there are times I've had to use advances to make sure the deal flowed. I fix the details later."

"Fix the details?" Randy-Randy said. "Pee-ul, what is this account called?"

"Suspense account," answered Phil.

Pete Morris was mute.

"You're going to be busy, Randy and Pete," the Pill said. "Randy, as of last night Morris has funded sixteen separate advances using the bank suspense account for thirty-three million."

"Jesus fuckin' Christ," Peterson prayed.

CHAPTER TWENTY

Billy was the first Johnstone to try college. He finished two years at Tarrant Community College in Fort Worth.

<u>North Dallas, Summer 1974</u>

Between years one and two of junior college, Billy Johnstone landed a job as a security guard at the construction site of Ken Thompson's eight-story office in Richardson. Ken Thompson, thirty-six years old and not yet CEO of a Texas Savings & Loan, inspected the site three times each week. Today was Billy's second day on the job.

Billy, with no plans for a career in finance, stopped Ken Thompson at the entry gate. The future CEO wore an emerald leisure suit; he was dressed like a lime lollipop. Billy digested this man and launched into his security act.

"That's right. No authorization badge, no entry." Young Billy Johnstone denied entry louder the second time.

"Son, I'm sure there is a way into this here site," Thompson stretched for his wallet, testing.

Billy got hot. He flat out didn't like this guy. The attitude pissed him off. Billy Johnstone used his clearest grammar, "Look, asshole, you're two seconds away from a physical explanation. Leave, now."

"Good job, boy," Thompson said. He wouldn't have to worry about material walking off this job site, "I'm going to let you in on a secret about me."

Goddammit, thought Billy, *this jerk ain't going to con me.*

Anger jammed the reasoning of the young man who would become the Chief Operating Officer of the Hamilton S&L, "I can see who you are. You're a pimp, passing yourself off as a queer."

That assault ruffled Ken Thompson. He didn't cater to queers and he didn't like to be called a pimp. This cowboy prick obviously hadn't taken a college course on gentlemen's fashion last semester. Thompson strained under a testosterone shock, "Your ass boy! Talk like that and you're going to be gone from this project."

Ken Thompson's words, as his attorney later explained, threatened the security guard.

Billy thumped his right index finger in the future CEO's chest, four pokes.

"Move, pimp," Billy said, "Move your butt back out the gate and down the street."

"Back off, boy. You got a surprise comin'," Ken Thompson said.

Billy Johnstone punctuated with one more thump. Air burst from Thompson's lungs. He couldn't spit his words. Thompson threw Billy's hand aside. Billy's hand snapped back into his chest.

The phone in the guard shack was fifteen feet behind Billy Johnstone. Billy Johnstone thought of the guard shack as his command center, off limits to civilians.

Ken Thompson lunged around the security guard, charging for the telephone.

Once the construction Super arrived, Thompson would conduct a manners seminar before he fired this security jerk. Billy camouflaged his intent with a half-step retreat then his fist, on a downward arc, hammered into Ken Thompson's jaw.

The knuckles of the security guard split the skin in the middle of the owner's right cheek. Billy's fist drove downward on a fifteen-degree angle from the point of contact. The sharp point from the two assaulting metacarpal knuckles cleaved the widening gash.

Billy's singular blow shattered Thompson's two right side bicuspids. They popped from their sockets. The surviving lower bicuspid twisted forty-five degrees.

Ken Thompson's tongue ricocheted inside his mouth. Constricting jaw muscles bit down at the precise moment his tongue catapulted between his clamping teeth, cutting into his own wayward tongue.

Blood pumped to the damage. His heart rate hurdled from eighty-five to 175 beats per minute, gushing energy to combat the crisis.

The owner lay on the ground outside the gate protecting his eight-story office; mouth smashed, thought impaired.

Blood ran below his shoulder and spit when he spoke from the slashed tongue.

The guard stooped, got a grip by the left shoulder and under the crotch. He cleaned and jerked Thompson's 185 pounds; throwing the owner's ass off the construction site.

Thompson's mumbled threats, as he hurled forward, couldn't be understood.

That was a long time ago. Now Billy served as Chief operating Officer of the Hamilton S&L, Ken Thompson's S&L. Billy was supposed to make sure that unwanted folks didn't get inside the Hamilton S&L.

Federal examiners were unwanted.

CHAPTER TWENTY-ONE

"Once someone possesses the magic power to create money, the temptation to creat too much is very strong. That's why banks need constant watching. Banks are too important to be left to bankers."

        John Gordon
        American Heritage Magazine

Dallas, The Savings and Loan Regulators

"To end up with a good loan, you need a good banker," the President of the Dallas Federal Home Loan Bank simplified.

"Hamilton doesn't have good bankers," replied the Pres' Number Two guy, "The only lender they have brought into the bank in the last year with any skill is Heather Montgomery."

Number Two headed the Dallas region for the Federal Savings & Loan Insurance Corporation, the FSLIC; *FIZLICK* in industry jargon.

"Is the Hamilton dead?" the Pres of the Dallas FHLB drilled his subordinate.

"You saw the examination report for the last quarter," Number Two said. "That was the Hamilton's first report since we switched to the

FDIC's standard for classifying loans. Thirty-two percent of the Hamilton's loans are classified substandard or worse. Hamilton doesn't have the talent to overcome their lending mess." Number Two sidestepped the Pres' question.

"Great," the Pres said, "then the Hamilton is bankrupt, no different than our other Texas S&L's."

The FHLBB, the Federal Home Loan Bank Board had three tasks; create, regulate and insure Savings and Loan banks. In Texas, each task reported to President of the Dallas Federal Home Loan Bank. His Number Two was in charge of Regulating; assuring the banks behaved.

Number Two, head of FIZLICK, pleaded, "Our guy Scamehorn has nailed the Hamilton cold. Their COO, Billy Johnstone, traded dead horses to Sunbelt Savings for dead cows. We want your *go ahead* to seize the Hamilton."

The Pres of the Dallas FHLBB measured his Number Two guy. The Pres' arms lay across his desk, not moving.

"Then what do we do?"

"What do you mean?" asked Number Two.

"The Federal Savings and Loan Insurance Corporation is broke," the Pres said. "*FIZLICK's* insurance fund is tapped. We don't have the money to repay bank depositors if another large S&L goes bust."

"Ah fuck," said Number Two, "Hamilton is fourth largest in Texas."

"Seizing the fucking Hamilton will kick off the next great American bank run," the Pres said.

The President of the Dallas FHLB slowly rose from behind his desk, "We've got 1,574 *FIZLICK* examiners, about half of them trained, in the entire fucking country to control 4,000 S&L banks. Thirty S&L's in the Dallas region haven't even been examined during the last two years. Five of your rare, qualified examiners are locked inside this Hamilton fiasco."

"The Hamilton is a zombie," Number Two replied. "The bank is dead and still receiving transfusions of new deposits. Deposits we insure. What happens if we don't stop the bleeding?" Number Two put the call right back in the lap of his Pres.

"Forbearance. That's what Washington calls the policy," the Pres said. "That's what the Bank Board in Washington has decided. If we can't seize the bank, Forbearance is our only option left."

Number two argued, "At least hit them with a cease and desist on new money out the door."

"Summarize your facts," said the Pres. "Put your report on my desk tomorrow.

Number Two stepped towards the door.

"And, Joe," the Pres paused. "Even though we can't seize the S&L, Washington wants to crucify one of these thieves running the bank. One of the guys right at the top. Felony charge. We're running out of time; need to scare the piss out of them."

Number Two nodded as he walked out.

CHAPTER TWENTY-TWO

Dallas, The Hamilton Savings and Loan

"I can't advance even one more dollar. Things have changed." Pete Morris wiped his forehead with his free left hand.

The Greek accented voice on the telephone instructed, "Yes, you can Peter. $3,000,000 tomorrow."

"No, Mr. Paulopnos. Things have changed. I don't have your loan approved by the committee yet. Jesus, the $5,000,000 I've already advanced to you on this deal has our auditors all hacked off. Nothing has been approved yet." Pete Morris was becoming repetitive.

"That's your problem, Peter. You are my banker. This is why I allowed you to participate for five percent. A participation with funds I lent you at zero interest and no repayment. Another $3,000,000 must be in my account tomorrow."

Dimitri Paulopnos did not bother to explain that he had deposited a check for the $3,000,000 in a Houston bank the previous afternoon. If his check arrived at the Hamilton Savings & Loan before Peter Morris deposited $3,000,000 in the Plano Mall checking account, Dimitri might have to defend his check writing procedure in court.

Pete pleaded, "I can't. This new workout guy is all over me. You've got to wait until I can get your loan approved by my loan Committee."

Dimitri Paulopnos said nothing for a moment, then asked, "How long will your approval process require?"

"Appraisal, narrative, loan notes, I can do it within three weeks if I hustle."

Dimitri rebuked the Hamilton Vice President in an instant, "No. Tomorrow. You live a nice life, Peter. You have a nice condo. You are better off now than you were last year because now you own five percent of the Plano Mall, real estate that will be very profitable for you and me. I like you. I wouldn't want to see your life disturbed. Tomorrow. $3,000,000."

The phone receiver clicked in Pete's ear.

Great fucking day so far, thought Pete. *First that fucking Pee-ul digs up the advances, now the Greek wants another three mill. I never should have left Ohio.* Morris checked the time. *Jesus, it's only 10 A.M.*

Thirty seconds later the VP's his secretary said, "Dimitri Paulopnos, he's calling back."

"Tell him I'm not here," Morris said.

Pete Morris recalled his original reluctance to fund the Greek's Plano Mall deal. This guy, this Greek sonofabitch, looked bad, mean bad. The rumors in suburban Dallas had the Greek, Dimitri Paulopnos, tied into the Dallas underworld.

Morris didn't want to make the next phone call. His demands on the Endres brothers would not make the morning any more pleasant. Phil, the Workout committee, instructed Pete to push the Endres on repayment of their debt.

He shuffled the phone messages on his desk as a way to waste time before he had to dial.

Morris' secretary stepped into Pete's office.

"Leonard Endres is holding for you," she said, "Says he is staying on the line until you take the call. Line two." She paused at the door, "You're losing that false Texas twang you've been featuring."

Pete punched the button releasing his second phone line, "Leonard?"

"Pete, what the hell ya'll doin' down there?"

From Endres' tone, Morris knew that the registered letter demanding Endres repay the bank had been delivered. The formal correspondence insisted the Endres Brothers begin weekly debt reduction; $500,000 each week. $500,000 every week until their Hamilton loans were reduced to the legal lending limit the Fed bank examiners defined for the Hamilton Savings & Loan. Eighty three consecutive weeks; $500,000 each week.

Pete interceded, "Len, you got my letter. Let me explain."

"I didn't get any fuckin' letter. I didn't get jack squat," Leonard Endres was not happy.

"How'd you hear?" Pete quizzed his largest, best customer.

"How'd I hear? The cunt has shown up at four separate projects holding what y'all call a special inspection. What do you mean how'd I hear? My fucking people told me, you simple asshole. Now, I'm in Phoenix trying to smooth her and I don't even know what the fuck you're doin!"

"What?" Morris said.

"Pete, I thought that $10,000 cashier's check I gave you for consulting covered any surprises like this. This happens again, Pete, and our relationship changes." Endres was emphatic.

Peter Morris was barely following, "Len, let me do some checking. Who is at your Phoenix project?"

Endres' voice came through the phone clearly from Phoenix, "Heather Montgomery, she says."

Morris was lost, "I'll get back to you." *What the fuck is a special inspection.*

"Better fix this, Pete," Endres demanded.

"Let me check," Pete almost hung up the phone.

"Len?" Morris said.

"What?" said Endres.

"Len, you're going to receive a letter. The bank is requesting you repay $500,000 each week," Morris said.

"Stick it up your ass, Morris."

* * *

Janis Lang discovered the dormant account report during the Texas Banking Commission audit four years ago. Customers of the Hamilton S&L who forgot they deposited money. The Texas Banking Commission treasure hunted for forgotten riches so the State of Texas could claim the neglected funds from banks and Savings & Loans. Money abandoned seven years, could be claimed by the State of Texas. Escheat, an aptly titled English legal concept, was precedent.

The Hamilton head teller listened as the Texas Bank Commission agent explained; she was enthralled.

"Seven years pass," the agent said, "and there's no activity in a checking account or savings account, state law assumes the person has abandoned his money."

"People forget their money?" Janis, who had been recently promoted to head teller of the Hamilton S&L, asked.

The Texas Banking Commission agent nodded, "Happens all the time. You wouldn't believe it. Guess how much money Texas claimed last year?"

Janis guessed, "Geez, I don't know. Maybe a million dollars?"

"Over sixty-two million bucks," the agent replied.

Hamilton's head teller was seduced, "What happens when the depositors finally show up to claim their money?"

"If they do, we give it back." The Texas man said. "Once we get the money, very few of the original depositors ever surface. Over the last ten years we've kept ninety-six percent of the dormant accounts for Texas."

"Only four percent of the money is claimed? Where do the original depositors go?" Janis asked.

"Most died without leaving a record," he said.

When the Texas bounty hunter asked Janis to document specific last activity dates, she skipped off to the fire-proof room storing the bank's hard copy records of deposit history. Janis xeroxed the dormant savings and checking account reports, the head teller noticed that the largest sum of money that had not been touched for over six months hid within Hamilton savings accounts.

Six months later she compared the inactive savings accounts, only the addition of interest had changed the balance. The head teller transferred one hundred dollars from a dormant savings accounts to a new checking account. A checking account she created in the name of Lucy Smith.

The head teller didn't sign the in-house money transfer tickets. The credit to Lucy's new checking account would be proof-read by a machine prior to entry into the Hamilton S&L computerized accounting; validity was based on the settlement amount, not the signature of a bank teller. After data input, computers swept away paper trails. Determining the origin on such a common transaction generated by paper, and lacking a specific teller signature, would be difficult, probably impossible.

That night the Hamilton computer withdrew the $100.00; converting the dormant account to active status; removing the account from the scrutiny of the Texas Bank Commission.

Two weeks later Janis returned the hundred bucks to the original account. The Texas Bank Commission did not require Hamilton S&L to report the $100 reimbursement.

Savings accounts had richer potential, but the interest earned was reported to the Internal Revenue Service. She would concentrate on checking accounts.

Janis rented a post office box in the name of Lucy Smith, paying cash. Her first automatic teller card arrived a week later. She would never forget her first withdrawal; the sensation, the thrill of forbidden fruit. Janis extracted two hundred dollars per visit, limited to one visit a day for each account. If the absent owner of the once dormant account re-appeared, he would be directed to the head teller of the Hamilton Savings & Loan Bank; Janis Lang.

She could make the missing money re-appear, the absent Hamilton depositor would be given an anonymous money order.

Janis' thrill ripened into addiction . . . and induced zealous attention to her duty as head teller. Fear of losing her position heightened her already high standard of performance. Janis had politely refused two promotions within the last year. Amid the ecstasy of scoring easy money, she had become a hostage to her job.

Janis steers her Bonneville up to the drive-through automatic teller machine at Sunbelt Savings & Loan. She slides her own legitimate ATM card into the slot. The screen says *Welcome Janis Lang.*

She deposits a thick envelope containing $800.00 and requests verification of her current balance; the automated teller says $108,632.58. No one has complained since Janis started stealing the money two years ago.

* * *

The Hamilton S&L

She read her boss' mail an hour ago. Randy-Randy Peterson has implausibly been drafted for the Hamilton A team. He received an invitation to the annual Fourth of July bash that Ken Thompson, the bank owner, hosts in Nassau. The only other Hamilton officer that has attended in past years is the Chief Operating Officer, Billy Johnstone.

He must have photographs of Ken Thompson screwing sheep, she thinks.

I hope he got that loan arranged, Randy thought. Peterson needed the money for the down payment on his new home in Plano.

The Denver loan broker had explained to Randy, "The Silverado Savings and Loan has assets of $2.5 billion. The Denver market is too small to place all the money they have available." The loan salesman surrendered a million dollar smile. "Silverado has a solid understanding of Texas because of the George Bush, Neil Bush involvement."

"Great!" said Randy. *God, what a deal, he thought, doing business with the Vice President of the United States.*

"Silverado wants to expand its presence in the Dallas market. They need a Texas partner."

"Let's try a couple a small deals and get to know one another," suggested Randy.

"I've got Colorado borrowers that need $800,000 for energy equipment on western slope projects." The financial intermediary from the mile high city pushed supporting financial information on the loan request across the conference table to Randy. Four loan requests that eight Colorado banks had already denied.

"Randy, I've also got pre-approval for you on that $25,000 personal loan." The Denver middleman brokered quid pro quo.

Except for Pee-ul's Workout Committee, things looked bright for Randy right now. Peterson visualized the impact the Nassau trip could have on his career. Ken Thompson entertained a lot of his Washington cronies at the party.

I gotta lose some weight before Nassau, he promised himself.

CHAPTER TWENTY-THREE

In Dallas, doing the deal, creating wealth, is power. The Powerful of Texas were fewer than media legend portrayed; yet their reach was extensive.

Fortune was a one-way street in Texas during the early 1980's. Money flowed in, labor arrived, deals got done. Wealth was created. Dallas S&L owners learned quickest.

* * *

Ken Thompson left SMU after the fall semester in 1959, at the school's insistence. He'd almost completed three years of college.

The future CEO of the Hamilton S&L headed for the oil fields of west Texas with his avarice-blue eyes wide open. In 1960 fate was blowing dusters where opportunity once shadowed west Texas wildcatters. Yet, not every petrol-filled anticline had been tapped. Ken Thompson committed to a 20% share in a proposed new hole, Midland Westridge #3. His share cost fifteen grand; he raised it all from six frat brothers still enrolled at SMU. Midland Westridge #3 hit oil at 3,800 feet.

After Midland Westridge #3, Ken Thompson suggested his *PARDS* "come along" on four additional holes.

Thompson secured mineral rights on 700 acres immediately east of Midland Westridge #3. He agreed to pay the land owner $1,400 per year, or one out of every eight barrels, if he hit oil. He swapped another eighth to the guy drilling and transporting the oil he expected to recover. He kept the other 75% for his group; 50% for himself, 25% split amongst his six *PARDS*.

Well Two spigoted a stratigraphic trap at 3,200 feet. Well three punched a reservoir twenty-two days later.

$2,200 arrived in the mail for each student/partner every month during their senior year at SMU; nice return on front money of $2,500 each. During the winter of 1961 Ken Thompson's legend grew at every TGIF party at SMU.

Thompson netted $218,000 in 1962, comfortable for a young Texas oil man of 23.

* * *

In 1973 Arab graduates of American business schools concluded the basic tenet of economics, elasticity of demand, did not apply in every situation. Their professors at Harvard, Dartmouth and Wharton had lectured that when the price of a commodity goes up, demand goes down. That is price elasticity.

Price elasticity is the foundation of economics. If the student didn't accept that increasing the price reduced demand, they flunked Econ 101.

These native sons of Saudi Arabia, Kuwait, and the United Arab Emirates absorbed American business disciplines. Arab fathers instructed their male heirs to learn how to manage the family oil reserves; the stored wealth of their country.

After graduation, the young sheiks reunioned at meetings of the Organization of Petroleum Exporting Countries. In Vienna in August 1973, OPEC announced a demonstration for the tenured economists of the West. The young Arabs speculated that price elasticity, as applied to crude oil, was bullshit.

They introduced their market test. Along the way they spawned some very wealthy Texans.

The OPEC theorists demonstrated that oil at $6.00 per barrel was more desirable than oil at $3.00 per barrel. At $10.00 a barrel this crudely, seductive commodity would incite car owners to form lines around the block, just for the rapture of topping-off the fuel tank.

American economists, when asked to explain why demand for oil increased as the sultans and sheiks jacked up the price, had an economic answer; Price Inelasticity, an economic phenomenon.

America's car-owning public didn't care.

As OPEC manipulated the cost of crude oil to higher ground, Ken Thompson, the future CEO of the Hamilton S&L, had twenty-two active wells. He was 35 years old. When oil rose to $12.00 per barrel, Sun Oil knocked on Thompson's door; they needed more crude. They cut Thompson a check for $23,000,000.

Thompson, turned east, to Dallas and the real estate market. By 1979 Kenneth Thompson had accumulated a unit; a net worth of $100,000,000 in Texas-speak. A unit bought a seat at the table of power.

Thompson served as Chairman of the Board for his empire; The Hamilton Group. Assets included Hamilton Homes, the second largest residential home building company in Texas; Braniff Airline; Hamilton Insurance Co, the country's fifteenth largest insurance company; and Hamilton Saving & Loan, with assets of $6,500,000,000, the fourth largest savings bank in Texas.

DOING THE DEAL in Texas always includes civic involvement. Information passes freely amongst civic leaders minding community affairs. Thompson found that although economic power administered easily through his north Dallas office dispensing political power required a Washington base. His private telephone line rang into both Dallas and DC. Thompson believed in free enterprise; free to do whatever he damn well pleased.

An empire only had one boss and at The Hamilton, Ken Thompson ruled.

CHAPTER TWENTY-FOUR

<u>Washington. D.C. The Tabard Inn</u>

"Something in the corner," Jack Richardson requested of the maître d' guarding the small Tabard dining room. They had been paged from their seven-minute wait and were being led to their table in the garden cocktail bar.

Jack Richardson turned to Brendan, "Big hangout for journalists. That can be good or bad. Tonight we don't need their prying ears."

After a year of Caribbean langouste and grouper of the day, Brendan anticipated a cholesterol filled repast. The chef grilled the eight ounce filet mignon, rare, perfect. Richardson, perhaps in deference to Brendan's rib-poke greeting that afternoon, ordered a salad containing enough grilled chicken to satisfy Wily Coyote.

"Problem," said Richardson as he forked a radish aside favoring the last piece of glazed chicken. "Since '86, thrift examiners are technically employed by the banks they examine. The examiners' boss, the president of each Federal Home Loan district bank, who, keep in mind, is an appointee of the member banks, is also the principal supervisory agent in charge of keeping the local S&L's honest."

Richardson understated, "This is not a good system."

"The chickens are pretending to be fox," Brendan said while maintaining a secondary vigil on the athletic brunette dining alone on the far side of the room, thirty feet away. She signed an American Express tab.

"Exactly. Until sixteen months ago. S&L examiners did not have a standard schedule, like we have at the FDIC, to classify loans according to the likelihood of repayment. The rationale was that S&L's made mortgage loans and mortgages were always repaid, or the house was foreclosed, the property sold and the loan paid from proceeds."

Brendan pondered the regulator's dilemma through the depths of the ruby Chateau Margaux 1978. He inhaled the bouquet from the oversize tulip wine glass.

"S&L's started making commercial loans in 1982, how did FSLIC determine the probability of loss if assets were not classified?" Brendan asked.

The waitress poured Richardson a second glass of the Bordeaux. "Fizlick didn't know diddle until ten months ago, when the results started coming in that included classified loan totals. S&L exams during the last six months have forty percent of loans classified. FSLIC is going crazy."

"Jesus, the highest classified ratio I ever heard of, Jack, was fourteen percent in upstate New York and the FDIC seized that bank. Does Fizlick have the reserves to cover that magnitude of bad loans?"

The brunette brushed her hand along the temple of her boyish haircut. Brendan thought he caught her glance.

"Not a chance," Richardson said, "That's my concern. Sooner or later this mess will be dumped in my lap. Treasury is ultimately responsible for national finances including the Federal Savings and Loan Insurance Corporation. Treasury is going to dump this mess on my FDIC. This is going to be a fucking fiasco unless this S&L swindle comes to a screeching halt."

The waitress removed the remnants of dinner and tried to interrupt to suggest desert. Brendan's wave dismissed her for the moment.

"Jack, can't you get a hearing before the House banking committee and pull the plug?"

The chairman of the FDIC plucked the dessert spoon from the white linen to orchestrate his lesson. "The Fed Home Loan Bank Chair, Ed Gray, petitioned the house committee in early 1984 with three logical requests. Authority for insurance surcharges on risky S&L lending, power to issue cease and desist orders halting unsafe bank practice, and Fizlick independence from the OMB . . . independent of executive budget control, like the FDIC is." Richardson's shaking head dramatized his bewilderment.

"And?" Brendan prompted.

Jack's eyes met his friend's, "And Congress said no, no, and no. After Congress denied Gray, Stockman, for emphasis, sent Ed Gray this memo." Richardson reached inside his shabby attaché case for the document. He boosted the papers above the stem water goblets, "Stockman's memo stating that 700 examiners could easily supervise 4,000 S&L banks. Note that the magnanimous starting salary for rookie bank examiners was frozen at $13,500. OMB really wanted the cream of the MBA crop, didn't they? As follow-up, David Stockman, with Reagan's blessing, leaned on the Fed Bank Board to replace monthly reports S&L's submitted to the district DS with quarterly reports; reduce paperwork. Fucking idiots."

The waitress had approached. Hearing Jack's crudity, she by-passed their table.

The FDIC director continued, "S&L's are pumping millions of FSLIC insured dollars into congressional reelection campaigns. They've got more political influence than the banks do."

Brendan listened. Responsibility for every dollar deposited in a national bank fell in Richardson's lap. His war against the S&L outlaws had become a vendetta.

"Why didn't Gray say no?" Brendan asked.

"He is a presidential appointee," Richardson said, "Who does he say no to?"

"Okay, so Ed Gray, assigns all his S&L examiners to the district offices of the Federal Home Loan Bank. What's morale like in the trenches?"

Twenty-five years of fiscal professionalism slipped away from the head of the FDIC.

"Peachy, just peachy. Turnover rate for thrift examiners is fourteen percent. Twenty-six percent in the Dallas district. We can't train people fast enough. Junior guys are being paid $13,500 to confront the most blatant financial criminals America has spawned in sixty years. The thrift examiners aren't that good to start with and the next week they're offered $25,000 to join the S&L as new lenders."

Get up and leave now, Brendan's inner voice advised, *before Jack locks the door.*

Instead Brendan asked, "How can FSLIC operate when examiners defect at that rate?"

When the brunette stood, Brendan swiveled his head a few degrees. About five-feet-six-inches. She possessed the body of *an athlete.* Brendan's eyes tracked her through the garden bar. *Thirty-two,* Brendan guessed.

"Ed Gray is a political man. He has to be, his regional Fed Home Loan banks are outside the control of OMB. Gray cranked salaries to recruit select senior examiners. Key guys from here, from the Comptroller's office and the Federal Reserve are abandoning ship to swim to the district Federal Home Loan banks. Guys making $100,000 a year are reporting to people making $50,000. So in summary, I'm losing key people, Ed Gray has a major fucking politico-bureaucratic moral snafu, and David Stockman is Washington history."

Brendan and Richardson consumed the last of the wine during dinner. Brendan beckoned and the waitress approached timidly.

Brendan ordered Drambuie, up, for himself and Jack.

Richardson demurred, "Can't drink that, allergic to it. Make mine a B and B."

"What's your plan?" Brendan asked after the waitress delivered the thick liqueurs, one a deeper gold.

Jack Richardson inhaled to assure the waitress hadn't confused his drink order. "Digest what you've learned today. Tomorrow at 8:00 A.M. we'll resume in my office."

The remainder of the evening was private gossip, tattling and confessions shattering the four year veneer since their personal lives last intertwined.

CHAPTER TWENTY-FIVE

Dallas, Texas

Heather lingered in suspension as dawn emerged in her unlit bedroom. Curled, lying on her right side, joined hands compressed within her thighs, Heather opened one eyelid to register the time displayed by the clock radio. Eight silent minutes until the 6 AM jangle. Her left hand tapped the radio; no alarm necessary. She slid her hand back under the covers and employed it as a fulcrum to roll onto her back. Settling, Heather pressed her palm into her groin.

Heather hadn't taken a sex partner since Detroit. She wondered; *would a male body someday again stimulate?* A hint of the sun evident behind the closed curtains broadcast dawn.

The snoop-tour Heater had completed yesterday left her beat. No appointments at the Hamilton until 10 A.M. this morning, although she had to talk with the S&L's Workout guy before then.

Nine AM will be fine, Heather thought. An hour-and-a-half later than her norm, but she had earned the ninety minutes. The out-of-town inspections had sapped her.

Heather lay still in the darkened room for three minutes; she slid her panties down her legs, tossed the garment on the oak rocking chair. For background she tuned the radio to Texas Public Radio. The morning news had not yet begun. Her hand reached beneath the bedside night table recognizing the Wahl SuperSage II. The vibrating massager remained plugged into the power, untouched since the machine's previous exercise. Heather pushed her right hand through the two pliable metal straps; the soft rubber back of the massage unit fit comfortably. Texas Public Radio announced Bedrich Smetana's composition; The Bartered Bride Overture. Heather had two choices; she selected the hushed timbre of the slower vibration.

Her hand, pulsing to the meter of the opus, rested upon her stomach. The folk-flavored Smetana music launched to the dancing tempo of subdued violins. Absence of heterosexual foreplay was absolved by her quick strokes to the music. Heather's mental readiness, lagging her biological head start, accelerated in a bid to catch up. Heather rode the music to achieve symmetry of body with mind. As the music carried her within mental striking distance of her physical readiness, she met the mounting sensation.

She guided the machine into the zone, ironing her fingers against the expectant flesh. Sexual sensors welcomed the incoming pulse. The symphonic overture playing on the radio depicted with melodic excitement the joy of medieval villagers welcoming a carnival troupe. Brass horns joined the violins four and half minutes into the overture, Heather's mental state was in harmony with her physical eagerness. The Bartered Bride Overture continues five-minutes and forty-five seconds before the crescendo commences. Smetana's crescendo plays on another forty-five seconds. Heather joined the crescendo just a few seconds late and finished with the orchestra.

Fuck! Pete Morris silently saluted the morning. *What else could get screwed up today?*

Pete had twisted through the last two hours of night creating inadequate escapes from his immediate S&L problems. He swung his legs from the bed, walked to the window for inspiration and found none.

Sunrays pitching through his window confirmed dawn. He sat on his bed and stared at the telephone. He swore at the receiver as though it had betrayed him, he dialed.

"Hello," Heather said.

Morris didn't care if he woke Heather. From her breathy response, she must have been working out.

"Heather, Pete Morris. Hope I didn't wake you?"

Heather shook the SuperSage vibrator from her wrist, "No, no I have been up for some time, although you are the first person to call this morning."

"Yeah, well sorry about the hour, but I am jammed today. Heather, Leonard Endres was all over my ass yesterday. Why were you poking around his building in Phoenix?"

"Pete, it is a little early," This wasn't the debriefing Heather anticipated. "Let's talk at the Hamilton."

"Heather, let's talk about this before we get to the office," he said. "There are a few things we should straighten out, and the Hamilton might not be the best place to pursue this discussion."

Heather's sudden transition from pleasure to irritation erased whatever receptive courtesy Heather may have been willing to entertain. She cut him off.

"No, Pete, I'll see you at the office," she hung up.

Morris slammed the telephone into its cradle, "Bitch," he said.

For the last two years, White Chevy Cavaliers had been General Motors' number-one selling combination of vehicle and color. Rental car agencies and law enforcement agencies bought them. Jim Kowalski had stashed his unmarked, white, department-issued Cavalier next to the tennis courts in the park, four hundred yards behind him.

Kowalski wore his Dallas Police Department uniform beneath the less prestigious, but often more welcome, uniform of a Waste Management garbage man. If this assignment fell within the jurisdiction of the Dallas SWAT, he would have swaggered. But, he was executing for the Greek.

This wasn't his kind of operation. His field pack fit within one simple Army green garbage bag. Hanging from his right arm the plastic pouch almost reached the ground. His weapon hid within the trash liner. Smaller and lighter than most pistol- caliber submachine guns.

Kowalski drew $32,000 as a member of the Dallas SWAT.

Last year he earned another $40,000 a year dispatching private, off-hour assignments for the Greek. And he got paid for doing what he did best, squeezing a trigger. Kowalski had not fired a shot while on duty for six years, since that doped-up nigger jerked a pearly handled Jennings pistol on him.

Give me back the shotgun . . . if I still had that baby, my insurance agent wouldn't be livin' so high off my fuckin life premiums. Fuckin congress, bent on disarming us all, thought Kowalski. Kowalski was toting an FIE semi-automatic LAW-15 shotgun aimed at everything the black man owned and would want to protect. First shot from fifteen feet ended the confrontation; second shot was just for emphasis.

This was dumb, too. Killing in daylight with a witness. But the Greek had been specific.

Kowalski accused and prosecuted as he traversed the field. Dewey Stokes, Howard Metzenbaum, Kennedy, Biden and their ilk had taken his chosen weapon of defense out of his hands. Outlawed the LAW-15 shotgun because they said it had no sporting purpose.

They ought to be on the street with me. I'd show them a sport, stayin' alive when a cocaine-crazed suspect ignores the aerosol restraint spray that was supposed to have incapacitated him and is charging you with his fifty-nine dollar Raven 25, two hours off the store shelf. That's not target practice, senators.

Inner voices began before Heather replaced the telephone receiver. The Hamilton rumor mill labeled Pete Morris as the focal point of the regulatory probe, and the Feds had turned up the heat. Because Heather had agreed to act as investigator on this unannounced bushwhacking of the Endres out-of-town loans, she looked like she had sided with the bad guys, the Hamilton Workout guy, The Pill.

As she lay in bed she questioned whether Morris' invitation had been an open door of opportunity that she had too hastily slammed shut. If she could get Pete Morris to open up about whatever the hell it was he was doing, this might be her shortcut out of the Hamilton S&L mess. A conversation, in private, might be conducive to discovery.

Heather wanted out of this Texas financial mess as soon as possible.

How does Pete Morris think of me? Heather asked herself.

Her fellow Hamilton staffer, Pete Morris, probably knows three facts, *I'm bright, I haven't been at the Hamilton long enough to get my fingers dirtied and I have just conducted a special inspection of his largest customer, the Endres Brothers.*

Heather dialed.

Morris answered, "Hello."

"Pete, it's Heather. It has been a bad week. I was hasty. What did you have in mind?"

"What's going on? You're on a special inspection of my customers?" Pete Morris breathed deep. "Heather, we're part of the same team at the Hamilton.

"Pete, I've got some questions of my own," she said.

Morris didn't want to defer his understanding of the situation further, "Let's meet for breakfast."

"Where?" she asked.

Pete looked at blue sky out his window. He wanted this bitch on his home playing field. Morris started to describe Andre's Bakery Restaurant, his traditional business breakfast stop. There, restaurant employee and coffee-drinking Hamilton customers deferred to him. No, the conversation he had in mind required privacy. Total privacy.

"Here, at my place," he said. "We can talk without interference. Here's the address ..."

Heather looked at the clock. 6:20 AM. She would have to hustle to catch the Hamilton Workout guy by 9:00 AM.

"OK, but it has to be soon. Is 7:15, OK?" she said.

Normally, for a breakfast meeting, Heather would have worn something conservative. Not today. This morning she wanted Pete Morris off balance. She picked the pale silk blouse.

Kowalski navigated through a quarter mile of knee-high weeds to the condominium site. A stream trickled from his forehead; his Dallas PD under-uniform was soaked. Safety pins affixed the Waste Management tag to his brown coveralls. A myriad of potential garbage tasks at the cluster condo endorsed his presence.

He had staked the target's condo last night; from dusk until almost eleven. His chosen firing site offered the least angle if he had to shoot through glass; glass could deflect the shot and fuck the whole deal.

"Be very accurate," the Greek had said.

Kowalski, disguised as a garbage man, emerged from the adjacent field onto the condominium property. He fell to a push-up position and slid beneath the shrubs. If discovered, a condo owner would be impressed with the diligence of this garbage man. Jim Kowalski reached into the green plastic to caress the La France M16K.

The weapon was unique, SWAT teams wanted a lightweight weapon when entering, stopping power when inside and when all hell broke loose, the hog option; automatic fire. The M16K's distinct gas system yielded bulls-eye control when the good guys shifted to full-auto fire. Kowalski didn't need a burst of fire power this morning. He'd fire the weapon at maximum accuracy, one well-placed shot.

He fingered the select-fire options.

Pete Morris walked to the sliding glass door of his condominium, leading his coffee-colored cocker.

"Fuckin' perfect," Kowalski withdrew the weapon and checked the range for eighty eight feet.

Kowalski squinted down the site, "Come on back, baby." Kowalski urged his target and Pete Morris.

Two nearby sprinkler heads threw a steady spray into' the air that rained onto the plants hiding Kowalski. The Electro-film finish of the submachine gun, molybdenum disulfide dry-film lubricant, rendered the weapon waterproof. That his weapon was impervious to the rain was irrelevant. He instinctively tucked his head and covered the SMG.

Kowalski raised his head to survey.

"What do you know?" The guy was setting the table on the deck for breakfast. This would be easy.

Pete's cocker spaniel raised his head before the door buzzer sounded at 7:23. The two of them greeted Heather Montgomery, who had set a personal morning record for her shortest time to prepare.

"Heather, I'm really glad we could meet." Peter Morris registered the sheerness of her sand-colored silk blouse.

Pete's start suggested to Heather it could be a good morning to ask the right questions, keep her mouth shut and listen. She had two simple strategies: don't waste time on pleasantries and whet Pete with a few real facts.

"Pete, we should try to work together," she said.

"Right, right," he said. "Come on out back. I've got breakfast set up on the deck." Morris snapped a leash on his dog and led Heather to the twelve-foot-by-ten-foot deck, elevated a foot above the ground. Orange juice filled two glasses and an urn of coffee simmered on the table.

Morris pulled a chair for her. He tethered his dog to an eye ring in the wood deck planking. The spaniel trotted as far as his leash permitted, claiming a shady position to nap under the table.

He poured her a cup of coffee, "Let me get breakfast. I'll be back within two minutes. Sam will keep you company." With the mention of his name the dog's head lifted for just a moment.

Kowalski, the false garbage man, lay under the dripping green plants. The sprinkling had ceased. He fidgeted, he had been on site too long. The woman on the deck looked pretty tasty. Too bad he didn't have more time with this assignment. She had her head back to soak in some rays. Kowalski sighted the La France M16K between her breasts.

"English muffins, sliced oranges and bacon," Morris announced his return. "Not classic, I wasn't planning on hosting breakfast this morning."

"It's fine," said Heather.

Morris placed the food on Heather's side of the table, "What's with this special inspection of the Endres out-of-town projects."

Heather wanted to ask the questions. She reverted to the second part of her strategy. *Whet his curiosity with fact.*

"Pete, it was something that Phil Kamerov told me to do. He may have suspected documentation inadequacies ahead of the examiner's next visit. But, the question may be, what have you been doing to control these loans?"

"What do you mean?" Pete got dumb.

Kowalski's right thumb and index finger traced the select-fire options. He clicked into semi-automatic.

Time to *get this done with and be gone.*

Kowalski attached the Blair High Frequency silencer.

"OK everybody, line up just right for me."

Kowalski sighted on the glass of orange juice Pete Morris held to his mouth, re- adjusting for seven feet less than his previous set. Kowalski rotated to Heather, centering her throat. He watched her neck muscles ripple as she swallowed. He moved the barrel almost imperceptibly. The woman slid her chair backwards across the wooden deck. Was she leaving?

NOW, he squeezed off one shot.

"Straight through the living room and turn right," Pete Morris directed Heather.

Heather scratched her chair backward and rose from the outdoor table. "I'll be right back." Sam, despite being a mere cocker spaniel, showed proper etiquette by standing as Heather pushed her chair back from the table.

The cocker exploded. Dog blood splattered her skirt. The blast blew the cocker spaniel towards the condo . . . as far as the leash stretched.

At the slight pop, Pete's head jerked up; he might have seen something rustle the shrubs. His attention refocused at Heather's gurgling.

Pete stepped towards Heather, tripping over his dog. Sam, always aware of Pete's whereabouts, didn't move. A pool of blood surrounded his dog.

"Oh no, that bastard." Pete Morris began to cry as he knelt next to his dead friend.

Heather's stomach heaved before she could stumble to edge of the deck.

CHAPTER TWENTY-SIX

Dallas, Texas

Water so hot it steamed showered Heather's body in the stall of the athletic club. She scoured her leg for a fourth time. Physical revulsion had surrendered to fact.

Someone deliberately shot Pete Morris' dog. Sick!

There had been a noise, a pop. *Oh, God, someone is shooting.*

On her hands and knees she vomited at the edge of the deck until her stomach emptied. Heather raced to her Mercedes, sprinting through wet grass, a mindless dash to the parking area. Never saying one word to Pete.

Pete, back on the deck of his condo, on his knees pleading with his dead cocker spaniel to recover.

No goodbye, no what the hell, just escape. The tires of the white Mercedes signed out of the parking lot with an illegible, screeching black rubber signature. She should have been jailed by the Dallas cops on a reckless driving charge for wild rush to the Richardson Athletic club. Heather would have welcomed the police if they had stopped her. At the Richardson AC, her club, two blocks from the Hamilton S&L, she raced to the Ladies' locker room. Heather twisted the shower valve to HOT. She stripped right there, slinging her blouse, bra, and panties on the hook outside the shower intended for towels. She threw her bloodied slacks in a heap on the yellow tile floor. Heather scrubbed. After two soapy purifications Heather walked, dripping, to the rack and grabbed one of the fresh white towels and re-entered her shower stall. She siphoned soap into the wet towel from the wall-mounted reservoir and scrubbed her face, her hands, her legs. The sight of the dog wouldn't wash away. Forty minutes under the torrent, she still felt contaminated.

Heather pumped the liquid soap dispenser in her shower stall three more times. The syrupy cleaning solution oozed onto the soaking towel. She draped the over-size wash rag around her neck and rubbed through it. A wave of nausea rippled her visceral muscles. Hands on her knees, she braced her slumping shoulders. The tile shower stall amplified her gagging. Nothing. Nothing more to expel except the putrid memory.

* * *

Shock had evolved into rage. Pete Morris energized his rage and swore revenge. After four minutes of clenched fist grief for Sam, his lifeless dog, Pete stood. He drove from his condo to his office at the Hamilton S&L; vowing to dismantle the finances of Dimitri Paulopnos. Arriving at his office, he realized he could do nothing. Call the loans, the Greek would laugh.

"Dimitri, you mother fucking immigrant cocksucker."

Calm, the European accent devoid of emotion, Dimitri Paulopnos responded, "Good morning, Peter. I expected your call to confirm the $3,000,000 had been deposited to the Plano Mall checking account."

Morris shot his left hand across his desk and yanked the signature pen from the desk set. Pete's left hand bent the black Cross pen thirty degrees before it snapped. Saliva lubricated Morris' words, "You went too far, you mother-fucking bastard. You'll regret this."

At the other end of the telephone connection, the Greek smiled. *So far, so good,* he thought. Jim Kowalski had telephoned thirty minutes ago to confirm that the dog had been killed as Pete Morris watched.

Peter Morris now understands there can be sticks in this game as well as carrots, Paulopnos thought. The Greek had transported the Hamilton VP to the edge. *Time* to *bring the young man back,* Dimitri Paulopnos said to himself. *There are tasks for Mr. Morris to accomplish.*

"Peter, my limousine will be at the side door of the Hamilton, the exit to your employee parking area, in thirty minutes. Please join me, we can resolve our business matters," the Greek said.

Pete Morris hammered the phone into its cradle on his desk at the Hamilton Savings & Loan without answering Dimitri Paulopnos' invitation.

Get control of yourself, get control . . . then fuck the Greek prick.

The Hamilton VP arrested his hyper-ventilating breath. Sweat tracing his spine fell into his undershorts. His hand swept the papers on his desk to the floor. From inside his office he slammed the solid oak door. The shot the door delivered sounded like a cannon within the Hamilton. Relying on touch he found his way to the swivel chair behind his mahogany veneer desk. Morris collapsed into the leather seat, dropped his head into the bed of his arms and squeezed his eyelids in an effort to dispel reality.

* * *

Heather side-saddled into the blue leather driver's seat of her white Mercedes 450SL. Before she settled into the baking leather, her right arm extended to set the air conditioner control for maximum high. With her feet resting outside the auto on the black parking lot pavement, she started the automobile's engine. The passenger side door remained open. The air conditioner's introductory blast trumpeted one-hundred-sixteen-degree air into the car interior . . . without lowering or raising the temperature.

Heather bent towards the cellular car phone. Grasping the receiver, she punched seven digits into the phone's transmission board, then rested the telephone on her lap, waiting for the Mercedes' inner temperature to drop below one hundred degrees Fahrenheit.

Her physical effort of dressing, then walking across the roasting asphalt from the athletic club to her car, had drained her minimum reserves Heather still possessed.

Had she really witnessed Morris's dog being shot on the deck this morning?

Stupid Heather, she scolded herself, *you try to get closer to Morris and you almost get yourself killed! What the hell was Pete Morris into? Was the killing of the dog related to the Hamilton S&L?*

Heather had enough quandaries of her own. She didn't need to bear the problems of other Hamilton employees. Lending money as a career choice didn't include dodging bullets while eating breakfast.

This sucked.

The Hamilton wasn't real, these people weren't real. Heather pressed the SEND button on the telephone option board.

"Mr. Johnstone's office," the secretary answered.

"Good morning, Becky." Heather reacquired her professional tone, "Is Billy in?"

"Hi, Heather." The Chief Operating Officer's secretary, Becky Riley, and Heather Montgomery respected each other, though differing professional responsibility had prohibited development of close friendship. "He's meeting with your boss, pork belly Peterson. Should I interrupt?"

"Does it look like their discussion will end soon?" Heather asked.

"Hold on, I feel the ground tremble under heavy footsteps as we speak."

The phone went silent. Heather swung her legs into the white German car and under the steering column. She pulled the car door closed. The temperature inside the auto dipped to a cool ninety three, two degrees below the ambient temperature. Heather adjusted the fan propelling the air from the conditioning unit to fifty percent of maximum in order to hear better.

Less than one minute later Johnstone spoke, "Heather, hope I didn't keep you holding long?"

Heather took one deep breath, "Billy, I've got a problem and it is affecting my ability to represent the Hamilton S&L. I don't have proof, but I suspect the problem may be the Hamilton S&L's problem, too. If I am going to work with the Hamilton to solve the problems we have, I need to have certain facts on the table. In the open, with the responsible people present."

"Should you and I meet? " Billy asked.

"Yes, and the meeting has to include Randy Peterson and Peter Morris," she said.

Johnstone reached for his appointment book, "Heather, why don't you confirm the time with the others? I'll make myself available. Let's meet in my office. What if I pencil off a week from tomorrow at 2 P.M.?"

"No. Billy, too important, too important to wait until next week. I'll gather Morris and Peterson. It's imperative we meet now. Today or tomorrow morning at the latest."

Billy Johnstone held the receiver at arm's length in front of him and stared at Heather's request through the phone piece, "What's your proposed agenda, Heather?"

"People dying, people being shot at, powerful customers with falsified documentation for their loans, regulators. We've got enough regulators in the bank to seize Panama. My agenda: What the hell is going on? I'll tell you, you tell me."

"Tomorrow at 8 A.M.?"

"That will do," she said.

"My office, Heather. I'm writing the time in ink. I'll assume you'll corral Pete and Randy?"

"I will." Heather hit the button on her phone marked END. The interior temperature of her automobile was eighty-four degrees.

* * *

The Hamilton S&L

Pete Morris accepted he would suffer injury. That he would be arrested and spend time in jail was inevitable. He'd conclude this part of life honorably.

The tenebrous, black, stretch Lincoln owned by the Greek loomed ominously at the private side entrance for staff of the Hamilton Savings & Loan. The Hamilton VP exited exactly thirty minutes after hanging up the phone on Dimitri Paulopnos. Killing Paulopnos didn't bother Pete. The beating Morris would have to endure, he had to endure because· killing the Greek with his hands wouldn't be instantaneous. Sweat rivulets stream from Pete's armpits, draining down both sides of his chest. The muscles lining Morris's neck cramped.

The Hamilton VP thought about getting a gun when he arrived from Ohio, the Texas guys all had guns. Pete Morris had never shot a gun. Pete weighed puncturing the Greek's heart with a knife.

God, that would be a bloody mess, he concluded. Pete figured he didn't have the skill for a knife. His plan is hasty, but spontaneity might support his inevitable legal plea , if he can bargain the charge of murdering Dimitri Paulopnos.

As Pete walked to the elongated auto, Paulopnos' uniformed chauffeur opened the rear door. Windows tinted deep blue hid Dimitri, unaware he was living his final minutes. The dark glass on the limo will confuse witnesses that testify at Morris' murder trial. A trial the death of Dimitri Paulopnos will surely merit. Pete reminds himself to keep his hands high when he enters the back seat. He contrives a false adjustment to the label of his sport coat, getting his hands up. Slowing the pace of his stride, he compacts his leg muscles for push-off. He scans one-hundred eighty-degrees to see if there is a potential witness. The only observer in sight is the skinny Mex raking the plant beds sixty feet to his right. Pete can't see through the opaque glass into the automobile.

Pete anticpates the Greek's chauffeur will thump him from behind, trying to stop the death struggle. Pete will have to withstand the chauffer's pummeling, he has to kill Dimitri.

Get a grip on his neck, hold, squeeze his fucking neck until the bastard breathes his last mother-fucking breath.

Morris will use the strength of his legs to kick the chauffeur away. If Pete feels the chauffeur is overcoming him he'll fracture Paulopnos' trachea.

How long could it take the fucking Greek to die; a minute?

Reaching the attended open rear door of the limousine, Morris stutter-steps to suck air, then lunges into the rear of the auto. Wailing an Indian war cry, meant to alarm not warn, Pete scrapes his knees across the limousine's floor. Morris reckons Paulopnos will react to his Comanche yell by throwing his hands upward, shielding his Greek face. Extending his raging scream, Morris scrambles, on his knees, deeper into the limo. He wedges his foot into a fulcrum against the front bench to leverage his right fist. Upper thigh muscles bulge and he plunges under the Greek's defensive hands to deliver one punishing thump. Just one thump that will ram every cubic liter of oxygenated air from Paulopnos' lungs.

Morris's gruntal alarm sounds a terrible warning to the slight Mex gardener. The Hispanic had swum the shallow Rio two miles north of Ojinaga two months ago and immediately assumed a high-strung lack of presence. The three-truck landscape company paid him cash at days end.

The Mex did not like working at the busy banco. *Too many people, so in the open.*

The illegal laborer understood some English, but had admitted it to no one. He'd much rather be working in the backyard of a private casa. His obsidian eyes keep vigil.

Gianni Cortese sat alone in the back seat of the limo. His boss, Mr. Paulopnos, had cautioned Gianni that Pete Morris grieved over the loss of a friend.

"He'll be upset, Gianni. Don't hurt him though. Deliver him back here in one piece," the Greek said.

Gianni Cortese prized his job as Mr. Paulopnos' bodyguard

Gianni didn't ask, but figured Morris' grief couldn't be too great because he, Gianni, didn't do the job. The boss must have employed that redneck Pollack asshole, Kowalski, for one of his commando assaults.

"Porca Miseria," Gianni mumbled as he watched Morris knee-hop towards him along the floor of the backseat in Palopnos' limo.

You gotta look at me if you wanna hit me, Gianni thought.

Cortese's lifts his hands in mock defense as Morris screams a TV-Indian cry. Gianni separates his hands twelve inches to view Morris's ineptness. He watches Pete's eyes as Pete locates a foot-hold on the floor of the back seat.

Never take your eyes off the target, che pazzo, Gianni thinks.

The Italian security man slides right as though floating on his leather seat, catches Morris' incoming fist of the Hamilton VP, transferring the force of Morris's intended punch. Gianni pulls Pete forward, trussing him face down, Morris' nose poking the adjacent spot on the black leather bench just vacated by Gianni's ass. Gianni Cortese, jerks both arms behind Pete's back and yanks Morris' limbs upward, stretching ligaments, tendons, and muscle to the point where they'll be useless for five minutes but not permanently damaged. With the Hamilton VP immobile, Gianni spins him counter clockwise a half revolution. He slaps Pete three rapid whacks to the right side of his face. A finishing rap to the back of Morris' head gains command. The last knock forces Pete to sniff the leather seat again.

Pete had accurately gauged the protective action the chauffeur would initiate. The driver did come from behind. He sauntered around the back of the car, stopping to watch the Mex gardener light-foot through the freshly raked plant bed and dash across the parking lot.

Man, that little spick can travel, the chauffer observes. The chauffer saw the agitated illegal gardener burst from the far side of the Hamilton parking lot and run straight through a dense eight-foot evergreen hedge.

The Greek's motorman stepped to the far rear door hoping to assist the bodyguard. Inside, Cortese jerks Pete's right arm, spinning him half circle. Together, they yank Morris upward, parking his ass on the bench seat. The chauffeur snaps Pete's seat belt for safety.

Gianni smiles. "Sit back, kid. The ride won't be long. And relax. I assure you I'm not the guy you're mad at."

The body guard catches his reflection off the tinted window, smooths the hair on his right temple with his four fingers.

CHAPTER TWENTY-SEVEN

<u>Dallas, Texas</u>

Pete Morris didn't attempt to speak to the Greek's bodyguard during his back-seat journey. The course the limousine's chauffeur navigated suggested this trip would conclude at his own condo. As the black auto made an eight mile-per-hour entrance into the parking lot of the Hamilton VP's condo, Pete Morris confronted the butchery he ran away from this morning.

Sam, dead on the deck. Who do I call to remove a dead dog? God, I can't look at it again.

To Pete Morris's right, Gianni Cortese folded his arms before speaking, "Look, we are going into your place. Don't matter to me how we do this, but we are going into your condo. Why don't we just do it easy 'cuz I got no reason to get hard on you?" The eyes of the Italian foretold of Mediterranean bias, honor by edict.

Morris twisted his head just far enough for a peripheral impression of the Italian bodyguard. Gianni Cortese didn't seem to notice.

"Maybe I don't want to go in," the Hamilton VP said.

"That has nothin' to do with anything," the Greek's man said. "We're only talking method."

The limo pulled into an empty parking slot in front of Peter's condo. The chauffeur exited the car posthaste; opening the left rear door. Gianni clamped his left hand around Pete's upper right arm; the two men marched towards Peter's condo. Pete dug for the front door key.

"No need," Cortese's free right hand twisted the unlocked doorknob and allowed Peter the honor of first entry.

Morris passed through his short foyer into the living room.

Drawn curtains darkened the room and the air conditioning cooled to seventy-three degrees. "Good morning, Peter," said Dimitri Paulopnos

Steel fingers from the Italian hand re-clamped into the Hamilton VP's upper arm, arresting Pete's charge at the Greek; the man responsible for killing his dog that morning.

"Peter, your reluctance to fund my loan yesterday could have cost me a great deal."

"Fucking prick," Pete Morris spat at the Greek.

Gianni Cortese's open right palm rattled the Hamilton lender's head, dispensing an etiquette refresher.

Paulopnos delayed a moment while Morris composed himself.

"In fact, Peter," the Greek said, "I do not exaggerate when I speculate that your failure to fund our deal might have cost me all I've worked for during the past ten years. You were not honorable in your end of our arrangement."

"You prick," Pete Morris said, "You don't fucking shoot a dog because your loan takes a few days longer to fund than you anticipated."

Gianni Cortese was right. The boss had used that Pollack soldier of fortune. *That mercenary asshole must have loved this assignment . . . shooting a fucking dog. Incazzato. I wonder if he dressed in camouflage to sneak up on the dog.*

"Peter, I've got payments that will hit your bank today, checks I've already written. Plano Mall is under construction. The project can't wait three weeks. You've funded half the loan. Timing is essential. Money is made by meeting schedules. You've interrupted my schedule. It's time we get back on track. Put the three million in the Plano Mall account today."

Pete Morris stood accused, being tried in the living room of his own home. "Dimitri, listen to me. The rules are changing. I've got examiners all over my ass." The cadence of Pete articulation went monosyllabic, "The rules can't be bent."

The Greek cut the Hamilton lender off, "Peter, I can't concern myself with your dilemma. Put the money in the account."

Dimitri rose from Peter's couch. A yip from outside broke the silence in the room. Behind the closed living room curtain, the door to his deck must have been open.

It couldn't be that . . . no, Morris thought. *Sam was dead, there was no mistake.*

Then another weak bark from just outside the sliding glass door leading to the deck. Peter Morris' eyes interrogated the Greek; Paulopnos had all but admitted to killing the dog. Paulopnos walked past Peter, stopping in the foyer. Gianni Cortese released Morris's arm and opened the front door in anticipation of his boss's departure. Peter could see the back of the chauffeur through the open door, standing at attention on the front walk overseeing the safety of the parked limo.

"$3,000,000, Peter. So important I can't express it in words. And I won't express it in words. Call me to confirm the transaction." Dimitri didn't wait for Peter's reply. The bodyguard shut the apartment door.

Morris stood. *Why in the fuck did I get into this?* The faint bark induced Pete to walk towards the deck. As he approached an alcohol smell assaulted his nostrils. He couldn't pull open the curtains.

Jesus, could his dog, could Sam still be alive? No, the dog died. Peter's head slumped. Crisis jumped back into his life. Peter yanked the curtains open. No dog. The spot where Sam had been shot was immaculate? No evidence remained, no Sam, no blood from the tragedy of that morning.

Peter walked onto his deck, to the exact site of the carnage. He stooped down. His fingers ran across the fresh wood stain. The evidence of Sam's demise had been removed. Whatever didn't wash away had been sanded clean. The pungency of the oil-base stain permeated his senses. Fresh light grey wood stain, applied an hour ago, meshed with the deck color. The muffled yip sounded again. Peter had no defense for his tears. They flowed without warning as he dropped to his knees. Peter wondered when the echo of his companion would cease. Was he going mad?

After three minutes Pete raised himself to full height. He tilted his head upwards, eyes closed, attempting to siphon courage from the power of the sun. *How do I get things straightened out?* he asked a nameless god. He dropped his head and opened his eyes. As Pete turned towards the door into his living room the six-week-old rust-colored Cocker Spaniel pup, cowering in the shadow of the condo, shed its fear.

Trailing the new red leash, the cocker spaniel pup trotted towards Peter.

CHAPTER TWENTY-EIGHT

Dallas, Texas

Except for the heels she wore, Heather would have run to her car. She ignited the engine, finagled the car from her parking spot, and exited the Hamilton Savings & Loan employee parking area. 4:15 P.M. Fifteen minutes until her scheduled meeting with the Number Two at the Dallas Federal Home Loan Bank; the guy in charge of regulating S&L banks in Texas. The Dallas FHLB, Heather had decided, would be her plan B.

Heather pressed the telephone button, dialing the head of the FDIC in Washington, D.C. One ring later Jack Richardson picked up his private line.

"Hello," Jack Richardson said.

"Deal's off. You guys do your own footwork. I'm out," Heather said.

"Heather?"

"Yes, this is Heather," she confirmed.

"You sound harried?" A thousand miles away in Washington. Jack Richardson perceived her frazzled state.

"Even the protection you offered me last night isn't enough of an umbrella." Heather was inhaling so fast and deep her oxygen supply was dwindling.

"Hold on, Heather. Take a deep breath." Neither spoke for twenty seconds.

"Now, explain," the chairman of the FDIC instructed.

Heather recited all relevant detail since talking to Richardson on her way home from the airport last night. Concluding she said, "So that's it. No one can protect me when some maniac shoots from God know where while I'm eating breakfast."

"Heather, calm down. I will get you protection. Whether you like it or not, you are involved in this mess," Richardson said.

"I'm not involved in anything I don't want to be in," she said. "And I am out. Officially."

Richardson tried soft sell, "If you leave now, your reputation will be tarnished when we finally bring Thompson and the Hamilton down."

Heather wanted to hang-up the phone, but something probed her subconscious. "What do you mean Thompson? I thought the Hamilton is your target. You want to nail the Hamilton's CEO?"

The FDIC Chairman had spoken too quickly, "The Hamilton is our target," he said. "Ken Thompson is the majority stockholder. Regulator's way of viewing this bank problem."

"Well, you are on your own. Regardless of who, or what, your target may be," she said.

"Heather, you are an integral member of my team. I need you to finish."

"No, I am not part of your team. Good-bye, Mr. Richardson, and best of luck." Heather operated her Mercedes left-handed, her right hand flipped the phone over. She located the END button that would terminate this conversation, cutting Jack Richardson off.

Before Heather's thumb depressed END, words she hoped never to hear again sieved from the speaker of the telephone.

"DETROIT." The telephone receiver lay belly-up on her thigh. The voice within the phone, so faint, reached her ear. His word struck like thunder quaking the night.

The phone remained in her lap. "What!" Heather challenged the voice. Heather yanked the receiver against her right ear.

"There is a question regarding the accusations you presented in Detroit," Richardson said.

Heather squeezed the receiver, "What question?"

"Heather, I talked to Peter Quist recently."

"How did you happen to talk with Peter Quist?" Heather snarled.

"Heather, the FDIC is responsible for national banks. Peter works for a prominent national bank. Extorting money from a national bank is criminal."

"I don't understand." Heather was not going to lead this dance.

"Mr. Quist insists you do understand. I would just as soon let the issue remain buried." The chairman of the FDIC paused to let Heather evaluate.

Heather snapped back, "What issue in Detroit?"

The Chairman of the FDIC paused to let Heather evaluate, "You are part of my team aren't you, Heather?"

Another crisis; again the male world wasn't playing fair with Heather Montgomery.

* * *

Another day, Heather jabbed the elevator button pointing up. She spun her left wrist, 1:57 P.M. Great, three hours behind a schedule that didn't include a single appointment.

Yesterday's threat from the FDIC Chairman to re-explore her accusation of rape in Detroit had occupied her last hour. Heather concluded that she had to continue spying for the feds. If she walked out now she would forfeit her carte blanche cover from the Feds and one great resume line. Plus Detroit had to stay in the closet. She'd walk both sides of the street. Heather decided to adopt a second guardian while she meddled inside the Hamilton; she had contacted the Texas S&L regulators; the Dallas Fed Home Loan Bank. But first, she would tattle the details of the money Endres Brothers had received and wasted to Phil Kamerov, Hamilton's Workout guy. The elevator chimed, the doors split.

"Hi, Janis," Heather greeted the incoming passenger, the Hamilton's head teller.

Janis Lang bobbed her head in response.

Heather retreated within, unrequited memories, *Jesus, what kind of people is Morris screwing with? Shoot his dog!*

A sniffle from the head teller interrupted Heather. Self-control ebbed from Janis Lang with each ping as the elevator climbed floor-by-floor towards Phil the Pill's office. Her sniveling mutated into chattering sobs. "I'm sorry," Janis murmured.

Heather assumed the grieving passenger had addressed her.

"For what?" Heather asked.

Janis' couldn't stem her weeping. Her words sputtered through gaps in her sobs. "I'm meeting with Mr. Kamerov, to tell him. "

"Phil can be a pill, but he's not worth getting worked up over," Heather said. *What the hell is Phil doing with the head teller?* Heather mused. "What do you have to talk to him about?"

Janis' sobs baffled Heather's attempt to interpret, "Money, dormant,"

Heather patted Janis shoulder, "Calm down."

At Heather's touch Janis' confessed, "I'll give it . . .didn't mean it. Money, didn't hurt."

The babbling from the teller defied interpretation.

"Janis, I'm on my way to The Pill's office. Walk with me. He's a squirrelly little guy, but he's not as bad as you seem to think he is."

CHAPTER TWENTY-NINE

<u>Dallas, Texas, The Hamilton Savings and Loan</u>

His right hand stabbed outward, "Janis, I'm Phil Kamerov, chairman of the Workout Committee." Phil the Pill stood outside the teller's gate. The head teller gripped his hand with dread.

Pete Morris had exposed the truth to Janis; the Workout guy was a spy for the examiners. She feared that eventually Phil Kamerov would trace the missing money; the money she had stolen from the dormant accounts.

"Hello. I heard you joined Hamilton recently," Janis feigned congeniality, "What does a Workout Committee do? Sounds like group exercise!"

Phil Kamerov needed to recruit the Hamilton's head teller. Janis Lang could be the informational shortcut to Pete Morris's unauthorized loans. *How is the Hamilton lender funding the commercial real estate deals without the loans appearing on the records of the Hamilton S&L?*

"Chairman of the Workout Committee? I, uh, locate financial problems, then fix them," The Pill said.

Vertigo slid over Janis like an avalanche, "Oh!"

Phil studied the head teller of the S&L, "I assure bank policy is being carried out properly by Hamilton Employees."

Images collided in Janis' mind.

"Cure inconsistencies, misapplication of funds." The Pill removes his clean bifocals for polishing with his handkerchief.

"Does that keep you busy? Everybody here seems in tune?" Go *away*, she silently begs.

Phil the Pill understands that Pete Morris' indiscretions could wreak havoc upon this woman's existence. He dramatizes the consequence of bank fraud, then leaves her an escape hatch.

"There are problems. More than the examiners realize. Are you aware of misapplication of funds?"

Janis' reaction confirms to Phil that she understands her complicity in Pete Morris' fraudulent advances. Janis knows she is a criminal, Phil knows she isn't.

A single truth devours Janis; she is going to jail for stealing from those dormant checking accounts, dead people's money. She pictures Phil Kamerov latching stainless steel hand cuffs around her wrists; hears the irrefutable click.

"Janis, let's discuss this privately in my office," the Pill says.

Tears cloud her vision. She nods, submitting to his suggestion.

"2 P.M. an hour from now," he says.

Lang, Hamilton S&L's head teller, shakes her head in affirmation. *Oh god, he knows about every penny.*

CHAPTER THIRTY

<u>Dallas. Texas. The Hamilton S&L</u>

Billy Johnstone, COO of the Hamilton S&L, took the phone call at his secretary's desk.

"Billy," said Ken Thompson, CEO of the Hamilton S&L, "there is chatter on the House Banking Committee that Treasury intends to make an example of a Texas S&L." Ken Thompson had a problem.

Becky heard her boss, the COO of the Hamilton say, "I'll be there."

"Becky, I'm going to need a flight to DC tomorrow morning for a hurry-up meeting. Gather the files on our executive review with the FHLB and the FDIC examiners." Billy Johnstone half- instructed, half-asked his secretary.

"What's the scoop? The quarterly board meeting isn't scheduled for two more months," Rebecca Riley said.

"Don't know exactly. Our CEO is uptight about the S&L regulators. They are on our back but, it's more than that. Ken got word of something through his political pals in Washington. He wouldn't talk about it on the phone. Just the chief, our D.C. attorney and me at tomorrow's meeting." Johnstone stated.

"Tell me what you need."

Billy opened his personal file. He traced through the FDIC audit of the Hamilton S&L.

"Becky, get a hold of Heather Montgomery and tell her our appointment for 8:00 A.M. tomorrow has to be rescheduled."

Becky spent ten silent minutes collecting the files the Hamilton COO required for his meeting in Washington the following day. Billy Johnstone didn't speak as he read the summarization of the FDIC's exam completed a month ago.

Becky couldn't let her boss leave for DC without discussing it. She had waited all day for Billy to bring up the newspaper story. She had to talk about her feelings.

"Billy," she said, "this has nothing to do with your meeting and maybe it's not the time to discuss it, but what about the story in the yesterday's Dallas *Morning Times* on the bomb exploding in London last week?"

Billy was absorbed, reviewing his notes on the FDIC exam in prep for tomorrow's meeting.

"Didn't read Sunday's paper. Wasn't in town," the COO said

"Didn't you see the picture of the hotel explosion?" his secretary asked.

"No, I don't think so." Billy Johnstone's tone suggested his mind had wandered.

"A bomb exploded in London," Becky's voice trembled. "It killed four people. They were all American. Billy, the people killed were federal bank examiners. They were in London to examine a branch of a U.S. bank."

Billy's head swung, his eyes widened, "I can't say I'm distraught after what those examiners have put us through this past year." Billy felt a warning jangle on the skin of his back, a warning that bad news was imminent, "Anybody we know?"

"Yes. Julie Weidener, his secretary said. "You remember. She was here for two weeks last month with the FDIC people. I took her out for a drink after work one night." Becky stopped.

Billy look down at the file, re-reading his concluding recommendation; the confidential memo he authored. A recommendation for the eyes of Ken Thompson only, the Hamilton CEO; *Weidener and her FDIC team are challenging our lending, accounting and management procedures. Use your Washington contacts to have her removed from the Hamilton examination.*

Becky interrupted his speculation, "Billy, she's dead."

Billy's internal electronics processed this data at full throttle. This changed Hamilton's problems. Weidener led the FDIC exam team. At her summary review, Ms. Weidener forewarned the COO of her scathing indictment on managerial deficiencies. Her report was to have been presented to the FDIC brass this week. Billy didn't believe in luck or coincidence.

Weidener's death could be linked with her penultimate assignment.

"That's enough for tonight," Billy said.

Becky observed his mood change. She wanted an answer to the question she hadn't asked. She cleared her desk.

CHAPTER THIRTY-ONE

Early morning sun filled the sixth floor office of the head of the Federal Deposit Insurance Corporation, Jack Richardson. Brendan stepped to the window; a US Air 737 climbed from Washington National and rotated towards the Midwest. The FDIC man, his old college roomie, had served up the evidence accusing the Savings & Loan industry.

Neither man looked at each other, Brendan asked, "That's the case, what is the plan, chief?"

"Tackle the bastards now," the FDIC guy said. One question had not been discussed. "Brendan, our FDIC bank examiners were assassinated in London. My exam team was loaned to the S&L guys at the Dallas Fed Home Loan Bank, the Texas S&L guys needed FDIC experience with bad lending practice."

Brendan yearned for his yacht anchored in that far away Virgin Island harbor.

Richardson, the FDIC Chairman continued, "My examiners will resign rather than be assigned to a Texas S&L. The prez of the Dallas FHLB says his examiners don't know how to get tough with the S&L's, they are in lock-down. I've got to break this standoff. When the Savings banks fail, this mess will fall back on the FDIC."

"Shouldn't the solution come from the head of the Fed Home Loan Bank, Ed Gray?"

"Talk is that the White House is encouraging Ed Gray to resign as Chair of the Fed Home Loan," said the FDIC head, "Gray is under pressure, a group of five senators called a private meeting with Gray; told him to back off on S&L's."

"How do I contribute," Brendan said.

"Facts on the S&L fraud have to be gathered from inside an S&L, by someone with the power of god. You can't believe the political clout these criminals have bought. I need to hang one of these thrift sonofabitches; a public hanging of the most notorious bastard. The United States can't afford to have the Savings & Loan industry fail."

Brendan turned from the window, "First step?" he asked.

"Go down to the land of the two step and long neck beers. Texas," Richardson said.

"Jack, I've been away from the banking game for twelve years."

The chairman of the FDIC came around his desk and clamped his arm on Brendan's shoulder from behind, "You'll have help. We've identified the worst of the worst. Six S&L's misappropriating insured deposits, looting the treasury. Each thrift has assets exceeding six billion dollars. Two are in California, one is in Arizona and three are in Texas. One guy has his hands in the pockets of at least five senators. Even congressmen have to be accountable."

"Who is that?"

"Ken Thompson, he controls the Hamilton S&L in Dallas."

The midnight-blue Cadillac limo negotiating Washington's early rush hour could be identified as U.S. government by the unique license plate.

Brendan said to the head of the FDIC, "Logical start is the S&L's accountants."

The limo swung south on 20th Street, towards Washington National.

"Yeah," responded the FDIC head, Jack Richardson, "but isn't. Arthur Young's senior partner on the Hamilton S&L signed off on a clean audit last year. For emphasis he authored a letter to Texas Senator, Jim Anderson, accusing the Fed Home Loan examiners of lacking the financial skills to critique Texas real estate lending."

"How did he arrive at that conclusion with thirty two percent of the loans classified?"

The chauffeur spun the stretch Cadillac past the Lincoln Memorial and across the Arlington Memorial Bridge. The driver was on loan from the Secret Service.

"He was bought. The accountant left Young two months after the Hamilton audit, started a consulting business. First client, the Hamilton S&L at $480,000 a year. Stay away from Hamilton's outside accountants. Arthur Young is circling the wagons with the Hamilton."

"Who is on your side in Dallas?" Brendan asked. The limo passed over the muddy channel flowing from the Potomac into the Pentagon Lagoon.

"First, contact the Director of Supervision at the Dallas Federal Home Loan Bank; he is the number two guy and heads examination of all S&L in Texas. He is expecting to be contacted, but doesn't know it will be you," Jack handed Brendan a confidential report addressed to the Secretary of the Treasury.

Brendan scanned the cover; FRAUD, SELF-DEALING, CONFLICTS OF INTEREST leaped from the page.

"Second, there are two people inside the Hamilton who are cooperating with me." Jack Richardson wrote a single name and phone number on the last page in his pocket calendar. He ripped the single sheet from the wire binder and tucked it into Brendan's shirt pocket.

Richardson said, "There is only one name on the sheet I gave you. The second contact inside the Hamilton is through Treasury. I need their approval to disclose."

Brendan nodded.

Jack Richardson said, "Third, you'll have a guardian angel. Your angel will connect with you in Dallas. All he will say is *I'm here to protect you*. Easy to remember."

Realization smacked Brendan that he had been drafted, not volunteered.

"Anything else?" Brendan asked.

"Yes. If you have to push these pricks, contact me. If you get stonewalled I will inform the Hamilton CEO that my office may recommend that deposit insurance be revoked for the Hamilton S&L and his lack of cooperation might provoke a leak to the *Washington Post*. Depositors will run away from the Hamilton."

"Doesn't that blow our investigation?"

"Announcement is to be reserved as a last, a final resort." The limo pulled into the curb announcing Departures at Washington National.

CHAPTER THIRTY-TWO

Washington. D.C . - The Mayfair Hotel

The Federal Express driver had the front desk clerk of the Mayfair sign for the package at 9:30 A.M. The bellhop knocked on the door to suite 418 at 9:33 A.M. The FedEx label on the package did not list the address or the phone number of the sender. Purple and white wrapping protected an eight-inch-by-eleven-inch manila envelope just as Ken Thompson had promised. The assassin sliced through the end of the envelope clamped with the brass butterfly fastener. Jonathan placed each document on the rectangular two-foot-by-four-foot glass top coffee table in the $375 per-night hotel suite.

For thirty minutes he circled the low table, pausing to digest each of the eight pages of information. Jonathan Blair memorized three addresses: the Alexandria apartment, the Maryland home, and the sanatorium where the mother resided. Historical patterns provided probable itineraries of future journeys. Jack Richardson drove to the medical center in Maryland that housed his Alzheimer afflicted mother twice each month. Schedules, habits, rituals of the FDIC chairman became file records in Blair's mind. The information analyzed and committed to memory, the assassin retrieved the metal waste basket from the bedroom. He sat on the edge of the plush beige arm chair, straddling the waste container. The Mayfair provided matches in the drawer of the desk. Jonathan ignited one page at a time, holding the lower corner of the sheet until it was ash.

Jonathan Blair left his sixth floor suite of the downtown Washington, D.C. hotel and repaired to the public sanctuary of the District's grass Mall. Strolling the one mile union linking the United States Capital Building to the Washington Monument, he drafted his final plan. Rotating scenes in three dimensional analysis, exploring around corners, shifting drapes, lifting sewer covers.

Washington, D.C. outside FDIC headquarters

Jonathan Blair surveyed the fourteen character vehicle number through the tinted front windshield of the British racing-green BMW. He recorded each of the stamped numbers evident on the auto's dashboard.

In front of the car, painted black capital letters on a six-inch by twenty-four-inch metal placard, the parking space was reserved for RICHARDSON. The small sign jutted three feet above the turf. Assets of the Federal Deposit Insurance Corporation did not warrant the sweeping twenty-four-hour security its godfather organization, the Department of Treasury, received. The Treasury Building, six blocks away, opposite the White House, commanded protection from their in-house security; the Secret Service.

Jonathan Blair penciled the last four digits of the BMW's unique serial number on the single slip of paper. He folded the paper and filed it into the pocket of his light blue dress shirt. He committed to memory the eighty meter path between the parking lot and the entrance to FDIC headquarters. Gate crashing the offices of the Bureau of Engraving were money is manufactured, or barging in Treasury, would have been impossible. Yet, here at Treasury's subsidiary, the FDIC, anyone can stroll into the lobby. With a little ingenuity the intruder might arrive, without appointment, in the office of senior officials, interrupting insurers of the money deposited in America's banks.

The assassin climbed two series of four concrete steps on the short walk to the atrium of 550 Seventeenth Street, N.W.

CHAPTER THIRTY-THREE

<u>Dallas. The Hamilton</u>

"Phil, Janis Lang is cracking apart in your outer office," Heather told the Workout guy, "What did you do to her?"

Heather defended the broken teller waiting in the Pill's outer office.

"I need her." Phil the Pill rose from his scratched, undersized desk and tracked towards the doorway leading into the hall.

Heather intercepted his chest like a referee controlling a heavyweight title fight, her palm stopping him, her right index finger admonishing, "Wait a minute. Talk to me. Janis Lang is a harmless teller. She needs a psychiatrist, not a Workout Committee. What the hell did you do to her?" Heather had had it with intrigue within the male network.

The Hamilton Workout guy, attentive of propriety, rebutted Heather's implicit, feminine tone with wide, white-eyed insult. "Nothing, nothing, she knows the details to nail that deceitful VP of Lending, Pete Morris,"

Phil the Workout guy added, "This is not something I should be sharing with you."

Heather took a shot. She had no idea if her Washington contact communicated directly with the Pill, "Phil, our friend in Washington told me last night to trust you. I'm here with the goods on the Endres. You owe me the truth."

The Chair of the Hamilton Workout Committee assessed her. If Heather was in for a penny, she could have her pound. "Morris has been funding money to Hamilton customers without loan approval. The transactions are being buried in Hamilton's inter-bank settlement account. Janis Lang is creating the accounting tickets."

"How bad is that for Janis?" Heather asked.

"Janis was wrong. Morris was criminal. She doesn't know what Morris is doing. But, I want her under pressure, our head teller is the key to nailing Morris."

The Pill has no idea about the money Janis has stolen, thought Heather. .

"Phil, let me talk to Janis alone for a few minutes," Heather said.

* * *

Heather tracked down Pete Morris at Herman's Cellar where Pete was pitching Hamilton S&L's ability to finance the proposed LBJ Marriott.

"Morris, you simple bastard," she said through the phone. "What have you been doing?"

Morris shook his Rolex free; 4:12 P.M. Their breakfast meeting at his condo seemed like a week ago. When he last saw Heather, she was fleeing his condo after heaving her guts on his deck.

"Where are you, Heather? " Morris said.

"In my office with Janis Lang. She has just told me a tale of banking intrigue."

Pete Morris shifted into low voice. "Oh, Jesus, Phil Kamerov has been all over me about that."

Heather kept probing, "The Pill summoned Janis to his office. I intercepted her. She has only talked to me at this point. By the time Phil

Most Delicious of Privileges

and the examiners interrogate her, I think they'll shoot you, not your goddam dog." Heather rotated her eyes to Janis Lang, seated across her desk. Heather breathed deep, the Hamilton teller didn't flinch at the dog remark.

"Tell me exactly what in the hell is going on," Heather said.

Pete Morris wanted out of this mess. He needed to strike a deal with someone with power, or jail loomed. Since the Greek had offered the cocker spaniel pup in peace, Pete had examined how he could cut such a deal. Whatever the course, his arrangement had to be in place before Janis Lang squealed to the Pill.

"Heather, I've got to talk to Janis," the VP said.

Heather seized the opening, "Janis is only talking to me. If you want to swap information, I have contacts. Talk to me if you want a way out of this mess."

"Contacts?" Pete Morris asked.

"Excellent contacts," Heather said, "I need to know how much money you've distributed without loan approval. Specifically, talk to me about the three million you authorized for Plano Mall two hours ago?"

A deleterious deja vu flashed Pete, "Heather, meet me at my condo."

"Pete, no more condo. I've had it for one day. It isn't the safest haven in Dallas."

"It's safe now. We can't talk in public. Bring Janis Lang. Let's hash this out. I need to know about your contacts. Agreed?"

"Not your goddam condo." She surveyed Janis, who had regained partial composure. Heather had told the teller Phil the Pill didn't know a thing about Janis' theft from the dormant Hamilton checking accounts; the teller refused to believe this news.

Incredible! Lang says she got a hundred grand! The Pill's only interest was to crucify Pete Morris, whom Janis Lang regarded as a cocky Vice President at the Hamilton.

How's Phil ever going to discover the money Lang stole from the dormant accounts if those people are dead? Heather's question evaporated.

Heather reconsidered, "When will you be there?"

"The front door is open," Pete said, "I'll wrap this meeting up and be there at 5 P.M."

Heather replaced the receiver. Phil Kamerov walked by Heather's glass office panels. Without invitation The Pill stuck his head around the stained oak support frame.

"Can we have our discussion now?" The Pill asked.

Lang convulsed. The Pill reached forward to console her, touching Janis Lang's shoulder.

Lang's hysterical scream, so foreign to the five-foot-eight-inch dowdy staffer, juiced the Pill's like a mega-volt. He leaped backwards with the dexterity of a teenage break-dancer.

"Phil," Heather screeched, "touch that woman, I'll file charges." Six Hamilton staffers in adjacent offices glared. Through the glass walls they could inspect the Workout guy's transgression.

Lang's hard sobbing commenced.

Phil peddled backwards from Heather's semi-public sanctum.

"Call me when she's ready," he said.

Heather collected Janis Lang by the arm; first Peter Morris.

CHAPTER THIRTY-FOUR

<u>Washington, D.C.</u>

Ken Thompson's fist slammed the tapered end of the ten-foot conference table. The mahogany veneer held. He spit his reaction to Billy Johnstone's last recommendation, "I pulled chains in Washington that LBJ would have been proud to yank to get that FDIC bitch out of my bank and assigned to the Europe team." The CEO's words came slow, "Now, Billy, figure out how to show those examiners a couple of loan files and then move them quietly out the back door, or your ass is gonna end up back on the Texas prairie."

Billy's left hand accented his protest, "Ken, we've lost our edge on these bastards."

Ken Thompson's fist tightened, "Get somebody inside that taxpayer sieve."

"Ken," the attorney on retainer to the S&L said, "we're in a damage control situation." His calm was out of sync with the other two men, "Let Billy complete his report. Then we discuss action."

"G'wan, Billy. Don't hold back," The CEO cooled to simmer.

"What the examiners couldn't figure out, they classified," Billy Johnstone, Chief Operating Officer said, "Thirty percent of our loans are classified!"

"Hell, rookies, all of them," interrupted the CEO.

Billy responded, "Naw, these were the FDIC examiners that Treasury dropped on us."

"Do we have a claim against Treasury for interfering with the Federal Home Loan Bank system," Ken Thompson petitioned his attorney.

"We don't," the attorney avoided inflection, "FDIC applied national bank standards against the Hamilton. We tested bad. Treasury has the right to audit any financial situation they think undermines the system. The Fed Home Loan Bank is part of the system. Treasury has a broad brush to paint with, Ken. Rumor has it Treasury was invited to examine the Hamilton by the FSLIC. Legal action against the Department of Treasury is a losing proposition."

Billy continued, "The lethal salvo was fired when the FDIC examiners tallied our loans to the Endres brothers. As it is the Endres have fifty-seven mill in loans and FSLIC has recalculated our legal lending limit at six million."

"Hell, each of those boys has a rock solid financial statement that guarantees his loan." The chiseled jaw line of a younger Ken Thompson could be recognized beneath sagging skin, sun- damaged from his wildcat years in the West Texas oil fields.

Hamilton's attorney spoke, "Ken, they pledged the same building as collateral for four separate personal loans to the Hamilton."

Billy supported the attorney by reminding his CEO, "The shit hit the fan when the examiners found our accommodation letters to the Endres brothers."

"Guarantees, not accommodation letters," the attorney chastised, "Bona fide, illegal, guarantees."

"Guarantees, accommodation, it's just paper," the CEO's pitch fell on deaf ears.

The attorney had kept his charcoal suit coat on. He focused his blue eyes towards Thompson, vituperating at the canoe end of the partially filled table. The attorney more and more often, was questioning his involvement in this mess. He wouldn't accept blame and, yet, he was reluctant to extract himself. At $320,000 a year a lot of problems work out.

"Ken, maybe we've gone too fast in our attempt to compete with the banks," Billy Johnstone said.

"Billy, goddammit, boy, growth has been what's saving our butts. If we didn't earn on our new loans last year, we'd look sadder than a Mississippi puppy in June right now."

The attorney interceded, both hands framed his argument, "Billy's point, Ken, is that 65% of those earnings were accrued, not collected. Liquidity is being squeezed."

"We can broker the extra money we need from Merrill Lynch. Texas' economy will sort through this slump. Always does," argued Ken Thompson.

Billy's forearms tensed. He tried an alternative tact, "No, probably not, Ken. The fucking regulators are all over our back to stop the growth and shrink the loan portfolio. They want more documentation in the loan files, more training for our loan officers. The regulators are insisting on complete minutes of every loan meeting. We don't have the time or people to continue growing."

The starched collar of the attorney's white shirt constricted his neck veins. He seized the discourse from Billy Johnstone, "Ken, the Endres brothers are a golden calf to the FDIC exam team. That mess has got to be cleaned up."

The grey edges of Ken Thompson's hair were barbered every two weeks. His camel summer-weight wool suitcoat hung from the back of his chair, "Billy, you explained to our loan people that the regulators don't believe a brand new Endres partnership is justification for brand new loans?"

"Randy Peterson received that message very clearly, Ken, " Billy said.

"Are the Endres brothers helping us to solve their problem?" the CEO asked.

"Pete Morris sent the Endres a letter demanding $500,000 a week be repaid."

The attorney rephrased removing ambiguity, "Have the Endres brothers begun repayment of their loans?"

"Leonard Endres told Morris to fuck off," Billy said.

"What is the total?" asked the attorney.

"$63 mill, up from $57 mill last month. Austin and Phoenix are both partially complete."

Phoenix will need $4,000,000 additional to complete tower one. Stop building now and the space can't be leased."

Ken Thompson drew a circle with his pen. "What about the accommodation . . . the guarantees?"

"Down, decreased $37,000,000 to $33,000,000," reported Billy. "But for the wrong reason. We had to make good on an *ACCOMMODATION LETTER* for the Endres stand-by offer to purchase two hundred acres in Plano. That was the $4,000,000."

"Shit," their attorney to the Hamilton lost decorum, "So, we now have $96,000,000 in loans and guarantees to the Endres brothers? One customer?" The attorney's pencil summed the scribbled column of figures. "And we'll need to add another $4,000,000 more to complete Phoenix?"

"That's right, " said Billy Johnstone

The attorney preached to Hamilton's COO, "One hundred mill! The Hamilton's lending limit is six million bucks per borrower," He admonished from his legal pulpit, "We've got miles to travel before morning."

"We're fucked right now. There is no quick way out of this," Billy Johnstone preached back.

The attorney reloaded, "FSLIC ordered us to reduce Endres debt to six million. They are threatening a cease and desist order to stop all lending. The next step after that is they take over management of the Hamilton. What's the Endres plan, Billy?"

"After Endres told Morris to Fuck Off, I called Leonard Endres," Billy said. "He said they didn't have a plan. But, if we had one, they'd give it real consideration."

"Great," Ken Thompson muttered, "Anything else?"

The attorney said, "The Securities and Exchange Commission has received too many questions from FSLIC. They may be coming to Dallas."

The CEO seethed, "What do they want?"

"They're going to investigate Hamilton's involvement with your development, Ken, the Nassau Shores Resort," said the S&L's attorney.

"What's the problem?" The CEO of Hamilton S&L asked.

"They're suspicious Hamilton's investment bank, Drexel, Burnham, swapped $25,000,000 in junk bonds to the Hamilton for the money Drexel invested in your Nassau Shores time share," said the attorney.

"Tell the SEC to go to hell," Ken Thompson instructed his attorney.

The attorney asked, "Did Hamilton buy $25,000,000 of junk bonds from Drexel's within the six months prior to Drexel underwriting the $25,000,000 bond,issue for Nassau Shores?"

"We have an on-going business relationship with Drexel," Thompson feinted.

"Shit," the attorney responded. He got to his feet and stripped off the suit coat, the last man in the room to do so.

"Mother fucking examiners," Thompson muttered.

Ken Thompson's secretary interrupted to announce the phone call for Ken Thompson.

Walking from the conference room, "Five minutes," he said without looking back at his two executives.

His left hand swept the solid oak office door shut.

CHAPTER THIRTY-FIVE

Washington National Airport

The limo assigned by Treasury to Jack Richardson motored out of Washington National Airport and onto the George Washington Parkway. The Chair of the Federal Deposit Insurance Corp removed the cellular telephone receiver from its cradle, dialed the seven digits, and sent the call. Two miles away the second-ranking cabinet officer in the United States answered his private line without pleasantries.

"Yes."

"Mr. Secretary, Brendan Donahue has been dispatched," Jack Richardson said.

"Can he operate in the black?" the Cabinet official asked.

"He can. That he has been out of the country for almost a year lessens the likelihood he will be detected during his first week in Dallas. You ARE committed? I can't be hung out on this."

The Secretary of the Treasury did not hesitate, "You have my full support."

Jack Richardson confirmed, "He needs protection. Have you assigned someone?"

"Selection has been made. Assignment has already been executed. Identification of personnel is need-to-know, and you do not need to know who."

"I understand. Thanks," the FDIC chief said.

"Jack, keep me up to date. I only want verbal reports until we have definitive corroboration. No written communication, understood?"

"I understand very clearly. Good afternoon, Mr. Secretary."

Jack Richardson hung up the phone.

CHAPTER THIRTY-SIX

Washington, D.C., Thompson's private office

Ken Thompson, alone, sat down behind his nine-foot desk and lifted the telephone receiver to his unlisted line. His secretary had been instructed to interrupt the meeting for only one call, one congressman.

"Senator Anderson," the Hamilton CEO began, "thanks for returning my call."

The Texas senator's voice was guarded, "Ken, we never had this conversation."

"I understand. Did you get the report?"

"Yea, but my chief assistant had to lean on a House Banking Committee staffer. Listen very carefully."

The CEO listened to the confidential memorandum the chairman of the FDIC had sent to the chairman of the House Banking Committee following the FDIC's unannounced cross-over exam of the Hamilton S&L, an examination still open due to the death of the senior examiner, Julie Weidener, prior to presenting her summation report.

The Texas Senator read on, "*If the Hamilton were under FDIC supervision, we would act immediately. The FDIC would seize the Hamilton next Friday.*"

Washington. D.C.

Billy, Hamilton S&L's Chief Operating Officer and the attorney waited in the adjacent conference room for Thompson's return, both silent; Billy stood by the wall contemplating the Civil War drawing, the attorney worked through a sheaf of legal sized drafts.

Billy studied the black and white sketch; a view of the Mississippi in 1863. The desolate mood of that Civil War July 4, descended on Billy. He broke the silence, "I'm handling Hamilton's day-to-day issues. Where is the SEC heading?"

The attorney turned to Billy, "The SEC isn't paying a house call to sort out civil infractions, Billy. These guys are casting for criminal indictments."

The 1863 drawing depicted the Confederate surrender, the COO spoke without taking his gaze away from the sketch, "I don't want to appear parochial, but I assume the funding of Nassau Shores is a corporate issue, not a personal liability. I mean I can't be held," the COO's ten year career had been as a team player, Ken Thompson's team. His question broached divorce. He stuttered, "I can't be held liable if something has been transacted that I'm not part of?"

Billy presented his question as a declaration.

The attorney shrugged, he tendered Billy his upward palms in answer.

Billy recast his statement as a question, "The Hamilton is a corporation?"

"Billy, here is the straight dope. You are an officer of the Hamilton. You are absolutely liable as an individual if you perpetrate fraud, and potentially liable if you condone criminal fraud."

"Damn," Billy said, "Monday, the SEC requested all Hamilton records relating to the purchase of $25 mill in junk bonds we bought from Drexel."

The COO continued, "And they want a copy of every letter Ken wrote on Hamilton stationery during the last twelve months."

The attorney whitened, "Did Drexel work a swap? Was there an agreement that if the Hamilton bought $25,000,000 in junk bonds that Drexel would underwrite Ken's Nassau Shores resort investment?"·

"No, the $25 mill junk purchase was a stand-alone deal." Billy still stood, looking at the artist's interpretation of the day the South's glory ceased to be.

"That's good for now," the attorney said. "But we're still walking right on the line."

Billy stepped back to the black-and white lithograph of the Siege of Vicksburg. *How bad was starvation throbbing in Pemberton's gut that he would surrender his Vicksburg garrison to Grant?* The attorney stepped towards the illustration of confederacy's death.

Billy looked at the scene while he spoke to the attorney, "The S&L didn't buy the junk bonds, our insurance company bought the Drexel bonds."

"Shit," said the attorney for a record third time in one day as his heart pounded into anaerobic calisthenics.

CHAPTER THIRTY-SEVEN

Dallas, Texas, Morris' condo

The dog killer drove his plain Chevy back into the parking lot of Pete Morris' condominium. Inside the white, unmarked Cavalier the straining air conditioner battled the Texas summer heat. Brushed burgundy seating had absorbed hours of June sun.

Killer Kowalski had finished his shift for the Dallas PD two hours ago, at three o'clock. Post shift, he had downed five celebratory beers at The Shoot-Out, a bar on the yuppie north side that incongruously catered to law enforcement tipplers.

This morning had gone well. $2,500 for zapping a dog. Killer tapped the wheel to the thumping of a Huey Lewis song. He shouldn't be here.

After settling his tab at the Shoot-Out he slipped into the rest room at the Texaco station and re-dressed in his Dallas PD blues.

Kowalski eased up on the Chevy's six-cylinder engine, slowing to ten miles an hour, he checked Morris' deck. The Dallas cop, a twelve-year veteran, circled the asphalt driveway ringing Morris' condo project. Killer K was about to take his leave when he spotted the S&L woman's white Mercedes parked.

I woulda bet she wouldn't show up here for weeks, he thought. *Sonofabitch must be good in the sack.*

Jim Kowalski had two unhealthy addictions, each warranted therapy: pulling a trigger and women who didn't love him. His skewered code of chivalry regarding women relied on overcoming their protests of disinterest. His tactics; liquor, persistence and a little physicality.

Kowalski liked chicks that resisted; heightened his mood. Alcohol acerbated both of his addictions. He recalled Heather's cut silk blouse as he sited down the barrel this morning.

Killer K parked his anonymous Chevrolet in a slot three buildings removed from Morris' condo.

Dallas, Texas, Morris' condo

Heather rapped the door of Morris' condo. No one. She opened the door and both women entered. Quiet. Janis Lang seated herself at the far left side of the couch. Heather, battling inner screams of warning; went to the curtains hiding the deck. She pulled the thin cord. The drapes whisked open.

Nothing. No evidence of the dead cocker. She adjusted the drapes, leaving the curtain a quarter way open to let daylight into the living room.

"What's that Phil going to do to me?" asked Janis.

Heather was playing this afternoon's situation by ear, "Janis, what we have to do is get Phil to agree not to prosecute you for stealing from the dormant checking accounts. Give him the details on the money Pete Morris instructed you to deposit in the accounts of his customers. But, only after the Pill agrees to let you off the hook. You might avoid federal charges if you make restitution and the Hamilton buries the issue."

Janis got off the couch and fidgeted through Morris' dining area. She had wanted to trust somebody for a long time. Circumstance suggested that Heather had been delivered as her confidante.

"Should I get an attorney?" Janis asked.

"Not yet. Let's see if we can make something work for you."

Janis Lang's low sniffle developed into renewed sobbing. Janis looked around clearly confused, "Why are we here?"

Knocking on the condo door stopped Janis' weeping. Heather's finger over her lips mimed instructions for Janis to shut her mouth. Heather moved next to Janis.

"I'll answer it," Heather whispered, "Go into the bathroom, dry your eyes."

Janis retreated.

Heather peeked through the peephole. Spying the uniformed police officer, a rush of confidence overruled caution. Trusting authority, she unlatched the door, swinging it all the way open.

"Yes, officer," Heather said.

Changed her blouse. Changed from slacks to the skirt too, Killer Kowalski noticed. *Not half as sexy as what she wore this morning.*

"Just doing some follow-up on this morning's disturbance, ma'am. Is everything okay?" Killer said.

At least Morris is getting some protection, Heather thought. *That's what he meant when he said his condo was safe now.*

"Yes, it seems to be OK," Heather responded.

"We've made our presence known all day," Kowalski said, "Kept ourselves in sight. Not much to worry about now. I think I'll wrap it up for the day."

Heather did not want to be in Morris's condo. *How do I keep this guy on duty?* She wanted this scare-crow visible. *What's going to keep this cop patrolling for another hour?* She'd stay calm if this cop stood guard until she left Morris' condo.

"Thanks. Ah, I'm alone for another hour or so. Could you, could you stay on for that time?" Heather asked.

Could be fun, thought Kowalski. *She's givin' me a little invite.*

"That's after hours, ma'am," Kowalski the cop slowed his rhythm, "I am authorized to call this as I see it, but,"

"I'd really appreciate it, officer. Really appreciate it. I'm alone and still afraid." Heather's smile was a legal bribe, asking the sentry on duty to carry on his rounds.

Wants me, does she?

"Well, okay," he said, "For a while. When will the mister be home?"

Heather calculated. If this cop stayed on watch a couple of hours, she would be out of here. Hesitantly she coaxed, "Two hours?"

The cop slid his blue flat top service cap back three inches exposing his forehead. "Hmm, I'd have to cancel bowling at six." Killer K adjusted his reflective silver lensed Ray-Ban aviators. The left side of his mouth lilted in a condescending grin, "I'll take a quick walk around. Would it be okay if I used your phone to cancel my bowling? They don't like those kind of personal calls patched through the base."

Heather, you are managing like a charm this afternoon. Heather complimented herself.

"Sure," she said.

"And I would sure appreciate a coffee, ma'am."

"You got it, officer. Should take me about ten minutes, stop back," she said.

Heather didn't lock the door as the cop left.

CHAPTER THIRTY-EIGHT

Dallas. Texas. The Federal Home Loan Bank

Bobby Scamehorn, senior examiner at the Dallas Federal Home Loan Bank replaced the telephone receiver. "An officer of the Hamilton S&L requests to meet with examiners. This has got to be a first."

Nobody on his exam team had arrived yet this morning at the office; fifty-five unoccupied olive-green steel desks furnished the drab bullpen inside Dallas FHLB headquarters.

Scamehorn popped into his boss's office unannounced, the number two guy at the ninth Federal Home Loan Bank in Dallas, the Director of Supervision for S&L's in Texas.

"Heather Montgomery, the chick Hamilton hired from Detroit, called. She wants to meet," the examiner announced.

"She mention London?" Number Two asked.

"Not a word. And I didn't bring it up," Scamehorn said.

"Her request is timely." Number Two spoke deeply, his senior examiner leaned forward.

"Your Hamilton S&L bumped up to fourth on next month's Watch List. Quickest moving S&L in the Texas top twenty; up from number fifteen last month."

"It's not my *HAMILTON*," Scamehorn said

Bobby Scamehorn briefed his boss on the progress of his five-man team examining the Hamilton S&L. Number Two half-listened, eyes fixed on two stapled sheets aligned on the corner of his grey metal desk.

"Reach that report," Number Two said with a repressed wave of his right hand.

The examiner scanned the report. "Why even print the FSLIC Watch List. You have every problem S&L in the Ninth District etched."

"Our Pres shared the preliminary Watch List with me. Hamilton is in neck-high cow shit, Bobby. Handing out money they have corralled from brokered deposits . . . and your updated classified loan report isn't even included in this ranking."

The Senior FHLB examiner digested the S&L dishonor roll for the Texas region. "Four of these S&L's got a star after their name?" Bobby Scamehorn asked.

"Yeah, FSLIC is seizing the assets of those four on Friday," Number Two said.

"Since Washington forced us to classify the bad loans, net worth is coming up negative. Going to continue," Scamehorn said.

"Washington is having second thoughts about classifying loans," Number Two said. "They're running short on their capability to insure deposits and they don't have the people to seize four S&L's every month."

Scamehorn asked, "What has *FIZLICK* seized so far?"

"$7.5 billion in assets, seized just from fucked up Texas S&L's," Number Two rolled his gray tattered chair forward, "Four seized this month, four S&L's debut next month. And none of these idiots believe their own S&L's are terminal. All they need is fresh money, new deposits, and they'll work their way out of the problem."

Number Two asked, "What percentage of Hamilton's funding is from brokered deposits?"

The Senior Examiner answered, "Sixty percent, mostly through Merrill Lynch."

Number Two unveiled the tactic he proposed to the Federal Home Loan Bank Board in Washington six weeks ago, "FSLIC should cut off deposit insurance when an S&L is put on the Watch List. Announce to the public that no new deposits will be insured. As long as FSLIC guarantees deposits up to $100,000, the S&L's aren't going to stop."

"Will DC let us use public announcement as policy?" The Senior FHLB Examiner asked.

"No," Number Two replied.

"Maybe I should request a transfer," Scamehorn said.

"We need you in Texas," his boss, Number Two said. "We are re-enacting *War and Peace* with these dumb-fuck Texans; carts with the wounded are rolling out from Borodino while the cavalry comes down the road singing their way into the battle."

"We're pounding on S&L management as each exam finishes," Scamehorn said.

"Here's a new report." Number Two unfolded backwards into the shoddy vinyl chair. His left hand raising a two-inch-thick sheaf of paper.

"What is it?" the Senior Examiner asked.

"New document, courtesy of Washington, the FSLIC Warning List. Not the Watch List, Bobby, the new fucking Warning List. DC doesn't want us to lose sight of our priorities, so they limit the regional Watch List to the twenty biggest problems in Texas. Now we have a second tier of fucked-up S&L's, the Warning List. All moving down the road to the Watch List."

"Where does this Warning List come from?" Scamehorn asked.

"Your S&L exams are sent to the FHLB. Treasury was looking over their shoulder, made them send the data to the FDIC for . . . for positive criticism."

The FHLB examiner asked, "Since when?"

"Since six months ago. Your classified loan percentages scared the hell out of the Washington. FDIC is worried they might inherit our S&L problem."

"What are we supposed to do with this Warning List?" Scamehorn asked.

"Make believe it doesn't exist. There are 318 Savings & Loan banks operating in the Dallas district, 186 made the FSLIC Warning List," Number Two dropped the Warning List back into the bottom drawer of his metal desk.

"Why does the Hamilton woman want to see us?"

"She didn't say. She wants you to be at the meeting," the examiner said, "She mentioned you by name."

CHAPTER THIRTY-NINE

Dallas, Morris' condo

Heather gave Janis no choice. She instructed the teller to remain in the bathroom adjoining Morris' bedroom.

"I told the police officer I'm alone. I think he feels protective of a single woman. If he sees you, he's going to split for his bowling league," Heather explained as she tucked Janis into the bathroom servicing the master bedroom. "Don't come out of here for anything. He's coming back for his coffee. I'm just going to hand him the cup."

"Thanks." The cop reached to accept the steaming instant coffee from Heather. Heather walked out of the kitchen, towards the window overlooking Morris' deck.

Nice ass, Kowalski thought.

"Any ideas?" Heather would rather have him patrolling outside, not socializing in Morris' living room.

"Well, just a theory," he set the red cup on the end table and moved behind her.

Heather jumped as his hands grasped her shoulders.

"From here," he positioned Heather, "look at the plant bed at the corner of the 1489 building."

He inhaled the essence of the cheap liquid soap hung in every shower at the Richardson Athletic Club, Heather's club where she scrubbed herself that morning..

Kowalski focused her on the firing location, he released her shoulders.

Heather could not recall being touched by a cop. She couldn't recall seeing a cop touch anybody on TV.

His lips closed on her ear, promising to reveal conspiratorial secrets. "That is the probable firing site. Do you think the shot was aimed at you, or the mister?"

Heather spun and juked past the cop into the refuge of the kitchen. She resisted calling Janis Lang from the second bathroom. She didn't want Lang questioning the dog's having been here this morning. "Officer, I would feel safer." Heather second-guessed her intuitive warnings. "Excuse me, I don't even know your name."

"John, John Cortese," Kowalski lied.

"I'm still tense about today's circumstances," she said. "I would feel a lot safer with you patrolling. Checking the grounds."

"Sure thing," Kowalski drained the red coffee mug, "Here you go. Thanks."

Heather accepted the empty cup with two hands, turned, and carried it to the kitchen.

He moved behind her without a sound. Kowalski slid his hands under her armpits and locked her breasts in his palms.

"What!" Heather elbowed his stomach. Her effort exposed her breasts further to his mashing grip. He kneaded through her blouse, she hurt.

"Stop!" she screamed.

"Just relax," the cop coached. "Relax. Easy we go."

Kowalski's excitement surpassed that of his morning kill. He fingered between the buttons on her blouse, suddenly ripping.

Heather's cotton blouse peeled from her chest and shredded halfway down her arms. Heather lashed her half-shackled forearms in futile self-defense, but the torn blue fabric draping her elbows restricted her punches.

"You bastard, what the hell?" Events were so unforeseen that Heather had no rational defense. "Get out, GET OUT!" she screamed without control.

Kowalski snatched the front of her bra, ripping the snap apart so quickly Heather wasn't aware until her breasts unweighted.

"Damn, you turn me on," Kowalski leered. "We better do it quick or I'm going to come right here. Baby, you're gonna like this. Just let yourself go."

The Polish hit man snatched Heather by her wrists and pulled her towards him. She butted her head and swung her arms, resisting. He grabbed Heather's neck, squeezing it in a vise hold. He dragged her to the couch and packed her into the soft cushions.

Heather slugged for survival. Kowalski, his knees spread-eagle on the couch, loomed over her. He grabbed an upright cushion and pinned Heather's arms. His right palm cracked her left cheek, paralyzing her arms. The off-duty cop needed both hands to rip Heather's skirt above her waist. She jerked her right knee upward to mash his balls. Sensing her muscle contract for the incapacitating crunch, he lurched forward. Her knee thumped him in the ass.

"That would ruin the next half hour, now, wouldn't it?" His thumb and middle finger of his left hand clasped each side of her knee. He pinched inward, penetrating ligament and muscle underneath Heather's flesh until she cried.

The rogue cop instructed her, "No more dirty tricks."

Straddling her on his knees he unbelted his pants and unzipped his pants.

"Just enjoy." The aviator sun glasses he still wore reflected Heather's terror.

As he bent forward, Heather could smell beer through the coffee on his breath.

"Kiss?" the cop asked.

Heather pinched her eyes and wrenched her head away.

His weight crushed the breath from Heather as Janis Lang smashed the bottom of the hot silver coffee percolator into his vulnerable right temple. Killer dropped on Heather in a limp collapse; a soft landing.

* * *

Jim Kowalski, veteran of the Dallas PD, lay on the floor trussed to two bar stools when Pete Morris pushed through the unlocked door of his condo.

One stool, up-side-down, secured Kowalski's legs, spread eagle and bound. The cop resembled a wishbone with his legs pried eighteen inches apart to accommodate the base of the stool. His pants remained unfastened. The second stool, diametrically in line with the first, exposed Kowalski's chin jutting over the seat. The women had tied his extended arms around the top stool, then retied each wrist to the far-side legs. All his limbs lashed securely with Pete's yellow electrical outdoor extension cord.

The women had insisted the cop remain uncomfortably prone, straddled on top of the upended bar stools.

Janis Lang threatened to indent Kowalski's skull again.

"Move a fucking inch," she cocked the coffee percolator, "I'm going crack open your hollow head." A stunt she had perpetrated against his bloody cranium four times already. After her fourth undefended blow, he became very attentive, lay very still.

The women barely acknowledged Pete Morris enter.

Janis Lang searched for a tool. "Heather, find something narrow to hit him in the nuts with," the head teller ordered.

Heather had only fastened her bra as the two women scurried to tie the incapacitated Kowalski. She disregarded her undress when Pete arrived. The seriousness of securing Kowalski had restored some order to Heather's emotional state, but half-dressed with Morris in the condo she started slipping.

"Morris, you bastard. What kind of fucking life are you leading? This place is war."

"Something long, thin, smack his nuts off, Heather." The head teller grabbed a bottle of Fume Blanc stored on its side from Pete's wine rack.

"Jesus, this guy is a cop. What the hell is going on here?"

Heather cracked her palm across Pete's face.

CHAPTER FORTY

Washington, D.C.

The attorney and Billy had stood silent for fifteen silent seconds in the deserted conference room, each man's speculations colliding like fusional neutrons.

Ken Thompson pushed into his Washington conference room.

"Ready?

Their heads jerked towards the door in alarm.

Thompson fell into his seat at the head of the table, he reconvened, "Let's wrap this up. What's this about the Department of Insurance?" He looked at Billy and the attorney at the same time.

"Talk to TDI, Ken," Billy hadn't recovered. His voice was edgy, "They want written confirmation the insurance company won't transfer money to support the S&L."

The chair's roller wheels reversed Thompson eighteen inches.

The CEO's head angled towards his two associates. This time his direct gaze avoided both, examining the span between them.

"I depend on you two for conclusions and recommendations."

The attorney said, "My conclusion is *FIZLICK*'s ultimate goal is to seize the S&L."

Thompson probed the opportunity before confronting adversity, "How would *FIZLICK* determine value?"

"They don't. You don't get a penny. The FSLIC simply takes your Savings and Loan," the attorney explained.

"What is your recommendation?" demanded Ken Thompson.

"Time," shrugged the attorney.

"Time we don't have," said Billy. "These constant examinations are sucking the life out of the S&L. We're trying to cut expenses, fill in documentation, make new loans, and I've got eight people answering to these Fed examiners full time."

The attorney advised, "That's the recommendation, Ken. Time. We've got to get the examiners out of the Hamilton for a while."

"Let me consider this." Thompson's response adjourned the meeting.

"Billy, would you excuse us?" the attorney said. "I've got to talk with Ken privately on a separate matter."

Four years previous, when Ken Thompson purchased the Hamilton S&L, the FSLIC required a pledge to maintain adequate capital. FSLIC never defined "adequate". Thompson wrote the guarantee. The two-page document promised that capital from his insurance company, if needed, would support the S&L. With the nonchalance of a junior Hamilton Savings & Loan officer filing an accommodation letter, Thompson slid the "keep well" pledge into the locked drawer of his Washington desk.

During each annual audit for the past three years the Texas Department of Insurance asked if Hamilton Insurance bore any financial responsibility for the S&L. Thompson lied and said no.

Billy snapped his briefcase shut and left the room.

"Do I know everything?" Thompson pre-empted.

"Ken, you've got one solution to the potential problems," his attorney started. "The regulators are digging for racketeering charges. SEC, FSLIC and maybe even Treasury are going to hang someone, and you're a big fish in the waters they're trolling. Spin off the Hamilton S&L from your group. Divorce yourself from the S&L industry. Sell it. Get it away from you and do it fast. While you are selling I'll try and get a *drop all charges* agreement from the feds."

The CEO pondered his attorney's words, "How quick can it be sold for a profit?"

"Forget profit. Your S&L is a rabid dog that can bring you down." The attorney's tone left no room for debate. "Clean up the legal-lending limit infractions, prepare offering documents, find a buyer, sit tight through the buyer's audit, be prepared to negotiate the price down, and obtain the approval of the FSLIC. At least six months to wrap it up . . . I agree with Billy, we need time."

"This is a big asset to sell?" Thompson said in the form of a question.

"Ken, sell it to a large public company. Preferably a bigger bank, a much bigger bank." the attorney advised.

"Why?" asked Thompson.

"Because the last of Hamilton's problems haven't surfaced," the attorney explained, "A large bank with publicly traded stock just might hide a bad buy rather than publicly admit they fucked up."

CHAPTER FORTY-ONE

Washington, D.C.

Ken Thompson considered his attorney's advice to sell the Hamilton quickly; he had another idea, replace the head regulator, quickly.

The Hamilton CEO dialed from his Washington office. His Texas Senator understood the Savings and Loan industry.

"Yes," said the Senator, "White House Chief of Staff, Don Regan, confirmed this morning, Robert Henry has been cleared to replace Ed Gray at the Federal Home Loan Bank."

The senator spoke with swagger, "All clear, Don Regan will put it in front of the President."

Robert Henry, Atlanta attorney, had represented the Hamilton CEO on several matters, nothing was active or pending.

"Bob Henry is a good man. Understands the industry," The CEO said.

The FBI investigated all debt in vetting Robert Henry's personal financial condition; the Bureau's agent did not ask Mr. Henry about previous guarantees. Until six months ago, Mr. Henry, the proposed head of the agency overseeing America's Savings & Loans, guaranteed loans totaling $21,000,000; loans arranged by his associate Ken Thompson and held by the Hamilton Savings and Loan Bank in Dallas, Texas. At the last Federal Home Loan Bank examination, an outside appraisal was commissioned on the Georgia real estate supporting the loan guaranteed by Robert Henry. The value of the three, mostly empty, strip malls totaled $12,000,000. The S&L examiners classified the loan DOUBTFUL. Good lending practice would have been for Ken Thompson's S&L to demand payment on the $9,000,000 shortfall. The Hamilton CEO cured the shortfall with an alternative fix; he tore up Bob Henry's guarantee. Interest due was being paid from the Hamilton S&L's *RESERVE* fund, administered by Randy Peterson, Hamilton SVP.

The Texas senator said to his constituent and contributor, "Regan has the President's approval for Henry's nomination."

CHAPTER FORTY-TWO

<u>Washington, D.C., outside FDIC Headquarters</u>

His newly cut car key unlocked the driver's door on Richardson's BMW. Inside, Jonathan Blair's screwdriver popped the cap with the logo off the center of the steering wheel. The blade of the screwdriver wedged between the latch and the small metal stud. Straining down on the grooved yellow handle, the assassin pried the tool's tip upwards, disengaging the clamp from the steel peg. He repeated this procedure on the two remaining clamps on the column. Only the two bolts secured the steering wheel to the auto's permanent post. He easily ratcheted the three-eighths-inch wrench counter clockwise, removing the fasteners.

<u>Dallas, Texas</u>

Pete Morris watched the bound policeman squirm as he explained to the Greek. "His name is Kowalski. We know that from his license. Won't tell me a thing,"

Dimitri snapped his fingers. His Italian bodyguard picked up the receiver on the second telephone in the office. Cortese's rising finger activated the line with the stealth of a Napolitano sneaking out from a one-night stand at six A.M.

The Greek, calm, asked, "What does this have to do with me, Peter?"

"Everything, Mr. Paulopnos. Everything. Somehow he's yours. I'm not going to fuck around."

"You're sure he tried to rape the woman?" asked the Greek.

"He's in my living room strapped to two bar stools with his pants unzipped. Two women are debating which one gets to crush his balls with a bottle of Robert Mondavi. I'm going to do one of two things in the next three minutes, Dimitri: make a deal with the FBI as part of my last great confession, or make a deal with you. I'm a fucking banker, not a Mafioso hit man."

"Keep him tied, Pete. My . . . representative will retrieve Mr. Kowalski in fifteen minutes." Dimitri Paulopnos called Morris by his familiar short name. "Pete, you've done the right thing. The deposit was made this afternoon. Your personal problems have ended . . . and I will make financial remuneration for your troubles and those of the two women."

"Hurry, Dimitri, " Morris said.

Paulopnos hung up the phone. "Bring him to me, Gianni. In one piece. If he gives you trouble, settle him down. Take the limo."

Cortese couldn't get to Kowalski fast enough.

Washington. D.C .. FDIC Headquarters

Jack Richardson collected the separate folders from the four-person corner conference table in his office: a summary of last week's bank examinations from the Dallas Federal Home Loan Bank. Each Tuesday Fed Ex trundled the bad news into his office. The five preliminary reports displaced eight inches of inner space in his worn, brown, legal-size attaché case. 9:23 P.M., he could finish reading at least two of the Dallas FHLB bank exams at his Alexandria apartment tonight. The paper stuffed in the case, he snapped the clasp.

Thirty-five years of use caused the old elevator to groan as it ended Richardson's slow descent to the, first floor. The leather soles of

Richardson's wing-tip shoes tapped against the marble floor, creating an echo in the uninhabited late evening lobby.

The grey haired security man had removed his stiff patrolman's hat when he came on duty at 8 P.M. The cap sat on the top counter of his two tier podium-style security desk. Despite the approach of reverberating footsteps, the aging patrolman's gaze remained locked on the sports page perched on his shielded lower counter.

"Good night, Ralph," Richardson said.

The single sentry protecting the Fed Deposit Insurance Corporation building snapped his head up.

"Mr. Richardson, good night to you. I noticed your signature wasn't in the register and assumed you were still in the building."

"Sign me out, will you, Ralph?"

"Done." The sixty-four-year-old uniformed guard conspired to violate one of the very few security rules proscribed for the agency that oversaw the soundness of the US banking system. He printed the name John C. Richardson, noting the time was 9:34 P.M.

Richardson knew the revolving door had been locked since 6 P.M. so he blocked his shoulder against the swinging glass exit at the far left bank of doors. The dense, cooler air within the Fed building resisted Richardson's effort to push the exit door into the hot air outside. Daylight had disappeared.

June, Richardson thought, *longest days of summer and I can't get out of this place until after dark.*

He jitter-bugged through an opening in the doorway just wide enough for his body and his nine-inch-thick attaché. Hot, inrushing air vacuumed the door shut behind him. Eighty-eight degree heat in the D.C. night and twenty pounds of briefcase weight drew a quick sweat from the FDIC executive as he traversed the eighty-meter jaunt to the executive parking lot.

Richardson couldn't remember the last breeze strong enough to ripple the Potomac much less cool Washington's downtown. Tonight was no different.

Dallas

"Did you have a partner with you?"

Kowalski's head slumped. His performance had languished during the last thirty minutes. Blood leaked from the right side of his mouth. Cortese had been working Kowalski's left cheek.

The screamer at the condo, the woman swinging the bottle of wine, had pulped the right side of the Polack's skull.

"I've told you," Kowalski's tongue was thick, "everything."

Cortese's open palm slapped the flesh on the cop's damaged right cheek. Kowalski's face straightened. He glared hatred at the Greek's Italian bodyguard through eyes that rolled in foggy pain. Gianni Cortese stared right back at the bungling cop.

"Enough!" ordered Dimitri Paulopnos. "Leave us alone, Gianni." Paulopnos' Italian security man departed, as they had agreed he would. Time for Dimitri to be Jim Kowalski's benefactor.

"Kowalski, you have jeopardized all that I have worked for. I expected discretion from you. A policeman." Paulopnos looked around the unfinished interior of the Plano Mall. The concrete space would be the storeroom for a Gantos shop in four weeks. "Did anybody else know you were returning to Morris's condominium?"

"Not a fucking soul." Kowalski spat through the blood.

"What did you tell the Montgomery woman?" the Greek asked.

"Nothing, nothing," Killer Kowalski said.

Dimitri breathed deep. "But, you did tell her you knew about the dog being shot."

"Only that, though. That's just normal for a cop to know. This won't happen again, Mr. Paulopnos," Killer promised.

"No it won't."

The Greek walked away. At the steel fireproof door, Dimitri stopped. He smiled back at Kowalski, strapped to the chair. As he closed the door behind him, echoes reverberated through the unfinished store room.

Gianni Cortese leaned against the front panel of the black limo parked ten feet outside. He straightened as his boss exited from the mall onto the freshly laid asphalt. Cortese stepped towards the Greek, his steps soundless on the soft tar.

Paulopnos brought Cortese close by placing his left hand on Gianni's shoulder.

"I think he's told us everything, but try one last time," the Greek said.

"Here?"

"No, somewhere more private. You never have liked Kowalski, have you, Gianni?"

"No, sir, he's pazzo . . . crazy. In business, you can't have crazy. What do you want me to do after I talk with him?'

"Make him disappear, Gianni."

"With pleasure, boss."

FDIC Headquarters

American Yew shrubs grew in a verdant six-foot wall lining the north edge of the concrete path leading from the lobby door to Richardson's 1983 BMW 735i. Passages interrupted the woody hedge every fifteen feet. The thirty-six-inch cuts permitting entrance into the small park that spared twenty percent of the 17th street block from commerce. The Lilliputian green refuge bordered FDIC headquarters. Jonathan Blair positioned himself in the third break, thirty feet before Richardson would arrive at his dark BMW ... the only automobile remaining in the parking lot that evening.

Blair clenched the weapon in his right fist, he observed Jack Richardson exit through the half-opened door of the government building. Watching through the hedge, the assassin confirmed Richardson would pass his stationary observation post.

Twenty meters outside the lobby Jack Richardson stopped to switch the heavy brief case from his right hand to his left hand. He removed the suit coat and draped it over his right forearm, picked up the luggage, and resumed his journey.

The BMW steering wheel smashed into Richardson's face.

Jonathan Blair caught the crumpling Richardson as he slumped against the hedge. The attaché case remained sealed as it hit the concrete sidewalk. Blair soccer-kicked the briefcase and suit coat into the base of the hedge. Richardson's heels dragged as Jonathan backed through the opening in the hedge into the park. Richardson groaned when Blair dropped him on his back. His broken cheek swelled, pinching his left eye shut. Blair, in a crouch above Richardson's head swung the steering wheel a second time. Richardson's jaw broke, his body went limp.

Jonathan Blair rose, stepped to the opening in the evergreen hedge, and searched the parking area. Blair's head scanned in a slow three-hundred-sixty-degree revolution. No one.

Leaving Richardson concealed near the base of the hedge inside the park, Jonathan retrieved the briefcase and suit-coat. He punched the release button on the exterior of the trunk of Richardson's BMW and tossed the baggage into the cavity. Blair slid into the driver's seat and slipped the displaced steering wheel onto the two bolts extending from the steering column. The bolts guided the BMW steering wheel into the two precision-tooled slots that eliminated slack in the auto's turning performance. Blair snapped the three clamps from the column locking the steering wheel to the car's permanent post and screwed the nuts down tight. He capped the mechanical fasteners with the blue and white BMW logo cover.

Blair returned to the unconscious Richardson, knelt behind him and leveraged the body upwards; wrapping Richardson's limp left arm over his shoulder and lugged him to the back seat of the green German auto. The combined weight of the two men totaled three hundred ninety pounds. Thirty feet to the car in the heat of the Washington June evening consumed twenty seconds. At the green Beemer, the assassin opened the rear door and let Richardson slide backwards into the rear seat. Blair stuffed Richardson's feet onto the car floor and short-stroked the car door shut.

The executioner rounded the car to the opposite door of the backseat, stuffed the small pillow under the back of Richardson's slumping neck, tilting Richardson's head backwards. Blair snapped the forty-two inch section of nasal gastric tubing from his right coat pocket. He lubricated the probe end of the tube with a dab of K-Y jelly and threaded the pipeline into Richardson's nostril. Blair fed the tubing down Richard's esophagus brushing the vagal nerve. Jonathan plugged the stethoscope into his ears and pressed the sensor against Richardson's belly.

Blair cocked the syringe, filling the cylinder with air. He fastened the cocked syringe into the end of the nastro-gastric tube with a jab. As he squirted air into the tube, the rumble through the stethoscope in Richardson's abdomen verified the opposite end of the tube led into Richardson's stomach, not his lungs. Blair hung the clear five hundred milliliter gravity bag from the clothes hook above the auto's rear door.

He attached the tubing to the adapter on the bottom of the gravity bag; the sack contained sixteen ounces of Laphroaig single malt Scotch whiskey. Blair set the drip rate at one hundred twenty CC per hour.

Jack Richardson consumed the booze, neat.

* * *

At 1:30 A.M. no traffic was moving on the two-lane Maryland county road, except Richardson's dark green BMW. The 735i skidded to a stop on the gravel apron of the road, within inches of the two-hundred-foot roadside plunge. In the back seat, Jack Richardson, unconscious, had absorbed all sixteen ounces of the Scotch whiskey. The alcohol in his blood measured point one nine percent.

Blair repeated the procedure to disengage the BMW's steering wheel from the steering column. He let the car engine run as he rounded the back of the auto. He eased the tubing from Richardson's stomach up his esophagus and out his nose.

Blair lifted the drunk body onto his shoulder and dropped Richardson onto the gravel apron outside driver's seat of his 735i, propping his head on the pillow. Jonathan measured the distance and delivered two sledgehammer blows to Richardson's forehead. The assassin traced Richardson's neck for pulse. The stethoscope could not detect a heartbeat.

Blair reattached the steering wheel. He lifted and placed Richardson's body in the driver's seat of the BMW, seatbelt uncoupled. Blair shifted the transmission into drive, the BMW inched forward. Blair guided the car, reaching through the open window to steer the proper course.

Ten feet from the drop, the assassin stepped aside.

"Goodbye, Mr. Richardson," Jonathan Blair said.

The green BMW 735i rolled and crashed through the Maryland night, landing upside down two hundred feet down the cliff.

CHAPTER FORTY-THREE

Washington. D.C.

In his DC office Ken Thompson, CEO of the S&L, bounced the extended telephone cord. News of Jack Richardson's death had been broadcast two hours ago. Thompson pressed the receiver to his ear.

"Ed Gray, that cocky Chairman of the Fed Home Loan Bank Board is a goner," the Texas Senator said, "Sumbitch looked all five of us in the eye and said NO."

Robert Henry's dossier had been submitted by Ken Thompson to Texas Senator Jim Anderson, Republican, four weeks earlier. The Senator sent the dossier by congressional bicycle courier to the White House Chief of Staff, Donald Regan. Regan the former Merrill Lynch CEO, authorized the FBI background check. Robert Henry received a clean bill of character health. The White House evaluation was teed-up when WWDC radio's On-The-Hour at 9 AM reported the death of the Chairman of the Federal Deposit Insurance Corporation.

Ten minutes after the UPI news broke the story on Richardson's death spiral down a rural Maryland cliff, Texas Senator Jim Anderson phoned the White House Chief of Staff.

"Don, let's make Henry acting Chairman of the FDIC," the Texas Senator proposed.

For Don Regan, installing Robert Henry, in line to assume leadership of the Federal Home Loan Bank, as acting head of the Federal Deposit Insurance Corporation cleared one more issue off his desk. Regan listed FDIC Director on his agenda with the President for that day. Forty-five minutes later Ronald Reagan approved Henry as the new Chairman of Fiddick, the government arm that insures the deposits of America's banks. The FDIC chair is a presidential appointment; pending congressional approval.

Robert Henry, heir to the FDIC throne, owed lots of money. Borrowed money, invested in three suburban Atlanta malls. Malls eighty-five percent empty, not paying rent. Hamilton S&L had loaned the money to Henry; sort of.

Robert Henry quietly guaranteed he would be responsible for the $21 million Hamilton debt. His pledge was not evidenced in writing. Each day unpaid interest of $5,833.33 mounted.

The Texas Senator said, "Everything's done, Ken. Of course for the post to be permanent, Henry still needs Senate approval, but that's just a formality."

"Great, Jimbo. That's great," the Hamilton CEO recast the timbre of his voice, "Too bad about Jack Richardson. What's the scuttlebutt?" Ken Thompson never asked his assassin the manor of death.

"Drunk. Skidded off a gravel road in Maryland," Senator Anderson said. "Had a mother in a health care facility nearby. The E-units guys that cut him out said he reeked of booze.

"Too bad. Tough job, too much pressure for some," Ken Thompson said.

The Senator asked. "When will Bob Henry arrive in Washington?"

"His flight from Atlanta arrives in thirty minutes at National," the Hamilton CEO stretched his left wrist free from the white starched cuff,

"He is joining us for dinner at my place in Georgetown, just the three of us."

"Ken, we were damn lucky to have Bob Henry approved and ready to head up FDIC. He's gonna be a help solving this agency in-fighting about the S&L banks," the Texas senator said, "That leaves us short a candidate to replace Ed Gray as chair at the Fed Home Loan Bank."

"Let me consider that, Jim," the CEO said, "See you in Nassau next week. You got the date marked?"

"Yes, yes. See you on the island."

Dallas, Texas

Reality, Brendan thought. *Three days ago I was sailing the Virgin Islands.*

Outbound Dallas lunch-hour traffic was rolling off one-minute miles. Brendan Donahue's Hertz Ciera strained to keep pace. He glanced at the digital clock on the dash. He was meeting the Number Two guy at the Dallas FHLB at 1 P.M.

His phone call to Number Two this morning offered the Texas S&L regulator little information. When Number Two asked the purpose, Brendan simply responded, "Jack Richardson."

Brendan wheeled off the expressway and into a parking slot in front of the eight-story, golden glass building worthy of Vegas. A marquee sign announced that Dallas Cowboys executives worked here.

No security guard in the lobby, only a directory. In Texas, God helps those who help themselves. Brendan's thumb pushed the seventh floor button in the elevator.

"I'm Brendan Donahue," Brendan said to the FHLB regulator.

"Nice to make your acquaintance," Number Two responded. The Director of Supervision led Brendan into his office. "Been expecting you, been expecting somebody."

Brendan liked the ease of the Number Two guy at the Dallas Fed Home Loan Bank. His demeanor suggested their impending task might be less onerous than Brendan anticipated. Number Two explained his connection to Jack Richardson through his time at the Comptroller of Currency, his previous station.

"If the carnage doesn't stop soon, Treasury is going to end up liquidating 4,000 S&L banks," Number Two said.

"Jack Richardson gave me your confidential report to Treasury. You're blunt about the Ninth District's problems. Your words . . . massive fraud, widespread self-dealing, conflict of interest. Your report didn't say that Treasury would end up owning Texas S&L's though." Brendan let his observation hang as a question.

The Director of Supervision used two hands to rise from his desk; he strode to the window. He looked at a cloudless azure sky while answering, "The report you read is three months old. The S&L's are sicker now and declining."

"You told Jack the only way to stop the carnage is to criminally charge one of the top guys at the big S&L's."

The FHLB regulator looked away, ""You used to examine national banks." He turned to Brendan. "What's the highest percentage of classified assets you ever, EVER saw?"

"Jack and I discussed that at dinner two nights ago. Fourteen percent. Bank was seized by FDIC." Brendan inspected Number Two's office for personal mementos. The office, though immaculate, was sterile.

"Here in District Nine, bad loans average nineteen percent. FSLIC is broke. The fix for Dallas has to come quick, or Teapot Dome will seem like lost pocket change."

The office door slammed open, the brunette secretary barged through.

"Sorry, call on your line. You better take it," the woman turned to Number Two's guest. "Are you Brendan Donahue?"

Brendan listened to Number Two's limited contribution to the phone conversation. The FHLB regulator's eyes swung to Brendan.

"Who is in charge?" Number Two listened.

He hung up.

"Shit, this isn't good," Number Two said, "Jack Richardson died last night."

* * *

Their connecting thread was the FDIC, through Jack Richardson. Brendan Donahue left the office of the Director of Supervision, seeking solitude. Brendan knew only what Number Two had been told by the FDIC administrative assistant who had phoned, an Atlanta attorney had quickly been appointed by President Regan as acting FDIC Chairman.

Brendan paused within the air-conditioned ground floor lobby, seven floors below the Ninth District FHLB, he dialed the public phone.

A woman answered the deceased Jack Richardson's Washington phone.

"FDIC," the woman said.

Brendan could not associate the voice with Jack's secretary. He stuttered through an introduction, "This is Brendan Donahue."

No recognition.

"Do you remember me? I'm Jack's friend." Brendan rechecked the telephone number for Jack Richardson's private line he held in his right hand.

"No, I'm sorry. I don't," the woman said.

"I was in Mr. Richardson's office yesterday. Am I speaking to Jack's secretary?" Brendan asked.

"I'm new as of this morning," she said. "Robert Henry is acting Chairman. He replaced . . . "

Brendan cut her off, "I heard that, What happened? What happened to Jack?"

"Just a moment," she banged him on hold so rapidly Brendan didn't have time to object.

A male voice came on the line inside fifteen seconds, "This is Bob Henry, with whom am I speaking?"

"Brendan Donahue. I am the . . ., " Brendan scanned for the precise description that would identify him to the acting chairman. " . . . the guy investigating the Hamilton S&L."

"Oh, yes, yes. Where are you now?" Henry asked.

Brendan assumed Henry requested his exact location in Dallas, "In the lobby of the Fed Home Loan Bank. What happened?"

The acting FDIC chairman spoke slowly, "Details are sketchy, Mr. Donahue. It was a car accident in Maryland late last night. They discovered Jack early this morning. You're at Fed Home Loan Bank here in DC?"

Affirmation that his friend Jack Richardson was dead dropped a pall over Brendan. He asked, "What do you want me to do now?"

"Aahh, two things," said the FDIC Chair. "Who is your contact at the FHLB? Second, update me on your assignment."

Brendan stared through the tinted glass in the suburban Dallas lobby. Heat rose outside from the baking black asphalt of the parking lot. Through the refracted light waves, memories of Jack reeled like a feature film. It struck Brendan that this conversation was backwards. Direction should be coming from the new Chairman. *There hasn't been time to accomplish anything since yesterday.* Brendan didn't speak for fifteen seconds.

"Anything wrong?" asked Robert Henry, his first day on the job as acting Chairman of Fiddick. Before she was awarded two weeks mandatory vacation, Jack's former secretary had given the new FDIC Chairman a vague idea that the Hamilton had issues, but she didn't know much.

"Forgive me. I'm just stunned," Brendan said. "How long had you worked with Jack?"

What does he mean, am I in DC? Brendan asked himself.

"Actually, I didn't know him. I was appointed yesterday. My appointment to FDIC was rather sudden. Mr. Donahue, please continue with your update."

How does an outsider get appointed chairman of Fiddick this quick? Brendan was wary. "Mr. Henry, tell me what you know then I can bring you up to date."

"Mr. Donahue I'm reviewing your file," The FDIC appointee lied.

Nerve ends jangled allover Brendan's back; there was no file.

"I'm calling from a public pay phone. Let me call you back, " Brendan said.

Henry's response was delivered quickly, "Mr. Donahue, hang on. FDIC will not be investigating Savings and Loan banks further. S&L's fall under the jurisdiction of the Federal Home Loan Bank. I would like to meet with you, this afternoon if possible."

Jesus, he has no idea of where I am.

Brendan lied. "I'll call you back in an hour."

* * *

Brendan Donahue considered Robert Henry's confusion; he called Number Two from the lobby underneath the FHLB Dallas headquarters.

Thirty minutes had passed since the jolting news that the FDIC chairman had been killed. Richardson had advised Brendan to keep a low profile in Dallas. Jack suspected somebody inside the Fed Home Loan Bank's Ninth District was snitching info to the Hamilton S&L. Brendan Donahue would be obscure until the pieces fit together.

Number Two answered.

"Brendan Donahue again, are you alone?"

"Yes," The regulator answered.

"Jack Richardson told me I could trust you," Brendan said. "Jack was a personal friend of mine."

"I'm sorry, I didn't know that," Number Two said.

"I just spoke to the acting FDIC chairman. He is vague on our investigation of the Hamilton. His name is Robert Henry. Do you know him?"

"Never heard of him before today," Number Two said.

"He didn't seem to know you either. I don't get it, his office called you with the news of Jack's death."

"The FDIC's office didn't call me," Number Two said. "The call you overheard came from Jack's secretary … after she had been told to take two weeks off. No options"

"Robert Henry says our probe of the Hamilton is over," Brendan said.

"Henry's office just scheduled a 3 P.M. conference call," Number Two said.

"I don't like it," Brendan said, "How does Fiddick have a new chairman so quick? Were your communications with Jack written?"

"No. We were talking across interagency walls," Number Two said. "We agreed that until a course of action was determined, all communication would be verbal. We believe the Hamilton has an informant inside our office."

"Henry doesn't know much," Brendan said, "Except that the FDIC won't be investigating the Hamilton . . . or any S&L. Something is wrong. Do you know of Julie Weidener?"

"I know she died in London. Brendan, I'll phone you after I talk with Henry. Sorry again about Jack."

CHAPTER FORTY-FOUR

Washington, D.C.

Robert Henry, on the job two days as the Head of the Federal Deposit Insurance Corp, had vetted his staff. Only the former secretary to Henry's predecessor, the late Jack Richardson, was aware of Brendan Donahue.

Four FDIC staff analysts had critiqued the confidential memo prepared by the Dallas Fed Home Loan Bank number two guy. Heather Montgomery, the Hamilton S&L VP, might have remained unknown to the new Fiddick chief, if she hadn't phoned the deceased chairman's office when she couldn't connect with him on his private line.

The distant end of Bob Henry's call rang twice before the Hamilton CEO answered.

"Some bad news and some good news. Which do you want first?" Robert Henry asked.

"Save the good news for last," said the Hamilton CEO.

"You have been marked. The FDIC and Jack Richardson concluded the S&L industry would end up in their lap if FSLIC went broke. Richardson, with info from the Dallas FHLB and *FIZLICK* created a hit list of six Southwest S&L's. Hamilton is at the top of that list."

Ken Thompson's fist pounded the mahogany, "That sonofabitch! How was the FDIC going to do this?"

Bob Henry looked down at the 3M square stuck atop his desk. Three names were penciled on the four-by-four-inch yellow post-it, "The opening thrust of the FDICs crusade seems to have been launched against your Hamilton S&L."

"What's in the file?" the CEO asked.

"There are no FDIC files. Nothing is documented. My conclusion is this was an ad hoc force commissioned at the whim of Jack Richardson."

"What has Fiddick done so far?"

"No one in DC knows," said the new FDIC Chair, "Specific action against the Hamilton would have required bureaucratic ass covering; memos, files, documentation. No record of communication with congress or fed agencies exists. Officially, nothing had commenced."

"Who is involved?" asked Ken Thompson.

The FDIC chairman drew a loop around one name on the note.

"Three people," the FDIC head replied, "I personally instructed each person that the FDIC has terminated this probe."

"Who?" asked Thompson again.

Robert Henry surrendered the woman, "Heather Montgomery, a vice president of your S&L." The FDIC Chairman penciled a thick slash through Montgomery's name.

"Who else?" The Hamilton CEO asked.

Henry in his two days running the FDIC had not bonded with DC's other regulators. The Hamilton was the fourth largest S&L in the Dallas Ninth District. Member S&L's elected eight of the fourteen directors overseeing the Dallas Fed Home Loan Bank. Ken Thompson and his peers had command authority over the S&L regulator on Henry's list; the Number Two guy at the Dallas FHLB.

Bob Henry stroked a quivering line through the second name.

"The Director of Supervision for your Ninth District FHLB in Dallas. Richardson had a pipeline to him. Communication between the FDIC and the Fed Home Loan Bank in Dallas is off the organization chart. Usually, the two agencies fight like cats and dogs over their separate turf."

The new FDIC Chairman had not researched Number Two's resume before betraying him. Inside-the-beltway advisors would have pointed out that Number Two had labored nineteen distinguished years for the Comptroller of the Currency, an office of the Treasury Department.

"You said three people," Ken Thompson said.

Bob Henry framed the remaining name between two block-style question marks.

"The other guy is Brendan Donahue. Don't know where he fits in. Worked for Richardson direct. Strange though; no record of employment. No record of anything other than Richardson's secretary mentioned he met with Richardson two days ago. I spoke to Donahue himself yesterday, called him off."

Thompson concluded his notes. "Thanks, Bob. Let's have dinner next week?"

Washington, D.C., 7:18 AM

Ken Thompson strolled through the small manicured park inside Washington Circle. Black wrought-iron fencing protected the inner bluegrass courtyard from DC's rush-hour traffic. Thompson waved at a passing midnight blue 1984 Caddy convertible; the Oklahoma senator flicked a wave back over the windshield. The Okie Senator at the wheel, spun onto Pennsylvania Avenue, smiled and recalled the ten grand campaign contribution last year.

Thompson traversed K street's boulevard. From the three-step depth of the Bagel Factory's front door, a second man stepped up and fell in pace with Ken Thompson step for step. The CEO didn't sense his shadow for threes strides, until the voice shattered his daybreak stroll.

"Good morning, Ken."

From across K Street, Brendan observed the sharp jerk of the CEO's head.

"My God Jonathan," said Ken Thompson, "We agreed not to be seen together in Washington."

"Sometimes what is visible is the least obvious," replied the assassin, "You are the only person here right now."

Thomson's neck tensed, his scan for work-bound congressional power brokers halted. "Our relationship requires caution."

Jonathan Blair spoke as though discussing the weather, "All went well, as you have undoubtedly heard. Mr. Richardson drove off the highway while drunk."

"I am grateful Jonathan, but you and I together in public is reckless."

"I have a personal request, then I'll be gone. Have your sources obtain a current profile on this individual, Blair slipped a folded paper into Thompson's shirt pocket, "He is a general in Cuba, one of Castro's inner circle."

Brendan Donahue had disguised his hunt by occasionally anticipating Thompson's walking route. Brendan stepped into an alcove entrance outside Radio Shack. He peripherally observed the S&L owner talking to the pop-in stranger. Brendan lacked sanction to carry on Richardson's quest. Alone, he began by observing the man Richardson was targeting; the S&L thief that Jack Richardson had said was stealing other people's money.

Brendan Donahue stalked the two men as they walked a short block, then Thompson's acquaintance hailed a passing taxi. The cab stopped an instant, the unexplained walker entered the rear seat. Brendan had no chance to follow.

Dallas, The Federal Home Loan Bank, 8:10 AM

In nine years examining S&L's, the collegial exclamation *FIRED UP* never burst into Bobby Scamehorn's day-break emotions as he anticipated his day. Scamehorn hunkered in the office of the Number Two guy at the Dallas Fed Home Loan Bank.

He scowled as his pissed-off boss fired directives.

Number Two asked his Senior Examiner, "Am I being explicit this morning, Bobby?" Number Two locked his eyes into Bobby Scamehorn. Bobby Scamehorn was *fired up.*

Scamehorn had been digging inside the Hamilton S&L exam for two unproductive weeks. His next fourteen days would be a hell of a lot more productive, Number Two was unleashing the weapons to counteract the Hamilton's deflections.

"Very clear."

Number Two paused, "I'm not calling off the Hamilton examination because some new guy at the FDIC says so, that order has to come down from the President of the ninth Fed Home Loan District."

Number Two continued, "Based on your prelims, what percentage of the Hamilton's loan portfolio will be classified?"

"If we find the delinquent South Metro loans that disappeared," Scamehorn recalled the facts, "… sixty-two percent."

Number Two clamped his jaw, "That, all by itself warrants our staying on this case. Justify your estimate in a memo to me. Date it last week."

Bobby Scamehorn penned another note. "Done. Should we send any of the guys to Garland Savings? They're on the calendar next."

"None, Bobby. Your five-man exam team stays in place. If they refuse an answer, mention criminal charges."

"What are we looking for?" Scamehorn asked.

"I don't know, but, it's there, " Number Two said, "What facts can you prove?"

"One of their vice presidents, Pete Morris, has been handing out money without loan approval, too. No promissory notes, no security agreements, no liens filed. We think he cooked the books in the bank's overnight settlement account for $143,000,000."

Number Two shook his head. "Morris must be a moron. Stay on Morris. What else?"

"Hamilton's letters of credit, none were approved or reported. The Hamilton people called them ACCOMMODATION LETTERS."

"What's the tally?" Number Two asked.

"We've found $114 mill so far. The SVP of commercial, fat guy name of Randy Peterson, isn't even offering an alibi," said the Senior Examiner Scamehorn.

"Dig every letter of credit from their drawers; classify every customer accommodation letter," Number Two said, "By the way, you are getting reinforcements. San Francisco owes me a favor. I've borrowed three of their top examiners. They arrive this afternoon. Put them to work."

Bobby kept his head down and whistled.

"Bobby, pull every one of our guys out of the Hamilton at noon today. Go back in at 4:45 P.M. for an all-nighter."

"Never done that before," Scamehorn said.

"I want every Hamilton official looking over their shoulder," said Number Two, "and advise Hamilton's COO Billy Johnstone, that we are extending the exam by at least two weeks."

CHAPTER FORTY-FIVE

Dallas, The Hamilton S&L

Heather Montgomery had been arguing with the Hamilton Workout guy more than fifteen minutes in his fourth floor office. Tattered furniture testified to the lack of esteem given the Pill by his Hamilton S&L colleagues.

The Pill refused. Janis Lang, the S&L's head teller, would not be granted carte blanche absolution. Such a request, inexplicably presented by vice president Heather Montgomery, implied that the head teller was guilty of something. Heather hadn't revealed what Lang's discretion was.

"That has to be the deal, Phil. If you want Janis Lang to tell you what she knows, you have the Hamilton agree she will not be charged with any financial violations."

"Tell me what Janis did that she thinks is wrong; maybe I can agree to your proposal," Phil Kamerov hedged,

Heather stood, "End of conversation," she said, "I can't trade on assumed forgiveness. I'll reconvene in Washington." Heather Montgomery strode towards the door.

"Let's say I agree on Lang," the Pill said, "If she discloses everything about the money Morris had her funnel through the bank's overnight settlement account."

Heather paused and turned to her one-man audience, "Morris also wants to make a deal. Trade info for immunity."

Phil's brown eyes magnified behind his dark frame glasses, "Didn't we just do this with Janis Lang? Where is this going? When were you appointed house counsel for every crook in this S&L?"

"Janis Lang was induced into administrative errors," Heather lied, "Peter Morris has knowledge of deliberate criminal bank violations."

The Pill snapped the wooden pencil he held, "Knowledge? Does Mr. Morris desire leniency, or would he like a full goddam pardon from the governor?"

Heather enveloped herself in feminine serenity, "The full pardon, Phil. He doesn't want to go to jail."

The Pill weighed the delinquent loans he knew the Hamilton COO, Billy Johnstone, swapped to Sunbelt Savings. He pondered the money the Endres Brothers had received from the Hamilton . . . through Vice President Pete Morris, for brick and mortar that was missing. *Morris must know where that money went!* He had Morris on the hook for improperly funding Dimitri Paulopnos $6 million for the Plano Mall project. Morris must know precisely where the fucking Accommodation Letters lay hidden, undisclosed in the desk drawers of Hamilton lenders?

"Assume I agree to a deal with Morris," said The Pill

Heather, still at the doorway, flinched at his use of the word *assumed*.

"How far upstream are you pointing? Randy Peterson?" The Pill asked.

"No, Phil. Randy is stupid and fat." Heather shut the door and back-stepped into his office, "Randy is a rung on the ladder; he's too stupid to be malicious."

Phil Kamerov moved away; he gripped the back of his chair and leaned over the top, "Then who?"

"Billy Johnstone?" Heather said.

Phil studied the woman, "Our collaboration is restricted and temporary. I will verify one person at a time. Understand?"

Heather nodded, "Agreed."

* * *

Heather's white Mercedes 450SL had recently been used more as a phone booth than for transport. Inside the car Heather Montgomery wrote her list of incriminations. Covert accusations she would trade to the Chairman of the FDIC, this catalog of financial misconduct inside the Hamilton S&L was her ticket out of Texas . . . out of the illusory S&L world. Her phone call would exonerate Heather from lingering whispers about Detroit.

She braced the list against the Mercedes' steering wheel.

Heather leaned back against the car's headrest, *$100,000.* She'd give Jack Richardson and his FDIC a sketch of Lang's and Morris' indiscretions . . . *then he and I will agree on my remuneration,* Heather anticipated. *This information is worth every penny. These people* are *crooks.* Heather would bear no allegiance . . .even Janis Lang was being surrendered.

Heather Montgomery had, with a little luck, gathered enough detail for Jack Richardson to prosecute the Hamilton thieves. The FDIC chairman could choose his target by himself; the owner of the Hamilton S&L or the crooks inside, her fellow employees.

Heather smiled at her indicting list again. Her passport to a year of nothing. Heather drifted to a French island. A sea-side cape shaded by swaying palm trees. Trade winds, creole spices, a thatched bar ten steps above the beach. St. Anne, Guadeloupe. Topless sunbathing on endless afternoons, lost amongst French-speaking attendants, rum blended with tropical fruit . . . Merci. She'd never travelled to the French West Indies.

She pushed the send button; the FDIC Chairman wasn't answering his cellular phone. She dialed his office number.

"FDIC."

"Jack Richardson, please. This is Heather Montgomery."

"Can you tell me what your call regards?"

Heather couldn't wait, "Tell Mr. Richardson I've got everything." Heather restated with syllabic emphasis, "EVERYTHING he requested on my Hamilton S&L report."

"Please hold," the receptionist said.

A part of Heather sailed back to her French beach.

The man answering wasn't Jack Richardson, "Heather Montgomery?"

The unidentified voice jarred Heather like a dose of smelling salts. "Yes, who is this?"

"Robert Henry. I am acting Chairman' of the FDIC. Please go ahead with your report."

"I asked to speak with Jack Richardson," Heather said.

"Ms. Montgomery. Unfortunately, there was an accident. Jack is dead."

Heather half-heard as the man asked again for her report on the Hamilton.

"Ms. Montgomery, the FDIC is closing our investigation of the Hamilton. They do not fall under our jurisdiction."

She was alone again.

Washington, D.C.

"FDIC must know something about this guy." Ken Thompson challenged through the phone. Bob Henry scanned mementos from his dead predecessor hanging on his office walls.

Henry's third day since Ronald Reagan appointed him chairman. Sixty percent of his time at the FDIC had been spent dismantling the covert probe on his caller's S&L. The remaining forty percent of each day had been wasted . . . wasted as he determined that few staffers at the FDIC knew anything about the deceased Jack Richardson's obsession with the Hamilton S&L.

"Ken, there is no record of Brendan Donahue. Don't worry though. I told him explicitly that there was no FDIC investigation of the Hamilton. He's gone, Ken. Gone."

"Okay, okay. It just seems this mysterious Donahue should be fully debriefed. He should be formally told Fiddick's probe is over. You've only spoken to him once?"

"Ken, he'll re-surface. I'll take care of the formalities.

"Keep me up to date," The Hamilton CEO said.

During the last three days Bob Henry's former guarantee on the delinquent $21 million to the Hamilton hung in the background like a cardio monitor. Henry anticipated the CEO would suspend interest accrual while he held the sensitive chairmanship of Fiddick. The three malls couldn't even pay the property taxes.

The men hung up their telephones.

Thompson punched seven digits. The phone call only had to travel seven District of Columbia blocks to the Senate Office Building. The senator's direct extension jangled.

"Jim, Bob Henry believes he has defused a conspiracy by the FDIC that included Fed Home Loan regulators. Jack Richardson was trying to screw our S&L's. Goddam bureaucrats are spending our tax dollars to chase windmills. Richardson had assigned three people to extra-curricular pursuit of the Hamilton. Henry located two. The third is running free."

Protecting constituents' rights was Jim Anderson's responsibility. However, the Hamilton S&L had become full-time work. The Texas senator's forearm propped his tired head.

"What do you need, Ken?" The enthusiasm in the Texas senator's voice was waning.

"Your help to ferret out a Brendan Donahue."

The senator twisted his gold-plate Cross pen. The inky point turtled out. Senator Jim Anderson printed the name.

"Plug into Hamilton's credit agency. United States senators don't locate missing persons."

"Tried, I ... we can't find this guy," said the S&L CEO, "not a credit app, no active credit card charges on the east coast or Dallas. Both Bob Henry and I want to reinforce to this Donahue that the Hamilton connivance is over." Thompson borrowed the implicit charge of the FDIC without authorization.

"I'm not sure what I can do, Ken."

"Jim," the CEO said, "you approve the budget for the biggest missing person bureau in the business."

Senator Jim Anderson, Democrat, Texas, shuddered at Ken Thompson's insinuation. "Don't even ask me, Ken.

"Have the FBI track this boy down for me."

"Ken, the FBI does criminals, subversives . . . I can't instruct them to locate a . . . missing consultant to the Fed Deposit Insurance Corp. Besides, I don't tell the Bureau what to do."

"Jim, goddammit, I don't ask for many favors. You control the money to operate the Attorney General's office. The FBI, last time I checked, reports directly to the AG. Tell them Donahue is a communist . . . FBI tracks commies. Tell them anything you like. This guy was dispensed to undermine the Hamilton . . . a $6 billion institution. You, better than most, know what that would do to the economy of Texas. How much more subversive do we need?"

"Calm down, just calm down, Ken. I'll see what I can do." The senator then asked facetiously, "Any other miracles you require today?"

"Yeah, uh . . . oh, yeah while you've got the FBI's ear, I need a biographical profile on an officer in Castro's army. Apparently still in Cuba. My information is sketchy, goes back to 1964."

Jesus Christ, the senator said to himself, *why can't there be some ribbons to cut somewhere?*

Jim Anderson, eighteen years in the US Senate, jotted down Thompson's request for information on Cecille's uncle Ramon; the man who had betrayed his own brother to advance his career in Fidel Castro's military.

At least this Cuban commando is a real commie, thought the senator.

Dallas, Federal Home Loan Bank Headquarters

The Number Two guy in the Dallas FHLB stood at the head of the conference table inside headquarters. His eight-man team examining the Hamilton S&L was in attendance; five sat, three hotshots confiscated from the San Francisco FHLB leaned against the back wall.

"Bobby, you've been inside the S&L two weeks, ever since the FDIC team headed back to DC," Number Two said, "What have you uncovered?"

Bobby Scamehorn, senior examiner coordinating the Hamilton pursuit, pointed to the tallest member of his Dallas exam team.

"Last week two Hamilton employees were racing shiny new Honda ATV's in the Hamilton's parking lot." The gangly examiner adjusted his glasses, "It was an odd scene, the ATV's were drop-shipped in the lot by Lone Star Honda apparently just for the lunchtime race. Lone Star Honda borrows money from the Hamilton." The junior examiner nodded towards his boss, "Bobby had us investigate the two Hamilton participants."

"Anything?" asked Number Two

"In a roundabout way," replied the tall FHLB examiner. He lifted his chin. "I visited the dealer, Lone Star Honda late yesterday, just before they closed." The twenty-six-year-old examiner unfolded his presentation with confidence. "The owners had gone home. Hamilton finances Lone Star's floor plan Hondas. Lone Star was supposed to have fifty-three ATV vehicles in their showroom. I counted seven. Title release documentation has been completed by the dealer and signed without verification by two lenders in Hamilton's consumer loan department; the guys racing in the parking lot. I couldn't locate records of an inspection . . . ever, in

Hamilton's records. We can nail two junior guys for falsification, probably get the department VP on mismanagement."

Number Two asked, "Are the Hamilton guys involved?"

"Yes, sir. Lone Star's accountant was still in the office during my visit last night. Little guy." The tall examiner straightened in his chair, growing a little taller. "When I realized I was forty-six Hondas short, I invited the little bugger into the empty showroom and suggested he explain or I would instruct the attorney general to issue a warrant for his arrest."

The examiner continued, "I was talking through my butt. Can we have warrants issued for a bank's customer?"

"No." Number Two pardoned the examiner's misrepresentation. "But, I won't tell anybody. Threaten the Hamilton lenders that signed the title releases on the Honda ATV's with potential criminal charges. When they admit, suggest we would be open to a deal . . . immunity . . . if they can remember and prove indiscretions by more senior Hamilton officials."

Number Two redirected, "Anything else?"

A five-foot-seven examiner from San Francisco trimmed with a five o'clock shadow stood; he spoke in a humorless tone, "We investigated the Endres Brothers, specifically Leonard, the older brother. Every other one of the Accommodation Letters being discovered in the desk drawers is written for the benefit of the Endres. And Leonard Endres serves as a Director on the Hamilton S&L Board.

The San Francisco examiner had tight black hair; central casting would have tagged him as ethnic, Italian. He continued, "Six months ago the Hamilton issued new shares priced at $12 mill and sold them all to Leonard. A month later Hamilton bought a parcel of land from Leonard Endres; paid $15 million for the property; declared it was for a future branch office."

"Something wrong with the transactions?" asked Number Two

The Examiner on loan from the San Francisco Fed Home Loan Bank used both his hands as he spoke, "Didn't seem to be," he said, "When an S&L sells stock to an insider, like Endres, then completes a transaction, like their purchase of property from Endres, it is a *report only* transaction, no audit required by the SEC, as long as 30 days elapse between transactions."

"So," said Number Two

"So, if the transaction occurs in reverse order; Hamilton buys the land for $15 mill, then Grimes invests $12 mill – the SEC audits the transaction to make sure there is no tit-for-tat."

"Go on," said Number Two

"I tracked Leonard's checking account, got copy of the check he wrote to the Hamilton for the newly-issued Hamilton stock. Hamilton held onto Endres check for 45 days, then cashed it and received the $12 mill."

'OK, so we can trigger an SEC audit," Number Two said. "Interesting, but the threat of an SEC audit doesn't shake the tree much."

The borrowed examiner removed his black framed glasses, "The $15 million price the Hamilton paid for the property was established by an appraisal; an appraisal prepared by an appraiser serving Hamilton on retainer." The examiner paused to make eye contact with the other seven examiners in the room, he continued, "I met with a State certified appraiser not connected to the Hamilton, explained he was being hired by the Fed Home Loan Bank; chatted about his good-standing as a licensed State of Texas appraiser," as the San Francisco examiner delivered his report his right forearm served as a metronome, four fingers bunched around his thumb.

"You must have made his day," Number Two said.

"My appraiser values the land that Endres sold to the Hamilton at $830,000."

Number Two leaned across the conference table. "So, land valued at less than a mill turns into $12 million in new equity for the Hamilton and $3 million for their Director Leonard Endres?"

"Yup, and the S&L flip flops the transaction sequence by holding the check. A Texas S&L special," said the SF examiner.

"SEC audit, fraud, and jail time. Good job. Schedule a meeting with Director Endres here at our office," said Number Two.

"Bobby, what about their VP, Pete Morris making unapproved loans?"

Scamehorn replied, "We've traced $6 mill he funded to the Plano Mall without loan committee approval. For a while I thought Hamilton's Workout guy, Phil Kamerov, was covering. Then yesterday, Kamerov, they call him Pee-ul, gives us a prize . . . the missing South Metro delinquencies."

"Where did they go?" Number Two asked.

"Across town at Sunbelt Savings. Swapped for delinquent Sunbelt loans. The Hamilton and Sunbelt boys were clever, along with the bad loans, they traded each other a sham interest reserve. They grossed up the bad loans to create an interest reserve. Enough fake money to pay interest for a year. Illegal as hell. When we correct the swap, Hamilton's classified loans will exceed sixty-five percent of all loans."

"Who can we nail on this?"

"Give me two more days. I am trying to pin the COO, Billy Johnstone."

"Bobby, split up the team. Give each of the San Francisco guys one of our junior examiners. Have you been able to coerce Heather Montgomery into cooperating with us?"

"Since she canceled our appointment, she's been mum."

Number Two rose from the head of the conference table. "This is the COO's test. He's either going to build a wall around himself, or jump over to our side. Billy Johnstone will start hearing from his employees that we're digging. Let Pete Morris understand the gist. Spread the rumor we've made a deal with an un-named Hamilton official; traded information for immunity. Questions?"

Bobby Scamehorn said, "That's pushing pretty hard. We're outside our authority."

Number Two finalized. "Whisper that the Attorney General's office has agreed to issue criminal warrants, to be served when we present our examination summary."

"Jesus, these people are just bankers," Scamehorn said. "We're going to scare the shit out of them."

"Exactly," concluded Number Two.

* * *

Ken Thompson's manipulations had been perfect. He anticipated awe in Billy Johnstone's positive response. The Hamilton CEO envisioned Johnstone's wide-eyed, admiring wonderment.

"Billy, you watchin' the hind-side of those fucking fed examiners as they march out the front door of my S&L?"

The CEO's thirst for retribution had been partially slaked.

Instructions from his vassal, Robert Henry, three days chairing the FDIC, should have been communicated to the examiners on the lowest rung of the Ninth District Fed Home Loan Bank.

In Dallas, Billy Johnstone, Chief Operating Officer of the S&L, paced beside the short side of his desk, stretching the telephone cord. He had postponed the call to his CEO, Ken Thompson, for eighteen hours. After Ken's explicit instructions at last week's meeting in DC to usher the examiners out the front door, Billy didn't have a satisfactory explanation for yesterday afternoon's news from the senior FHLB examiner, Bobby Scamehorn.

"Ken, that's not exactly the scenario here. The examiners seem to be settling in."

Thompson misheard his COO, "Say again, Billy"

"Ken, bad news. The examiners extended for at least two weeks," Billy swallowed deep and slow, "And they added three senior people from the FHLB San Francisco district. That makes eight of the sonofabitches pokin' and foolin'."

"Who the fuck authorized this?"

At least I can be accurate, thought Billy. "Their Senior Examiner, Bobby Scamehorn, told me instructions came down from the Number Two guy here in the Dallas FHLB office.

The name left a bile taste in Ken's mouth for the second time this week.

CHAPTER FORTY-SIX

July 3,

The Arizona congressman leaned fifteen degrees left, into the center of the narrow aisle aboard the G-4. In his mind he stripped the blonde flight attendant. Erin Colleen approached his seat on the right side of the private jet. Lecherous eyes betrayed his oxygen-deficient brain, blood homesteaded his penis.

Is that body part of this weekend's offerings? the silver-haired congressman from Arizona speculated to himself.

Erin Colleen displayed a nuance of lavender eye-shadow when she lowered her brows, stimulating a testosterone rush in the Republican rep. Her flirtatious bloom strained her resolve. An effort so well disguised, the Washington pol didn't notice her subtlety.

"With a twist," she delivered his drink.

He asked, "You will be joining us in Nassau for the Fourth?" The five-term Arizona representative was hopeful.

"No." Her blonde hair swung forward as Erin Colleen bowed her five-foot-eight-inch torso to serve him his fourth vodka and tonic since take-off. "The flight crew stays at Causarina, near Cable Beach. A safe eight miles from Mr. Thompson's Casa Del Mar."

"I'll have to talk to Ken about that. He's got plenty of room at Casa Del Mar."

"I've never seen Mr. Thompson's home," she said.

"A glimpse of Eden," said the Arizona congressman.

The reputation of Republican Representative Dennis Martini, Arizona, travelled with him like a carry-on bag. He had been anticipating his third trip to Lyford Cay for Thompson's annual Fourth of July party. Representative Martini revered this three-day weekend, away from his office, out of the U.S.A., and with his friends. And congressman Martini loved women. The politician never counted the rooms at Casa Del Mar, rooms he had explored in tandem. What a party Thompson threw! No wives, just the boys for a little R&R. Well, just the boys and the special ladies from West Palm that Thompson flew to the Bahamas for the weekend. The best part was being out of the country, away from the prying journalistic eyes that had caused so much domestic trouble for his political predecessors. "How about I pick you up at your hotel, say noon, on Saturday for the party? Saturday we always have an afternoon beach grill. Good food, sun and laughs to hurt your ribs."

"Against company regulations," Erin answered, launching her one-woman parade towards the front of the Gulfstream IV's fuselage. Dennis Martini tracked her until she disappeared into the cockpit.

She clicked shut the aluminum frame door of the cockpit from inside, sealing off the ten passengers in the aft cabin. She arched between the two men, resting her arms on the high back of each flight seat. "Jesus Christ, these guys were drunk with their power when they got on the plane, now the booze is kicking in."

"Want a TO?" the co-pilot asked.

"Yeah, Jimmy. Give me five-minutes." The flight attendant accepted the co-pilot's proposal.

The co-pilot reached above his right shoulder grabbing the transmitter for the intercom servicing the Gulfstream's passenger cabin. "Gentlemen, directly underneath our right wing through the steel blue smog, you can see the North Florida coast melting into the Atlantic ocean. We are cruising down to Nassau at an air speed of 560 miles per hour. The sixty-five-mile-per-hour tail wind makes us 625 over the ground. We anticipate landing in Nassau in thirty-five minutes. Miami Center's most recent weather advisory indicates that as we enter the Gulf stream breeze, the breeze that will cool you on New Providence Island this weekend, our ride may be bumpy. Therefore, I have turned on the Fasten Seat Belt sign. Please remain seated while the sign is on. We should be through the chop in approximately ten minutes." He replaced the transmitter. "There, you got an extra five minutes.

"Thanks. Let me know when we reach the Bermuda Triangle," Erin said. "There's one lecher back there I want to bury at sea."

"We can handle that for you," the co-pilot said.

"Oh, yeah? Tell me how."

"I'll tilt this bus sideways while you open the door and jettison the jerk?"

Jimmy offered a half smile as Erin met his eyes. Supporting herself in a deep knee bend between the two pilots, she laughed. Both pilots inhaled Erin's scent in the flight deck.

* * *

What began as a knock on the cockpit door degenerated into thumping. From the passenger cabin a voice clamored, "Anybody in there?"

The flight attendant checked the indicator above the co-pilot to assure the *Fasten Seat Belt* sign was still illuminated. It was. She stood, turned, and opened the cockpit door. Congressman Tony Welman, Republican, Texas, sixty-two-years old, fifty-five pounds overweight, was the knocker.

"How about a drink, sweetheart, before we land?"

"Congressman, you're not supposed to walk about while the fasten seat belt sign is on," she instructed.

"I know that." His tone was inebriately indignant. "But that goddam sign don't restrict you from walking about."

"Yes, it does," interrupted the co-pilot. "Company policy."

"That ain't the policy on my plane, we service our guests, bumps or no bumps, and we been flyin' twenty six years. Drinks roll unless we're driving straight through cumulo-nimbus territory . . . and from where I stand I don't see nothin' out your windshield but easy flyin'."

The flight attendant squeezed the co-pilot's left shoulder. Erin's grip stanched his next comment; a riposte she knew would be loaded with career-ending potential. Erin stepped past the senator, exiting the cockpit for her requested booze run.

"Fuckin' egotistical asshole," the captain said to the aircraft windshield.

* * *

<u>Nassau, Bahamas, July 3</u>

Sandy Herbert, the transplanted New Yorker, moved with the other passengers aboard the Delta 727 towards the exit and onto the tarmac at Nassau. Herbert, bald, egg-headed, tall, athletic, ran American Savings with integrity. His $12 billion San Diego S&L loaned people money for home mortgage loans. Sandy had reserved two weeks at Nassau's West Wind Condos, paying Bahamian summer's bargain GOOMBAY room rates.

Sandy's wife exited the Boeing 727 first, forerunning down the portable silver aluminum steps into eighty-eight degree island heat. At the base she waited, as wives sometimes do when their husbands trail.

Sandy sashayed off the final step with a youthful hop. He inspected the yellow masonry airport for island peculiarities.

Most Delicious of Privileges

Sandy Herbert had climbed to the pinnacle of California's financial industry by avoiding indeterminate risk. No home runs, just hit em' where they ain't. He spied the Hamilton S&L jet, bayed two hundred feet from the Delta. Rising letters up the tail-fin advertised Hamilton's ownership of the Gulfstream.

"Hmmph!" he snorted.

Sandy's wife misunderstood his exclamation as an opinion. Her husband cultivated a liberal attitude toward underdeveloped cultures despite a stone-carved conservative philosophy in his world of finance.

She asked, "Did you choke or was that an intended hmmph?" During their thirty-six years of marriage, she often challenged Sandy with benevolent argument.

"Dennis Martini, Arizona congressjerk, just staggered off that Gulfstream." He indicated direction with nod of his wrinkled forehead.

She followed his stare to the ten men grouped around the nose of the private jet.

"Those guys are unloading for Ken Thompson's Fourth of July carnival. More illicit back-scratching gets accomplished during their three-day binge on this island than the rest of the S&L industry performs in twelve months."

"No wives?" she asked.

"Hmmph!" Sandy's intone perfected by three and half decades of marital communication, suggested that this was not that kind of trip for the boys.

"Oh?" She couldn't have been more curious if this were a Geraldo Expose. "You mentioned Senator Martini! Is that ethical for so many politicians and bankers to spend the weekend together?"

"Not the way these guys do it."

Maybe better than Geraldo? "Is it a secret meeting?" she asked.

"Nope, everybody in the S&L business knows about it," said Sandy Herbert, CEO of the largest S&L in San Diego; an institution profitable for almost a hundred consecutive years.

Delicious, a scandal she thought. "What draws them here on the fourth? July 4th should be family time."

Sandy Herbert, financial conservative, answered his wife with a riddle: "Rumor is the candy man is attending this weekend."

Confused, she asked, "Sammy Davis?"

Sandy chuckled as they walked into the shade on the concourse beneath the airport's rain roof. "No. Michael Milken. He's Wall Street's messiah. Promised those jerks in Texas . . . they can eat the dishes."

Her husband's riddle leapfrogged her grasp. "I don't understand."

"Milken sells for a New York investment bank Drexel, Burnham. He peddles junk bonds. A security most aptly titled. Someday Milken is going to jail."

"Why?" she asked her husband.

His expletive shocked her, "Because he's participating in the rape."

CHAPTER FORTY-SEVEN

Nassau, Bahama Islands, July 4,

Randy-Randy Peterson slid the glass door open. He stepped onto the private concrete terrace outside his bedroom at Thompson's Casa Del Mar. Beyond the knee-high, green and white hedge formed by Cape Jasmine gardenias, the Bahamian sea rippled, stirred by a northbound whisper of gulf stream breeze. The Hamilton Senior Vice President was dressed like a little boy. He wore sky blue Bermudas, a fuchsia polo, ringed white socks stretched to mid-calf, and stiff, unscuffed Docksiders.

Slanting coconut palm trees anchored in Nassau's bleached sand waved along the shore. Mist from waves breaking on the outer reef bore a salt pungency that jarred Randy's senses. Seventy-eight degrees of sunrise perfection.

The purser, Ken Thompson's designation for the six-foot-two, uniformed Bahamian charged with directing the weekend guests, had briefed Randy when he arrived last night concerning dining arrangements. Each guest at Thompson's Casa Del Mar had been assigned a table on the pool deck for breakfast and lunch.

Dinner would be served under the white tent erected on the side lawn. Randy's eyes swept the distant pool deck. He estimated fifteen early risers already munched on breakfast.

The Hamilton SVP strayed from the narrow footpath for a tropical meander through Ken Thompson's manicured grounds. Randy Peterson had never visited the Bahama Islands before. He had no reference for the strange plants. The bright red petals protecting the east side of his walk smelled of perfume; he didn't recognize the shoulder-high bougainvillea. The small pruned lime tree rose above his shoulder. Randy felt at home spotting the dwarf cactus huddled amongst the white flowers and clean pebbles. He judged the weed bowed by wind at the back of the plant bed, the Bird-Of-Paradise, as ugly. His detour terminated at the sea wall, ten feet above the crystalline salt water. Randy pondered the undersea porcupine creatures, submerged in limbo on the coral sea floor.

Cooking bacon defeated the sweet scent from the Violet Clamshell Orchids lining the limestone trail leading to the pool deck. Randy was pulled towards breakfast, with the instinct of a salmon swimming upstream to spawn.

Randy had been assigned the second table from the shallow end of the pool, away from the ocean. Approaching the deck, he observed three men already seated at his stipulated table.

My table-mates are early risers, he thought. He could not identify faces and place names on the three gentlemen.

Peterson broadcast his arrival congenially, "Hi, I'm Randy Peterson."

The three diners studied Randy, but did not speak.

"Neat flowers here!" Randy said.

A black waiter in a fresh starched white jacket poured thick coffee in Randy's cup without asking.

Good-natured instructions sprang from under the uncolored straw Panama trimmed with a raised black band. "Pull up a chair, Randy. Looks like we're table partners for the next three days."

Peterson returned a fat smile towards the familiar Texas drawl on the opposite side of his table.

"Tony Welman, Texas," the man offered. "Have a seat, Double-R."

Congressman Tony Welman, Randy Peterson thought. *Five term representative and I'm having breakfast with him. Never would have recognized him in those shorts.*

Tony Welman, Texas congressman, dressed even more unforgivably than Randy, was the un-elected chairman of this table.

"Rule One, Randy," Welman said, "we never assume everybody knows each other. Now that all four of us are tableside this morning, we give each other a little resume." A confederate grin creased Welman's flush face as he nudged the younger man to his left.

Welman wore a print shirt featuring the colors yellow and orange, suggestive of far-away Pacific Ocean islands. The gaily garbed congressman spoke to his three table-partners, "And we forget everything we do on the island when we go back home." Welman's belly laughter mutated into choking; red-faced he regained control of the conversation at his table. Capping his convulsing lips with his linen napkin, he pointed to his right.

The gentleman in his fifties with wind-resistant gray hair extended his right hand. His teal-blue golf shirt bore the logo of a Scottsdale country club. "Jim Matthews, Attorney General for the great state of Arizona, Randy."

The server placed a bowl of sliced blood oranges ringed by fresh strawberries in front of Randy. Riding the breeze, a distant promise of fried bacon teased Randy.

The third man appeared younger, early thirties, Peterson guessed.

"Dennis Conley, campaign manager for Representative Martini, Republican, Arizona." Conley was dressed for athletic pursuits. His running shoes had enough wear to insinuate he hadn't been clothes shopping with congressman Welman. His white socks didn't cover defined calf muscles. Conley could have eaten the bacon Welman chewed without caloric concern.

As Randy concluded his personal synopsis, Welman flushed the pork with the thick coffee, "Well, boys, we are stuck with each other for three days. Let's make the best of it. The Purser has made a pretty fair match. Two from Texas, two from Arizona. He didn't put any fuckin' Democrats at the table. Randy, nice to have a patron here." Welman didn't disguise his wink at the younger campaign manager.

Randy-Randy pretended he understood.

Casa Del Mar, Nassau, July 4, 5:30 PM

All four table-mates for the Nassau weekend congregated at the diving-board-end of the pool patio. Late afternoon sun posed no threat to their pale skin.

Texas Congressman Tony Welman prodded Peterson's flabby waist with the hand carrying his bourbon, "Double-R, that's Eddie McBirney of Sunbelt Savings talkin' to your boss Ken Thompson. McBirney is Texas' answer to the Great Gatsby. You attend the Sunbelt Savings Halloween party a couple years ago?"

Randy Peterson's red Bermuda shorts stood out amongst better dressed invitees at the sunset S&L cocktail-hour. Beach attire had been suggested for Saturday evening's buffet . . . and ignored by everyone except Randy Peterson.

"No. Was it a good party, Tony?"

"Whoooeee! McBirney dressed as a king. Menu included lion, antelope, pheasant. Halloween was million dollar holiday for Sunbelt." Congressman Tony Welman, Texas, balanced two meatballs on a nacho. He shoveled the smorgas mouthward. Welman garbled through appetizer-packed cheeks, "Say, Randy, you're being beckoned."

Their Bahamas host, Ken Thompson CEO of the Hamilton, was signaling. Randy ventilated. His overweight gut shrank two inches. Randy pranced away from Tony Welman, with a jolly step.

"Later Tony," Randy said. He really liked his table pards.

Randy Peterson caught his CEO's concluding words as he approached the two Texas S&L owners. " . . . my Chief Operating Officer tells me the loan swap worked out well. Now, we both got solid, earnin' assets on our balance sheet."

McBirney, CEO of Sunbelt Savings in Dallas, responded, "Did work out good, Ken. And with the interest reserve we created, the loans can't go delinquent for at least another year. Good, creative bankin'. We ought to be swappin' more loans."

Randy beamed two steps askew of the financial deal-makers. Thompson paused, "Eddie, I want you to meet my head lender, Randy Peterson. Say hi, Randy."

Randy shoved his porky right hand toward the Sunbelt swindler.

Ken Thompson continued, "Randy, the Hamilton S&L is goin' to do some more business with Sunbelt Savings. Those South Metro Division swaps worked out real well. Cut loan delinquency for both our banks."

On his visual periphery Randy Peterson evaluated his three table partners. His status at Thompson's weekend party jumped from minor to major league. Once upon a time Randy suspected the Sunbelt-Hamilton loan swap might be illegal as hell, until Hamilton's accountants, Arthur Young, certified the trade.

Where is Billy Johnstone? Peterson wondered.

Casa Del Mar, Nassau, 6:30 PM

Randy Peterson gauged the meticulous Bahamian caterers with a carnivore's interest. Congressman Welman advised that Graycliff was Nassau's outstanding restaurant. Graycliff staff scurried under a blue and white awning, arranging trays of seafood on the lawn just off the pool deck.

Food should be good when it's finally ready, thought Peterson.

Randy had been watching Ken Thompson work the VIP cocktail-hour imbibers, forty political men, for the last hour. Interacting socially with the CEO of the Hamilton was a first for Randy Peterson. He leaned on his raised knee, his foot propped on the eighteen-inch limestone break-wall. Randy's thoughts roamed out to sea where a Carnival Line cruise ship pointed eastward, returning to Port Everglades.

He jumped when Ken Thompson spoke behind him.

"Randy, you havin' fun here at Casa Del Mar?" the Hamilton CEO asked.

Peterson's chunky neck swiveled, "Mr. Thompson, you bet. Great party. What a group of guys!"

"Good. You meshin' with your table partner, Congressman Welman? He's something, isn't he?"

"He's quite a gambler. Lassoed a small fortune at the Crystal Palace casino this afternoon. They're all great guys. The Arizona AG and Conley, he manages the election campaign for Arizona's senior senator."

"Heah, heah . . . did Congressman Welman get in any lady trouble?" Thompson winked.

Randy stutter-started his rendition of the blond flight attendant slapping Welman at the craps table, "slaghhhh . . . "

Ken Thompson's lifting hand forbade the tale, "No, Randy. Don't tell me if he did."

"Naw, naw," Randy said.

"Listen, Randy," the CEO said, "in addition to our funnin', we got a little S&L business to take care of this weekend. I need your help."

"Sure thing, Mr. Thompson." Peterson would have swabbed the decks if it meant a permanent invite to Thompson's Fourth of July Nassau bash.

"After the Graycliff caterers clean up the food tonight, they need to be paid. Pay for it on your Hamilton S&L American Express, would you?"

"Done, Mr. Thompson," Randy replied.

"Money elects politicians. campaigns need financing."

"Right, Mr. Thompson."

"These men, my guests this Fourth, need our help. A single business, like the Hamilton S&L, is limited to a contribution of $1,000. Each man at Casa Del Mar this weekend has an interest in our S&L industry."

Peterson's chubby head bobbed in confirmation.

"Our key employees can help these men. Conscientious Hamilton S&L employees will support the American political system, I know they will."

Peterson bobbed affirmative again, not understanding the S&L owner's direction.

"How?" Randy asked.

"Every Hamilton S&L employee who contributes $1,000 to a political candidate, a candidate of their choice, will be eligible for immediate salary review; that review will result in a $1,500 bonus."

"Gotcha," Randy said.

"Randy, I'd like to see at least seven hundred fifty of our S&L employees participate. This effort will be overseen as an ad hoc election year task force. You're the guy I want to run this Hamilton task force."

Randy Peterson accepted seven pages of instructions from his boss. Campaign contributions of $750,000 would make the Hamilton S&L a very political bank.

"Our people," the CEO said, "can choose whatever candidate they want, within limits. They can select any candidate on the recommended list. There are fifteen candidates."

"Where's the recommended list?" Randy asked.

"It's in your instruction packet," Thompson said.

Randy gave a quick glance at the fifteen names, looked like the group gathered on the pool deck for cocktails. "A lot of these men are here at the party."

"Every recommended candidate is here at Casa Del Mar this Fourth of July, Randy. Meet each one while you're in Nassau. Then, you'll be able to advise our S&L people when you get back to Dallas."

"Will do," Randy confirmed.

Ken Thompson slapped Peterson on the back and winked. Eight paces distant the Hamilton CEO linked arms with Texas Senator Jim Anderson.

Nassau, 7:30 PM

Darkening crimson hues on the western sea draped the horizon. Nassau's sun, even on the Fourth of July, set quickly. On the Casa Del Mar lawn, black teenage boys banged a melody from shiny capsized steel barrels. Two-step calypso bonged from the steel drums, accompanied by gleaming white rhythmic grins. The crash from the waves beating on the shore diminished within the Tower-of-Babel political chatter around the pool. White-jacketed servants scurried to replace empty trays, refill empty glasses.

Randy Peterson stood on the patio with his three Fourth of July table-pards. Saturday evening's Nassau feast was served as an informal, walk-around-the-pool buffet. Dennis Conley, the youthful Arizona campaign manager, scoured the crowd from his pool-side table. He wore a red blazer, white slacks, and a blue-striped oxford; no tie.

Conley leaned into the three other men, "Hey guys, Don Dixon of Vernon Savings just arrived."

Tony Welman, the gregarious sixty-two-year-old Texas congressman fond of young blonde stewardesses and aged liquor, chewed a gummy conch fritter. "Donald should be politickin' real hard this weekend. He's got some thorny S&L problems. FHLB examiners are threatenin' to classify ninety-six percent of Vernon's commercial loans."

Randy Peterson heard wrong, "Ninety-six percent? That can't be!"

The insatiable Texas congressman said, "Woulda thought so, too. Vernon Savings is on the verge of a new North American record for horse-shit loans. I don't even think our senior Texas senator, old Jim Anderson, has the pull to save Donald." Tony Welman repaired to the buffet line for more conch.

The subdued Arizona AG shrugged, "Anything is possible in Texas."

Casa Del Mar, 8:15 PM

After twenty-four hours in Nassau, Randy Peterson had acquired nonchalance. He sauntered into conversations as he orbited his boss, Ken Thompson. Guests sought out the Hamilton CEO as Saturday's dinner hour concluded at his Nassau estate. Randy studied as his CEO worked the patio; he guessed that Thompson had spent five quality minutes with every politico VIP during the pool-buffet. Randy, stuffed from over-plucking the buffet, stalked within five feet of his CEO. He enjoyed eavesdropping better than participating.

Ken Thompson's words, though spoken softly, jumped above the din.

"Well, if Dixon's got to be crucified, if his Vernon Savings absolutely can't be saved, let's make sure we don't trigger a domino run on our Texas S&L's."

Ken Thompson's confidant, the commissioner of the Texas S&L Department, answered contritely, "I'm sorry it has to be done, Ken. But if I don't close Vernon Savings, the feds will step over my head. Then Texas loses all control."

Randy's mouth hung. His boss condoned the condemnation of a fellow Texas S&L, an invitee to the Nassau party.

The Hamilton CEO's confederate, the Texas S&L commissioner, switched subjects and lowered his voice. Swirling Bahamian trade winds glommed on to the commissioner's private words and dispatched them towards Randy.

"Ken, I need some advice. I've got two million borrowed on an Austin condo development. Sales are slow. Sunbelt Savings, Ed McBirney's S&L, has my loan. I should get that debt placed outside Texas. Appearance, you know. Looks bad that I have a loan with an S&L that I regulate. What do you suggest?"

Thompson squeezed his fellow Texan's shoulder, "Done, Lin."

He looked around, spotting his SVP, hovering close-by.

"Say, Randy, Come on over here for a second. You ever met the head of the Texas S&L Department?"

"No, sir."

"Randy, you're doing some business with Vice President Bush's son at the Silverado Savings in Denver, aren't you?"

Casa Del Mar 8:45 PM

"Don't drink too much, Tony. Fireworks start at nine," said the Arizona Congressman.

His colleague, Congressman Welman, carouseled his glass; sluicing the ice with amber bourbon. "Don't worry about me, Dennis," The older Texan checked his watch, "I got twenty minutes of serious training."

On the pool deck at the Casa Del Mar, Bahamian sea breeze blended laughter with clattering food trays. Dirty jokes and embellished reminiscences had replaced deliberate political prattle.

Randy learned something new with each Nassau conversation this evening. "Fireworks? What fireworks, Dennis?"

The handsome, grey-haired attorney general from Arizona answered instead, "Hookers, Double-R, real high-class hookers, imported from West Palm."

Welman weighed his bourbon. He signaled a black waiter. No waitresses served at the Casa Del Mar this night. "Randy, wait until y'all see these girls. I think Ed McBirney is in charge of hooker procurement at your CEO's Thompson's parties. What do you think, Dennis?"

Conley corroborated, "Probably is McBirney. He commanded the fly-pull at Sunbelt Savings' hospitality suite in Vegas last year."

Randy Peterson loved his new friends' stories. He accepted his role as straight man to the humorous slander tossed around by Congressman Welman and Arizona campaign manager Conley.

"Dennis, what the hell is a fly-pull?" Randy asked.

"Double-R, a fly-pull is a Sunbelt Savings marketing technique to lock-in their best customers. Like the frequent flyer mileage American Airlines offers."

"Never heard of a fly-pull," Randy-Randy said.

"Well, Randy, listen and learn. Sunbelt Savings gathers twelve favored S&L customers in a fictional Las Vegas hotel room. Sunbelt CEO Eddie McBirney mounts the podium, that's the coffee table. He instructs his male customers to form a circle. McBirney calls for the house lights to be dimmed, anonymity is valued at Sunbelt Savings just like it is in Switzerland. All the lights are killed except for a sliver radiating from a crack in the bathroom door. That's so no one trips over the furniture."

"What is it, some secret Sunbelt Savings society?" Randy asked.

"Private, Randy, but not so secret. Quiet now," Conley, the campaign manager for his Arizona Senator said, "I'm tellin' the story." A small crowd formed to listen to Conley's retell.

Randy directed his incredulity towards the thirsty Texas congressman, "This really happen?"

Tony Welman accepted another bourbon, "Last October, Desert Inn, sixth floor."

Dennis Conley stilled their interruptive talking, "Hush, Randy. You're learnin' S&L history. I'm relating the Great Sunbelt Savings fly-pull," Conley resumed, "McBirney calls for the women. From the bedroom they enter the suite single-file and surround the twelve Sunbelt customers. Twelve of the best looking, for-hire girls I ever saw. Each stations herself next to a Sunbelt borrower and McBirney hollers 'FLY-PULL'!"

Welman and the Arizona AG split into laughter.

"What happened?" asked Randy.

"What happened? The whores pulled each guy's dick out. You want a box score, Randy? Three guys got laid, six guys got a blow job, two were so drunk they couldn't get it up, and one guy still swears he was never in Vegas that week."

Ten guests gathered to hear Dennis Conley's eye-witness recount of the much-rumored McBirney fly-pull. The group roared as they nodded confirming heads.

Trim Dennis Conley, working his listeners wearing his red Stanley Black blazer, tamped air with his suspended hands. The assembly hushed. "That's why I dearly hope, Eddie got the girls for tonight. That's Ed McBirney. He can pull off most anything. Hell, rumor is McBirney engineered placement of the new head of the FDIC, Robert Henry." This unexpected leak from the young Arizona political assistant stilled his appreciative audience.

Randy Peterson corrected the erroneous information the instant it escaped Conley's lips, "Don't be giving McBirney credit for the new FDIC guy," Randy called out, "My guy, Ken Thompson, wired Henry into the FDIC from the get-go." Laughter on the pool deck braked without a screech. Randy thought maybe he should have kept his mouth shut.

<u>Casa Del Mar</u>

At 9:00 P.M. white lights bordering the canvass awning flicker, then dim. Soft blue spot-lights revolve through Nassau's black sky above the Casa Del Mar. The hum of an internal combustion engine announced the 1954 Silver Dawn Rolls Royce as it drove around the sea-side villa. It braked on the sea-side lawn.

Thompson's Fourth of July guests circle the Rolls. Darkness shrouds the identity of the gawking men. Low intensity blue illumination throws dark shadows around the grey metallic automobile.

A uniformed chauffeur steps from the driver's side of the stretch auto. He stops to polish the glistening chrome door handle. Ignoring the forty leering men, he servilely releases the door latch to the rear compartment.

Randy Peterson unfastens his second button down his Polo golf shirt. He nudges past several people, edging to the front of the group near the car's left rear door.

Dennis Conley already stands in this prized position. "La belles, Randy boy," he whispers.

Blonde, five-foot-eight, white lace halter with more space than lace, steps from the car's back seat.

"Jesus fucking Christ!" Randy can't help his remark. Her red spandex mini-shorts fit like the peel on an apple. "God amighty, that's gotta be Farah Fawcett's baby sister."

Holding the chauffeur's hand, she tongues a shine on her painted lips, "Would someone buy me a drink?"

Dennis Conley bounds from his genuflection. He extends his right arm in a gentleman's offer.

In unison the other thirty-nine men crow, "Whooooo!"

Randy Peterson searches the crowd for his boss, Ken Thompson. Randy wants guidance before he waddles into this game. His CEO is nowhere in the night-time pack.

Randy suggests to the sweating Texas congressman on his left, "Tony, that was some woman."

"Don't come in your pants, Double-R. This here Silver Rolls holds seven more, just as purty." A tan, silky, bare, very feminine leg started to emerge from auto's rear door.

* * *

Randy Peterson couldn't read his watch in the Bahamian night, not through throbbing eyes.

Must be after midnight, he thought.

Peterson had told the Graycliff staff manager he'd settle the catering bill when the festivities ended. There isn't a sound. Casa Del Mar is sedated. Peterson craned his bulk upwards on the chaise lounge to a sitting position. His naked toes dug into beach sand.

Where are my shoes? Too much booze. His three weekend table-mates would hoot him for not grabbing one of the West Palm Beach hookers.

Damn those were good looking women, he thought.

With strain, Randy resurrected his 243 pounds to a stand; on wobbly feet he approached the scene of last night's buffet dinner. Underneath the tent-ceiling, Randy recognized the Graycliff staff manager soundlessly straightening chairs.

"Raymond, hey Raymond."

"Mr. Randy," the Bahamian food man demonstrated no anxiety about his overdue bill.

"I thought I missed you," Randy's right palm compressed his aching forehead, "Thought you left without getting paid."

"My staff left an hour and a half ago," the Bahamian caterer said, "I waited for you. Could we settle?"

Randy mixed through his pocket. "Yeah. There you go." He handed the American Express card to the caterer, "What time is it?"

"4:15 A.M," the caterer from Graycliff said.

"Jesus!" said Randy.

Raymond had already tallied the damage, "Your total is $12,400." The caterer recorded the amount at the bottom of the blank credit card slip, "And a twenty percent gratuity is to be added."

Randy, dumfounded, signed the check.

The Graycliff caterer slipped away in Nassau's pre-dawn shadows.

Peterson walked towards the ocean. Casa Del Mar sleeps.

White waves rumbled softly on the outer coral reef. Salty sea spray diluted the stale party scent as night washed into dawn. Randy sat on the low limestone-and-shell break-wall. Scenes from the previous evening twinkled within . . . deals, scams, and women.

"Hi." Her voice shot a jolt of internal electricity through Peterson.

"Uh, hi. Uh, kinda late. I, uh, didn't hear you," Randy said.

Peterson recognized Farah's baby sister, "Goddammit, you scared me."

She drowsily swayed towards him in the Nassau dark. "Sorryyyyyy," her apology dragged in a little girl voice, "You have a good time tonight?"

Randy thought of his night. He thought of the whole day.

"Yeah," he said, "Incredible day. Gambled, ate too much. Drank till I fell asleep."

"You didn't get laid?" the baby sister asked.

Peterson didn't even suck in his gut. It was too late, too dark. He misinterpreted her question about his sexual abstinence as approval, not concern, "No, I was good. Liquor got to me before I did anything immoral."

"What's your name?" she asked.

"Randy."

"Too bad for you, Randy," she stepped behind him and stroked his bulgy neck.

"Feels good," Randy said.

"How about a blow job, Randy?" she said, "That would feel even better, I bet."

"Me?" he said.

She stood the S&L lender on the break-wall, "Just let me," She unzipped his Bermudas.

"Oh goddammit," Peterson said.

CHAPTER FORTY-EIGHT

The phone in Heather's office rang, "Hamilton S&L, this is Heather Montgomery."

"This is Brendan Donahue, Heather," he waited. No response from the S&L vice president through the telephone line. No recognition. "I work with Jack Richardson, the FDIC chairman."

Heather had a vise-grip on her telephone, "Richardson is dead. Who are you, Mr. Donahue?"

"Jack was my friend," Brendan said, "I was to be your FDIC contact. I had just arrived in Dallas when," Brendan grappled with his explanation, "... when Jack died."

Heather's voice betrayed doubt, "For whom do you work, Mr. Donahue?"

"I was," Brendan's unraveling explanation had to be simple and precise,"... was recruited by the FDIC to investigate the Hamilton S&L."

She permitted Brendan Donahue no ambiguity, "According to Fiddick's new chairman, there is no investigation of the Hamilton S&L."

"That's what the new head of FDIC told me too," Brendan said, "He called you?"

"No," she said, "I called Richardson. I'm not sure Fiddick ever would have called me. Knowledge of my role was scanty when I spoke to Richardson's replacement."

"Heather, I don't believe Jack's death was an accident. I will be in Dallas tomorrow. Can we meet?"

Heather contested her unknown caller, "You didn't answer me, Mr. Donahue. Who do you work for?"

"No one at the moment," he said.

"No thanks on meeting, Mr. Donahue. I've got enough problems." Her telephone receiver moved towards its cradle.

"Julie Weidener's death was a result of her investigation of the Hamilton S&L," Brendan said.

His accusation poured over Heather like a rogue wave, "Who killed her?"

"I'm not sure, yet. Someone with power is pulling strings to keep the S&L regulators at bay. People, who blow trumpets outside the walls of your S&L, die. You're in danger, Heather.

"Danger! Mr. Donahue, yesterday a Dallas cop attempted to rape me. Day before I was shot at by a hit man. My only buffer, your mysterious FDIC boss, dies suddenly, you're telling me I may be in danger, you're a fucking genius."

Heather's frenzy decomposed into swimming dizziness.

"Calm down, Heather."

"Calm down? Two people investigating the S&L are dead! That leaves you, me and the Pill."

"Who is the Pill?" Brendan asked.

"Hamilton's Workout Guy. You know, our bad loan guy," she said.

"Jack Richardson said you were his only contact inside Hamilton."

"Phil Kamerov isn't working for FDIC?" she asked.

"I've never heard of him before now," Brendan said.

Heather explained, "Richardson told me to keep Phil up to date on what I was doing inside the Hamilton."

"Be careful what you say to him," Brendan said.

"Mr. Donahue, I'm not relishing this conversation," she said. "You're on your own." Heather slammed the phone into its cradle.

July 5, Nassau, Casa Del Mar

"Hey, Billy," Randy called, "Over here, on the beach."

Billy Johnstone squinted through the mid-day Nassau sun. He waved acknowledgement to his chubby Senior Vice President. The Hamilton Chief Operating Officer surveyed sunbathing bodies on the Bahamian beach in front of Casa Del Mar.

"Where the hell you been?" Randy Peterson lumbered up the four steps from the beach. "Man, some party goin' on here this Fourth of July. Billy, I got a hundred stories to tell you."

Half a bottle of number fifteen Coppertone sunscreen greased Peterson's body. He flapped a crimson rum punch as he jabbered at his tardy boss.

"Billy, you're two days late," Randy said.

"Fuckin' bank examiners decided to extend their stay, Randy. I couldn't get out of Dallas until this morning. I miss anything?"

Randy said, "You missed Friday, Saturday, and the best goddam party girls I ever seen."

On the veranda of Casa Del Mar, Ken Thompson appeared. His arm spooled for Billy Johnstone. Peterson trotted alongside his COO.

"Jeeeeesus, Billy! Gambled at the casino. Look here," Peterson exhibited his drink as though it were an uncut diamond he had unearthed in the beach sand, "Billy, grab yourself a rum drink."

As the two men neared, Ken Thompson said, "Randy, I need to talk with Billy, privately."

"Hey, Double-R," Billy Johnstone said, "grab me one of those rum drinks, will ya?" Pudgy Peterson pattered off towards the bar.

As Randy sauntered away, Ken Thompson asked, "How you doin' with those mother-fuckin' regulators, Billy?"

"I'll handle them, Ken," the COO of the Hamilton replied.

"Give me an update this afternoon." Thompson draped his arm around Billy Johnstone. He routed him to a cloistered spot on the estate's ocean-side lawn.

"Billy, a friend of mine needs a favor," Thompson said, "This is very confidential."

Johnstone had thrived fourteen years with Ken Thompson always being confidential, "I understand."

"Do we have contacts in Dallas that can influence people?" Thompson clarified. "Physically influence."

"You mean enforce?" Hamilton's COO asked.

"Yes. An acquaintance needs to employ physical persuasion. Do you know someone we could recommend?"

Johnstone slowly spun a three-sixty, as though he was bathing in Nassau's ambience. No one was within earshot, "There is a Greek guy, Dimitri Paulopnos."

Washington, D.C.

Ken Thompson was shouting into the phone at his attorney, "I'm cleanin' up the Hamilton so we can sell the S&L. Just like you recommended. And you were right, I need time. But my COO just told me them sumbitch regulators in Dallas ain't gettin' the message."

"The Dallas Fed Home Loan needs a personal message," advised Hamilton's attorney

"Bob Henry, our new head of the FDIC, told the Dallas regulators point blank," Ken Thompson said, "The Dallas guys didn't back off, they put more examiners inside the Hamilton. You're the lawyer, give these guys a legal lesson, get them out of my S&L."

The attorney looked out the window, tracking K street traffic, "Ken, a lawsuit against the two top regulators in the Dallas District has to identify monetary loss due to harassment outside regulatory guidelines. A personal lawsuit will be front-page news in tomorrow's *Wall Street Journal*. Negative headlines won't help sell your S&L."

"Tuck em', file the charge. Name the president of the Dallas Ninth and his number two guy. Get them out of the Hamilton, last week. How quick can you get the process started?"

"Three days. Two, if I tip the courthouse clerk a couple of bucks. Let me call the President of the Dallas FHLB and tell him we're filing. Maybe they'll back off?" The S&L's attorney shrugged, nobody could see him.

Dallas, Texas

His boss, the Greek, told Gianni Cortese to leave no doubt in the mind of Heather Montgomery. Compared to the Italian's typical enforcement for Dimitri Paulopnos, today's assignment had an indulgent warp.

Che Bella, the Italian thought.

Montgomery, the S&L woman, had been tangled-up with the Polack asshole cop, Kowalski. Eliminating Kowalski had soothed Cortese, a fringe benefit he received as the Greek's most trusted envoy. This assignment with the woman had a feel-good tingle too.

Cortese tested the front door knob outside Heather's apartment. He jammed the lock hard-right, then churned counter-clockwise. Locked! Gianni Cortese retrieved the single, newly fabricated master key from his pocket. Freshly cut, silvery edges glistened from the evening lamplight. He unlocked her metal front door. Inside Heather Montgomery's apartment, cooler air eased the heat of the Dallas summer twilight.

Cortese slipped-off his cordovan Fiorucci loafers. Fading light allowed Gianni to inspect her living room, dining area, then the two bedrooms. He didn't create a sound. Empty. Heather Montgomery at that moment was sweating her slim body on the Stairmaster at the Richardson Athletic Club. Cortese had tailed Heather to the RAC forty five minutes ago.

He snapped the master light switch on, then clicked-off each individual lamp in her living room except one, the marble and polished brass lamp next to the brushed cotton, burnt-orange Lazy-Boy. Gianni Cortese hand swept the chair's already clean surface and sat down.

Cortese extinguished the single electric lamp illuminating Heather's small living room. In Heather's dark apartment his fingers smoothed his Italian-black hair behind his ears. She'd be home in thirty minutes. By 9 PM he would complete his day's work.

<u>Washington, D.C.</u>

"$250,000 was wire-transferred to Zurich this morning, per your instructions," Ken Thompson said.

The assassin did not offer his appreciation. Ken Thompson resumed, "When do you depart for Milan?"

"This evening," Jonathan Blair replied. Eighteen inches separated the two men sitting on the iron bench in Lafayette Park.

"I envy you. Ten hours cocooned in an airplane. No telephones, no problems."

The assassin didn't respond. Jonathan never flew non-stop between his residence and his assignment; to do so would be reckless. He also never revealed his travel itinerary to anyone. The CEO's unanswered question faded away in Washington's dirty-brown haze.

Sweat leaked from the S&L man's brow. Washington's mid-afternoon temperature lacked three degrees from reaching the ninety-four degree forecast. "Jonathan, I have another assignment. This problem, this man, surfaced without warning."

Jonathan Blair surveyed the top third of the Washington Monument, "Another death, you mean you want me to kill," the assassin questioned.

"Yes. This individual is threatening my existence," Ken Thompson said.

"When?" Jonathan said.

"Now. Before you return to Europe. This man has to be extinguished."

"No. I do not have time to prepare," Jonathan said.

"This would be lucrative," The Hamilton CEO said.

"No." Jonathan's distant gaze fell on the White House gates, directly across Pennsylvania Avenue. He stood. Departing, he swiveled his head, "Absolutely not, Ken. Assassination is not a parlor game I play on a whim."

"Jonathan, if you could correct this problem for me, I believe I could lean on the FBI to accelerate their research on that Cuba information you requested."

"No, this is not for me," Jonathan Blair said for the third time.

The assassin left the Hamilton CEO alone on the black enamel-paint bench. Thompson stared without seeing the placard-carrying protestors across Pennsylvania Avenue.

CHAPTER FORTY-NINE

Dallas. The Federal Home Loan Bank

"In my office, now," The President of the Fed Home Loan Bank's Ninth District commanded through the telephone to his Number Two, the guy tasked with assuring proper financial behavior from Texas Savings and Loans. Number Two anticipated his boss would be pissed off. Eight days had passed since Number Two unilaterally cranked up examination heat on the Hamilton S&L.

Well, he thought, *I've got some facts.*

Number Two spoke as he marched through the Pres' open office door. "You catchin' flack on the Hamilton examination?"

"Big, jagged pieces, we are being sued by the Hamilton. Fucking S&L is paying their goddam $200 dollar-an-hour lawyers using FSLIC-insured money to sue us, their regulators."

"Suing us for what?" Number Two asked.

"For $36 million dollars. Thompson's attorneys say that represents lost profits due to Dallas FHLB examiner harassment," The President of the Dallas FHLB said. "Attorneys for Hamilton, just called, said it was a goddam *Courtesy Call.*"

"Can an S&L sue their Fed Home Loan Bank?" Number Two said.

"They are not suing the Fed Home Loan Bank; the fucking Hamilton is suing us, you and me, the two of us, personally."

Number Two leaned back against the door frame, "Holy shit!"

* * *

Heather's brunette hair was still damp, it drooped over her ears. In her right hand she portered a satchel of sweat-heavy aerobic togs. A small plastic Safeway bag holding hydroponic lettuce and cheddar cheese swung annoyingly from her left wrist. Keys hung on a ring that looped her right baby-finger. She shook the ring, isolated her familiar key, inserted and turned her door-knob.

Heather's fingers shaved across the light switch. Nothing. No light. Four lamps in her living room should have illuminated. She strapped the switch up and down three times.

Heather weaved her way through her unlit living room, bobbing the satchel protectively in front of her. Carpeting muffled each testing footstep. In the dark of her kitchen, she touched the stove-top. Heather punched the ventilator light; a dim thirty-watt bulb illuminated. Shafts bent around the corner, highlighting the living room's contours. She twisted the white grocery bag free from her wrist, depositing the food in the sink. Silence.

Heather retraced back to her living room. Fractional illumination paved her path. She flicked the one-hundred-fifty-watt lamp on her roll-top desk. The upright, dependable lamp refused to spark. She quietly pattered towards her front door.

Gianni Cortese sat tombstone-still, measuring Heather's silhouette.

Weak ribbons of light angled from the kitchen. Heather swept the living room, her eyes missed him.

Most Delicious of Privileges

Cortese fingered the Smith and Wessen 39 in his jacket. He'd rather execute the Greek's command without a weapon. She had to see his face. His left hand reached for the master switch controlling all electrical outlets in Heather's living room. As she turned, the Italian snapped the master switch on.

Light exploded. Cortese's line was rehearsed, "Remember me? I removed that dick-head cop from your friend's condo. Guy who tried to rape you."

Heather recognized the accent before recognizing his tan face. Her lower jaw hung. Heather tried to scream, but only a rasp came, "What!"

"You gotta' problem," The Italian said. He watched her in case she gets crazy and goes stupid.

Heather's hoarse scream had no volume, "What are you doing here?"

"Stay calm," Cortese remained seated in her reclining chair, "I'm not your problem. I'm just here to tell you, you got a problem. Give you a message. Do you a favor."

"How did you get in here?" Heather Montgomery's huffed.

"Can I stand?" the Italian asked.

Heather just stared.

The Italian stood. Heather back-stepped against the wall.

Cortese wandered behind the rust-colored Lazy-boy, away from Heather.

"This is a favor to you. My boss, the Greek, you know the Greek?"

She shook her head with short frenzied whips, denying knowledge of the Greek.

The Italian bodyguard continued, "Well, the Greek, see, he gets a request to shake you down. Message to you is, back offa' your talkin' with the FDIC. Normally, the Greek, he might handle a favor like this for a client."

"What's *shake me down* mean?" Heather sprang in one leap to the dark-stained pine Ethan Allan desk. She snatched the triangular wooden nameplate, once a marquee atop her desk at the National Bank of Detroit.

"Don't worry. I'm not gonna' shake you down, Miss Montgomery." Cortese's hands raised in a priestly suggestion of pastoral benevolence.

Roar, like the morning train, returned to Heather's voice, "What is a shake down?"

Cortese's courtesy slipped, "You know, I rattle you a bit. Make you think I'm gonna hurt you. Abuse you a bit. Maybe, punch you two, three times . . . places people don't see." Cortese could have been explaining to a kindergarten class how zebras get their stripes.

The Italian continued, "Anyway, the Greek, see, he decides he owes you one. You were quiet with that Dallas cop problem. The Greek pays his bills. So, I'm not going to shake you down. Instead, Miss Montgomery, you get a warning about the guy who requested that the Greek rattle you. The Greek is returnin' you a favor. Someone doesn't like you talkin' to the FDIC. Be careful, the guy who gave the Greek this assignment, he's powerful."

"Who?" Heather asked.

"Can't say, professional code. I gotta' be goin' now. Can I walk out the door without you crackin' me with that piece?"

Heather let the forgotten nameplate cocked in her right arm fall to her side.

"Go," she said.

"Two things. And I'm doin' this on my own, Miss Montgomery. One, when the Greek does you a favor like this, sometimes it's good to remember, in case you can do him a favor back."

"Fuck you!" Heather spit her words.

"Good. OK, that's healthy," the Italian said.

"Get out!" she screamed, her voice back in full.

Cortese stepped to the door. "Second, the man who commissioned us to shake you down is someone I would have thought was on your side. Me, if I were you, I'd take a walk from that place you work."

Heather, trembling, sank crying on the carpet.

* * *

The Federal Home Loan Bank

Number Two's boss, the President of the Dallas Fed Home Loan Bank, rolled the legal claim into a baton and flailed, "Washington is a broken record; FSLIC is broke.'" DC says they'll reimburse us for legal costs to defend against the Hamilton charges only if the verdict absolves us. No reimbursement if the verdict goes against us. We're armed with dull lead pencils to battle these S&L criminals. Now, our tops execs in DC leave us hanging." Number Two had no money to defend himself against the bogus Hamilton charges.

The Pres outlined the only non-monetary strategy, "We have to compromise with the Hamilton; get them to dismiss. I don't have the dough to hire a big-time attorney to defend."

Number Two, the head regulator at the Dallas Ninth, spiked a final challenge at his boss, "I'm not calling the exam team off the Hamilton S&L." He slammed the door, storming out the office of the President of the Ninth District of the FHLB.

"Goddammit!" said the Pres.

Washington, The Senate Office Building

Senator Jim Anderson, Republican, Texas, regretted hosting the five-man meeting in his office. By default he led the discussion, debating the President of the FHLB Ninth District, the Texas region.

"Are you purposefully antagonizing us, sir?" Senator Anderson asked.

"Senators, I need your support," the Pres said, "We need to halt this looming S&L disaster in Texas; the Hamilton S&L has been identified as the most serious problem," The lonely regulator rested his conclusion with the four US Senators seated at the conference table.

Senator Anderson pointed at the isolated regulator, "My constituent interest, the Hamilton S&L, is personally suing you for regulatory harassment. Do you understand Washington's policy of forbearance for our S&L's?"

"Forbearance is not an appropriate solution for the Hamilton," the FHLB Pres said, "Texas S&L's are looting America's treasury. My Director of Supervision and his examination team have discovered that the Hamilton S&L swapped eighty-five million in delinquent loans with Sunbelt Savings . . . for eighty-five millions of Sunbelt's delinquent loans."

"Is that a problem?" asked The Texas Republican.

Despite laboring air-conditioning, nervous sweat beaded down the regulator's ribs. He over-simplified, "Senator, a delinquent loan swapped for another delinquent loan is accounting magic. Past due interest on the delinquent loans at both S&L's is grossed-up, magically paid up-to-date." His regulator hands parted imaginary clouds. "Paid with new deposits flowing into the S&L because *we the people* guarantee those depositors will be repaid. The Hamilton is squandering other people's money."

Senator Martini, Arizona, asked, "Did Hamilton's auditors approve the delinquent loan swap with Sunbelt Savings?"

Exasperated, the President of the Dallas FHLB could only respond with the truth. "Yes."

"And why do you suppose a major CPA firm would sanction Hamilton's loan swap?" Senator Martini pursued.

"Because the Hamilton S&L is their client, Senator Martini," the Pres said.

The Ohio senator spoke, "Arthur Young, Hamilton's accounting firm, tells me your Dallas District has taken an unusually adversarial line with the Hamilton S&L."

Most Delicious of Privileges

Senator Alan Cranston popped his head through the door and interrupted the senatorial inquisition. "Sorry I can't sit in. Are we resolving harassment of the Hamilton S&L by the Dallas regulators?"

Malice screwed into the features of the solitary S&L regulator warring against the power of five U.S. senators.

Senator Cranston lasered the Pres of the Dallas FHLB, "I can't stay, but I want to let you know, sir, that I share the concerns of my fellow senators." His vote cast, Cranston departed for an unexplained political sabbatical.

Senator Anderson, Texas, invoked the prestige of his colleagues in asking, "Well, can we have your assurance the Dallas FHLB harassment of the Hamilton S&L will cease?"

Opposing the persuasive intent of the five senators, the regulator exposed another S&L crime. "Senator, Ken Thompson bought property from his director, Leonard Endres. In return, Endres purchased S&L stock. The Hamilton S&L paid fifteen million for land worth $875,000"

The S&L regulator waited, expecting this villainy to elicit damnation towards the Hamilton . . . and support for his Ninth District FHLB.

"I know Dallas land, sir," said the Texas Senator, "Real estate values are skyrocketing. Was the purchase supported by an appraisal?"

"Yes., but, " the Pres rebutted.

"But, nothing. Your duty is to keep our S&L's functioning. You are failing. Do you understand my message?"

"Senator, even Dallas land doesn't appreciate in value fifteen times within one year," said the man responsible for assuring that sound lending was being practiced by Texas S&L institutions.

Senator Anderson and his four Senate colleagues stared down the disagreeable regulator.

Senator Anderson recalled the $50,000 Ken Thompson had pledged to his reelection campaign last Sunday morning in Nassau; about an hour after the West Palm Beach woman slipped into her thong bikini and out of his room.

Senator Anderson's delivered the verdict without collegial discussion.

"No more gestapo tactics, sir. Forbearance, as it pertains to the Hamilton S&L, will be your mission. Am I clear?"

* * *

"Cecille, this is Jonathan," the assassin said.

"Jonathan. Where have you been?" Cecille followed her question with quick words, "OK, your rules, no questions. I've wanted to tell you. I got it, Jonathan. My theatrical break-through."

Passion chipped at the executioner's practiced granite emotions. His Washington, D.C., assignment had been discharged. Jonathan sensed his soul tip-toe to the rim of humanity.

"Whoa, slow down," he said. "I'm flying to London tonight. Tomorrow, you can bring me up to date on what has happened since I left you in London last week. We'll have all night."

"Jonathan. I won't be here. My dark skin has finally become an asset. The producer of *Miss Saigon* thought I looked exotic . . . oriental."

Jonathan's corporeal appetite stirred. Cecille's voice carried across the Atlantic in erotic tones. Her naked image played on a private screen of his internal cinema.

"You're in *Miss Saigon*, wonderful! We can celebrate with dinner at the Gay Hussar after the play."

"No, Jonathan. I got a part in the Broadway production of *Miss Saigon*. I leave for New York tomorrow. Rehearsal starts on Monday; we open at the Schubert in two weeks."

Jonathan tapped his Washington-New York-London-Milan airline ticket on the edge of the night table in his Washington Mayfair Hotel.

"Can you come to New York?" she said, "I've never been to New York. I've read New York has horse carriages," Cecille proposed suggestively, "We can ride through Central Park after dinner?"

Ephemeral craving blitzed through Jonathan Blair. Across the Atlantic he could smell her fragrance.

"I don't think so," he said. Jonathan throbbed for Cecille, passion conquering caution, "I'm in the States now."

Cecille interrupted, "Then stay. Meet me in New York. I'm booked at the Saint Moritz on 59th Street."

"When do you arrive?" he asked.

"Three tomorrow afternoon," Cecille said.

"You will have a message at the front desk."

CHAPTER FIFTY

<u>Dallas, Texas, the Federal Home Loan Bank</u>

Number Two barged into the delayed 5 P.M. meeting. The eight examiners assigned to the corrupt Hamilton S&L welcomed their supervisor with silence. Number Two's fist banged the conference table; bouncing three pencils onto the floor.

"Five US senators have suggested the Dallas FHLB end our exam of the Hamilton S&L. For emphasis, I'm being personally sued for regulatory harassment for $36 million."

His exam team maintained silence.

Number Two's skin tone moved up the color chart, towards acute crimson. The eight S&L examiners stared; Number Two, the man who had dispensed bullets to them instead of blanks, was being crushed by political weight.

"DC recommends our exam teams introduce *Forbearance* as policy," Said Number Two.

Bobby Scamehorn, the tin man on the Dallas exam team said, "We all understand. You gotta' back off. Fat ass Hamilton SVP, Randy Peterson, laughed when we brought up criminal charges; said we were playin' hardball in the wrong league. We'll exam the Hamilton again in eighteen months. We'll nail the S&L then."

Number Two carved Scamehorn with a knife-like stare.

Note pads, files, documents were stacked in front of the five discouraged young examiners seated at the conference table; the original Dallas five. Standing, the three hired guns from the San Francisco Fed Home Loan Bank distinguished themselves from the less experienced Dallas examiners. Aloof professionalism had been the trademark of the three San Francisco mercenaries during their seven day Hamilton stint. They would go back to California without the spoils, without the accolade of *WELL DONE.*

Number Two explained the directive from the DC headquarters of the FHLB, "The Federal Savings and Loan Insurance fund is going broke. DC won't front the money to defend Hamilton's legal charges against me."

The Dallas examiner team relied on Number Two for an answer. Scamehorn's gaze darted away. Embarrassed eyes dropped to the conference room floor.

"Washington is sucking congressional cock," the five-foot-seven San Francisco examiner had a Napoleon-like presence. His previous opinions had been presented with more dignity, "Nut cutting-time."

Number Two inspected the west coast ace; the examiner appeared dead-serious competent.

San Francisco's eyes locked on Number Two with the icy detachment of a high-noon gunfighter. He shoved away from the wall, spread his legs, and weighted equally on each foot. He drew his yellow legal pad. His second-in-command, another short California examiner, lifted a stack of collated papers organized inside a three-ring binder.

"Before you dismiss us eunuchs back to San Francisco and give up the kingdom to the infidels, we've uncovered facts you should consider. Might want to take em' to trial for public disclosure."

Number Two waited on the short San Franciscan's last word. The Californian's eyes never left Number Two; neither man flinched in the vacuum.

"You aren't being dismissed. I can't ante up the money to defend; all I can rely on are your facts. We're going to nail these Hamilton bastards."

An impromptu eight-man war-cry whooped throughout the quiet, barren, late afternoon halls of the Dallas Ninth Fed Home Loan Bank.

Down the hall, alone in his office, the President of the Dallas Ninth District was drafting his compromise to his superiors in Washington. His examiners would conclude their examination of the Hamilton S&L recommending *Forbearance with a Timeline*, in return, the lawsuit initiated by the Hamilton against the Pres and Number Two would be dismissed.

Hooting from the direction of the conference room sounded like Texas had scored a first quarter touchdown against Oklahoma in the Cotton Bowl.

"What the fuck," said the Pres.

Dallas, Fuddruckers Restaurant

Brendan Donahue called Heather from a pay phone at DFW before he retrieved his baggage. She accepted his invitation without hesitation; someone she called the Greek had shaken Heather's resolve. Heather stipulated she would meet Brendan Donahue at the very public Fuddruckers restaurant at 8:00 PM.

Heather Montgomery didn't trust Brendan, she didn't know him. But Brendan was the only person Heather knew that was looking for answers.

"Phil Kamerov and I have been scouring the Hamilton to dig out the loan crimes. How could The Pill NOT be part of the FDIC investigation?" Heather asked Brendan Donahue.

"Jack Richardson gave me two names," Brendan said, "yours and the number two regulator at the Dallas FHLB. Your Workout guy, Phil Kamerov, is not an FDIC contact."

"Phil must be working for somebody other than the S&L management," she said. Hamburger odors from the grill drifted to their table."

Brendan suggested to the brown-eyed woman, "Maybe, Phil Kamerov is just doing his job as the Hamilton's Workout guy?"

Brendan's sincerity had wedged a sliver of trust within Heather's stony core.

"I don't think so," she said. "The Pill is not buddy-buddy with Hamilton management. He wants to end the S&L's self-dealing; if that means nailing the sonofabitches, that seems okay by him."

Brendan Donahue and Heather sat on high chairs at the small round table in Fuddruckers bar. Brendan plowed his straw through blended, golden slush, of Fuddruckers' frozen, family-size Margarita. He had bought two drinks hoping the sweet Tequila concoction would soothe Heather Montgomery. She had ignored her cereal-bowl drink.

Heather recalled the deceased FDIC chairman's directions. "Richardson said all the details of my inspection should be shared with Phil Kamerov."

"Maybe Richardson did not want to raise doubt in Kamerov," Brendan said. "Have you and Kamerov discovered criminal violations?"

"We don't have hard proof on anything criminal by the top guys, yet." She considered the theft of the dormant deposits by the Hamilton's head teller. Heather stopped Brendan's next question with her upraised palm, "I did negotiate to get the Hamilton's head teller off the hook. Part of the agreement was that once the Hamilton VP, Pete Morris coughed-up his dirt, I would never mention our Washington contact, Jack Richardson again."

"Heather, did you refer to Jack Richardson by name?"

"No, just as our contact in Washington. I always protected his identity, if that's what you're asking."

"When did you first mention your contact in Washington to Phil Kamerov?"

Heather sipped her icy Margarita without tasting,

Brendan leaned across the small circular table, "Can you remember your exact words to Kamerov?"

She recalled her comment to The Pill precisely, "*Our friend in Washington told me last night to trust you. I'm here with the truth on the Endres. I think you owe me the truth,*" she said.

"Heather, Ken Thompson, the CEO of the Hamilton S&L, keeps an office in Washington. If Phil Kamerov is reporting directly to Ken Thompson, your comment could have been misinterpreted. Phil Kamerov would have accepted you as another inside source reporting to Thompson."

Heather searched the other eleven tables in Fuddruckers. "Aw Christ, The Pill would figure out that I had nothing to do with Thompson the next time they talked."

"Thompson's only conclusion, based on your comment to Phil Kamerov, would be you were feeding Hamilton data," Brendan said, "Feeding the Dallas Fed Home Loan Bank info from inside the Hamilton."

"Oh God!" Heather followed Brendan's trail, a trail that started with the death of Julie Weidener. "And when it's time to shut me up . . ."

"Ken Thompson commissions a thug to change things," he finished.

"To shake me down . . ."

<u>Washington, D.C., Lafayette Park</u>

"I'm beginning to believe you, Jonathan," Ken Thompson, CEO of the Hamilton S&L said, "The most obvious can be the least visible." Thompson stared at the White House across the wide street.

This was their second encounter of the day, again seated in Washington's petite, yet prominent, Lafayette Park.

"As long as one doesn't overstay," Jonathan said.

Thompson's K street office was a five-minute walk from the one-acre public common. The assassin's sudden change, considering Ken Thompson's new assignment, had surprised the CEO.

"Have you overstayed, Jonathan?" the CEO asked.

"Without doubt. Your request is dangerous, Ken. Dangerous and foolish."

On the far side of Pennsylvania Avenue's four lanes, twelve unsanitary liberals protested in a haphazard parade. They had arrived at a verdict against the White House tenant, Ronald Reagan; guilty of Iran-Contra misdeeds.

Jonathan Blair, assassinator of two banking regulators, kept his focus on the protesters from his seat on the Lafayette Park bench, he said, "Assassination is not a continuing preventive action. Death can send a powerful message . . . one time. If you employ its tragedy too frequently, authority will resist. You've delivered your message twice. Another death will rouse their vengeance. Revenge will become a factor for authority. Your objective should be their submission."

"I'm requesting your services," Ken Thompson said, "My immediate problem requires termination."

"Jack Richardson, head of the FDIC died. The FDIC is informally tied to the highest thrones of power in Washington. You're not immune to retribution." Late afternoon haze dunned the U.S. Capital Building.

"I've explored their conclusions on Richardson's death," Hamilton's CEO said, "Nobody suspects anything more than a drunk driving fatality. Will you nullify this Brendan Donahue for me?"

Jonathan Blair contemplated Cecille. Tomorrow she would be in New York; in his native country. He would introduce Cecille to New York City, the top of the World Trade Building, the aroma of pastrami-and-dill at the Carnegie Deli.

Jonathan said, "Do you have information for me on the Cuban?"

"Can you remove Brendan Donahue?"

"Where is this Brendan Donahue?" the assassin asked.

"He is in Dallas." The CEO passed a note to the assassin, "This is his location and appointment calendar for the next 24 hours."

Ken Thompson withdrew an envelope from his inner coat pocket. Inside five typewritten pages, on FBI stationery, profiled Cecille's uncle

Ramon, still a ranking generalista for Fidel Castro. The Hamilton S&L CEO passed the envelope to his assassin.

Swiftly, Jonathan tucked the envelope and note into his shirt pocket.

"Tell me what you know about Brendan Donahue."

<u>Dallas, Federal Home Loan Bank, Ninth District</u>

The Number Two guy at the Dallas Fed Home Loan Bank, the Director of Bank Supervision, assessed his S&L exam team; his only line of defense against the legal action brought by Hamilton's attorneys.

The eight examiners in the conference room at the Dallas Fed Home Loan Bank had been split into four two-man teams; the three San Francisco pros each led a team and they stood. Bobby Scamehorn, the senior guy on the Dallas FHLB exam staff, and a Dallas rookie comprised the 4th exam team.

"So I explained to the accountant at Lone Star Honda," said the Dallas examiner working on Exam Team One, "that forty-six vehicles short on a financial affidavit usually draws five years from the judge. The accountant cried . . . I waited him out."

The senior San Francisco examiner on Team One nodded to his Dallas intern. The Dallas examiner continued, "I suggested we trade, information for immunity, even-up. The accountant told, me rumor at the Hamilton was Pete Morris, the Hamilton VP, got $20,000 kickback on a loan deal Morris funded in Phoenix; said word got out around Memorial Day."

"Anything," Number Two asked.

The San Francisco examiner heading Team One dropped a manila folder on the conference table, landing in front of his junior team mate, The SF guy said, "Copy of a check for $20,000, deposited in account of Peter Morris, signed by Leonard Endres. Date deposited at Sunbelt Savings, that's where Morris kept his account, is stamped on the back of the check."

The other three exam teams drummed the conference table in support.

The Dallas examiner on Team One said, "I promised the Lone Star accountant he was off the hook."

"He might have to testify," said Number Two. He didn't want to know how they obtained a copy Morris' $20,000 check.

"Team two," Number Two said.

The shortest of the three San Francisco examiners, their spokesman since the Californians arrived, stepped forward. His thick black hair was slicked straight back, he looked more Italian than Naples. "Facts," the examiner said looking directly at Number Two. The examiner turned to the Dallas examiner assigned to him, "Talk."

The Dallas examiner in Team Two said, "Endres Brothers received $35 million from the Hamilton to construct an office building in Phoenix. VP Pete Morris authorized each draw. $25 million never went to build the Phoenix office, it was diverted to the Endres ranch, called the Wandering E, outside Corpus Christi. Used the money to build themselves an air-conditioned barn and buy twenty-eight classic cars at auction."

The lead San Francisco examiner heading exam Team Two started the day wearing a Brooks Brothers' navy blue suit. He had shed the coat. His sleeves were cuffed midway up his forearms. The pocket of his blue dress shirt was embroidered in capital letters; SOL, but those were not his initials.

The SF examiner said, "Morris could have run the money through the Phoenix construction account, but he didn't. Shoulda' been lien waivers, affidavits – financial docs that would have got Morris off the hook. Check went directly to the Endres. Civil court will convict Morris for time and money. Endres aren't liable for anything except being jerks."

The junior Dallas examiner on exam Team Two slid a neat folder to the center of the conference table, "Hamilton checks, $25 mill in total, signed by Morris on behalf of the Hamilton, deposited at Frost Allen in Corpus Christi."

Number Two didn't even want to speculate on how copies of the checks were obtained.

"Next," said Number Two

"Not yet," said the San Francisco examiner with the slick black hair, cuffed sleeves, and inaccurate initials on his shirt pocket, "I said we had facts. Plural."

Seated examiners drummed the table, pep rally style. The Californian had everyone curious, the rest of the examiners grew church quiet. Anticipation blossomed on their faces.

"Leonard Endres serves as a director on the Hamilton board, he sold his $875,000 property to the Hamilton S&L for $15 mill," the San Francisco examiner said, "Then bought $12 million in Hamilton stock."

Number Two said, "You were going to confront the Hamilton appraiser with your info?

The SF guy continued, "Showed the S&L appraiser, David Appraisal, my re-do number of $830,000. Hamilton's COO, Billy Johnstone, promised his appraiser he'd get all Hamilton new appraisal work if Endres property was valued at $15 mill. The Hamilton's appraiser confessed the property is worth only $830,000; confessed on tape."

The Dallas examiner, junior member of Team Two whisked a cassette from his shirt pocket and waived it above his head.

"We owe the Hamilton appraiser exclusion," said the SF examiner heading exam Team Two, "we've got Hamilton's COO for tampering."

The Dallas Fed Home Loan Bank Number Two nodded, the conference table reverberated.

"Next," said Number Two.

"Not yet," the San Francisco examiner with the slick black hair, cuffed sleeves, and embroidered shirt pocket said for second time, "Facts is plural, sometimes means more than two."

He continued, "The minutes approving the Hamilton's purchase of Endres property were altered. Here are signed affidavits from three Hamilton directors testifying they were neither presented with an appraisal, nor approved purchase from the Endres property at Hamilton's December board meeting. We've seized S&L's for less than this."

The junior member of Team Two presented hard copy of the last offense, the evidence travelled the length of the conference table hand-to-hand.

One junior Dallas examiner started to clapped politely; the others in the room joined. Nodding his head, suppressing a grin, Number Two tapped fingers against palm in appreciation.

Applause stilled, "Next," Number Two said, turning back to Team Two, led by the stocky Italian-looking regulator on loan from San Francisco, "with your permission."

The two examiners designated as Team Three had assumed the same posture as each team headed by a San Francisco examiner; Dallas was seated, SF stood

"Here is a letter agreement from Ed McBirney, CEO of Sunbelt Savings. Counter-signed by Hamilton's COO, Billy Johnstone. These two letters document Hamilton S&L's swap of delinquent loans with Sunbelt. Each bank grossed-up the loans to create an eighteen-month interest reserve; a regulatory infraction for privately owned Sunbelt Savings. However, publicly traded Hamilton violated SEC rules when they didn't disclose the interest reserve gross-up in their first quarter financial statement. SEC can nail the Hamilton, and lead the charge for civil penalties; dollars and jail time – Billy Johnstone is the guy on the hook at the Hamilton – 5 years minimum."

Number Two asked, "How did you get the McBirney letter from Sunbelt Savings?"

The San Francisco guy smiled cryptically and shrugged. He jumped to fresh news, "We documented the hide-out where Pete Morris balanced the $6 million he advanced to Plano Mall without loan approval. He debited the money into Hamilton's overnight suspense account. Being a fucking S&L moron, Morris left the debit balance in the account."

The San Francisco guy leading Team Three was carrying his audience.

Number Two asked, "$6 million?"

"$6 mill that transaction, Morris buried a few other unapproved loans in the overnight suspense account."

"How much?" asked Number Two.

"Morris has dispensed $33,000,000 of the Hamilton's money without loan approval," said Team Three's leader, "Evidence." He slid a manila envelope down the table.

"Nice work," said Number Two.

Bobby Scamehorn, the only Dallas examiner leading a team, caressed the manila envelope of damnation he held.

Bobby on behalf of the all-Dallas, exam Team Four introduced their results, "We've got some outside help for your defense against the Hamilton?"

"What do you have, Bobby?" asked Number Two.

"The Hamilton Group's insurance company, Hamilton Insurance, bought $25,000,000 in junk bonds from Drexel, Burnham, Lambert – the New York investment bank," Bobby said, "The next week Drexel invested a coincidental $25,000,000 to Thompson's Nassau Shores time-share development?"

"Can you document anything wrong, Bobby?" asked Number Two.

"The Drexel bonds were fifteen days from going stale, would have been deemed junk. Drexel write-down would have resulted in a $5-8 million loss; the month before annual bonuses were due the Drexel partners. Sale docs don't show that, but we've got internal memos from two Drexel partners that explain the consequences if Drexel doesn't make the deal."

Bobby, pushed the condemning evidence forward on the table.

Number Two was stunned, "Bobby, where the hell did you get internal Drexel memos?"

The San Francisco examiner with the black hair, rolled cuffs and initials on his shirt pocket said, "There is enough for the SEC to pursue civil crimes; Texas Department of Insurance can get the Hamilton guys on criminal charges. Thompson goes to jail. His attorney will be his cell mate. They can play doubles tennis with two prominent Drexel partners."

Number Two repeated, "Bobby, how did you get memos from inside Drexel, Lambert?"

Standing against the wall, the brick-like SF regulator with the slick black Mediterranean hair answered, "Good coaching," he said.

CHAPTER FIFTY-ONE

Dallas, the Barrio

The skinny Mexican answered in inner-city rap, "Hey, man, no pra-blem'. I be takeen' all dee' reesk."

Jonathan Blair had difficulty understanding the twenty-two-year-old illegal immigrant. He had never before subcontracted an assassination. Killing Brendan Donahue would be a fool's game; a game he would not play. Brendan Donahue would die by another's hand.

This runt will be caught within an hour, Blair forecast to himself.

Blair punched the twentieth hundred dollar bill into the greedy brown palm. "Two thousand dollars. The other four thousand when the Dallas newspapers verify the man died."

The American assassin and the Mexican pretender stood alone in the narrow alley.

"Si, senor. Quest hombre e muerde. No pra-blem. I blow heem away."

"How you accomplish it, I don't care," Jonathan said.

The raven-haired, beige man squiggled his nose in confusion at the assassin's inverted English phrase. The sun had set three hours ago on Dallas' southeast barrio. Two phone calls had directed Jonathan Blair to

Most Delicious of Privileges

La Playa Azzurra, a cacophonous bar where illegal aliens had engineered a sentry network that would have done justice to Fort Knox. Jonathan Blair had breached the Mexican bar alone.

"How do I know I geet dee raist of dee mo-nee, man?"

"Because I assure you that you will get your mo-nee," Jonathan said, "You do this job right, you kill this man, there will be more jobs. More money."

When the younger man grinned, his rotten teeth sullied the already stagnant ghetto alley. Youthful years sucking on raw wild cane had decayed his smile beyond hope of dental repair. His breath smelled of fermented cactus blended with mashed corn, a foul mulch. Sassy in his Spanish-speaking barrio, the five-foot-six mercenary taunted the six-foot-one assassin.

"Suppose I yus' keep your mo-nee?"

Jonathan unveiled the future for the small cocky Mexican absent emotion.

"Then you will die this Friday."

The little man's sneer vaporized. He spit brown flem on the dirty asphalt. "I keel heem. You breeng my mo-nee then."

"You must not be caught," Jonathan said.

"Doan worry, I nay-ver be caught," the Mex boasted.

"Can you get away? Do you have a car you can trust?"

"Even you cood not catch me in thees car. Not even thees Fridee," The Mex slapped the rusted 1968 Mustang under his right hand. Tacked on the blue front panel was a chrome 289 insignia.

Jonathan circumnavigated the, aging sports car, the pride of the late 60's at Ford Motor. He slapped the side panels on the far side of the car, testing the body's soundness. From across the car he peeked into the metal air scoop sculpted onto the hood. Jonathan nodded approval as kicked the left rear tire.

Jonathan's hired Mexican soldier of fortune propped both fists on the hood. He beamed with parental pride from the right front headlight of his auto.

Jonathan bent at the rear fender. He knocked loudly three times, so the Mex could hear.

"Soleed? Yes, senor?" said the Mex.

Jonathan slid the magnetic transmitter under the rear bumper, "Yes, this is a good car."

"Thees car will never be caught, senor."

CHAPTER FIFTY-TWO

Dallas, Texas

Neither had eaten even half of their oversize hamburgers at the oddly named Fuddruckers restaurant. Brendan Donahue leaned into the glass door leaving Fuddruckers. Heather Montgomery slid past him, out the door. Lower Greenville Avenue traffic ran at a hectic pace in the July night.

"Brendan, your suspicions may be correct. Phil Kamerov may be reporting directly to the S&L owner. And Ken Thompson . . . maybe his crimes are so grievous he has sunk to murder. But, I'm done. I can't take any more Hamilton S&L thrills. I won't be a pawn in this chess game."

Lawn sprinklers misted along Fuddruckers' sidewalk; Brendan had parked his rental car in the rear lot.

"Heather, you've been assaulted more this week than Mr. Bill. I need you inside the S&L." Brendan stopped walking. Too many questions remained.

"No. I'm leaving. Goddam Italian hood slithers into my apartment to warn me there's a contract to shake me down," Heather shook her head negatively, "I was supposed to be the good guy gathering info for your FDIC. I'm leaving, getting my butt out of this bizarre S&L world."

Without a signal they resumed walking towards the restaurant's parking lot in the rear.

A deliberate, slender woman, five-feet-six-inches stepped from the shadows, blocking their route. Her commanding hand slapped against Brendan's chest. She halted him by gripping his blue cotton dress shirt. She screwed her fist around two middle buttons. If she hadn't been so lithesome, Brendan would have resisted her grasp.

"Stop, now!"

Recognition flashing through Brendan's mind. She offered no smile, no greeting as she arrested their progress.

Her brown eyes darted to Heather, "You too."

Short brunette hair on the severe, yet appealing thirty-ish woman prodded Brendan's memory. In the night her eyes seemed black, her cosmetics veiled. Identifying credentials waved in her left palm.

Brendan shuffled forward, pushing against her grip.

"Stand still. Mr. Donahue, I am here to protect you," she said. "That is the code phrase Jack Richardson chose."

Brendan recalled this authoritative woman. His last Washington dinner with Jack Richardson, the Tabard Inn. Richardson had promised a guardian angel to protect Brendan. Brendan had forgotten, assuming the pledge of protection ended with Richardson's death.

Four fingers on her right hand flickered. In the night a six-foot-four-inch man rustled from behind a cedar shrub taller than he was.

"Are we clear to detonate?" she said.

"All clear," the man confirmed.

Brendan's heartbeat raced. Heather bumped against his back and stuck. Brendan's voice pealed in alarm, "Detonate what? Who are you?"

The athletic woman dining alone at *the Tabard Inn in DC.* Brendan thought. *What is she doing in Dallas?*

Most Delicious of Privileges 269

"Secret Service, Mr. Donahue. I'm assigned to you. I'm agent Mollie Leep." In the night Brendan couldn't verify the license framed in her raised left palm.

Heather blinked back and forth suspiciously between the woman and Brendan.

The Secret Service woman levered herself and jabbed them two steps backward. "Mr. Donahue, someone baked you a distasteful dessert. Brace yourself, Miss Montgomery."

With a three quick strides, the man who would detonate the bomb closed, "Agent Olsen, Secret Service." His emblem reflected light from the eleven blue and yellow neon letters glowing on Fuddruckers' sign.

Neither Brendan nor Heather verified its authenticity.

"Let's get this over, Olsen," she said, "Before anyone else comes along."

Secret Service man Olsen decreed, "Look at my shoes."

A shower of flame convulsed the Dallas night. Brendan's rented Cadillac Seville ignited. Rushing heat assaulted the four people at the edge of Fuddruckers' parking lot. Hertz's 1987 GM auto incinerated. Not another vehicle was parked within fifty feet of the burning Caddy.

"Jesus Christ. Did you do that?" Brendan hollered over the crackle.

Wailing from the siren of a Dallas squad car muffled the Secret Service woman's attempt to reply, "Mr. Donahue, while you and Miss Montgomery ate, your car was rigged by a small time hood. We re-wired the bomb so we could detonate it without having to turn the key. You were supposed to die . . . possibly you too, Miss Montgomery."

Heather crumbled on the bright concrete sidewalk. She gasped, tearless sobs barely audible above the fire's surging crackle. "Nooo, no, no . . . no more!"

The Secret Service woman's clarification didn't mollify Heather, "I'm pretty sure, Mr. Donahue, that you were the objective." Red and blue police lights strobed as Dallas cops ran interference for the racing fire truck parked in the alley.

Brendan shivered in the eighty-five degree Texas night.

"Tried to kill me. Where . . . where is the bastard? Who rigged this, this bomb?"

"I let him escape," the Secret Service woman said.

Brendan spit his protest. "Why? Why did you explode my car? Why is the bastard gone?"

"If someone wants you dead, you are safer being dead."

Heather, lying on the sidewalk, shrieked, "What the hell's going on?"

Pressurized water sizzling in the flames drowned explanations. The quick-arriving fire engine extinguished Hertz's flaming Cadillac within sixty seconds.

Secret Service agent Mollie Leep shouted, "We have little time. Miss Montgomery, agent Olsen will escort you home. He'll stay with you. I will contact you," she pointed at Brendan, "Mr. Donahue, you're coming with me."

Brendan's world spun. Death's specter decayed his resolve. He was vulnerable to systematic acceptance of blind orders.

"Let's go!" she ordered.

Her command spanked Brendan's senses. He shouted, "Where?

"We have a flight to Washington. It leaves in forty-five minutes." The Secret Service woman clamped Brendan's elbow. Her thrust left him no option.

CHAPTER FIFTY-THREE

<u>Washington, D.C., The Senate Office Building</u>

Ken Thompson listened from the visitor's side of the refinished antique oak desk. Senator Jim Anderson, Republican, Texas, recapped the five-senator grilling of Dallas' top S&L regulator. Anderson's secretary, Peggy, intercepted all telephone calls. The Texas congressman concluded, his Senate Office Building sanctuary still as a Sunday dawn.

Ken Thompson approved, "Sounds like you got our message across very clearly to the regulators, Jim."

"It's not often four United States Senators convene, Ken, to debrief a S&L regulator." Senator Jim Anderson took pride in his judicious, firm deployment of congressional power. "Ken, there's a caveat to getting the regulators out of your S&L. You gotta' drop those goddam personal law suits against President of the Dallas FHLB and his Director of Supervision."

"I don't think I can responsibly do that, Jim. Those sonofabitches have cost me real money."

"Shit, Ken, those damn law suits are bold-type headlines in the business section. The whole goddam country is questioning not only your S&L industry, but the economic health of Texas."

The Hamilton CEO's fingers constructed a meditative steeple. He peered from above, "I'll drop both lawsuits on one condition."

The Texas Senator sighed his question, What's that?"

"The Director of Supervision, the number two guy, has been a prick. I don't trust him. He's a loose cannon on my deck. Fire him. Not transferred, Jim. Canned. Dismissed from the FHLB system. Out of Dallas permanently. Minute he's gone, the lawsuits will be history."

"Jesus Christ, Ken," the Senator asked, "what did you hear?"

"That the Director of Supervision was going to file criminal charges against some of my people at the Hamilton? His arrogant examiners have been mouthin' it around my S&L. Fire the number two at the Dallas Ninth and I drop the lawsuits."

Senator Jim Anderson drummed his pen. He picked up his telephone, "Sit and listen, Ken."

Ken Thompson crossed his right knee over his left. Texas Senator Anderson dialed the lame duck chairman at Washington's Federal Home Loan Board.

"Give me Ed Gray, please."

CHAPTER FIFTY-FOUR

Treasury's Lear 35 had landed at Andrews Air Force Base at 3:45 AM, three hours earlier. Brendan Donahue had not slept on the flight from Dallas.

Brendan stood framed within the six-foot Treasury Building window. From his fifth-floor view he gazed across the street to the front lawn of the White House. Wisps of wind stretched America's red, white and blue banner in the slanting dawn sunlight.

Behind the desk the Secretary of the Treasury answered Brendan's question. "How long? You've had Secret Service protection since the evening you had dinner with Jack Richardson. At the Tabard Inn, here in Washington. Four days ago."

"I didn't see you," Brendan said, turning to the woman.

No explanation was offered by the Secret Service woman. She had been his guardian angel since that evening.

She semi-smiled concurrence, "You weren't supposed to see me."

Brendan turned from his window view of the White House, "How did I rate Secret Service protection?"

"Because that crook, Thompson, is being stalked with my approval. You were Jack Richardson's great hope," explained the cabinet officer, "Secret Service is part of Treasury, Donahue. You're tackling people with spectacular power. Sometimes they employ that power. Jack Richardson sent you to Dallas with spectacular protection. I approved his request."

"Jack?" Brendan revolved. He looked out the oversize window constructed in 1869.

"Brendan, bring me up-to-date on your Hamilton S&L investigation," Mr. Secretary said.

Brendan glanced at a navy-blue limo passing through the east gate of the White House, then walked from the window. He collapsed in the chair fronting the massive oak desk.

"Nothing really to tell. The investigation was called off before . . ." Brendan mourned the senseless death of his friend Jack Richardson. ". . . before I got started. Jack's death severed my connection to the FDIC. I didn't have authority to continue. I was floundering as an amateur spy."

Agent Leep informs me you tracked Ken Thompson yesterday morning."

Where on K Street had the Secret Service woman been? Brendan thought.

"Long-shot." Brendan shoulders shrugged, portraying futility. "I didn't know what I was looking for. I didn't discover anything."

The Treasury Secretary and the Secret Service agent exchanged a glance.

"Was Jack Richardson's death an accident, Mr. Secretary?" Brendan asked.

"The autopsy report is definite," said the Treasury Secretary, "Jack Richardson died from trauma to the head. He drove his BMW over a two-hundred foot embankment in the Maryland night. His blood alcohol was point-one-nine. Jack's head rattled off the steering wheel all the way down the embankment. He was drunk, Mr. Donahue."

"Bullshit. Jack drank, but not to the point he'd kill himself," Brendan said.

"The autopsy was done by the Navy's top forensic guy at Bethesda. He's very good at details. I personally read his autopsy report; Laphroaig Scotch. The forensic docs can ID single malt whiskeys from a speck. There was an ounce of undigested scotch in Jack's stomach. Forensics concluded Jack must have been drinking while he drove."

Brendan's gyrating head denied the Secretary's conclusion, "Was there a struggle?"

"No evidence of a struggle," The Secretary of the Treasury said, "There were skid marks from Richardson's tires on the dirt road. Started fifteen feet from the precipice. Too little, too late! Maryland cops say Richardson's BMW would barely have slowed in that distance. Autopsy report is conclusive: drunk driving."

The second ranking Cabinet officer stood from his desk. He walked to the corner of his office where the Secret Service woman sat. His factual recounting of the damning autopsy staggered Brendan's adamant loyalty.

"Jack spoke of you occasionally, Brendan," the man said.

Brendan's answered with pain, "Jack Richardson was a good friend."

"Jack Richardson was the most realistic sonofabitch overseeing our finances in Washington." The five-foot-ten-inch Secretary of Treasury turned toward Brendan. He ignored Secret Service agent Mollie Leep. His vagabond reflection digressed, "Over the last fifteen years, Jack and I resolved many partisan problems outside our respective domains. sometimes over a medicinal after-hours cocktail," said the Treasury head.

His words harpooned Brendan like a long, sharp sword.

The Treasury Secretary continued, "Jack Richardson was murdered. His commitment to the FDIC cost Jack his life."

Brendan, rattled, locked his eyes into the Treasury Secretary, "What do you mean murdered?" he said, "You said Bethesda's autopsy is conclusive."

"It is, Mr. Donahue. Jack Richardson died with fifteen ounces of very expensive Scotch whiskey diluting his blood."

Memory of their dinner at the Tabard Inn screamed at Brendan. He inspected the Secret Service woman. Visions of apparent flirtatious glances they had traded flickered; glances that were just workday observations for the watchwoman.

After dinner, what was it?

"At the Tabard Inn, after dinner, Jack refused the Drambuie." Having deduced the answer to the Treasury Secretary's riddle, Brendan's words locked.

"That's right, Brendan. Jack Richardson didn't drink Scotch. He was allergic to it. Forensics noted splotches on his face and neck. I might have forgotten."

"Motherfucker!" Brendan said.

The Secret Service woman disregarded Brendan's vulgarity.

"Are you angry enough to continue pursuing the Hamilton S&L, Mr. Donahue?" asked the Treasury man.

"Bastard, goddam bastard," Brendan said.

"I will assume that is affirmative."

"Yes, goddammit!" Brendan confirmed.

"Good. You now work for the Department of Treasury. You have a sanction. Mine. First, we have to find out who killed Jack."

"How?" Brendan asked.

"You are undercover still, Mr. Donahue. I don't want this S&L crook burying his thievery. "

The Treasury Secretary's pointing finger condoned his Secret Service woman, "Quick thinking by our Secret Service has convinced someone that you died in a tragic car explosion in a Fuddruckers parking lot in Dallas last night."

"Have you picked up the guy who wired the car?" Brendan asked.

The Secret Service woman and the Treasury Secretary exchanged glances. "Can't, I'm afraid," she said, "The man, he was a young Mexican –

in the country illegally, was killed six minutes after the bomb was triggered. Two shots through the heart."

"Jesus!"

"Agent Leep will continue to be your protection on this assignment," the Secretary of Treasury said.

"Secretly? Or, will I see her?" Brendan asked

"I may surface when appropriate," she said.

The Treasury Secretary disregarded her probational innuendo. "Agent Leep will guide your initial exercise."

"Which is?" Brendan said.

"Mr. Donahue, I want the identity of the assassin who killed Jack Richardson," he said, "Within twenty-four hours."

Brendan just stared at the man who demanded the impossible.

CHAPTER FIFTY-FIVE

Washington, D.C., Department of Treasury

Their footsteps clapped off the marble floor and masonry walls. Reverb echo from the Treasury Building's twelve foot ceiling shot back; two boomerang pings for each leathery step.

"Law Enforcement Coordination, acronym LEC; part of Treasury-world, Mr. Donahue." Secret Service Agent Mollie Leep's deliberate deportment partially assured Brendan.

"How can LEC help us identify the assassin?" Brendan asked.

"LEC is the US representative to INTERPOL," she said, "We've got a wizard, a computer genius, on staff. You're going to help him massage assumption into fact."

"INTERPOL?" Brendan said.

"INTERPOL's computer in Paris has the most comprehensive bank of criminal stats," Mollie the Secret Service woman explained, "Even better INTERPOL has negotiated access to lots of other data banks that are off-limit to even the best computer hackers."

She marched him through the first floor hall of the Treasury Department, located on the corner where 15th Street crosses Pennsylvania

Avenue. Undercover for the Secret Service woman meant no uniform. Her pleaded tartan skirt whirled to mid-calf. She preceded Brendan by a vigorous half-stride. If the Secret Service woman wore make-up, it blended well. She opened the door for him.

She presented Brendan to the Wiz with uplifted palm, "Mr. Miller, meet Mr. Donahue."

Harry Miller wearing a green cotton pull-over, khaki trousers and high-mileage Asic running shoes, greeted Brendan with a handshake.

"Mr. Miller is Treasury's computer Wiz," Secret Service Mollie said.

"Hello, Mr. Donahue. Mollie is gracious . . . and correct," the Wiz said, "I understand we have a job with a twenty-four-hour deadline."

Dallas, The Federal Home Loan Bank

"Ed Gray just called me," the President of the Dallas FHLB said to his number two man; his guy supervising S&L's in Texas.

"Did you give him my *'grow a dick'* message?" asked Number Two.

"He didn't give me time. Gray told me to fire you. Unfortunately, I've got to do it," the Pres said, "I don't agree with this."

"That's it? That spineless chairman of the Fed Home Loan is my judge; you're his hangman? It's over?"

"Somebody pulled rank on Gray," the Pres said, "Gray said you had pissed off certain powers and that his order came from the top. You're fighting United States Senators. I'm sorry."

Questions and challenges raced through Number Two's mind. He controlled his kaleidoscope emotions for two minutes. Only one rational question surfaced, "I've never been fired. What's the procedure . . . two weeks and out?"

"No, today is your last day," said the Pres, "Take my advice; don't fight it. Go on to something else. Pack it up. You've got thirty minutes."

* * *

Within forty-five minutes Brendan and the computer Wiz completed their conjectures. A profile of Richardson's death on the back roads of Virginia, the murder of Julie Weidener in London and the Dallas car bomb targeted at Brendan had been scrolled inside three dates and six assumptions.

"Best subterfuge for a terrorist is to disguise himself while executing his deed. Then he can roam the world utilizing his real identity. Travel on his own passport. Much easier to plan one's itinerary."

"You mean the assassin lives a . . ." Brendan's head cocked as he questioned the Treasury computer Wiz, "a normal life?"

"Precisely, if he is an intelligent man. And our man is very intelligent."

"Then, murder would be his hobby?"

"More than a hobby. His avocation. He controls the drug, it does not dominate him."

"What can INTERPOL's computer tell us from our assumptions?" Brendan asked.

"Not much," said the Wiz, "But, INTERPOL can retrieve airline data. Most airline reservation systems, like American's SABRE, wash historical airline passenger data twenty-fours-hours after the actual flight arrives.

'You're leading me somewhere?" Brendan said.

"INTERPOL will instruct American Airlines, and every air carrier into, or out of, our three cities, to reload historical reservations for the dates we specify. Interpol's computers will sort the airline passengers according to our assumptions. If your assassin used one name, we might get lucky. If he is very good . . . and very confident, perhaps, he travelled under his own name."

"How do you figure?" Brendan asked.

"FBI, in Quantico, set up NCAVC. Travelling under his real name is their profile assumption for high intellect terrorists."

"Who is NCAVC?" said Brendan.

Most Delicious of Privileges 281

"Sorry, National Center for Analysis of Violent Crime. FBI unit collaborating with the University of Virginia. Got the leading psychologists, sociologists and criminologists creating psychological profiles."

Brendan whistled three-tone intrigue.

"We're using intellect as a weapon, Mr. Donahue," the Wiz said.

Brendan double-checked their assumptions. Scan and store airline passengers from all incoming flights to Heathrow and Gatwick. Limit the names to the three days prior to Weidener's murder in London.

"God, how many people fly into London each day?" Brendan asked.

The treasury Wiz tom-tommed his computer keyboard. "Lots. FBI mind-men at the National Center for Analysis of Violent Crime, the government's back-room psychiatrists, insist terrorists arrive at their site with only enough time to prepare and discharge their horror. Our scan will be limited to three days preceding."

"Then they leave?"

"And quickly, according to BSSU," the Wiz said.

"What is BSSU?"

"Behavioral Science Services Unit. Part of NCAVC," explained the Wiz.

"Sure, OK."

"After we store the names of all London arrivals we'll sort airline passengers departing either Gatwick or Heathrow within twenty-four hours of Weidener's death . . . she died at approximately 5 PM." The Wiz keyed the limiting assumption onto the screen," the Wiz continued, "From that list, we eliminate all air travelers except those flying into Dulles, National, or Baltimore/Washington during the three days prior to the FDIC man's murder. This is where our list shrinks. INTERPOL staffers will not be happy Parisians. We're going to hog a lot of their computer memory during our initial scan and store."

Treasury's computer Wiz chanted his input one-word-at-a-time in a cheerful sing-song pitch, "Sift out the group ticket purchasers and passengers specifically requesting to be seated with a companion passenger." His fingers fox-trotted across the keyboard.

Harry Miller, Treasury's genius stopped. He lectured didactically, "That'll reduce our target group by sixty percent."

Brendan peered over the dressed Wizard's shoulder at the screen, "Assassins travel alone?"

"Always, say the FBI's mind-benders," confirmed the Wiz.

"Is this theory or fact?" Brendan asked.

"Fact, based on limited data. ISU is asking captured bad guys not only why, but how they were caught and what mistakes they made."

Brendan didn't ask Miller to interpret the ISU acronym. "Will you eventually stop assassination?"

"No, but we're going to shorten careers," said the Wiz.

Brendan validated yellow letters jumping on the IBM screen.

Treasury's Wiz spoke, "Disregard first class passengers. Too noticeable. Same with passengers requesting special meals."

His fingers soft-shoed across the trampoline keys; parameter followed assumption.

"FBI's esteemed psychologists insist that in contradiction to the constabulary axiom that a criminal returns to the scene of his crime, terrorists get out of Dodge City in a hurry. So, having sorted down the Washington arrivals, let's search for the hypothetical assassin who departed Washington by commercial airline within twenty-four hours after Richardson's assassination."

Suddenly, the Treasury man gunned his straight-back chair in reverse. The chair tilted, sports-car-style chair, into a semi-recline. The Wiz dissected his real-time quest, "Finally, the Dallas report. Expert opinion based on the modus operandi in London and Washington suggests your assassin erred in Dallas. NCAVC postulates a high-intellect assassin must murder three times before his pattern is detected. I'm skeptical."

"Skeptical of what?" Brendan asked.

Most Delicious of Privileges 283

"Your assassin is very good. The Dallas car bomb attempt on your life is an anomaly. Something went wrong. You should be dead, Mr. Donahue."

Dallas, The Federal Home loan Bank

Bobby Scamehorn's casual saunter into the Director of Supervision's office pronounced him guilty before he spoke. He jabbed the package forward.

"Here," said Bobby, the senior Fed Home Loan Bank examiner assigned to the Dallas office.

"What's this, Bobby?" Number Two was packing his scant personal items in his office. He rejected the thick envelope Bobby Scamehorn shoved forward.

"A memento of affection from your Hamilton examination team. Put it in your briefcase."

Number Two refused the bulging envelope, "I can't accept it, Bobby. I'm not departing the Dallas Home Loan as a hero. I've probably screwed up the next three salary reviews for the guys working on the Hamilton S&L exam team."

Scamehorn's body shielded his covert transmittal, "Put this in your fucking briefcase, before someone walks in here. This present may come in handy."

"Yeah, what is it?" said Number Two.

"Hamilton loan documents. Loan agreements, security agreements, and most importantly personal guarantees. Seems FDIC's new chairman, Bob Henry, guarantees $21,090,000 in loans that are in default to the Hamilton S&L."

Number Two stuffed his going-away present into his briefcase.

The Treasury Department

Brendan had left the Wiz at Treasury six hours earlier, he snapped awake as the phone in his hotel room rang. He ended the call, splashed water on his face, didn't bother to change clothes and ran the four Washington blocks from the Hyatt Regency back to the Treasury Building in less than three minutes. He flashed his security clearance at the entrance and dashed up the stairs; huffing to a halt in the doorway of the Wiz.

Computer wizard Harry Miller's feet rested upon his desk, scruffy running shoes next to his played-out keyboard. Black coffee steamed from a ceramic cup advertising that PROGRAMMERS DO IT IN THEIR MIND. His computer screen was off; the screen an inanimate grey-black.

"Get a name?" Brendan wheezed.

"Brendan," The Treasury Wiz prefaced his professorial analysis, "INTERPOL is very unhappy about the eight hours of computer sort time I confiscated from their perpetual day."

"Did you get a name?" Brendan's arms plugged across the door frame. His hands held. He propped himself, panting.

The Wiz ignored Brendan's panting question, "But six of the hours we usurped were after 6 pm in St. Cloud, France. Very slow time of day, over there in the Paris suburbs."

Brendan inhaled, "What do you have?"

"Had twenty-four names after the sort identifying airline passengers arriving in Washington three days prior to Richardson's death. Then . . ." The Wizard's hands swan dove through the air.

"Then what?" Brendan said.

"Then, every passenger, all twenty-four names, washed-out on the assumption our assassin departed Washington within twenty-four hours of Richardson's death."

Brendan sank to a deep knee squat in the doorway. Sweat trickled into his eye sockets. "Sonofabitch." The Secretary of Treasury's demand for a twenty-four turnaround on the identity of the assassin would be unfilled this afternoon.

Most Delicious of Privileges 285

"The more I questioned your avoidance of death by car-bomb in Dallas," the Wiz said, "the more apparent it became that botched attempt to eliminate you was a second-rate effort."

"Thanks, Harry. Gives me a chance to buy some life insurance," Brendan said.

"That's not my concern," continued the Wiz, "My job is to sort down to one name, one airline passenger. The attempt to end your life in Dallas was second rate, half-hearted, as though the assassin didn't really relish this assignment. A quickie if you will, our assassin was distracted, his focus was diverted."

"Your profile assumed a man who lives for the kill?" Brendan said.

"Yes, that disturbed me," explained the Wiz, "The Dallas assignment, your termination, was so poorly handled, it may have been a spur-of-the-moment assignation. So, I directed the INTERPOL computer to disregard the twenty-four-hour Washington departure assumption."

"What does that mean?"

"The twenty-four names were put back into memory," the Wiz said, "I jumped to the Dallas sort. All air passengers arriving at DFW within three days of the mismanaged kill that by all rights should have ended your life."

"And?" Brendan said.

"Six names," the Wiz explained, "But, I was outside a consistent psychological profile of the intelligent assassin."

"Unless you're right about Dallas being spur of the moment."

"Precisely, Brendan," said the Wiz, "You're getting the hang of this game. Spur-of-the-moment suggests time became a confining factor. So, I instructed INTERPOL to determine if any of our six Dallas-arriving passengers flew to the big D non-stop from Washington DC; something your assassin should have avoided. Put simply, I postulated that he made a second mistake."

"And?" Brendan asked.

Treasury computer Wiz Miller launched a paper airplane towards Brendan. "Here's your info; Jonathan Blair, Investment banker living in Milan, Italy. Texas roots date back to college at SMU. INTERPOL will deliver a photo facsimile to the Secretary of Treasury's office within two hours."

* * *

Number Two mentally replayed the financial misdeeds at the Hamilton S&L exposed over the past two weeks by his former exam; could he have done something different?

A year-and-a-half ago he had been lured away from his job with the Comptroller of Currency's with a stern mandate: bring financial law and order to the FHLB's Dallas Ninth District. Texas S&L's were growing wildly, swollen with brokered deposits, crippled by inept management and mutilated by bad loans.

Forty-one years old, the former Number Two executed his duties and lost his job; his resume forever scorched by his unceremonious firing. Texas S&L's threatened to undermine the country's financial system. FSLIC the US agency insuring S&L deposits, begged for competent regulators. Now, they had canned their Director of Supervision, maybe the best. He was out of work, flying back home. Washington, DC didn't generate inner nostalgic warmth.

His old boss had left the Comptroller's Office; he was now minting money for Salomon Brothers in New York City. Number Two's potluck telephone call to the Comptroller's office yesterday elicited the lackadaisical suggestion he fly to Washington for a courtesy interview.

Well, Washington had once been home for eighteen years. So, like a dying elephant, he clomped his remembered path.

Southwest Air's 737 descended over the stoop-shouldered, aging West Virginia mountains toward Maryland's rolling green hills. Urban haze obfuscated the horizon past three miles. Banking right, the fat jet crossed the Potomac upstream from the city, into Virginia airspace. He peered out the right side of the Boeing jet. Hydraulic gears dropped the plane's wheels. Dipping below the lowest cloud, Arlington appeared below. He exchanged long-distance gawks with lunchtime diners watching the plane descend from their tables inside the restaurant atop the Arlington Marriott. Just past the 14th Street bridge the stubby jet banked, flaps-down, seeking Washington National's east-west runway. From his secluded window seat, it seemed the plane would ditch in the muddy Potomac River. Number Two gripped each arm rest.

Number Two had never been fired. Irrationally, guilt sifted into his emotions. He had been dismissed for over-performing; being canned connoted failure.

What could I have done differently? he thought.

Inner questions assaulted him. Fighting the urge, he replayed the last eighteen months in Dallas.

Upon landing, busy procedures occupied him; sterile stewardess good-byes, gates, baggage, taxi stand. Whereas Dallas in the summer baked, DC, a river town, steams. He dripped sweat by the time he arrived at National Airport's taxi stand.

From behind, on his left, the woman's soft proposition startled him, "May I help you with your bags?"

Her right fist gripped the handle of his swamp green, pseudo-canvas carry-on. He tugged back. She disarmed him with a contagious smile. Her slim spryness, green eyes framed by cropped brunette hair, gained her a moment. Her thin neck supported an imaginative jaw.

"Ahh, I'm not sure," Number Two said.

Both his left and her right hand competed for his cheap carry-on. Agent Mollie Leep snapped open her left palm. After eighteen years with the U.S. Treasury's Comptroller of the Currency, Number Two digested her Secret Service credential as though sipping a cool gulp of mountain stream water.

"I'm your ride. You have a job interview," she said.

Number Two smiled for the first time in twenty-four hours.

"Am I qualified for this job?" he asked

"The Secretary of the Treasury believes you are," Secret Service Mollie said.

CHAPTER FIFTY-SIX

<u>Washington, Treasury Building</u>

Paper airplane in hand containing the identity of the assassin, Brendan Donahue ignored Treasury's ancient elevator. He flung open the grey metal fire door sealing the deserted stairway. For the first three floors Brendan vaulted up two steps each leap.

At the fifth floor he barged through the door. Racing down the marble hall, he skidded to a screeching, rubber-sole halt at the closed door outside the Secretary of the Treasury's office.

The calm demeanor of the woman serving the third ranking Cabinet member of the Reagan administration, suggested most of the Treasury's visitors arrived in equal haste.

"He said that only you are permitted to interrupt. Go in," she said.

Sucking in a liter of fresh air, Brendan stepped, knocked and entered.

Three familiar people suspended their conversation. Brendan expected the Treasury Secretary and the Secret Service woman. He did not expect the Number Two guy from the Dallas Fed Home Loan Bank.

The Treasury Secretary spoke, "Welcome Brendan. Harry Miller at LEC just called. The Wiz said you were on your way to my office with interesting information."

"He identified the assassin," Brendan said.

"So I understand. Our computer Wiz is something, isn't he?"

Blood surged to Brendan's head from the dash, leaving him dizzy. He shuffled to where the Secret Service woman sat and folded himself into the tan leather couch.

The Secretary spoke, "You remember the Director of Supervision from the Dallas Ninth?"

Brendan started to stand. The Texas S&L regulator who once worked for Jack Richardson, already stood at the couch. The men shook hands.

"He has just been dismissed, Brendan. His vigorous pursuit of the Hamilton S&L rattled a certain Texas senator."

When Treasury's Wiz had awoken Brendan from his nap at the Hyatt Regency Brendan wore a red cotton pull-over and khaki-colored shorts. Slipping into Converse tennis shoes did not refine his attire. The Secretary of the Treasury didn't appear offended.

"Our former Director of Supervision in Dallas shared your problem, Brendan. When Jack Richardson was killed, his support had been eliminated. "

Brendan's head swung in sympathy, "Hope you did better than I was doing."

"I was doing so well, I got fired," Number Two said.

"He has some interesting facts documented, Brendan," Treasury said, "I am resurrecting your effort as a two-man team. You're now working together for the United States Department of the Treasury."

Brendan spoke, "To do what?"

"Very simple, gentlemen. Your mission is to stop the financial carnage at the S&L's. My objective is to send the worst S&L thief, Ken Thompson, to prison."

Number Two sat across the Secretary's six-foot-wide desk.

Brendan, his blood re-oxygenated, perched on the edge of the leather couch. The Secret Service woman had not spoken. The Treasury man handed Brendan and Number Two a legal pad and a pencil, "Take notes."

His listeners scribbled as the Secretary spoke.

Brendan drew a large question mark; he circled it four times with number two lead. He asked, "Can't you just seize the Hamilton?"

The Treasury Secretary's answer suggested annoyance, "No, Treasury can't seize the Hamilton; and FSLIC can't either because they are broke. A Thompson appointee is chairman of the FDIC. Treasury, unfortunately, is playing left field in a rigged game for the moment. That is what you two will change. We must sever Ken Thompson's support. He has to be isolated. Too many people stand between me and the Hamilton crook. I need absolute control when the Hamilton S&L is seized. Four people must tactically be eliminated."

Brendan slid back on the slippery leather, "Your Wizard loosened my earlier doubts. I'm a semi-believer."

"Good. First, dispose of the acting chairman of the FDIC, Bob Henry," Treasury said.

Brendan penciled Henry's name on his lined pad of paper. He sketched another block-letter question mark.

Number Two reached into his briefcase. He balanced the dull yellow envelope wrapping his going-away present from the Dallas FHLB. He set the package on Treasury's desk and responded with the confidence of a Wheel of Fortune contestant, "Done," Number Two said.

Brendan's head snapped up, "Done?"

Even the Secret Service woman tuned in to Number Two's affirmation.

The Secretary of the Treasury didn't ask for details, he continued, "Tactic two, neutralize Thompson's COO at the Hamilton S&L."

Number Two confirmed, "OK."

Brendan arched his eyebrows, cocked his head, shrugged and said, "OK!"

The Secretary of Treasury thumped his oak desk. "The power of Texas Senator Jim Anderson must be abrogated. Anderson's potency increases exponentially with each senator he recruits to defend this goddam S&L boondoggle."

Brendan studied Number Two, seated in front of the Treasury man. Number Two didn't confirm this surgery. His head stayed down.

The Treasury Secretary's soliloquy continued, "And Thompson's hired assassin must be eliminated."

Brendan snapped his pencil. Eliminating the assassin who murdered Jack Richardson was an assignment he craved. He leaped over impossible demands of the Treasury man's implausible blueprint.

"Then what?" Brendan said.

"Then I will order the FDIC to seize the Hamilton S&L; my directive will be based on the data provided by Julie Weidener's FDIC team we sent into the Hamilton last month. But I cannot act until someone I trust heads the FDIC, not while an amoral assassin kills freely, not while a coalition of senators defend these S&L bastards, and not until we can grab the Hamilton S&L without their senior executives destroying the key records we need to prosecute Ken Thompson."

"Mr. Secretary, I'm willing to try," Brendan Donahue said, "What's your plan?"

"My plan? I'm not a banker, Mr. Donahue," said the Treasury head, "You and our recently canned regulator from Dallas are financial experts. You will have Secret Service protection. You have my authority to grant immunity to low-level managers in order to nail the top people. Put a plan together. I want to review it with both of you in two hours; by the time the fax photo of our assassin arrives. Get to work."

Brendan asked, "Sir?"

"Meeting is over. Oh yes, Brendan. Whose photo is Interpol faxing to us?"

He mumbled, "Jonathan Blair."

* * *

The license to prosecute his persecutors, delegated by Treasury to the former Number Two at the Dallas Fed Home Loan Bank, produced an avaricious, if temporary, G-man. He wanted to ensnare them all. Secret Service woman, Mollie Leap listened as the two men plotted.

Based on his delinquent $21 million held by the Hamilton S&L, convincing the recently appointed FDIC chairman, Robert Henry, to go away seemed possible.

"Brendan, divulging confidential info obtained during our Hamilton exam should rub me the wrong way, but it doesn't, here," Number Two surrendered loan documents on the three Atlanta strip malls, including a memo signed by Billy Johnstone reducing interest on the loan to zero percent and suspension of all payments due from Robert Henry, Chairman of the FDIC and guarantor on the loan.

"You think this is enough?" Brendan asked.

"This information is a weapon. It's a start," said Number Two.

Number Two continued, "We'll use Hamilton's swap of delinquent loans with Sunbelt Savings. Tell their COO, Billy Johnstone, that this deal lands him in jail. That'll move him to our side."

Brendan jumped ahead, "So, you're betting Billy Johnstone gives us Ken Thompson."

"No, once the Hamilton belongs to the government, we'll have an Easter basket full of criminal charges against Ken Thompson. Johnstone, The Hamilton's COO, has to be persuaded to cough up information to strip away Thompson's support people; to incriminate Senator Anderson of Texas and eliminate the assassin, Blair."

Brendan drew a line through Billy Johnstone's name. A question mark hung alongside Senator Anderson. Only the assassin, Jonathan Blair, lacked a disabling tactic.

"Jonathan Blair?" Brendan asked.

"I think we can separate our roles. I'll work on freezing the Hamilton managers. You eliminate Thompson's support people; the Texas Senator and the assassin. I don't know how to neutralize an assassin." Number Two had entered uncomfortable territory.

Secret Service woman Leep reminded them with exactness, "The Secretary didn't say to neutralize the assassin. He said to eliminate Jonathan Blair."

"Eliminate? Kill this man?" Brendan said.

Stony, dispassionate eyes dug into Brendan. She said, "This man killed Jack Richardson. He savagely murdered four FDIC bank examiners in London. Mr. Donahue, he tried to kill you in Dallas. Do you think he should survive?"

Brendan started to ask, "Will you . . . ?"

"No, Mr. Donahue," she said, "I won't kill your assassin. Unless killing Jonathan Blair is necessary to save your life."

Cold electricity bolted down Brendan's spine.

* * *

"INTERPOL faxed the photo of Jonathan Blair," The Secretary of the Treasury pushed the black and white reproduction across his desk, "The man has no record."

"Jesus, that's the man who met Ken Thompson on K Street last week," Brendan said.

The Secret Service woman peered around Brendan's shoulder, "Yes, same man."

The Secretary of Treasury said, "We've uncovered a woman that Jonathan Blair visits occasionally. Her name is Cecille."

Dallas, Texas

"Ciao, Gianni. Come va?" Discovering good Italian food in Dallas would have been impossible, if not for the San Francisco regulator's cousin, Gianni Cortese. The five foot-seven inch regulator needed one favor before departing Dallas. He needed his cousin to steal; an act he knew his cousin was pretty good at. Steal one condemning piece of the Hamilton S&L jigsaw puzzle.

Eddie Ciraff, baptized Edoardo Ciravegna in the Piemonte town of Bra at the foot of the Italian Alps, had pipelined almost enough information to the Number Two guy at the Dallas Fed Home Loan Bank to crucify the Hamilton S&L CEO. One last illegal promise, locked in Thompson's private office, would complete his prosecution. Eddie just had to get his hands on the letter Ken Thompson wrote to the Texas Department of Insurance . . . and pass it on to the former Number Two at the Dallas Ninth.

"Edoardo, stai bene," Gianni said, "You stayin' in Dallas?"

"No, Gianni. My job is over," Eddie replied, his slick black hair combed straight back, "Bigwig fucker pulled strings to get me out of his S&L."

"Cazzo," Gianni swore, "I was hoping you'd stick around Dallas couple more weeks?"

"I'm flying back to Frisco tonight." Eddie Ciraff circled the undersized spoon on the white linen table cloth, a tiny spoon meant to stir thick espresso coffee. His parents had migrated to San Francisco four weeks after his birth, settling in the North Beach neighborhood; Little Italy. His uncle emigrated from Italy a month after Eddie's parents, somehow Gianni's father landed in Texas.

Eddie had never asked a favor of his relatives. He avoided the system of honor that kept a significant faction of his extended family on the illegitimate side of society.

"Gianni, I got a criminal by the balls. Bastard pulls strings to get me out of town, back to Frisco. My gut tells me that if I don't nail this guy, my career takes a major fucking leap backwards. I've worked too hard to let some connected sonofabitch take me down." The cuffs on the shirt of the San Francisco examiner were rolled up to the elbow; he tapped the inside of his left forearm with the backside of the first three fingers of his right hand.

Gianni's clicking fingertips propelled, agitating the air between the two cousins. "Hey Eddie, you tell me, how I can help you? No one fucks with family, eh," Gianni leaned across the table and gaveled his cousin's forearm, "You know, I got to be careful though. Can't bite the hand, you know what I mean. I work for the Greek. What do you need? Maybe a hooker so we get this shmuck in a dirty photo, eh?"

Eddie drew circles on the white linen tablecloth with the miniature spoon. He lifted his eyes, "I need a letter, Gianni. A letter locked in a desk inside a private office a couple a floors above K street in Washington, D.C."

"Porca Madonna, Edoardo. Only thing I know about Washington is the fuckin' White House is there. Breaking into a private office, stealing letters means beating a security alarm. That takes local pull."

Eddie waved away his presumptuous request, "Capisce. I shouldn't have brought it up."

"Maybe, I can put you in touch with someone in DC, Eddie."

"No, Gianni. This has got to be handled by someone I trust," Eddie cast his appeal. "If it's not you, I let the chips fall."

"It's that critical, eh?" the Greek's sentry said. Gianni chuckled at the three initials stitched on the pocket of his cousins shirt; SOL.

"It's that complex, cousin," Eddie Ciraff said.

"Whose office am I stealing this letter from?" Gianni asked.

"Real connected guy, Gianni. Guy name of Ken Thompson, owns an S&L here in Dallas, the Hamilton. Connected big-time to congress."

"Porca miseria," Gianni said, "You tellin' me that fuck Thompson is the guy who's dickin' you?"

"Fuckin' me and half of Texas. You know him, Gianni?" the San Francisco regulator asked.

"Yeah, I know him, know about him," his cousin said.

"He's the guy who's going to fuck my career, Gianni. He's already forced out the top S&L regulator in Texas. Thompson is ear deep in financial horseshit and fuckin' the good guys trying to stop his stealing."

Gianni bent towards his cousin, he confided, "Thompson's riff-raff has occupied a great deal of my working time in recent weeks. Thompson is a sotto mano sonofabitch, Eddie. I'll get your letter, my pleasure. Thompson goes away and I can stop shaking down women and burying dead dogs."

Eddie stymied curiosity about his cousin's peculiar rational, "Gianni, stai attenti. Rumor in Fed circles is that Thompson took out a couple of people who annoyed him."

"Non c'e problema," the Greek's employee said.

CHAPTER FIFTY-SEVEN

Dallas, The Hamilton S&L

Billy Johnstone should have felt better. Two days ago the Dallas examiners suddenly disappeared from the Hamilton. At 10 AM Tuesday morning the wimpy senior examiner, Bobby Scamehorn had called saying the FHLB examination of the Hamilton S&L had concluded. Scamehorn's written report would be reviewed with Hamilton's executive management in two weeks. Problems would be discussed, but nothing grievous. No sanctions would be recommended.

An inner burr pricked Billy Johnstone. Heather Montgomery was acting like a zombie. She had been locked in her office for two days. Pete Morris hadn't been seen in the S&L during the past six days. His secretary reported that he was calling on customers. The four personal loan guys eye-shined their shoes every time Johnstone toured their department. Respectful "Yes, sir's" and "No, sir's" replacing their secretary-baiting fables of gargantuan sexual organs.

Silence gnawed at Johnstone.

Billy Johnstone pushed out the S&L's revolving door. His white coupe baked under Dallas' cloudless 5 PM summer sky.

The side windows hummed as they lowered. The Hamilton COO started his Cadillac Eldorado and gunned the engine; closing his eyes, he imagined cool air . . . not the invader who confiscated the passenger seat.

"Billy Johnstone?" Brendan Donahue slid into the leather front seat of Johnstone's Caddy.

Billy Johnstone, a stocky thirty-six, snapped his eyes open.

Reacting, he grabbed at the intruder with his right fist. The quickness of the well-dressed trespasser surprised Johnstone. Billy's fist pinched against the leather console, his forearm locked.

From outside the open driver's-side window, two slender fingers stabbed through skin and muscle on the back of Billy's lower neck. His paralyzed arms slackened. He couldn't even wiggle his fingers.

A sedate woman's voice instructed, "Calm down, Mr. Johnstone. We're here for a discussion." Her stiff fingers rotated his pliant head counter-clockwise. From his neck up, Billy ticked around. He came face-to-face with the Secret Service woman.

She slapped her credentials to close to his face to read, "Secret Service. We're the good guys, Mr. Johnstone. Permit me to introduce Brendan Donahue; currently on assignment with the Treasury Department."

Electrified pain arched through the Hamilton's COO from shoulder to shoulder. Not believing that this one woman had him pinned helpless with a single hand, Billy Johnstone searched past her for other hands.

"What do you want?" Billy Johnstone said.

Her left hand with the credentials disappeared, "Can I count on you to behave?"

Billy nodded. *I'll strangle this bitch,* he thought.

"Good. I like a man I can trust," she said. Her left hand reappeared caressing a Walther PPK. She wedged the barrel of the hand gun into his auditory canal and blew on his lobe, "Because if you even sneeze, I'm going to soil Mr. Donahue's suit-coat with your brains."

Billy stiffened as the weapon violated his ear.

She instructed, "Now, Mr. Johnstone, devote your full attention to Mr. Donahue's questions." Secret Service Mollie nodded at Brendan.

Brendan side-saddled on the white leather, "Billy, you are going to jail."

"Fuck you," the Hamilton COO said.

Her gun barrel dug painfully deeper. The Secret Service woman whispered down the barrel, "Bang."

Brendan explained, "Our attorney projects that you will be in jail at least fifty-four years. Let me outline your crimes. Swapping $85 mill with Sunbelt Savings. Evidenced by Ed McBirney's letter dated February 26."

Billy's head whirled towards Brendan Donahue. The Secret Service woman's Walther jabbed into the base of his neck, pinpointing the exact location were Johnstone's brain became spinal cord.

Brendan continued, "Siphoning $36 million into a slush fund for delinquent real estate borrowers. Money came from the sale of Hamilton's DFW land. Except you have agreed to buy back the land from McManus after thirty-six months. Your slush fund is tapped-out. Now, Randy Peterson, your plump SVP, needs another $30 million."

Billy stared out the front windshield. Secret Service agent Mollie Leep nuzzled the gun barrel under his lower left jaw. Johnstone tried to disguise his reaction to the facts Brendan recited.

"Purchase of Drexel junk bonds by Hamilton Insurance. How am I doing, Billy? Purchase of junk bonds on November 11 last year. Authorized by you. Next week Drexel funded Thompson's Nassau Shores project. Fraudulent use of depositor's funds."

"What is this, a government lynching?" Billy Johnstone said, "Doesn't Treasury allow the accused man an attorney anymore? Hasn't the government been battered enough trying to harass the Hamilton S&L?"

Brendan's voice pitched to a guttural condemnation. He knifed his index finger an inch into Johnstone's soft lower jaw. Johnstone's nose brushed the Caddy's felt ceiling. "Assassinating Julie Weidener, an FDIC bank examiner in London."

"What? No way," Billy protested.

"Murder, Mr. Johnstone. You go to jail forever," Brendan said.

"You're wrong."

"Conspiring to kill Jack Richardson," Brendan said.

"Not even close. I had nothing to do with any murder," The Hamilton COO said.

"Murders you suggested and conspired to commit."

Billy started to deny these crimes.

"Murders ordered by Your boss, Ken Thompson," Brendan said, "and executed by Jonathan Blair."

The name stunned Billy Johnstone,. Billy Johnstone knew Jonathan Blair as an old investment partner of Ken Thompson.

"Mr. Johnstone. You are in deep caca," Brendan said.

The heat rose inside Billy's Eldorado. Billy Johnstone analyzed. No wonder his managers had recently lacked conviviality. These Treasury people had the facts and dates correct. Somebody inside the Hamilton S&L had delivered very accurate data to these Feds.

"I am not involved in anybody's murder." Billy Johnstone needed an attorney.

"I can build a case that you *are* intimately involved, Mr. Johnstone," Brendan said.

"Where do we go from here? Am I the focus of your allegations?" Billy Johnstone, COO of the Hamilton S&L asked.

"Not exactly, Billy."

Johnstone's head spun from his accuser to the woman with the gun pressed into ear, "Then what am I doing in my car with a pistol aimed at my head?"

Air conditioning futilely spewed 70-degree air.

Perspiration drained down the Secret Service woman's thin, pale neck. Billy silently damned Ken Thompson for the Drexel money sent to

Nassau. Damned Thompson's Washington political pals. Damned Thompson's request for an enforcer . . . The Greek.

"Billy, Ken Thompson has powerful friends. I need to neutralize two of those people. If you have the right information, I may forget this conversation."

Salvation pounced into Billy's mind, "Have Treasury indemnify me. Then we can talk."

"No, Billy. No deals. You've done what you've done. You give me what I need on Senator Jim Anderson and Jonathan Blair, I go away. You will never see me again. You refuse, and every fact I just recited, you will hear again in court."

"How long do I have?" Billy Johnstone asked.

"About two minutes. Then I call for a warrant. I can't stop that process once it starts," Brendan said.

Seated between the Department of Treasury and the Secret Service woman, Billy had few choices.

"Jonathan Blair I know nothing about. If your disappearing from my life is contingent on Blair, I can't help you."

"Senator Anderson?" Brendan said.

Billy Johnstone took a deep breath and looked sideways. Six inches from his nose the Secret Service woman glared.

"If I told you the Hamilton S&L had sluiced $800,000 into his campaign fund, would that get you on your way?"

"Properly documented, this would be our last meeting."

<u>Washington, D.C.</u>

Vehemence seethed through the telephone, "Ken, I just got a call advising me not to miss Jack Anderson's column in the *Washington Post* tomorrow," Senator Jim Anderson, Republican, Texas, said.

Ken Thompson responded with adult-child condescension, "Why are you telling me this, Jim?"

Senator Anderson's voice climbed the decibel ladder, "Two reasons. Sonofabitch said Jack Anderson will be featuring your Hamilton S&L. Says he provided *Post's* reporter with the facts for tomorrow's story."

"Jack Anderson writes exposes," Thompson, CEO of the Hamilton, said, "What is he going to say about the Hamilton?"

"He didn't say. But Anderson doesn't write endorsements, Ken. Guy says I will be the feature character in Jack Anderson's column next week unless I meet with him."

"Was your caller from Anderson's office at the *Post*?"

"No Ken, he was not," answered the Texas Senator.

"Then don't worry. Jim," The Hamilton CEO said, "Why does Peggy let crackpots like this get through to you?"

The Texas congressman's voice hissed like a coiled rattler's tail, "Because the sumbitch quotes to Peggy that cashier's check number 86234-LB drawn on Lloyds Bank for $50,000 cleared my campaign fund account at Texas Commerce on July 9. That's the check you handed me in Nassau, Ken."

"What else did he say?" The Hamilton CEO asked.

"That he'd call me tomorrow to arrange a meeting. This isn't some goddam know-nothing. What the goddam hell is going on?"

"Do you have any idea who the man is that called you?"

"A real good idea. He told me. It's the guy I had the FBI trace for you, Brendan Donahue," The Republican Senator said.

"Impossible! Donahue's dead," Ken Thompson stated.

Senator Anderson hollered through the phone, "What?"

"Nothing, nothing. I will call you back."

The Treasury Building

The ex-Number Two and Brendan Donahue each had his own copy of the *Washington Post*. Brendan sat on the couch in The Secretary of Treasury's office. Number Two read out loud highlights of Jack Anderson's scathing editorial report on the delinquent loan guaranteed by Robert Henry, FDIC acting Chairman. The Treasury Secretary paced the perimeter of his spacious, fifth-floor office.

That morning the entire country read that acting FDIC chairman Bob Henry guaranteed a loan totaling $21,000,000 due the Hamilton S&L based in Dallas, Texas. A delinquent loan that the S&L's owner, Ken Thompson, had *adjusted* to zero interest and no payments, two days after Ronald Reagan appointed Henry chairman of the FDIC.

The *Washington Post* columnist thinly disguised specific quotes by Bobby Scamehorn's from the Ninth District's examination report. *Washington Post* reporter, Jack Anderson, concluded his disclosure with a self-pardoning recommendation that S&L examination summaries should be public information.

Robert Henry, on the calendar for his Senate confirmation hearing, scheduled for next week, was dead. He would resign rather than face interrogation.

The Treasury Secretary scolded, "Brendan, Henry would have resigned if you simply threatened to release this information. I fear you have alerted our ultimate target, Ken Thompson."

"Henry is gone as FDIC Chair," Brendan said, "But I need Thompson to make another mistake. I'm betting Anderson's column infuriates Thompson. Ken Thompson can deliver the assassin, Blair, to us. An added benefit of the *Washington Post* expose, is that I now have absolute credibility when I meet our Texas Senator, Jim Anderson to discuss his future."

"Three birds with one stone?" Said The Treasury head.

"If Thompson panics," Brendan confirmed. "If the CEO feels threatened enough to lead us to Blair. Announcement. Just before his death, Jack Richardson told me it was his one effective weapon."

"Let's turn the screws. If we are to prosecute Thompson successfully, the FDIC has to seize the Hamilton S&L as soon as possible."

The Treasury Secretary dialed his phone, "Senator Proxmire, please."

He exchanged minimal openings with the Wisconsin Democrat, Senator William Proxmire, chairman of the Senate Banking Committee. Proxmire, Congress' passionate watchdog of banking, would hound his colleagues about Anderson's expose.

"Bill," Treasury said, "Did you read Jack Anderson's column this morning?"

The Secretary of the Treasury listened, then responded, "Good, good. Senator, if you should request a criminal investigation into the Henry-Hamilton S&L matter, Treasury would endorse your appeal."

The Treasury Secretary looked at Number Two and Brendan while Proxmire responded.

"You have scheduled a press conference for 11 AM?" said the Cabinet member responsible for the finances of the United States, "Yes, and yes. Draft a statement that Treasury supports you. Fax it to me," Treasury listened, "That is for the best." He hung up.

"Bob Henry just resigned as FDIC chairman. Well done, Mr. Donahue. Now, I control the FDIC."

"How did that happen?" Brendan asked, "Who replaces Henry?"

Number Two and the Treasury Secretary exchanged colluding smiles.

The Secretary spoke, "Brendan, did you study government in school?"

"It wasn't my best subject," Brendan replied.

"The Comptroller of the Currency is a department of Treasury. The Comptroller is a permanent member of FDIC's board of directors. President Reagan and I agreed that the Comptroller would assume temporary chairmanship of the FDIC . . . should Bob Henry resign."

"We still have to eliminate the assassin and the senator," Number Two reminded.

The Treasury man added, "And I must have the Fed Home Loan bank surrender jurisdiction for the Hamilton to the FDIC. I won't act until our Texas Senator is neutered and the assassin is eliminated."

"Mr. Secretary, what do you mean by *eliminate*? Brendan said.

"Brendan, did you study reading comprehension in school?" Treasury asked.

CHAPTER FIFTY-EIGHT

The Hamilton S&L

Randy Peterson padded a corkscrew route around Phil Kamerov's dank basement office. As he slogged, sweat bubbled on his pudgy upper lip. Every fifth step he toweled the sweat with a cleansing sweep of his right shirt cuff.

"Pee-ul, goddammit, I've never ratted on my boss, but I'm afraid Billy Johnstone is fixin' to jump ship."

Phil Kamerov nodded with false compassion. The Pill reckoned he had snared Randy Peterson. He dug for every detail Peterson possessed, with the modulation of a voice from within confessional darkness, Phil asked, "Why would Billy do that?"

"Those goddam examiners talked criminal indictment, Pee-ul. Billy stopped talkin' to me. It's been two days. Billy is my man."

Randy's flat-footed, out-of-sync gait drummed across the Pill's office floor. He paced three steps away, turned, and yanked the knot loose on his tie. His partially tucked shirt draped his left hip.

"Do you have anything to worry about, Randy?" the Pill asked.

Randy-Randy stopped directly in front of Phil Kamerov's grey metal desk. Peterson tucked the loose flap from his wrinkled shirt too tightly under his brown leather belt. A fleshy overhang testified to his two hundred-forty-three pounds. "Pee-ul, we've done a couple transactions that might not fly with the regulators. I want to make sure I don't get squeezed if the Feds seize the Hamilton."

"What would you be liable for?" The Pill said.

Peterson whisked a gale from his lungs. He wiped early sweat from his agitated upper lip. Collapsing into the chair in front of Phil the Pill, he clamped each hand on a thigh and said, "It's not what I did, it's what I'm doing for Billy. Phil, will you do the right thing with this information? I mean, I just got to talk this out."

Phil Kamerov slid open his confessional window, "Randy, changes are in store for the Hamilton. If the COO of the Hamilton is implicating you, declare them now, or you have to make your own deal."

Randy Peterson edged his butt to the front of the chair. He pulled a list from his blue striped shirt pocket. "I want to make sure we cover everything. I want to just . . . just stop worrying all fucking day."

"Let's go slow, Randy," the Pill said, "First, Billy Johnstone. Do you know about the loan swap with Sunbelt Savings?"

"Oh Jesus, I don't know how Billy pulled that one off," Randy said.

Randy Peterson confessed to the Workout man for more than an hour.

* * *

Phil Kamerov stacked his notes from Randy Peterson's confession, rose from his desk, walked to the door and glanced down the fluorescent-lit hallway for trespassers. Quietly, he closed his office door, returned to his desk and punched the Washington phone number.

"The Hamilton SVP just divulged enough information to put Billy Johnstone in jail for a long time," the Pill said.

Most Delicious of Privileges

Instructions from the Washington end of the phone line startled the Pill, he listened closely, not sure he could act out this game.

"I don't think I can comfortably make that phone call," The Pill said to the former Number Two at the Dallas Fed Home Loan Bank.

Number Two dangled the carrot of a clean bill of health sanctioned by the Comptroller's office, "You have to Phil. That's my deal if you are to come out of this with a commendation from the Comptroller's office. Call Ken Thompson and layout the charges."

"What about the crap Billy Johnstone has been perpetrating?"

"I'll take care of Johnstone," Number Two said.

Phil inhaled deeply, "OK, but I want your promise to me in writing . . . on stationery from the Comptroller's office."

"You'll have it, Phil. There is one other name I want you to bring up in your conversation with Ken Thompson."

* * *

Phil Kamerov looped the telephone cord in a continuous nervous circle. "I don't like having to tell you this, Mr. Thompson, but I thought you'd want to hear it direct. Randy Peterson has created quite mess here in Dallas."

"But you don't think Billy Johnstone is involved?" Ken Thompson checked again.

"I don't have evidence that Billy even knows," Phil the Pill said, "I don't really have the authority to question Billy."

"Phil, I appreciate your call," said the Hamilton CEO, "You did the right thing. If Randy goes around Billy to the regulators hoping for some kind of immunity, the Hamilton will be left hanging. Phil, keep me posted if anybody at the S&L gets too jittery."

"I will Mr. Thompson," the Pill paused. This is where Number Two had instructed him to test the name. He spoke with natural uncertainty, "I'm checking my notes,"

"Jonathan Blair," Phil the Pill mumbled.

"What did you say?"

"Jonathan Blair," Phil, the Hamilton Workout guy uttered the name as one might do when completing the last letter of a new word on the Scrabble board, just as Number Two had instructed him to do. "Somebody Randy Peterson mentioned a couple of times. I don't think it's relevant."

"What did Peterson say about Jonathan Blair?" said the Hamilton CEO.

"Nothing I could make sense of. I got the impression this this Jonathan Blair might be an attorney."

"Why is that?" asked the CEO.

"Peterson said as a final defense he might have to use this Blair. What else could he be?"

Thompson stayed silent at least five seconds, "Thank you, Phil. Keep me posted."

CHAPTER FIFTY-NINE

Dallas

"Randy got his Rolex from the Endres Brothers. Their thank you for his approving the $8,000,000 loan on their twenty-story building in Phoenix." Pete Morris exposed his boss's felonious acquiescence while standing face-to-face with Heather. A beige counter, separating his tight kitchen from the just-as-small breakfast nook, served as their no-man's-land. Heather tested Morris's eyes for lies. Pete ignored Heather's probe, he couldn't rebut her questioning stare. His own participation condemned him also.

"Any other trinkets that fat Randy grafted from his customers, Pete? Incriminating Randy Peterson is your ticket to an immunity deal."

Her flippant attitude worried him. "Just remember, Heather, get an agreement of immunity for me. The Endres left a Rolex under my Christmas tree too. This is just as damning to me, as it is to Randy Peterson."

"What else did Peterson take, Pete?" she asked.

"Heather, I funded $33 million in unapproved loans. That money is still outstanding . . . unpaid. I have to be absolutely sure you cut a deal for me. Exactly who will be granting me immunity? "

"Don't worry, Pete, your deal is firm. You have immunity from the regulators. I just have to deliver your facts that incriminate your boss Randy Peterson."

"Which regulators, Heather? Two different Fed agencies have probed the Hamilton S&L during the last month." Pete's capacity for trust had evaporated; he suspected Heater might be using his information for her exclusive benefit.

"Fed Home Loan, the Dallas District," Heather lied, "What else do you have on Randy Peterson?"

"Randy got a $25,000 kick-back from a loan broker in Denver. Some guy affiliated with the Silverado S&L. Randy was all excited because Neil Bush and the Bush's family connections in Dallas," the Hamilton VP appraised Heather with the eyes of a jeweler.

Heather Montgomery scribbled Morris's revelation, "How do you know Randy received $25,000?"

Peter Morris snapped open the twin locks on his aging brown attaché. He tossed the thin, light blue second copy of bank telex paper on the beige counter between them. "Because I swiped Peterson's copy of the wire transfer to his checking account. Dumb jerk left it on his desk last week."

"Jesus, Pete. You are a wonder."

* * *

Brendan Donahue liberated Heather Montgomery, "You're out. Walk away this afternoon, Heather. No more Hamilton S&L. Your job, and mine, is finished."

Heather had reported Pete Morris's incriminating evidence on Randy Peterson and Billy Johnstone to Brendan. "I need two things before I go, Brendan."

Heather had debated whether to sacrifice Janis Lang. No one had yet discovered her theft of the dormant checking account money. Heather

Most Delicious of Privileges 313

had decided for the moment that Lang's crimes would remain a private matter between the two women. She studied Brendan's blue eyes. This mercenary from the Treasury had slivered his way into her trust. Across the table in the cocktail lounge he sipped his second Lone Star from its long neck bottle.

Brendan propped his unshaven chin atop his closed left fist, "What two things, my S&L spy."

"Exoneration in writing. I've cooperated since the Secretary of Treasury called me. Now, I want a letter from him. The letter should say something unequivocal like: *Heather is free for all time*."

"Fair enough request. You'll have it this afternoon. What else," Brendan said.

"I'm not walking quietly away until we agree the Detroit issue will never surface again."

"What Detroit issue?" he asked.

"Don't play games with me, Brendan," Heather said.

"Heather, I don't know what you're talking about."

That's it, she realized. *I am free . . . out of this*, "When will you have my letter?"

Washington, D.C.

Leaning on his podium desk on the ground floor of the deserted office building, the security guard hums the tune so slowly that it could tax Gianni Cortese into sleep. Ignoring K street darkness outside the two barriers of locked glass doors, the grey-haired watchman follows his fingertip through this evening's *Washington Times*. Cortese's hunt is hushed by the rubber-soled, green-and-yellow running shoes he wears. He stalks the preoccupied sentry from behind, stifling even a whisper of breath. Creeping within three steps of the old man, Cortese lurches forward, jamming the pistol between two ribs, deep enough that bone stretches.

"Eyes forward," Cortese clamps the back of the man's neck.

"Aghhh," the old guard's wail stops the instant Cortese's open palm thunks against his skull. The crack of Cortese's hand peals around the small lobby.

"How are you tonight, Mr. Hamill?" the Italian said.

"What? Who are you?"

"I am a thief, Mr. Hamill," The Greek's sentry said, "Tonight I am stealing from your building. My advisers at the CIA have recommended that I kill you. Nothing personal, it's just so you can't be a witness," Cortese waits.

"Whaaa, "

Gianni augers the pistol, "Stop. Another word, I squeeze the trigger. Bang. Do you feel my gun? Cortese plugs the barrel deeper, "Right between your ribs, aimed at your heart. Cortese feels the Smith & Wessen pry apart protesting rib bone.

As Cortese digs, the security man arches forward, "Aghh!"

Gianni Cortese rang the guard's ear with another whack, harder this time. "Quiet, eh. Tonight while I'm stealing, maybe I don't need to kill you. I don't know, maybe I shoot you anyway, but maybe I won't. It doesn't really matter. Cept' the government is my best customer and they say *no witnesses*. You see I gotta get something from the upstairs. Just a piece of paper the CIA needs. Guy cheating the government, his own country. You believe that?" Cortese eases pressure on the piercing barrel enough that the guard risks one deep breath.

The hostage guard shakes his head; Cortese cuffs the man. "Don't look back, not even sideways. You see me, you're a witness. You're a witness, bang. Understand?"

Nodding affirmatives.

"See, I gotta' steal this paper because the government needs it. They're the good guys. Probably don't seem so good to you because they recommend I kill you, but it's nothing personal. Anyway nobody's ever going to report this paper being gone. No one's ever going to investigate. See what I mean? Just nod."

Condensed nods confirm understanding.

"So I'm thinking why kill this nice man?" Cortese whips a photograph in the face of the petrified man. He forces the old guard to study the black-and-white photograph of the guard's wife from the close span one utilizes when reading a map, "Cause then your wife, she's a widow and your murder gets reported and maybe I get some local police zealot on my case. It could be a real pain in the ass. Know what I mean?"

The old man waggles several mechanical yeses.

"But if I steal my paper and no one ever reports it and you live, what's the problem with that. You agree?"

Swift up-and-down nods.

"Good. Can you deactivate the alarm, get me upstairs and open the office?" Gianni says.

The guard telegraphs continuous confirming signals.

"Good, good, then maybe I don't kill you." Gianni pats the old man's shoulder; without provocation Cortese's jammed his gun deep again. "You understand that if you report this, I come back like a bad dream and kill your old lady?"

Racking nods convulsed through the guard's shoulders - swift up-and-down nods.

"Good. Deactivate the alarm, get me upstairs and open the office?"

Dallas, Texas

Heather and Brendan hid deep within Fuddruckers discussing the end of their conspiracy. For the fourth time she re-read the fax copy of the letter from the Secretary of the Treasury. Heather squeezed the paper, afraid it might be suddenly snatched away. Her thoughts strayed to warm, foreign, tropical shores.

Brendan joked, "Did you commit any S&L crimes?"

"Huh?" Her mistrust overruled his attempt at humor.

"What crimes did you commit, Heather?" Brendan chided.

"No crimes, sorry." Heather never considered graft. She had been too busy elbowing her way into the respectable financial world dominated by men. Heather remembered Julie Weidener, Julie died believing she was succeeding in a man's world.

"Well, don't slip from your noble wagon and do something wrong after today," Brendan said.

"Why?" Heather challenged his advice.

"Read your letter from Treasury," he said, "Your immunity is only good for crimes committed through today. Tomorrow will be too late in any case."

The Feds are going to seize the Hamilton tomorrow, aren't they," Heather said.

Brendan glanced away, confirming her suspicion.

"It's tomorrow, isn't it?" she said. Relief she felt moments ago turned to anger. A rage that she almost died in a botched car bomb, that someone commissioned a gangster to shake her up, witnessed the execution of a dog . . . read about a new friend's execution in London.

"Heather I need a favor. I want you to schedule a meeting with the COO, that slovenly SVP, the lender Morris and the Hamilton's Workout guy for 4 PM tomorrow at the Hamilton."

"What for?" she said.

Brendan took a deep breath, "You're right. We are seizing the S&L. Tomorrow at 4 P.M. I want each of those guys inside the Hamilton S&L."

"Jesus!"

"Listen, I want you in the bank too," Brendan said, "You are to appear as a culprit. But you are not to arrive until 3:45 in the afternoon. Here's what you need to say to the US Marshall when he comes to your office."

"U.S. Marshall! What for?"

"To arrest you," Brendan said.

Heather's icy stare froze Brendan. "Who killed Julie Weidener?" Her question chased Brendan's eyes away. His silence revealed that he could answer her question. She didn't want his answer, all she wanted to know was that Julie had been revenged.

"The same man who killed Jack Richardson," Brendan said.

"Why did he kill Julie?"

"Because Ken Thompson contracted him to kill Julie Weidener."

CHAPTER SIXTY

New York City

Eight A.M. hotel sounds stalked lazily through sleep's custody. Jonathan Blair forbid his eyes to open; his other senses whet his indulgence. He inhaled the Giorgio that Cecille patted on her ebony neck ten hours ago. He caged the fragrance, allowing its escape slowly so that his ebbing chest did not bump the sleep from her head as she lay on him. He over-ruled a distant voice that warned him to run, to escape before desire chained him.

Muffled Spanish voices and whining steel castors from the carpeted hallway announced slow-moving housekeepers tidying disheveled rooms already vacated by the St. Moritz's earliest risers. Eyes shut; the assassin blindly skimmed the smooth skin behind Cecille's neck and traced down her upper back.

Cecille slept naked against him. Early New York City sunlight filtered through the shear, gauze-like curtain guarding the hotel room's sole window. Her breath so slight it teased the hair on his chest; this feeling, so foreign he should refuse it.

From 59th street, three-floors below, hoof-beat percussion from carriage horses, prancing curb-side on Central Park South, echoed. Honking horns hammered by impatient cabbies fused into New York City's inharmonious post-dawn vitality. Jonathan absorbed Cecille as he listened to New York wade into another day.

He bent his head to her shoulder; the assassin's amoral being was under siege. Cecille had become important to him. *Is there a God?* He wanted to run away with Cecille, escape to a private place where others wouldn't hear him confess that she had hurdled his wall.

Their room on the St. Moritz's third floor was booked in Cecille's name. Blair, the assassin, sheathed in the anonymity of a kept man. Jonathan calculated his feelings, stripping his emerging desire from the course he had always pursued. Cecille would now perform on the world's premier stage, Broadway. Last night as she confessed her zeal, he accepted her intensity, touched her craving, spliced into her dream-come-true. Jonathan had approached the edge of hunger.

Without jarring her, Jonathan spiked his elbow on the king-size bed and elevated his head into the cup of his left hand. Under the ironed white cotton sheet Cecille approved some inner sensation.

"Mmmmm," Half-awake, she snuggled into the assassin, cementing their early-morning bond. Sleep began its evacuation. Cecille kept barraging his soul; even as she slept. Some benevolent god absolved his sins.

She felt his breath on her back; Cecille's first conscious sensation of the new day. She shivered to the welcomed small patch of human warmth. Cecille rolled on her side and delivered a drowsy, crooked morning smile. Her disheveled black hair veiled half her face. The thin white sheet contoured her breasts.

Their love-making last night had outraced the St. Moritz' air-conditioning, but this morning the room had cooled to a nuzzling seventy degrees, necessitating the sheet's insulation for only the last hour before dawn. Cecille understood a door into Jonathan's soul once closed, had been unlocked.

She challenged his silence, "What?"

Jonathan slowly leaned into her vulnerable neck. His warm breath soothed her like an August country breeze carrying the heavy scent of fresh cut alfalfa.

"When did you become so affectionate?" Cecille had savored this new Jonathan last night. Until then their love-making had been dramatic, their conversation adult. A relationship limited by dispassionate boundaries. Last night Jonathan held her a little longer.

Jonathan locked into her eyes, studied her mouth, her nose, her chin. He slid his fingertips around her neck, feeling her skin, not just touching. He raked her black hair, uncloaking Cecille's dark eyes and held the long strands. His lips bumped her forehead.

He did not answer her question.

"I don't know what changed you, but I approve," she said, "You're not getting out of here just yet to go back to Italy, Mr. Blair," Cecil crawled on top of him.

Jonathan rolled backwards, conceding her mount. Her tongue forced his lips apart. He stroked her bare lower back in encouragement. Cecille let the full weight of her willowy body indent Jonathan. She nestled her breasts into him as her legs skinnied between his parting thighs. Her head bobbed up to study this changing man from close range.

"You can't leave me today, not tomorrow," she said, "not ever. Now that I am a star on Broadway, I'm going to support you. All you have to do is be here in my room for me at all times." Cecille excavated her hips deeper into the valley of his legs. Sometime during the last twenty-four hours, his affection and passion had evolved. Cecille knew he would not speak the word. Neither would she. She would communicate with whatever he would accept.

* * *

Unrushed sex in the morning light lingers with more intimacy than lust chasing through night's anonymity. Afterwards Cecille drifted towards restorative sleep. Jonathan's fingertips scratched her back until her breath deepened.

A vacuuming plop in the hotel hallway announced delivery of Saturday's *New York Times*. He drew the sheet over her body and scooted out of bed. Naked, he quietly stepped on the balls of his feet, opened the door ten inches, and retrieved the newspaper. He skimmed the front page as he returned to the bed and sat against a single pillow he propped against the headboard. Cecille awoke, delivered a fleeting kiss, and vanished into the bathroom. Jonathan ogled her naked rear as she disappeared around the room's corner.

Jonathan Blair flipped to the Business section; the headline read *FDIC CHAIRMAN RESIGNS*.

Jonathan's contentment dissolved, his labor had been wasted.

"Shit," He slung the thick newspaper, scattering the several sections. Jonathan snatched the telephone off the nightstand and punched the number of the private line to Ken Thompson's Georgetown townhouse.

Thompson answered on the third ring, "Yes."

"Ken, this is Jonathan, the New York Times reports that your FDIC Chairman resigned yesterday. This concerns me."

Jonathan would not tolerate other's mistakes that could track back to him. His sprouting passion for Cecille shriveled like a day lily greeting dusk. This longing for Cecille, proved ephemeral.

"Jonathan, we have a problem," the Hamilton CEO said, "a problem that unfortunately you will have to involve yourself with."

The assassin recaptured his amorality. Jonathan offered no compromise, "No, Ken. My assignment is complete. I'm leaving for Italy this afternoon."

"Brendan Donahue is alive," the Hamilton CEO said, "He did not die in Dallas."

"Are you sure?" the assassin said.

"Unfortunately, I am absolutely sure," Thompson confirmed. "Donahue leaked information to the Washington Post that forced Henry to resign from the FDIC."

Cecille stifled his lust for killing. Assassination's thrill deserted his physical demands. He understood that desire subverted calculation, passion undermined resolve. Indifferent coldness gripped his psyche.

Jonathan did not challenge Thompson's assertion that Brendan Donahue still lived. He had never failed before. He spat a seething annulment through the telephone, "And nothing, Ken? We are through. Donahue is your problem now."

Ken Thompson said, "And, the resurrected Brendan Donahue implicated you by name in the death of Jack Richardson."

Thompson heard the other end of the telephone line bang; followed by a woman's distant cry, "Jonathan, what's wrong?" she called.

Ken Thompson continued, not knowing if Jonathan heard, "I believe you have one more task to complete before returning to Italy."

CHAPTER SIXTY-ONE

<u>Dallas, Texas</u>

Weekend room occupancy had been dismal all summer at the Rodeway Inn and Conference Center on North Highway 360 in Dallas . . . until yesterday when sixty-three rooms had been booked at the last minute by the Washington Glee Club. When the amateur singers checked-in, front-desk registration clerk Jeanie Babel remarked how nicely they dressed.

The Deputy Comptroller of the Currency tapped his gavel. Clamor in conference room B halved. Forty-five attorneys from Sidley & Austin's Chicago office had been rushed to Dallas by the FDIC. Sidley's for-hire attorneys would be on contract in Dallas for two weeks. Seven FDIC employees sat at the dais.

The FDIC would seize the Hamilton S&L with mercenaries. Seven United States Marshals stood; hands clasped behind their backs, they emitted chiseled law and order stares.

The Deputy Comptroller outlined seizure procedures; seal the bank records, dismiss Hamilton S&L employees, lock the doors. After they locked the Hamilton's doors, the attorneys would begin inspecting the records. He tapped again, requesting silence.

"Seven Hamilton S&L officers will be arrested this afternoon." Din ceased. Sidley's young attorneys perceived their 4 PM storming of the S&L as a cowboy adventure; arresting management spiced this Texas escapade.

The Deputy Comptroller continued, "These seven men on my left are United States Marshals. Warrants have been issued. Seven arresting teams will be assigned. Each team will consist of an FDIC official to explain, a US Marshall to arrest, and a Sidley attorney to secure all documents."

Tumult rumbled through the room.

Hush fell as the seven lucky lawyers were named. The younger Chicago attorneys exchanged back-slaps and a couple of "Yippee Kay-oohs."

"We seize the Hamilton at 4 PM. Remember, SEIZE," the man representing the Comptroller office said, "You are in absolute control from the moment you crash through the S&L's door. We will next meet as a group Sunday evening at 6 PM, right here. Any questions?"

One hand hoisted. A twenty-eight-year-old attorney from Sidley. He wore a grey wool suit; hand-tailored in Rome. Three monogrammed initials adorned the sky blue right cuff of his custom dress shirt. Polished black Balley shoes sparkled as clean as Switzerland; a double-Windsor knot cinched his silk Paisley tie tightly to the collar. His 24 karat ring tipped off others in the room that Princeton hadn't flunked anybody in the class of 82'.

The young Sidley attorney stood, "Sir, could we conduct our Sunday meeting at the Fairmont Hotel?"

"We are staying at the Rodeway," the Comptroller man said, "Why would we meet at another location?"

"This place is uncivilized," the Sidley attorney said, "last night I dined next to twelve people sharing a single room and a motor home parked outside. Their dinner resembled a food fight. Afterwards, I repaired to the terrace patio, where apparently orphans train hoping to gain admission to Wet & Wild. Room service, an inexcusable sandwich board, ends at 10 PM at this . . . this Rodeway?"

Most Delicious of Privileges

A smattering of applause supported Patrick's eloquence. He rested his case.

The Comptroller man asked, "What are you suggesting?"

"The Fairmont has twenty-four-hour room service, an excellent menu, and a superb wine selection. Their weekend rate is a very reasonable $129.00 a night. Some of us have taken a room at the Fairmont. Meeting there Sunday evening would be convenient."

"Who else in this room has checked into the Fairmont?" Approximately thirty of the Sidley hands signaled they had upgraded.

Treasury's Deputy Comptroller turned from the microphone, "Fucking prima donnas," he muttered under his breath.

He pulled the mike to his lips, "We'll meet here at 6 PM Sunday night." A groan followed.

He checked his watch. 2:56 P.M. "We will proceed to the Hamilton at 3:15."

Rodeway Inn, The Arresting Teams

"One Hamilton S&L official has government immunity. He or she has cooperated with Treasury on this investigation. Our informant will identify himself when you enter his office. Once identified, call me for confirmation."

"Then what?"

"You will parade our informant out of the S&L. His mock arrest has to appear legitimate. Treasury promised protection. To other S&L employees, our informant will be dragged away as a Hamilton crook."

"Why don't you tell us who has immunity?"

"Because information leaks. This way only three people know the identity of our informant," The Deputy Comptroller's eyes swept the seven three-man teams, "Not twenty-one people, not forty-five pampered Chicago lawyers staying at the fucking Fairmont Hotel."

"What do we do with your stool-pigeon?"

The Deputy Comptroller winced, "Bring him back here."

"Got it."

"Gentlemen, the seven people you are arresting are the big fish. They control the documents FDIC needs to prosecute. Move quickly. Don't let Hamilton's people react. Somehow management always seems to know the instant the Feds crash through their front door to seize the S&L. If the elevators don't work, run up the stairs."

CHAPTER SIXTY-TWO

The Hamilton S&L

Billy Johnstone stood at his window of his office inside the Hamilton S&L, his back to his desk.

Five floors below, Friday afternoon traffic escaped Dallas on the North Central Expressway. An early release program for weekend commuters.

The growing dilemma during the last six days gnawed from inside; either he had to betray his CEO or rebuild his own lost ethics. As Chief Operating Officer, he was walking the edge. Sooner always preceded later. His conscience, under twenty-four hour assault, refused the next step.

Johnstone ignored the seven-car parade as the vehicles drove into the Hamilton's parking lot one after another. From five floors above, the procession began to unfold as clearly as a Dallas Cowboy third-down passing play. Johnstone tracked fifteen plain cars parking randomly in the S&L's lot.

All rental cars, he thought.

Below, sixty well-dressed passengers emerged. They gravitated into one mass, a Friday afternoon get-together.

"Jesus Christ!" Billy Johnstone sprinted for his phone. He rammed in the three number extension for the Hamilton's main floor manager.

* * *

Heather read the small sign outside the door identifying Hamilton's Wire Transfer Department. The back of her neck pinched from cramping anxiety. She jerked to a stop in the hall, breathed deep, willed her hands to stop shaking, and pushed through the door.

Walls in the Wire Transfer room were constructed of concrete block, amplifying the ticking chatter from the teletype, requiring Heather to callout louder than she preferred, "Patti." Heather saw the three assistants spin their heads.

Reams of paper confirming the day's money relocations between the Hamilton S&L and their correspondent banks lay in undisciplined rolls behind the perpetual clicking printers. Patti Konger, Hamilton's overweight, red-headed Wire Transfer manager, whirled at Heather's call.

"Heather, don't see you in here often." Patti's loose green-print dress made no attempt at a tuck in the waist. Pedestrian traffic rarely walked into Wire Transfer. Patti's widening brown eyes trapped Heather in an expansive query.

"Patty, the Federal examiners are seizing the bank," Heather said, "They are in the first floor lobby, you can call the lobby to verify." Heather prayed that shock would prevent Patti from making such a call.

"Oh my God," Patti collapsed backwards to the edge of her ancient metal desk.

Heather lied, "Patti, the US Marshall has requested that you report to the first floor immediately. An FDIC man is there. Introduce yourself, tell him what you do, then wait for his instructions."

"Just leave the wire transfer room?" Patti said.

Heather pressed her quaking arms against her hips. She lied again, "I am to remain here for the short time it takes until the Feds secure this office. Now go. Take your assistants."

Patty didn't need to repeat Heather's instructions to her staff. Shock dampened Patti's trademark spunkiness She led the other three clerical lambs, who had swallowed Heather's every word, out the door with a confused hand motion indicating they follow her.

Heather's shivered at the chance the federal agents would burst into Wire Transfer, exposing her deception. She banked on priorities being confused as the Feds seized the S&L, confusion that would eclipse immediately sealing off Wire Transfer.

Staccato chattering from the four teletype machines ticked through the room. Heather sat in the swivel chair facing the dedicated line linking the Hamilton to Banker's Trust in New York City.

Her tight fingers pinged instructions, relaying her order through the dedicated phone line to mid-town Manhattan. She commanded that Banker's Trust transfer the money immediately to Banco Populare de Panama. Sweat rippled down her ribs as she validated her instructions by punching in Ken Thompson's four digit, three character authorization code sanctioning the transfer. Knowledge of the CEO's code had been confined to three people; Thompson the CEO; Patti, manager of Wire Transfer; and the Hamilton's head teller, Janis Lang. An hour ago Heather received the only code enabling Banker's Trust to transfer an unlimited amount of Hamilton money to other banks. Heather and Janis Lang had made a deal.

Sending the command, Heather shook her stiff fingers, trying to expel the stress. She begged the teletype, "Hurry, get this done."

Heather's eyes ping-ponged between the sweep second hand of the wall clock and the monitor screen wired into Banker's Trust Wire Transfer Department in Manhattan. Forty-five seconds later from a subterranean bank office in mid-town New York, an $18,000-a-year wire transfer clerk teletyped confirmation back to Dallas.

$40,000,000 CHRG TO HMLTN CRSPDNT ACCT. SENT BNC PPLR, COLON, PANAMA. ACCT NO. 7641-3429. 16:04. CNFRMD 16:08, CLRK BT-6159.

As the last digit typed, Heather ripped the hard copy acknowledgement and darted out the door of Hamilton's Wire Transfer Department.

* * *

"Leave the line open and your phone off the hook," said the Hamilton COO. For twenty-five seconds Billy Johnstone heard only Friday afternoon banking sounds from the first floor lobby inside the Hamilton S&L; then a tinny, distant voice through the receiver, "I am with the Federal Deposit Insurance Corporation. We are seizing control of the Hamilton S&L."

Chatter suspended. Billy hung up.

He galloped from his office to the elevator bank. He punched the buttons of each elevator control panel, commanding each unit to the fifth floor. As each elevator arrived, he jammed a chair between the open doors, locking down all units.

* * *

When Sidley attorney Janet Sellers ran 10K road races, she attracted a tailing pack of lean men. At her eight-minute-per mile pace the guys behind her loped along easily. Some Saturday morning jocks jogged all six miles behind the swaying blonde hair of the five-feet-eight woman with thirty-four-inch hips.

"Elevator is stuck on five. Dammit," the attorney swore.

The middle-age FDIC man assigned to her three-person arresting team jabbed the useless elevator button.

The US Marshal declared, "Let's use the stairs. We've wasted four minutes. Pete Morris could have started a bonfire by now."

* * *

Randy Peterson, the Hamilton SVP, hoisted his feet onto the top of his desk. The Athletic Club brochure intrigued him.

Gotta' lose twenty pounds, he thought.

Randy inspected the bodies of the two perfect tens lifting dumbbells in the club's color photo. He stood from his tattered chair, calling to his secretary as he walked out his office door, "You ever do this aerobics? Doesn't look too difficult."

Randy bumped into the first man.

"Randy Peterson?" the man asked.

"Yes," Randy said.

"This is US Marshal Andrews. You are under arrest."

* * *

Heather Montgomery divulged no emotion as the US Marshal began his droning speech. Heather weaved past him; the Marshall grabbed her arm. She rebuked him with her free right hand.

"Don't worry," Heather said as she closed the door to her office.

She turned and spoke in suppressed voice, "I am to instruct you that the Secretary of the Treasury has indemnified me."

Adrenalin pumping in the three men switched off. The twenty-four-year-old Chicago attorney picked up Heather's phone. He dialed the Rodeway Inn, verifying that the government's informant would soon be arriving.

* * *

The three-person team arresting Phil Kamerov, the Hamilton Workout guy, fucked up. Hamilton's first floor directory did not list the Workout Department. A bewildered teller recommended they try the fourth floor, but the elevators were locked down. The three men hoofed up the staircase.

"Pee-ul? He's in the goddam basement," Fat Randy Peterson, hands cuffed in front of him, betrayed his Workout guy. Randy shouted after the three men trotting to the stairwell, "Arrest Pee-ul, too. He's been a gawd-damn pain in the ass since the day he got here."

Their running, five-floor cascade, down to the Workout guy's office sapped their wind. The three-man arresting team staggered into Phil the Pill's office with scarlet faces, huffing.

"Phil Kamerov?" the Marshal said, sucking for oxygen

"Yes," said the Pill.

The 28-year old Sidley attorney, adorned with a Paisley neck-tie and a gold ring announcing Princeton, assigned to the three-man team arrived last. He circled the office, inspecting the shabby furniture; with disapproval he asked, "Is this your permanent office?"

"Yes," Phil the Pill answered the Sidley attorney.

The FDIC man resumed, "Phil Kamerov, you are under arrest. The Deputy US Marshal had collapsed against frayed green wallpaper, unable to speak. He just waved the warrant as evidence.

"Hold on," Phil the Pill said, "I have immunity."

"Good," said the Marshall, he crumbled onto the Pill's substandard two-seat couch.

Patrick, the Sidley attorney, disdained the available chair, continuing his assessment of The Pill's office, "Don't you have any art for your walls?"

Most Delicious of Privileges 333

"Hey, Chicago, don't be such a prick," the Marshall said, "Call the Rodeway, tell him our guy is the one with immunity."

* * *

Janet Sellers, the Sidley attorney, exploded into Pete Morris' office, well out in front of the other two members of her arresting team. Morris, preparing for his 4 PM meeting in Billy Johnstone's office, jumped to his feet.

"Pete Morris?" she said.

"What can I do for you?" the Hamilton VP said.

Janet didn't have any words to offer. Her role was to secure documents in Morris' office. The Deputy US Marshal would arrest, the FDIC man would explain. Neither had kept pace.

"Just a minute. stay right here," She barricaded the door with her willowy arms.

She searched back down the hall for the Marshall and the FDIC man. No sign of the either man.

* * *

Inside the Dallas, Rodeway, the four man team coordinating the S&L seizure was operating in controlled pandemonium. The Deputy Comptroller of the Currency hunched at his table. His FDIC counterparts scurried more chaotically than fourth graders at nearby Six Flags Over Texas.

Shouting into the live telephone in his left hand, the Comptroller man verified, "It's Montgomery. Heather Montgomery. She is the one who has immunity from the Secretary of the fucking US Treasury. Get her back here, now."

He crushed the telephone home. His assistant handed him another live telephone.

Patrick, the Sidley attorney, cheerfully spoke through the phone, "We've got the guy with immunity, chief. Phil Kamerov, the Hamilton's Workout guy."

"Kamerov doesn't have immunity," the Comptroller man said, "What the fuck is going on there?"

"Workout guy seems pretty confident," the young Sidley attorney said.

"Who does the Workout guy say granted him his fucking pardon?" asked the Deputy to the Comptroller of the Currency.

"Ahh, the Comptroller of the Currency's office, your office, sir," replied the Sidley attorney, "He's even got a name in Washington he wants us to call."

"Whose name?"

Patrick repeated the name of the Pill's contact at the Comptroller's office and said, "You guys ought to get your shit together before you storm these S&L"s."

"Fuck you. Haul Phil Kamerov's butt down here to the Rodeway, pronto."

"Have you reconsidered meeting at the Fairmont Sunday evening," the Sidley attorney asked.

The Comptroller man threw the telephone against the wall, "Mama-fucking-Mia. The right hand doesn't even know where the left hand is."

* * *

<u>Washington, D.C.</u>

Sweat drained from each man's forehead. "4 P.M. in Dallas. Let's go," the FDIC man said to his two associates.

Most Delicious of Privileges

For thirty minutes they had waited, communing in the haze on K Street. Washington DC's relentless summer heat sapped.

They pushed Ken Thompson's office door open and entered. They did not require Thompson to identify himself.

"Ken Thompson, you are under arrest," said the FDIC guy, "Charges stem from financial infractions relating to the Hamilton S&L. This is US Marshal Symkowski."

Thompson remained seated. He swiveled sideways from his desk, "I don't think so, gentlemen. You have obviously made a grievous mistake."

"There is no mistake. I am arresting you, Mr. Thompson," the Marshall said.

"You are making a mistake," the Hamilton CEO replied, "I have an agreement. Allow me a single phone call. You will be assured."

Thompson's reference staggered the resolve of the three-man arresting team. They did not expect the owner of the Hamilton to be the one with immunity.

"Make your phone call," the Marshall said.

Ken Thompson dialed; the other end of the line rang in the office building housing Washington's ultimate lawmakers.

Texas Senator Jim Anderson's secretary answered.

"Peggy, get me the Senator immediately," the CEO of the Hamilton said.

* * *

Washington, D.C.

The attorney to the Hamilton S&L saw the three men, one an attorney, enter the outer area of his DC office and surround his secretary. The attorney to the Hamilton and its CEO, Ken Thompson, could single-out a fellow lawyer from a hundred meters. He bounced from his desk to intervene.

"Is there a problem?" the Hamilton attorney addressed the newly arrived group of three.

"You are under arrest for crimes relating to the Hamilton S&L in Dallas," the US Marshall said.

"Come in my office, gentlemen," the Hamilton attorney said. He led the four-man parade, closing the door behind the group. He ignored the Marshal and the FDIC bureaucrat.

"Who are you?" the Hamilton attorney directed his question to the third man in the office.

"An attorney with Sidley, Austin. I'm assigned to the FDIC."

"You gentlemen apparently have not been well informed," said the Hamilton lawyer, "I have immunity from the Texas Department of Insurance."

The Marshal, Sidley attorney, and FDIC man traded an unspoken question. The Marshal spoke, "Nobody said anything about the Texas Department of Insurance."

"I am cooperating in TDI's investigation of Hamilton Insurance; the Drexel, Burnham junk bond, Nassau deal."

The FDIC man stumbled, "The immunity deal is through Treasury, not the Texas Department of Insurance."

The Hamilton attorney said, "If you will telephone this number, TDI will confirm our arrangement."

"Shit, wait until the Comptroller guy hears this!" said the FDIC guy, "Who wants to make this phone call?"

The US Marshal and the Chicago attorney declined.

* * *

The Hamilton S&L, 5th floor

Billy Johnstone listened and agreed as the Security and Exchange Commission man on the other end of the phone line outlined each demand. Billy confirmed, "As you proposed, you will receive copies of all correspondence relating to the junk bonds. I will identify the two Drexel vice presidents who authorized the Nassau Shores twenty-five million."

From New York, the SEC man explained the rules, "I am taping this conversation, Mr. Johnstone. Our offer has sat on your table for five days. This is not a game. Drexel has been eluding the SEC for some time. If you fail to provide the documents, I will bring obstruction charges against you."

Commotion in the hallway distracted Billy Johnstone from his phone conversation. His office door remained closed. He had instructed his secretary to deny entrance to everyone. Someone pushed against the door. The chair Billy had wedged under the inner knob held.

"I won't fail. I have the documents, letters and memos in my office," the Hamilton COO said, "I suggest you hop on a plane to Dallas pronto and retrieve my information."

"Consider it the SEC's information now, Mr. Johnstone."

"For the record, while we're on tape," Billy said, "let me repeat our agreement that the Securities and Exchange Commission will indemnify me against any and all charges relating to the Hamilton S&L."

"Through this date, providing the documentation is as you represent. That is the SEC's guarantee, Mr. Johnstone. You're lucky. Drexel is a bigger fish than you are. Overnight the documents to me."

"I'm afraid I won't be able to mail the documents," the Hamilton COO said, "The Hamilton S&L is being seized as we speak. In moments, the Feds will control your SEC documents. You better get here quick."

Wooden chair legs bowed, then snapped. Billy Johnstone's office door burst open; three men entered.

"Billy Johnstone, you are under arrest," the FDIC guy said.

"There is someone on the phone who wants to speak with you," Billy said as he handed the receiver to the baffled FDIC man.

* * *

<u>Washington, DC, office of the Hamilton S&L CEO</u>

Ken Thompson shouted through the telephone, "Peggy, get Senator Anderson on this goddam telephone."

Peggy sobbed. Her crying words flowed one syllable at a time, "Isn't, this, ter . . . ri . . . ble. Eighteen years." She blew her nose.

Thompson glared back at the doubtful eyes of the three accusing men standing in his DC office, "Peggy. I don't know what is so terrible, put the senator on this goddam telephone."

"I didn't know," the Senator's secretary convulsed, "Did you know, Mr. Thompson? I, I . . ." Her words fell away.

"Peggy, what the hell is going on there?" the Hamilton CEO demanded.

"Oh, Mr. Thompson, the news conference, Senator Anderson resigned. Just quit. Why? He is reading a statement on TV now. CNN is here. He is saying, his resignation, is . . . effective immediately."

"Shit!" Ken Thompson slammed the telephone down.

"Hands together, in front of you, Mr. Thompson," the Marshal said.

* * *

<u>Dallas, The Rodeway Inn</u>

A single telephone extension cord snaked down the hall at the Dallas, Rodeway Inn. The portable car phone had been lifted from the Rodeway manager's Buick Regal. All three phones operating in the command center at the Rodeway Inn were engaged.

Most Delicious of Privileges

Fifteen feet down the table, the FDIC man shouted to his Comptroller counterpart, "Arresting team one, at the Hamilton, says they are bringing in the guy with immunity."

The Deputy Comptroller of the Currency searched through disorganized papers for his assignment roster, "Surprise me, goddammit. Who has immunity now?"

The FDIC plugged the phone back into his ear. He scribbled for brief seconds, "Billy Johnstone, Hamilton's COO. The Securities and Exchange Commission in New York has just confirmed Johnstone's deal with our Marshal."

"Fucking A," screamed the Comptroller guy, "The COO of the S&L, he's our target. Get the SEC on the phone."

Standing in front of the Deputy Comptroller, the front desk assistant held back until their exchange ended; she winced at the Deputy Comptroller's vulgarity. Marcie was seventeen, serving as the afternoon registration clerk at the hotel was her first job. She felt invisible, despite standing two feet in front of him. She clasped her hands in front of her beige Rodeway blazer.

"Excuse me," Marcie interrupted so politely, he ignored her.

"Sonofabitches," the Comptroller guy said, "three people at this S&L think they've cut a deal for immunity."

Softly, she vied again for his attention, "Excuse me, sir. Are you the Deputy Comptroller?"

"Unfortunately, I am," he confirmed.

"There is a call holding for you at the front desk. The man said he is a US Marshal from your arresting team in Washington. It concerns the man with immunity."

"COCK-SUCK-ER," the Deputy Comptroller shouted.

Marcie gasped. In tears, she ran out of the conference room.

* * *

Government men tipped poorly. Water glasses in the Rodeway conference room remained empty. The coffee had been drunk. None of the Rodeway wait staff served the conference room voluntarily.

The Deputy Comptroller ignored the ringing phone; and FDIC assistant answered the incoming call.

"Headquarters in DC," the FDIC guy whispered.

The Deputy Comptroller listened to the Rodeway side of the FDIC's phone conversation with Washington.

The FDIC guy said, "The Deputy Comptroller is away for the moment, I'm taking his calls."

"Who?" said the FDIC guy.

"From whom?" said the FDIC guy

"Just a minute," said the FDIC guy.

He turned to the Comptroller man and asked, "Chief, you know about an immunity deal Hamilton's VP, Pete Morris, struck two days ago with the Dallas Fed Home Loan Bank?"

The DC shook his head wearily, "In-fucking-credible."

CHAPTER SIXTY-THREE

<u>Washington, D.C., The basement of the Treasury Building</u>

Secret Service agent Mollie Leep, shot her arm upward, stifling the four vigilant men into absolute silence.

Brendan, lifted the headphones, gently fitting them over his ears. Muffling his breath he listened to the tailing voice of Ken Thompson, CEO of the Hamilton S&L.

" . . . Jonathan, we have a problem, a problem that you will have to involve yourself with."

Waiting for the assassin to reply, Brendan felt his own heart beating, an awareness he had never before experienced. The Secret Service had been eavesdropping on the Hamilton CEO's Georgetown residence for two days. Treasury had not sought authorization to tap into the phone line. Before the Department of Treasury dethroned the CEO, his assassin had to be eliminated. And until now, the Secret Service hadn't been able to locate the man the Treasury Wiz had identified as the probable assassin; Jonathan Blair.

Brendan pressed his palms against the headphones, shutting out the noiseless room.

The assassin replied, "No Ken. My assignment is complete. I'm leaving for Italy this afternoon."

Brendan pressed the headphones tighter.

Down the long table, beneath the DC headquarters of the US Treasury, three Secret Service men studied a digital map of the eastern United States. The area on their screen zoomed to smaller geographic zones, enlarging the local detail with each leap. Technicians raced against time to track this call, to pin-point the location of the assassin. The computer screen leaped a fifth time, shrinking the map of New York State, narrowing in on telephone area code 212; Manhattan and the Bronx.

"Brendan Donahue is alive. He never died in Dallas," the Secret Service agents listened to the Hamilton CEO, their techies kept tracing to the source of the phone call.

Paralysis gripped Brendan's lungs as the CEO informed his assassin that Brendan had not died when the car bomb exploded in the Dallas parking lot.

"Locked," the Treasury techie pinging the monitor called.

The voices in Brendan's headphone dimmed until indistinct. Brendan strained to decipher Thompson's fading words.

"We're done here," Secret Service Mollie said, "What's the location?"

"New York City, 59th Street, St. Moritz Hotel," said the Treasury techie.

"Let's go," said the Secret Service woman. When Brendan didn't move she prodded, "Any doubts, Mr. Donahue?"

"None, none." Brendan rose, sapped of strength.

"Brendan, this is the man who killed Jack Richardson," Secret Service Mollie said, "Let's go!"

Manhattan

Cecille had insisted on window-shopping down the west side of Fifth Avenue. They reversed course at the city library and trickled back up the opposite side of Fifth Avenue, towards the Plaza Hotel. Three hours had passed since Jonathan had slammed the telephone off the wall in their room at the St. Moritz Hotel. Cecille watched Jonathan's mood decay into insulated seclusion. Jonathan had isolated her outside his inner-being. When he refused to discuss the call, Cecille stopped prying.

She led him by his hand, winding them through Fifth Avenue gawkers, elbowing him and issuing a smile when a young couple braked on the congested sidewalk for an unrehearsed kiss. Jonathan did not acknowledge. She had lost him. Cecille prayed that his feelings had been shoved, not lost, to some unknown. As they approached 58th Street she searched for words that could salvage the emotion she uncovered last night.

Jonathan spoke as they crossed at the common fronting the Plaza Hotel, "I have to leave you. I must return to Washington."

Cecille smothered her craving to beg him to stay, "Talk to me about it, Jonathan."

He stared straight-ahead through creeping yellow cabs, looking towards Central Park, "No."

"Jonathan, share your life with me," Cecille said.

"This part of my life doesn't share," he said, "Don't ask me to try."

She squeezed his hand and tried to pull him forward, across 59th Street.

Cecille pleaded, "I won't see you again if I let you go now."

Jonathan didn't respond.

"Come, walk with me, just for a few more moments," Cecille bumped into his chest, her arms surrounding Jonathan. She faced him, clenching him against to her, trying to thaw his stone facade. Cecille tucked into his chest, "Hold me, Jonathan, please."

He clutched her shoulders, but released her so quickly she protested, "No."

Releasing her, he yielded to her request. They entered the mid-town oasis; Central Park had assumed its daytime personality. Five minutes north of 59th Street's bustling traffic, Cecille stopped and looked up at Jonathan.

"Can you believe we're all alone? Not another person, not a sound of traffic," Cecille examined the only man to whom she had ever desired to commit herself.

The assassin looked past her.

"Talk to me goddammit, Jonathan. You are going to leave me and I don't know why," She beat her fists against his chest.

Jonathan Blair ended her drumming protest by tugging her close, stroking her silky black hair.

Cecille's stoicism fractured, her tears flowed, "Talk to me, what can I do?"

From a short distance a woman's command shattered the late morning serenity in Central Park, "Freeze. Don't move, Secret Service," orders enunciated with precision, "Jonathan Blair raise your hands," the woman called.

Jonathan's arms draped Cecille. She nuzzled into his chest, fearing the mysterious threat. He spun, his chest disappeared. Cecille's head snapped up as Jonathan Blair grabbed the back of her hair with one hand and yanked her face upward. The assassin's other hand shackled her neck. Facing the sky Cecille served as his armor. Wheeling in two quick gyrations, Cecille slanted her eyes downward and saw four people; three men and a woman.

One of the men ordered, "Surrender, Blair, you are under arrest by the US Secret Service."

Jonathan recognized Brendan Donahue, the man he failed to kill in Dallas, braced fifty feet away.

"And kill this woman?" the assassin said, "How would you explain her death?" His left forearm tacked Cecille against his chest. He absorbed her shivering. His right fist grasping her straight black hair slackened.

"The woman is expendable if that what it takes to arrest you," said Secret Service Mollie

Jonathan burned from the pain of using Cecille, "No, she is not expendable," the assassin said, "You and I understand that." He bent to Cecille's ear, "I am sorry. So sorry you'll never know." He agonized, wanting to free Cecille, to preserve this woman who loved him. Yet, without her physical shield he stood no chance of escape.

"Let her go, Blair," the Secret Service woman commanded, "She doesn't have to be harmed."

Jonathan released his straining grip on Cecille's hair, slinging his arm under her breasts he whispered, "I wanted to love you. Remember that."

Cecille pushed backwards, into his imprisoning arms, fusing herself into him, "Keep me," Cecille begged, "I'm your escape."

He disguised their inverted embrace, hoping Cecille appeared to be the locked hostage of his choking hold; not two lovers in a farewell embrace.

Molly Leep sighted down her Smith & Wessen, aiming eight inches below Jonathan's collar. She whispered low, "He won't let her go, she's his only chance out of this. "

Brendan whispered in response, "He has to let her go. Every man has his Achilles; she is his."

Secret Service Mollie said, "Brendan, remember this man has been commissioned to kill you. If he challenges our arrest, hit the ground, quickly." Drawing a bead with her right eye, the Secret Service woman edged her weapon a degree to the right, squinting down the sight at Jonathan Blair's chest, "He won't let her go," she said, "killers profile the same, Brendan, no emotional attachment."

Standing rigid, Secret Service Mollie shouted across fifty feet of stomped grass, "Blair, last request, let her go. Hands in the air."

Her demand crackled through Central Park, snapping Jonathan's attachment from Cecille. He wrenched Cecille into his chest and whispered, "I have the information on your uncle in my top pocket. Remember that."

"No, Jonathan. I don't want to remember, I want you."

Jonathan shouted back, "Save your commands, we're walking out of here."

"No you aren't Blair," The Secret Service woman's unequivocal denial refused Jonathan escape, "We will stop you."

Jonathan kissed the back of Cecille's neck. He buried his face against her skin and breathed in the vanilla oil moistening her skin. His eyes closed for an instant, "I have never felt so alive." The assassin listened to Cecille's sobs, felt warm tears splash on his forearm. "It never could have been any other way Cecille," he said, "I met you too late."

"Use me Jonathan," Cecille said, "We can get away, we can be together somewhere else." She swiveled her head, locking into his eyes.

The assassin met her stare and spoke, "There is nowhere else for me. Remember the information in my pocket," Jonathan swallowed, "Remember Cecille, remember that I only loved once in my life." Grabbing her wrist he yanked her in a violent corkscrew and whip-sawed her away. Cecille tumbled in a heap ten feet from him.

Jonathan plunged his right hand into the inner pocket of his jacket.

Brendan dove flat-out onto the bare turf. Secret Service Mollie Leep's single shot boomed through south Central Park before Brendan skidded to a landing. Sniffs of smokeless cordite powder scented the air. Brendan's sight raced back to the assassin. The Secret Service woman's reflexive shot had shattered Jonathan Blair's chest.

Cecille whipped her eyes back to Jonathan as the lead bullet thumped through flesh. She recoiled in isolated horror as his arms fluttered. Jonathan staggered backwards a half-step, his fingers surrendering the envelope. A puff of wind floated the paper towards her as he collapsed. Despair collided with love, creating within Cecille a chaotic denial. Her screaming rejection pitched beyond the scale of human hearing.

"Nnnoooooo!"

On her knees she crawled in anguish, her fingers scraping Central Park's matted soil. Cecille crawled forward in a shrouded pilgrimage.

Brendan reached Jonathan Blair before Cecille. He bent and picked up the envelope. One name addressed the envelope; Cecille. He pealed open the envelope and read the FBI profile on the general serving in Castro's army.

Washington, D.C.

Sitting at his desk in the National Security Agency, he traced electronic money transfers leaving United States banks for deposit in Panama. Every day he screened the dedicated phone lines into thirty-seven Panamanian banks, trying to follow drug money to the source of the product. At 4:04 PM his screen flashed that $40 million dollars had zipped out of Banker's Trust in New York City.

The NSA computer prioritizes information on emigrating dollars. The largest transfers pop to the top of his computer screen. Amounts exceeding $10 million flash in yellow letters. When the sum transferring is greater than $25 million, the information defaults into capital letters.

"Three-alarmer, Banker's Trust. $40 mill into Banco Populare," the NSA agent barked.

"Name?" his boss demanded.

"No name. Numbered account." The Treasury man's tapping fingers called the known-account list into a window on his monitor. He whistled, "Oh, oh! No match on anything we've seen before. New account at Populare. Set-up yesterday."

"Give me the account number at Populare," his boss at the National Security Agency said.

The National Security Agency man hollered the number, "Better hurry, this looks like slippery money."

His boss already had Banker's Trust on the other phone line.

Dallas, The Rodeway Inn

The FDIC guy sharing oversight of the seizure of the S&L called to the Deputy Comptroller of the Currency, "Chief, it's Morales, the Marshal we sent to the Hamilton's Wire Transfer room."

The Deputy Comptroller grabbed the phone, "What the fuck did you find?"

"Nothing. Wire Transfer is empty," reported the US Marshal.

"Jesus Christ, Morales," the Comptroller man said, "somebody wired $40 million through Banker's Trust from that fucking S&L twenty minutes ago, after our guys started seizure procedures. The instructions came from that room."

"No one is here, Chief. There is no verification of transfer, no goddam hard copy. The woman who runs Wire Transfer won't talk, except to say that she and her three assistants left the room just before 4 pm."

"She's lying," the Deputy Comptroller said.

"They are telling the truth," the Marshal replied, "We logged-in the four Wire Transfer people in the S&L's main lobby at 4:01, three minutes after we came through the door."

"Goddamit, what time did we seal off Wire Transfer?" The Comptroller guy asked.

"Well, that's a problem. We didn't seal it off, not until you called with the news that the $40 mill had been wired out. Nobody understood that fucking Wire Transfer had been abandoned."

"What else could go fucking wrong at that S&L today?" The Comptroller guy said.

"Chief, maybe we can pin it down," the Marshall said, "I tracked the authorization code. Guess who?"

The Comptroller man at the Rodeway command center said, "Morales, this isn't fucking Wheel of Fortune."

"Ken Thompson," said the US Marshal from inside the Wire Transfer room at the Hamilton S&L, "the CEO of this place, maybe he executed the transfer himself."

"Thompson is under arrest in Washington DC. Christ, $40 million slips away after we seize the fucking S&L."

CHAPTER SIXTY-FOUR

South Ocean Bahamas Resort and Country Club is a thirty-minute ride from Nassau's downtown straw market. Arriving guests walk under a fifteen-foot portico through an ambient hall. The covered walk by-passes reception and leads to the pool terrace. Emerging from the arcade, South Ocean's blue pool ripples as the Gulf Stream pours in from the east. Beyond the terrace, the sand stretches a hundred feet down to the shore.

The late lunch pool-side terrace hummed. Chaise loungers and chatting diners filled the clay tile pool terrace. Golfers, dressed in colors they wouldn't wear at home, joked at the bar. Sunbathers abused their skin along the outer reaches of the terrace. Fifteen-knot gusts plucked conversation and indiscreetly carried the gossip to ambivalent third parties.

The bartender's shirt was an explosion of Bahamian color; matching the yellow, red, and blue drinks he mixed.

The trade winds snatched the Texas accent, broadcasting the twang towards the bar. Yet, only an occasional word escaped from their group of four.

"Back to Toledo," Peter Morris shrugged, "Not glamorous, but it's home. I've had my fill of deals, power and Texas? Dallas is not for me. I get a second chance."

Pete Morris, former Vice President of the Hamilton Savings & Loan, tilted his face to absorb the penetrating midday Bahama sun. His teal blue shirt, Ocean Pacific shorts and Asic running shoes were all purchased the day before. Peter Morris, once a hotshot dealmaker at Dallas' most notorious S&L, fondled the euro-dollar certificate in his cargo pocket.

Nine million dollars in the Grand Cayman branch of London's National Westminster bank, Pete thought.

Each week the NatWest bank trustee was instructed to purchase another seven-day US Treasury bill in a nominee name and deposit the previous week's interest in Peter Morris' personal account. Last week Pete earned $9,500; he'd earn another $9,500 this week. The Grand Cayman's do not tax income.

A gust of wind tousled Heather's dark hair, "It will work for you, Pete," she said.

Heather turned to the smallish man, "Phil, you've been quiet?"

Phil the Pill Kamerov, Hamilton's once-upon-a-time Workout guy, scraped the folded paper in his right hand against the bare flesh of his thigh; his deposit receipt from Scotiabank. He never expected to be rich. Three days ago Heather delivered startling news; $9,000,000 had been deposited in his name at Lloyd's Bank in Nassau.

"District 11," the Pill said, "the Federal Home Loan Bank in San Francisco, is in deep financial caca, Heather. They asked me to join them as a special agent on S&L examinations. Some of their California S&L's are as messed up as the Hamilton was."

Heather raised her eyebrows.

"What the fuck," the Pill said, unexpectedly, "I like being *The Pee-ul*. I start next week."

The Pill nodded towards Billy Johnstone, the former Chief Operating Officer of the Hamilton S&L.

Billy Johnstone confirmed with a Texas accent, "We start next week." Billy lassoed his index finger at the black waitress approaching their table. His gesture saved her ten steps. The waitress rotated back to the bar to re-order her table of four another round of early afternoon drinks.

Heather Montgomery asked wide-eyed, "Billy, you and Phil are both going to work for the California Fed Home Loan Bank?"

The former COO extended his right hand, "Partner," Billy said. The two former Hamilton executives grinned at Heather and Pete Morris.

Billy Johnstone explained, "They wanted someone who could get inside the head of the guys driving their S&L's to the verge of collapse."

"What about you, Heather?" Pete Morris asked, "Where should we send your invitation for the annual reunion to celebrate our," Pete Morris grappled for words to describe their unusual exodus, "our graduation from the Hamilton?"

Heather's short brunette hair had been trimmed almost boyish. Her ivory shorts exposed three quarters of each tan, athletic leg. She had been holed-up on New Providence Island for a week. Heather had lost six pounds on her Bahamian diet of Conch and Grouper. Her royal blue blouse had captured the attention of each golfer seated on the distant stools at the bar. Heather, at twenty-eight years, looked her age today.

"Not a chance of a reunion, Peter," Heather said, "not a chance."

Heather recalled her letter written by the Secretary of the Treasury absolving her from all culpability in the Hamilton S&L. Yesterday, she had transferred eight million nine hundred thousand dollars to Credit Lyonnais in Paris. Inside the purse slung over her left shoulder was a traveler's letter of credit for five hundred thousand French Francs and American Express travelers checks for another hundred grand in the French currency.

"But, if you pass through Guadeloupe in the French West Indies, wander out to the Club Med in St. Anne. I'll be there until," Heather had committed through the winter season, "until I tire of West Indies sunshine. After that . . ." Heather tossed both hands, palms up, in the air.

Pete Morris asked, "Club Med? A permanent vacation?"

Heather wrapped her smile around the clear straw as she sipped the last of her golden drink, "No, Club Med is going instructional. I am the *gentil organiseur* of Finance," Heather said, "I will instruct a beach-side session on financial investments for forty-five minutes each week day. I get room and board . . . no salary. A new life, a new country. If you guys can't visit, don't write."

The Bahamian waitress returned with four drinks. Heather accepted her second Yellow Bird. Phil the Pill got the bright Virgin Mary. Pete Morris reached for his clear vodka and tonic before the waitress could set the highball glass on the table. Billy Johnstone's locally brewed Kalik beer was sweating in its see-through bottle.

"Here's to us!" offered Billy Johnstone, "And here's to you, Heather."

Heather raised her glass, acknowledging each man's silent thanks for his nine million dollars. She sipped her mixture of crème de banana liquor, rum and tropical fruit.

Billy Johnstone, former Chief Operating Officer, said, "Too bad about Randy Peterson."

Peter Morris, former VP, drained half the gin and tonic. Moisture dripped from his tall cocktail glass darkening his teal blue golf shirt, "Well, Randy did accept the Rolex watch."

The Pill, ex-chairman of Hamilton's Workout Committee stirred his Virgin Mary, "And Randy accepted $25,000 from the Denver loan broker connected to the Silverado S&L. It was a bribe; the Denver loan broker kicked-back twenty five grand from the loan proceeds to Randy."

Billy Johnstone added, "Double-R controlled the slush fund we set up to pay delinquent interest," Billy closed his eyes against the trade-winds and knocked back the Kalik.

Heather Montgomery gibed, "Yeah, Billy, but you instigated the slush fund."

Billy Johnstone inspected the three remaining ounces of the amber Bahamian beer. "Randy Peterson should have known better; he thought it was his way to a promotion."

"How much time will Randy spend in jail?" Peter Morris asked.

Phil the Pill wiped harmless non-alcoholic tomato juice from his lips, "The guys in San Francisco say maximum fifteen years, minimum of five."

"You know, Phil," Heather confessed. "I wasn't sure in the final days if you were working for the FDIC, or you were reporting directly to Ken Thompson."

The Pill ogled the frosty, Kalik beer in front of Billy Johnstone. "Heather, we discussed the FDIC. That was our strategy."

"No, we always talked about Washington," Heather said, "That could have been the CEO, Ken Thompson."

Heather asked herself, *I wonder if these guys know I wired $40 million dollars of Hamilton S&L money to Panama that last day, not the $36 million we split.*

"What's going to happen to Ken Thompson?" Heather asked.

The Pill, Hamilton's former Workout guy, soon to join California S&L regulators, said, "The judge denied bail; decided that Ken Thompson is a flight risk."

Phil Kamerov conducted his own internal conversation, *Nine million dollars, stowed across the border in Canada, living in Canada would be okay.*

The Pill continued, "At fifty-two years old, Ken might never get out of jail."

Heather asked, "Phil, the newspapers didn't mention Janis Lang. Did she cut a deal?"

Phil the Pill swirled his warming Virgin Mary. "Our head teller, Janis, negotiated her own deal with the Comptroller of the Currency. Janis couldn't stop herself, she had to tell someone she took the money. She told me. After the Hamilton was seized, she told the Feds."

The Hamilton's former Workout guy continued, "Comptroller's office made Janis a deal; spill all she knew, give the money back and she would walk. Janis Lang told them what she knew."

Peter Morris clanked gin scented ice cubes around his empty glass, "So, Janis Lang gave it all back?"

The Pill pivoted uncomfortably in his deck chair, "If she did, she's off the hook."

Heather goaded, "Pee-ul, you're not telling us something."

The Pill averted her question, he continued, "Before the Hamilton was seized, Janis told me about taking the money. She asked if she could keep the money. I pointed out, she risked going to jail."

"She would never have gotten away with keeping the money," Pete Morris said.

"Maybe not, unless the owner of dormant checking account was dead," The Pill said, "a statistical probability on some of the accounts. Close the account, clear out all money with a cashier's check payable to CASH, omit the remitter on the Hamilton's copy of the cashier's check. Correspondence from the Hamilton to the deceased halts, Hamilton stops reporting to the IRS, if the Cashier's check clears before the Hamilton was seized . . . the account would be buried."

"Pee-ul did you explain this to Janis?" Pete Morris asked.

"Maybe we don't want to know," Billy Johnstone, former COO said. Billy Johnstone raised a lazy hand for a third round of drinks. "Don't understand how Ken Thompson let himself get so far out on a limb. When the Texas senator resigned, Ken Thompson's support was yanked out from under him?" The ex-COO of the defunct Hamilton shook his head. Ken Thompson had been his mentor, until Billy Johnstone understood Thompson was using him.

The bar waitress arrived.

"What are those large red drinks?" Phil the Pill pointed at a nearby table.

"Goombay Smash. Dey good, mon, but very strong. Made wid Vat rum," the Bahamian waitress replied.

"Goombay Smash for me," said the Pill.

"Me, too," Heather said.

Phil Kamerov returned to the COO's question, "I was feeding info to Treasury, to the number two guy at the Dallas Fed Home Loan Bank, guy in charge of S&L exams. When he got canned, he took documents and details on a $21 million loan guaranteed by the new head of FDIC. The new FDIC head had quashed the Hamilton exam; his $21 mill loan with the Hamilton S&L was in default. The Dallas Fed guy passed the delinquent loan info to Brendan Donahue. Donahue gave the whole story to the *Washington Post* piranha, Jack Anderson. The Post published just ahead of the Senate confirmation hearing for the new FDIC chair.

"So, Ken Thompson's puppet at the FDIC resigned rather than face fifty US Senators?" Pete Morris asked,

"More like forty-five Senators," Heather said, "Five guys in the Senate were acting as cheerleaders for the S&L industry."

Phil the Pill continued, "Next, Brendan Donahue threatened the Texas Senator that he would feed the *Washington Post* facts on $800,000 that Ken Thompson dropped into the senator's campaign fund. An envelope delivered by Randy-Randy. By the time the Feds arrested Ken Thompson, his DC support system had been dismantled."

"You guys left Ken high and dry," the former COO said.

Billy Johnstone instructed the waitress delivering round three of drinks, to put it on his tab. Wedged in his shirt pocket was an envelope-size airline ticket to Zurich via London. He would depart Nassau at 4 P.M. this afternoon. The tattered brown briefcase under his left foot protected a negotiable letter of credit from the Nassau office of the Barclay's Bank. Tomorrow at 2 P.M. Billy Johnstone had an appointment at Credit Suisse. He planned to deposit his severance pay. Johnstone's nine mill would never touch the shores of America.

Heather sipped her Yellow Bird.

Most Delicious of Privileges

The rolling Atlantic had become bluer, the wind settled. She surveyed the sea's horizon, where illusionary waves leapt improbably high. Splashing from the pool, cloaked their privacy.

Over the horizon, southwest from the South Ocean Beach Club bar, the Bahamian out-islands separated Heather Montgomery from the Greater Antilles.

Heather said, "What happened to Brendan Donahue?"

No one at the table could answer her question.

PENULTIMATE CHAPTER

"Here's your mail, *Emily's List*," The mailman said. He thumped eight letters on her desk.

"Thanks, George. Hot outside today?" She didn't look up at the friendly, fifty-ish, black US Postal Service man. Every day the temperature outside hurdled ninety degrees, George brought the mail inside.

"Like an oven," George the postal carrier said.

Dust-blue shorts quarreled with his faded US-issue postal-turquoise shirt. Black socks and scuffed, thick-soled walking shoes completed the mailman's uniform. He was not the best dressed man on Washington DC's 16th Street.

"Maureen, what kind of a name is *Emily's List* for a business?" the mailman asked, "What kind of business do you all do?"

"We're a women's donor network," she said, "A political action committee."

The mailman's wrenching face suggested that her explanation had sailed a foot over his head.

She tried again, "*Emily's List* raises money for women trying to win election to Congress. Like Barbara Mikulski, our woman senator from Maryland."

"Don't understand why womens needs hep. They run the world now," the mailman said.

Maureen Mulcahy had joined *Emily's List* three years ago, just after Ellen Malcolm had founded the political organization for women candidates. Malcolm force-fed her nascent political idea through its embryo phase. *Emily's List* had funneled $350,000 to women in the 1986 election.

Maureen mimicked the mailman's chauvinistic sarcasm, kindly, "We needs hep, George, because we've only got twelve women in the US House. The number of women in Congress has been declining for fifteen years." She sorted through the mail, searching for incoming money.

Three years since *Emily's List* began . . . and balancing the checkbook was still a monthly adventure.

"Can't remember when a woman didn't run my life," the mailman said.

Inside the thin Riggs National Bank window-envelope, the folded notice loomed. *Not* an *overdraft!* Her heart skipped. She ripped the bank envelope open.

The postman jumped at her cry.

"Jesus, Mary, and Joseph!" She slashed at the telephone that could link her with Riggs National Bank's, 16th Street branch.

"I'm positive. Riggs Bank confirmed it," Maureen said to her boss, "There is no mistake, Ellen."

Ellen Malcolm, founder of *Emily's List* is a realist as well as a feminist. There were no tooth fairies. Malcolm committed her political fund raising machine, *Emily's List,* to electing ten pro-choice Democrat women to Congress this year.

Ellen collapsed behind her desk, "That's all it said, Maureen?"

"I asked the wire transfer clerk at Riggs Bank at least ten times," Maureen said, "It simply said, *For women, they will enact wiser banking law than the male Congressional classes of 1980 through 1986. Contributed in memory of Julie Weidener*. Riggs Bank says the money came from a numbered account in the Bahamas. And that's all they say."

"Who is, was . . . Julie Weidener?" the founder of Emily's list asked.

"I don't know, Ellen. But $4,000,000 was wire transferred into *Emily's List* bank account, $4,000,000 that can elect women to Congress . . . in Julie Weidener's name."

LAST CHAPTER

OUR CATS FLY read the logo over the entrance door leading into the lobby of SunCat Sail headquarters in Clearwater.

"Mr. Donahue. We've been expecting you. Follow me." The lobby receptionist jumped to her feet before Brendan could introduce himself.

The receptionist led Brendan down a short, narrow hall, then extended her arm. She pointed to the small office of Jay Goldberg, Chief Executive Officer of SunCat.

"Mr. Donahue, right on time. Have a seat," Goldberg offered.

"Thank you," Brendan said.

"It's not every day the Secretary of the Treasury calls me to introduce a client. How might we serve you?"

SunCat's CEO wore a short-sleeve red pullover, loose-fitting beige slacks, and the obligatory rubber-soled moccasins designed for traction on a wet, fiber-glass boat deck. Goldberg leaned against the corner of his desk with his arms folded.

"I need a boat," Brendan said.

"We have dealers," Goldberg paused, directed his gaze into Brendan's eyes, and waited for his unspoken question to be answered.

"This boat requires unusual specs. The design will be unique and the cost to fabricate will price the boat outside the range your typical customer might expect to pay," Brendan said.

"Why did you select SunCat?" The CEO was intrigued.

"Because your Cats Fly"

Brendan let the executive enjoy the compliment, "And your chief engineer has a unique background."

How did he obtain that information?, the SunCat executive asked himself.

"What you have in mind, Mr. Donahue."

* * *

Three months later. Paso De Los Vientos. Cuban waters

When the ensign rapped on the stateroom door to Brendan Donahue's cabin, the working freighter was rounding Punta Maisi on the eastern shore of Cuba. Three knocks and then nothing. Sleep had never come. Brendan rose from the chair and walked to her bed. When he touched Cecille's shoulder, her eyes popped open.

"Time," he said.

"Finally it is time." She rose, walked to a wall with no mirror and squeezed her eyes shut.

* * *

SunCat Sail, Clearwater

Mike Novak had been on the job as chief engineer for SunCat for eight months. Treasury's computer wiz tracked him down. The government file defined Novak's previous job description as Structural Composite

Analysis, Stealth Engineering, United States Navy; *on loan to Northrup Industries*. His current resume simply read; Engineering.

Novak led Brendan on a thirty minute tour of SunCat's manufacturing plant explaining technical feasibility.

Novak, at twenty-eight, combined naval experience with technology expertise. Brendan posed the only question that mattered, "Can the technology be applied?"

"To a boat?" SunCat's Chief Engineer asked.

At the engineer's incredulous response Brendan's enthusiasm waned.

Mike Novak didn't wait for Brendan to retort. The engineer's blue eyes danced. "Already is, Mr. Donovan. The British, as well as our Navy, have extensive naval stealth research in beta test. Stealth technology won't hide a vessel within visual range. But, on a moonless night, well, the bad guys on shore will get a hell of a jolt when the sun rises."

* * *

<u>Cuban waters</u>

From the exterior wing of the bridge, Brendan gauged the cargo freighter was pointing at two-hundred-sixty degrees; bearing west and maintaining enough separation from land to be safely in international waters. The trade winds that distinguished the passage between Cuba and Hispaniola had dropped to five knots apparent on-deck. The 20,000 ton vessel motored with a following sea at seventeen knots.

"How much longer?" Brendan asked the Captain.

"Those are the lights of Guantanamo," The captain's hand went to two o'clock. "Ten miles west is your drop, my friend."

"Are you sure?"

"I've sailed this passage to Jamaica longer than you've been a man."

The dark man's calypso voice left no room for doubt.

* * *

<u>SunCat Sail, Clearwater</u>

"You'll be commissioning an expensive little sail toy. A hell of a lot pricier than anything SunCat has ever constructed," the engineer said.

Each man pulled a chair and sat facing each other at a table in the vacated employee lunch room. The spotless floor glistened a layer of enamel covered the concrete. Their voices ricocheted through the room, they spoke in low tones.

"Do you want to know the price?" asked the SunCat engineer.

"No, I want to know when the boat will be ready," Brendan said.

"How sophisticated you want to get. Tell me what you want the radar picture to look like; I can give you the time-line by the end of the day."

"That quick?"

"Yes, sir. Mr. Donahue, I've done this, something like this, before. The crux is your technology trade-off versus increased visibility?"

"I don't want to be seen. Period," Brendan said.

"Impossible. You'll always be visible," The engineer countered the challenge. "I can reduce your radar cross-section. I can't eliminate apparent size. To halve your radar profile, the vessel's cross-section must be cut ninety-four percent. We can achieve satisfactory reduction of detective range. Three sensory factors determine . . ."

Brendan cut-off Novak's dissertation, "Whoa, Mr. Novak. Go slow. I'm not an engineer."

"Sorry, Mr. Donahue. Naval stealth was my life, my passion. Seems like . . . like an old girlfriend, who once jilted me, has returned."

"Another thing. Don't call me Mr. Donahue. It's Brendan."

"Yes, sir. Yes, Brendan. Anything else?" the engineer said.

Brendan continued, "Yes. Halving the boat's profile is not good enough. I don't want to be seen."

"You don't want to be recognized, Brendan," corrected the younger man. "We'll disguise the signature of the boat by reducing apparent size."

"Go slow, Mike," Brendan commanded.

"First, we'll redesign the craft to avoid efficient reflectors," SunCat's engineer sketched on his pad of yellow legal-size paper as fast as he spoke.

"Will I lose any sea worthiness?" asked Brendan.

"Negligible, there will be some loss of convenience. I'll eliminate flat surfaces, cavities, sharp angles and irregular protrusions. Below the water line all marine engineering will remain intact. Any questions?" The SunCat engineer waited.

"I'm hanging with you," Brendan said.

"Second, the hull, mast, and rigging will be manufactured from absorptive or refractive material. The hull won't be too costly. However, if we cast the rigging from gold, it would probably be cheaper than what we're going to manufacture," Novak finished scribbling. He looked up.

"Keep going," Brendan said.

"The next item is tricky. The Air Force has developed a paint that digests radar. You can't buy this stuff at the hardware store. I might be able to," Novak's broke into a devious grin. Brendan recognized the grin as the engineer's seal of assurance, "to requisition a few gallons."

"I don't think I want to know how you accomplish that."

"You don't and you won't, "the SunCat engineer said, "Lastly, I am going to hide your electromagnetic signature," Novak paused, "Now, let's balance the technical trade-offs with a cost you can tolerate."

Brendan looked at Mike Novak, "There will be no technical trade-offs."

* * *

Cuban waters

In the moonless night the ship's crane timorously lifted its unwieldy cargo. Thumping combustion from the diesel disturbed the blanket of night. On the open Caribbean Sea, twelve miles from Cuba's south shore, the cargo freighter slow danced to and fro.

Brendan Donahue dug his left hand under the canvas harness strap as the composite SunCat elevated off the deck of the ship. The crane operator held the sailboat twelve inches above the freighter deck. Satisfied that the crane's sling would support his small boat, Brendan extended his right hand.

"Here," he said.

Cecille reached for his hand, grasped, and climbed to the tarpaulin.

"Is this the most dangerous?" she asked.

"I would like to tell you yes," He flicked the pencil flash just once towards the crane operator, "Hang on."

Brendan guided her hands under the rayon hand hold.

The crane's hum went up-scale an octave as the pricey SunCat rose above the deck of the *S.S. Madrigal.* Cecille buried her right arm under the rayon hand hold, and dug the top of her feet under the strap running the length of the tarp. She welcomed Brendan's arm when he clamped her tight.

He said, "Pretend you're on a swing in the park."

The crane's slow rhumba refused to follow the non-synchronous rhythm of the ship. The stealthy catamaran was hoisted, swung astern, then lowered over the side of the ship.

* * *

<u>SunCat Sail, Clearwater</u>

"Is this a black project?" asked Mike Novak, SunCat's engineer, "Can we discuss the strategic objectives of the craft?"

"No, Mr. Novak, it isn't black. Although there are people who do NOT want to know what I am doing."

The engineer did not follow up.

Brendan perused Michael Novak, "Why did you leave Northrup?"

"Because instead of building the B-2, the government paid me to sit on my ass."

"A lot of people might envy such a position," Brendan said.

"Not at twenty-seven years old. Northrup sectionalized the teams working on the B-2. When one compartment couldn't overcome a technical dilemma, the next compartment sat. Sat and waited, playing gin rummy."

"What were you working on?"

"Materials engineering," said the SunCat engineer, "We were experimenting with composites and ceramics to optimize strength, absorption, and weight of structural material."

"Sounds to me like you could stay busy twenty-four hours a day. What kept you sitting instead of working?"

"Concurrence, an Air Force policy. B-2 aircraft were produced before testing was fully complete."

"How do you fly a B-2 before testing is finished?" Brendan asked.

"You don't, *concurrence* doesn't work for high-tech projects."

"What went wrong?"

"Northrup had the B-2 program compartmentalized," the engineer said. "One engineering team didn't know what another team was doing," Novak let out his frustration for the first time since he had left Northrup, "The B-2 design wasn't just a new generation; stealth is an innovation. The first proto required a 'fly-by-wire' computer control system to compensate for the unconventional aerodynamic controls. When the computer adjusted the aerodynamics in flight, the structural composites fractured. The extensive wiring the computer required leaked electronic noise like a foghorn. Electromagnetic emission was more readily recognized than radar."

"What did Northrup management do?" Brendan asked.

"Wasn't their money being wasted. Programmers tested while material twiddled our thumbs. Material worked while the aerodynamics well, you get the picture."

Two weeks had passed since Brendan Donahue had given the SunCat engineer the go-ahead. Brendan stroked the gray, starboard, honeycombed hull in SunCat's design shop.

Novak explained, "Instead of extending to the deck, the rudder will end twenty-four inches below the tiller arm."

"What's that do?" Brendan asked.

"Keeps the flat surface below the water line, so it can't reflect." Mike Novak's hands coddled the partially completed boat. This Design area had been off-limits to all others the past fourteen days.

"I've eliminated the overhang on top of the pontoons. You won't have as much protection from splashing waves, but potential concave radar whip from the joint, should the boat lift onto a single hull, is voided."

Brendan's hand slid along the ashen carbon fiber hull, "What are the fittings made of?"

"Ceramic. We've shrunk the radar cross-section by ninety-seven percent."

"Looks like . . . like a sailboat. What am I going to notice when I'm sailing that's different from a stock SunCat?"

"The deck will be slippery. The top of the pontoons have more curve. There won't be as much noise. The ceramic fittings and carbon fiber stays eliminate metallic stress."

"Do you guarantee that I'll be able to slip ashore undetected?"

"The only bad guys developing anti-stealth are the Ruskies. Are you assaulting Russia?"

Brendan responded, "No, but Russian technology may be photographing me."

I was right, thought the SunCat engineer. *This baby is sailing into Cuba. Well, Fidel,* Mike Novak said to himself, *too bad you won't be able to see what America can produce.*

"Anything else different?"

"It'll be the strongest goddam catamaran on the seas. The composite material will withstand any waves you dare test. And, it will be faster than our stock boats. The graphite in the composite reduces friction with the water."

"Were you able to procure the non-reflective paint?" Brendan asked.

Novak's face broadened into his signature grin. He pointed to two unmarked five-gallon drums in the corner.

"I have a suggestion. You wanted black. I recommend navy blue. The blue won't look any different than black at night . . . and during the day blue will camouflage the boat from overhead surveillance."

"Navy blue it is. Have you got a final cost?"

Novak released the compartment door located starboard at mid-hull, where metal antennae of the Global Positioning System would be installed.

"Brendan, I hope you're a wealthy man."

* * *

<u>Cuban waters</u>

The freighter's crane swung the navy blue craft towards a landing in the Caribbean Sea. *Jesus, don't drop this,* Brendan prayed.

Since departing Miami, Brendan had taken eight readings from the GPS located inside the port pontoon. Each reading matched the location indicated on the Global Positioning System of the mother ship.

Brendan recalled his last conversation with the SunCat engineer as the catamaran was loaded onto the truck bed.

"Good luck," Novak massaged his creation. Visible pride manifested as the engineer's vessel was loaded.

Brendan extended his hand, "Thanks."

Novak hesitated, "Brendan, maybe I'm out of line, but you said this is not a classified project. After it's over, stop back someday and tell me what we've . . . what you've done."

"I will," Brendan expected Novak's grin of appreciation. "Mike, you promised me a final analysis of my profile."

"Here is the read-out, Brendan. Your radar cross-section has been reduced 98 percent." Novak handed Brendan five printed pages.

"Mike, give me the bottom line. What am I going to look like on a radar screen from a half mile off shore."

Mike Novak cocked his head toward the printed analysis Brendan held. He reread the final page, then stepped away. Novak's gaze elevated towards the heavens, he pivoted, "From a half mile you'll have the radar profile of a dove."

Novak grinned, "A midnight blue dove."

* * *

Brendan had vetted the crane operator; the guy was seasoned. The SunCat sailing vessel slowly lifted, swung over the rail of the cargo ship and descended towards the Caribbean Sea. Even with care, and despite anticipation, the jolt when the boat banged onto the sea nearly knocked the wind from their bellies.

Brendan used the push rod to shove the catamaran out of the sling; giving a final shove to clear the freighter's wake. He let the catamaran drift until the cargo ship was five hundred feet distant.

"Mother," Brenda said into the handheld VHF radio, "I'll be home in three hours."

Cuban surveillance wouldn't be alarmed by the English spoken in these waters; Castro's troops had been monitoring the US Navy on this southeast shore even before the 1959 New Year's Eve revolution.

"No later, or I won't fix you dinner," replied the Captain of the SS Madrigal from his stand on the bridge.

"O.K. I promise," Brendan secured the marine radio in the port locker.

Twinkling lights defined the shore of Santiago De Cuba fifteen miles to the north. The catamaran could tear through the sea at twenty-three knots per hour sailing a dead-reach . . . and easterly trade winds fueled a dead-reach in both directions on the north-in, south-out course.

"Hang on tight," Brendan said to Cecille.

Brendan yanked the stern line, releasing the self-furling head sail of the catamaran. Wind filled the sail. The cat immediately pushed forward; Brendan held a tight reach limiting the speed to four knots. He locked the tiller and scrambled on his knees to the base of the mast. With an effort Cecille couldn't see, Brendan hoisted and cleated the main sail in fifteen seconds. The SunCat burst into overdrive. Cecille's dug her hand under the strapping across the tarpaulin deck.

Lights from the entrance to the port of Santiago De Cuba, capital of Oriente, provided an easy rhumb line tack. Five miles off the coast Brendan veered twenty degrees east.

Ten minutes later he nodded, "Those are the lights of Daiquiri. Are you sure?" he asked. Dropping a woman into the Caribbean Sea off the coast of a hostile country did not mesh with the internal principles.

Wind obscured Cecille's words. Brendan leaned towards her, she moved towards Brendan at the same moment. He felt the warmth of her breath.

"Your concern is needless. This is my destiny. Don't be bothered." She touched the back of his hand.

"Sorry, an old habit to be concerned," Brendan said.

"Someday, someday I will thank you," she replied.

"You can always change your mind," Brendan said.

Brendan tillered the slow-turning catamaran windward. The boat hung still, calm in the night breeze.

"We're here," Brendan said, "I am having a hard time believing I made this promise. I'm having a harder time delivering on it."

"Good bye." Cecille disappeared over the side with a splash.

As Brendan brought the sailboat about, beyond the wake of the cat he watched Cecille stroking through the water towing her buoyant waterproof case.

"Make your peace, Uncle Ramon. The shark of death swims in your waters tonight."

AFTERWORD

Regulators shuttered 1,030 S&L's in the years 1986-1992. In 1989 regulators seized 327 S&L's; six each week. The FDIC calculated that bill to repair this financial damage cost American taxpayers $150 billion.

Dick Thornburgh, Attorney General 1988-1991, commissioned four hundred prosecutors and investigators to sift through the S&L industry. The largest platoon was dispatched to the Dallas Bank Fraud Task Force.

Most Delicious of Privileges is fiction. Names, characters, places and incidents either are the product of the author's imagination or are used fictionally. Use of names of actual persons, places and characters are incidental to the plot and are not intended to change the entirely fictional character of the work.

The people below are real.

Charles Keating, CEO of Lincoln Savings, was convicted in California on securities fraud. Lincoln failed in 1989. Charles was sentenced to twelve years; he served four. Before Lincoln Savings, Charles departed American Financial under the cloud of an impending SEC investigation regarding a preferential loan. Charlie's palace on Cat Cay, Bahamas was a sought after invite.

Janet McKinzie, assistant to the CEO, North America S&L, Santa Ana, California, submitted phony invoices for her personal use; draining $16 million from the S&L. Janet's chairman died before her trial. Lucky Janet was sole beneficiary on his $10 million life insurance policy. The judge said to Janet, "Twenty years." She served six.

Janis Lee handled new customer accounts at Surety Savings, Vallejo, California. She skimmed $100,000 plus for herself from dormant customer accounts.

James Reagin, a real estate developer in Dallas pleaded guilty to flipping land; the sale of land back and forth to justify increased, albeit false, value.

His bankers, Timothy Heuer, owner of First Savings of South Beloit and Alan Kirchner, President of Bank of Alma, were indicted with Jim.

Robert Farmigoni, Senior Vice President, First Financial, Lutcher, Louisiana, supplied his client, Loretta Lustig, with $5,000,000 in unauthorized letters of credit that she used to obtain real estate loans. Loretta slipped Bob $50,000 for his help. Loretta and Bob got three years in separate pens.

George Bonfanti borrowed $20,000,000 from Sunbelt Federal Savings, Baton Rouge to build apartments and an office. George lied to Sunbelt about progress; the Sunbelt guys didn't check the job site. George drew up phony leases; the Sunbelt guys didn't verify the leases. George fabricated phony construction charges when he needed spending cash; the Sunbelt guys – well, who knows? Sunbelt wrote-off $12 million, George got five years.

Ralph E. Strader, a real estate developer in Houston, received a $17 million loan from Sunbelt Savings. Ralph justified his draws with false invoices from fictitious companies. Hi, ho, hi, ho, off to jail Ralph went for ten years.

Jack Lee Odom, President, Sioux Valley Savings, Cherokee, Iowa, found his regulators annoying. He set up a slush fund to bring delinquent loans current. He had his secretary alter Board minutes to indicate loans that had never been presented, had been approved! The secretary copped a plea deal offered by the regulators, she got 80 days; Jackie Lee got six years.

Patrick G. King, President, Vernon Savings & Loan, Dallas, reimbursed his officers $55,000 to cover their personal campaign contributions to favored politicians. Before joining Vernon, Patrick served as Director of Regulatory Supervision, Texas Savings & Loans. Vernon S&L failed in 1987. It cost taxpayers $1,300,000,000.00. The judge assigned Patrick to five years in the Regulators wing of the penitentiary.

Kaye Scholer, a New York law firm, settled civil charges seeking $275,000,000 with the Office of Thrift Supervision for $41 million. The OTS claimed the seventy-five-year-old law firm "aided and abetted regulatory violations" by Charlie Keating's Lincoln Savings & Loan Association.

The **National Security Agency** began monitoring transfers of money from the United States to Panama using numbered electronic instructions in the mid-1980's. After the S&L meltdown, the **Treasury Department** established an interagency financial intelligence unit, FINCEN, to investigate money-laundering.

The **Federal Savings & Loan Insurance Corporation** (**FSLIC** referred to as Fizlick by insiders) was created by congress in 1934 to insure S&L deposits. Fizlick was overseen by the Federal Home Loan Bank Board (**FHLBB**). Congress dumped $15 billion into FSLIC in 1986; another $10.75 billion in 1987. By 1989 **FSLIC** was too insolvent to save. Congress abolished **FSLIC** in August 1989 along with **FHLBB**, and transferred S&L deposit insurance responsibility to the **FDIC**.

Emily's List: In 1988 two women supported by Emily's List were elected to congress on the Democrat ticket, reversing a fifteen-year decline. In 1990, Emily's List, dedicated to *electing Democratic women to office,* with a boost to their war chest, championed five congressional women winners and two governors. Texas Gov. Ann Richards' campaign received $400,000.

Acknowledgement

Bankers who have mentored, influenced or laughed with me;

Alan Packman, Ulysses Giberga, Tim McGinnis, Todd Smallwood, Deborah Widener, Peter Lind, Peter Mills, David Banks, John Proctor, Mike Hogan, Bern Kroupa, Gianni Cortese, Craig Studwell, Alvise Alvara, Eduordo Ciravegna, Doug Blair, John Canepa, Phil Battershall, Ralph Garlick, John Erickson, John Paul, Randy Peterson, Scott Raymond, Rob Shuster.

View comments, or write your comment, at
www.mostdeliciousofprivileges.com

Made in the USA
Lexington, KY
09 June 2014

De todas las formas de psicosis, la psicosis paranoide es la más común. Este tipo de psicosis es un trastorno mental que se caracteriza por una modificación del sentido de la realidad y esa modificación genera un delirio alucinante que se concreta como discursos inconexos e incoherentes acerca de los hechos objetivos.

Existen Los delirios son creencias fijas que el vecino con este trastorno tiene, de una manera muy firme y determinante y que no las cuestiona, aunque la realidad, la evidencia o las valoraciones del resto de las personas de su entorno, le demuestren lo contrario y nieguen la existencia real. El vecino delirante está convencido al 100% de que lo que piensa es absolutamente real y no tiene la más mínima duda de ello.

Estas creencias solo las acepta el vecino delirante, porque nadie con un leve sentido de la realidad lo hace. Sus delirios que por definición, son completamente imposibles y son típicos en este tipo de vecinos. Por ejemplo; los dos más típicos son, que los personajes del cine y la televisión son reales y forman parte de su vida. Estos personajes se hacen reales a través de la antena de la televisión o de la pantalla de cine. El segundo más típico es que otro vecino lo persigue y/o lo espía todo el tiempo, aunque ese otro vecino no tenga el menor interés en este.

Existen diferentes modalidades de trastornos delirantes:
- ✓ La celotipia; son los celos extremos
- ✓ El persecutorio; es el más común
- ✓ El somático; tiene que ver con las alteraciones del propio cuerpo
- ✓ El erotomaníaco; creer que alguien famoso o importante en su comunidad está enamorado de este tipo de vecino

Debo señalar que el delirante no es consciente en forma alguna de estos falsos juicios, por lo que es sumamente difícil intentar razonar con él o siquiera establecer una conversación básica al respecto.

IDENTIKIT DEL VECINO FIEL A SU IDIOSINCRACIA

Para entender mejor este tipo de vecino, hay que entender la idiosincracia de la sociedad mexicana, desde un punto de vista práctico. Esta idiosincrasia es la que define y se instala a escala en los centros de trabajo públicos y privados, y en todos los lugares donde vivimos,- se trate de una zona residencial o de una colonia popular-.

La idiosincrasia del mexicano, está determinada por las huellas que su pasado ha dejado a lo largo de su historia y que tiene características específicas que la norman y que conforman su identidad como nación o como región.

Esta identidad está determinada por los valores, rasgos, costumbres, tradiciones y un sin fin de hábitos y creencias.

La idiosincrasia "temperamento particular" es el conjunto de características hereditarias o adquiridas, las cuales definen el temperamento y carácter de una persona o un grupo colectivo. Las relaciones establecidas entre los grupos humanos de acuerdo a su idiosincrasia influyen en el comportamiento individual, y también en el comportamiento social de las personas, en las costumbres sociales, en el desempeño profesional o en los aspectos culturales; y como parte de estos, el cómo conviven en un colectivo.

Una característica muy marcada de la idiosincrasia del mexicano es vivir en un completo desorden, la impuntualidad, postergar todo para después, no ahorrar, no educar a sus hijos, y algo muy importante y que impacta a sus vecinos, jefes y compañeros de trabajo de manera permanente, es que cuando algo es NO, este interpreta SI.

Según Octavio Paz, el mexicano lleva el sentimiento de inferioridad, una soledad que despierta en la adolescencia y trata de sobrellevar con el uso de máscaras, caras ajenas a nosotros con las que nos presenta.
El mexicano "trabaja para vivir" y no a la inversa.

Asegura el autor de *Vecinos Distantes*, Alan Riding, que "nosotros los mexicanos huimos de una realidad que no podemos manejar y entramos en una de fantasía, donde el orgullo, el idealismo y el **egoísmo social**, florecen con seguridad, además de que la pasión domina sobre la razón".
Este es el telón de fondo del vecino fiel a su idiosincrasia.

- Señora,- le dije a aquella mujer que estaba de pie, junto a mí, en el condominio exclusivo en el que vivíamos.

Ahí está el bote de basura; después nos quejamos de que se inunda el condominio.

- La respuesta de aquella vecina fue decirme, de manera airada, que me metiera en mis asuntos, después de haber tirado su botella de refresco fuera del bote, y a pesar de tener uno junto a ella. Tan sobria respuesta me desconcertó y le contesté, que mantener las áreas comunes libres de basura que obstruyen las coladeras, es un asunto de todos.

En México no se reacciona de buena manera cuando se trata de que alguien nos llame la atención sobre nuestro accionar ambiental y obligaciones cívicas.

Es casi seguro que de inmediato señalemos a quiénes también lo hacen o a la condición social como detonantes de este tipo de actitudes.

Sin embargo, las estadísticas señalan a personas de alto nivel socioeconómico e instruccional, lavando sus banquetas por horas, tirando basura en las calles, quemando desechos, permitiendo que sus niños molesten a los demás y maltratando a sus mascotas, etc. Y dejando de lado todo aire moralista, el punto toral no es juzgar dichas acciones, sino entender la razón de ellas para mejorar nuestro medio ambiente.

La destrucción del lugar en el que vivimos, ¿es el resultado de nuestra idiosincrasia o una adaptación al medio de la superficialidad del pensamiento cotidiano, que nos impide meditar sobre las consecuencias de nuestros actos?

Porque… ¿cómo explicar que aun sabiendo las consecuencias, no se modifiquen varias de nuestras acciones sobre el entorno en el que vivimos?

Nuestra idiosincrasia es un factor negativo para el cuidado ambiental?

Parecería que todo termina circunscribiéndose a un asunto que bien se puede denominar de idiosincrasia ambiental.
Es decir, la comodidad de tirar los desechos (o de otras diversas acciones irresponsables), simplemente porque "vale madre", es una actitud de irresponsabilidad. Esto parece confirmar que la conducta humana está hecha de incertidumbre e irresponsabilidad, y que cotidianamente adoptamos decisiones y acciones que comprometen nuestro futuro.

Si bien es cierto que nuestro libre albedrío nos "permite" actuar como queramos y que lo que queremos es generalmente actuar con desidia, e irresponsabilidad, también es cierto que dicha libertad debe ajustarse a un marco cívico y normativo orientado hacia el bien común.

Por lo anterior, y considerando que la responsabilidad con que tomamos nuestras decisiones de convivencia cívica, no tiene que ver con la información y el conocimiento que poseamos al respecto, se podría considerar si dicha desidia se debe a falta de información.
Pero; actualmente en México la educación ambiental forma parte del sistema educativo en todos los niveles.
Esto sugiere que teóricamente lo que condiciona el comportamiento contrario a una

cultura de cuidado y respeto común hacia la naturaleza, no es la falta de educación o información, o ambas, sino la idiosincrasia mexicana, y en donde principalmente detona esta idiosincrasia, es en la forma de educar a los niños y en la falta de cuidado ambiental.

Este es el telón de fondo del vecino fiel a su idiosincrasia.

CAPITULO 3

UNA PEOR FORMA DE VIVIR

Me parece importante insistir en las causas que favorecen la mala convivencia de los mexicanos con sus vecinos.

Para ello, debemos revisar la cadena de explotación de los países del tercer mundo, en el que el peso de la burguesía local era más relevante que el de las multinacionales y de los gobiernos de los países del Norte.

Galtung afirma que un grupo de pueblos se transforma en una civilización, cuando tienen las mismas convicciones, los mismos valores, y la misma visión cosmológica, con respecto a seis aspectos vitales:

1. Las relaciones interpersonales
2. Los fundamentos del conocimiento
3. El concepto del tiempo
4. El concepto de espacio

5. Las relaciones de las personas con la naturaleza
6. Las relaciones de las personas con las divinidades

Entonces vemos, que de acuerdo a este importante investigador, los mexicanos somos incivilizados, porque solamente cumplimos con uno de los aspectos; el de las relaciones de las personas con las divinidades.

En las relaciones sociales de los mexicanos, las emociones son un requisito indispensable e inevitable. Y son estas emociones las que las personas no pueden controlar, ni positivas, ni negativas.

Evadimos nuestra responsabilidad a causa del miedo, golpeamos porque estamos enojados, nos paraliza la sorpresa y nos deprime el dolor. Y es esta forma reaccionar, la que se ha institucionalizado y consecuentemente permitido en todas las modalidades de relaciones sociales, incluidas las vecinales, que también forman parte de nuestra cultura, - o de nuestra falta de cultura-.

El fracaso casi absoluto de una buena convivencia vecinal, es imputable a una ausencia total de identidad cultural. Y el telón de fondo de esta falta de identidad cultural, se remonta a nuestro pasado histórico. Dado que las civilizaciones locales fueron derrotadas por la civilización Occidental, las élites de estos países quedaron incapacitadas para elegir las soluciones adecuadas para su pueblo.

Entonces surgieron civilizaciones híbridas que imitan a la civilización Occidental, pero en esta imitación, no pudieron integrarse con la población indígena.

Este modelo de relación social, es el que vivimos todos los días.

Para *Galtung*, que nuestras emociones nos dominen las relaciones entre pares, nos convierte en un país "perdedor", en el que el reto más difícil de lograr, no es el crecimiento económico, sino más bien, la equidad y la identidad cultural.

En México, este concepto tiende a ignorarse, del mismo modo que el de cultura, porque hoy día la cultura se constituye por partes; "cultura de la violencia", "cultura juvenil", "narcocultura", "cultura del no pago", cultura tecnológica...

Para las ciencias sociales el concepto de identidad cultural es un concepto indispensable. Sin este concepto no se podría explicar la menor interacción social, porque todo proceso de interacción implica, el reconocimiento recíproco de nuestras respectivas identidades, y con ello, el principio de una interacción respetuosa entre nosotros.

No es posible pensar siquiera la sociedad sin el concepto de identidad, porque sin interacción social no hay sociedad.

Y es en los vecindarios, los barrios, los condominios horizontales o verticales, las unidades habitacionales, los conjuntos residenciales y la ciudad en su conjunto, en donde podemos ver en vivo y a todo color, las distintas prácticas de identidad cultural entre las personas que a pesar de tener conciencia, memoria, instintos y buenos sentimientos, se comportan como si no los tuvieran, como si no vivieran en sociedad y como si no formaran parte de un grupo.

¿Cómo se define a un ser social?
Cualquier persona ocupa siempre, una o varias posiciones en la estructura social. Las personas son indisociables de las estructuras y siempre deben verse como "actores-insertos-en-sistemas.
En el espacio urbano, por ejemplo, no podemos ni siquiera concebir un actor que no esté situado en algún lugar de la estratificación urbana o de la estructura socio-profesional urbana. Y eso significa ocupar una posición en la estructura social.
Ningún actor se concibe sin la interacción con otros, y esto es especialmente cierto sea en términos inmediatos (cara a cara), como en un condominio de cualquier tipo.

Por lo tanto, no se puede ser un actor social urbano que no esté en interacción con otros, ya sea en espacios públicos, en un vecindario, dentro de un barrio, dentro de una zona urbana especializada o a escala de toda una aglomeración urbana.

Todo actor social está dotado de una identidad. Y es ésta identidad, la que ejerce en el lugar que vive. Es la que va a "usar" en su relación con sus vecinos. Y es aquí precisamente donde tenemos el gran problema, porque esta identidad es una identidad inacabada y borrosa.

El proyecto de grupo está íntimamente vinculado con la percepción de nuestra identidad, porque deriva de la imagen que tenemos de nosotros mismos y, por ende, de nuestras aspiraciones.

Como parte de un grupo, y con esta percepción, el nuevo mexicano de finales del siglo XX ha entrado en un movimiento de imitación extranjera, asociando el lujo, el dinero, el poder y el consumismo como estándares de éxito, y ha dejado de lado el lado humanista, la convivencia familiar y vecinal armónica, y por supuesto, la cooperación solidaria con el vecino.

Entre los mexicanos, existe una conciencia desigual, -de origen,- de la igualdad grupal que se gesta en la independencia, se refuerza y acrecienta en los períodos de intervención extranjera y en las etapas de rescate de las raíces autóctonas.

México vive atrapado en su historia. Y nuestro pasado, no es un pasado glorioso, es trágico. Los aztecas abusaron de las etnias que conquistaron, y los españoles cometieron todo tipo de atropellos con los indígenas. De hecho, no se apostaba a la mezcla de dos grandes grupos raciales, con enormes diferencias culturales, y se pensaba que era imposible crear una nación. Así surge el mestizaje y el laboratorio racial que era México. La Colonia legó al siglo XIX mexicano, variadísimos experimentos raciales y una subcultura de la discriminación, en la que los españoles discriminaban a los criollos, los criollos a los mestizos y los mestizos a los indígenas.

Así, el México mestizo se apoderó de los muralistas y de la educación gratuita, pero no del bienestar social. Y este es el inicio de uno de los grandes y graves problemas.

Los mexicanos siempre estamos mirando al pasado, y no al futuro. Somos expertos en el arte de improvisar y odiamos la planeación.

Y esta forma de hacer, tiene sus bases en la conquista española.

Los españoles no descubrieron en el nuevo continente, una nación como tal, lo que descubrieron, fueron distintos grupos étnico-culturales con profundas diferencias linguisticas, religiosas, artísticas y culturales.

De estas diferencias destacaban la cultura azteca, la maya y la inca.

Los "americanos", -como nos llamaban, carecían de una autoconsciencia integral de su existencia y de sus valores comunes, lo que hacía que no funcionaran de manera colectiva.

Por eso, entre otras cosas, para los españoles fue tan fácil, incorporar a los mexicanos, a su historia. De esta sangrienta fusión, nace la historia de México.

El choque de culturas y la dominación de una de ellas sobre la otra, crearon en la sociedad mexicana, muchos defectos de origen.

El indio tuvo que esconder su cosmovisión, sus tradiciones y su apariencia.

El mestizo también aprendió a ocultar muchas cosas.

Por eso, es que la nuestra, es una sociedad que, cotidianamente simula y aparenta lo que no es. Y esta simulación también alcanzó a los criollos, que debían esconder sus realidades a los españoles.

Las raíces indígenas son algo así como un milagro, que sobrevivió a la imposición de una cultura ajena.

Cortés y sus soldados, inmediatamente después de su victoria sobre Moctezuma, Cuitláhuac y Cuauhtémoc, destruyeron Tenochtitlán, la capital azteca, sobre la cual se edificó la actual ciudad de México.

Este modelo, significó una tremenda ruptura, en la que predominó la destrucción y no la visión constructiva y vemos que mientras que los habitantes de Atenas y Roma descienden de griegos y romanos, y que las dos capitales se fueron construyendo sobre la cultura de sus antepasados, pero sin destruirlas, la actual ciudad de México, se edificó sobre las ruinas de la capital azteca.

En un instante se destruyó la vieja cultura.

Es muy posible que esta destrucción quedara en la psique de los antiguos mexicanos, como un factor cultural primordial; hay que destruir, no construir.

De ahí que los mexicanos vean con absoluta normalidad la capacidad de destrucción de lo colectivo, en sus ciudades, pueblos, calles, barrios, unidades habitacionales y condominios.

Y es esta capacidad de destrucción, además de la llegada de la modernidad, que favorecen la mala convivencia, de las personas con sus vecinos, además de la cadena de explotación de los países del tercer mundo, el peso de la burguesía local mucho más relevante que el de las multinacionales y de los gobiernos de los países del Norte.

Esta forma de reaccionar, se ha institucionalizado y consecuentemente permitido en todas las modalidades de relaciones sociales, incluidas las vecinales, que también forman parte de nuestra cultura, - o de nuestra falta de cultura-.

El fracaso casi absoluto de una buena convivencia vecinal, es imputable a una ausencia total de identidad cultural. Y el telón de fondo de esta falta de identidad cultural, se remonta a nuestro pasado histórico. Dado que las civilizaciones locales fueron derrotadas por la civilización Occidental, las élites de estos países quedaron incapacitados para elegir las soluciones adecuadas para su pueblo.

Entonces surgieron civilizaciones híbridas que imitan a la civilización Occidental, pero en esta imitación, no pudieron integrarse con la población indígena. Este modelo de relación social, es el que vivimos todos los días.

A ello habría que agregar, que somos impuntuales, postergamos todo, no tenemos la cultura del ahorro, ni la cultura de la conservación y cuidado del medio ambiente. Interpretamos SI, cuando es NO y este esquema impacta a nuestros vecinos en la convivencia.

Galtung afirma que nuestras emociones dominen las relaciones entre pares, y malinterpretar casi todo, nos convierte en un país "perdedor", en el que el reto más difícil de lograr, no es el crecimiento económico, sino más bien, la equidad y la identidad cultural.

Es difícil imaginar dos países menos compatibles que México y Estados Unidos. El maridaje geográfico entre la potencia más poderosa del mundo con un país subdesarrollado, con profundos problemas de identidad y autoestima, fue el telón de fondo de la globalización, que por si fuera poco, nos alcanzó , y con esta, las transformaciones de la identidad como acción colectiva a partir de los cambios impulsados por los procesos típicos de globalización económica. Y además, la globalización ejerce una dinámica que complica las identidades culturales, reconfigura la geografía de los territorios y reinventa la gobernabilidad a nivel macro y micro. En el nuevo orden globalizado, los grupos pluriculturales necesitan construir una nueva identidad que sustente las bases de una participación social.

Estos procesos de construcción de la nueva identidad cultural son opuestos a los procesos de la globalización económica, los cuales profundizan más las fracturas sociales. Para *Huntington* , la cultura e identidad cultural dan forma a los patrones de cohesión, desintegración y conflicto en la posguerra fría.

Este a su vez es otro paso de la hipermundialización, la que según *Laïdi*, es una realidad más inquietante, en donde los Estados, las fronteras, los sistemas sociales o los sistemas educativos y las identidades culturales y políticas no tienen ya más sentido a nivel nacional, y mucho menos a nivel de grupos sociales.

Las formas de transmitir los estilos de vida en una sociedad globalizada están generando contradicciones sociales muy fuertes, que fragmentan, dividen y marginalizan a grupos sociales que a su vez, contribuyen a formar altos niveles de incertidumbre en sus identidades sociales, políticas y culturales.
La convivencia asimétrica con tantas identidades fracturadas ,- ya tocadas por los procesos de globalización-, se transforman una y otra vez, en múltiples identidades y en múltiples expresiones .

Nuestra crisis de identidad nos mantiene fracturados, perdidos en el individualismo y el egoísmo tontos. La falta de solidaridad con el vecino se debe en gran medida, a esta crisis de identidad y de pertenencia que se originó en el choque de civilizaciones y que ha perpetuado la desigualdad económica, y en la que ni discriminadores, ni discriminados, se sienten en su casa.

¿Por qué y para qué establecer relaciones de armonía y de confianza en un lugar al que no pertenecemos?

Las personas experimentan cada vez más diferencias culturales debido a la globalización y junto con la fragmentación, reinician este ciclo de construcción-destrucción de la identidad, en el que prevalecen la inseguridad, la ansiedad, y la incertidumbre.

Y por si esto fuera poco, llegó la globalización, y con esta, las transformaciones de la identidad como acción colectiva a partir de los cambios impulsados por los procesos de globalización económica. Estos procesos, de manera natural, fragmentan y diversifican la identidad social, política, cultural, comunitaria y colectiva para ajustarla a las tendencias de los mercados globales, agravando la crisis de identidad nacional y consecuentemente, la crisis de identidad comunitaria.

La fragmentación de las identidades culturales, étnicas, religiosas, políticas, y la falta de consciencia ciudadana, es una de las razones de los profundos conflictos entre los grupos sociales en las ciudades, calles y especialmente en los barrios, unidades habitacionales y condominios.

La globalización dinamiza y complica los arreglos de identidades culturales, reconfigura la geografía de los territorios y reinventa la gobernabilidad a nivel macro y micro. En el nuevo orden globalizado, los grupos pluriculturales necesitan construir una nueva identidad que sustente las bases de una participación social.

La globalización además, acrecienta los problemas de identidad, de fragmentación del aparato interno de respuestas de la individualidad y ha creado retos enormes en relación a esta identidad.

El resultado es más inseguridad personal, ansiedad e incertidumbre.

Para enfrentar los retos que plantea esta diversidad de identidades, esta desigualdad, necesitamos desarrollar habilidades para la administración de esa diversidad, para manejar la incertidumbre y la identidad.

Esta desigualdad también se manifiesta en la concepción que de lo mexicano se tiene en las diversas regiones geopolíticas del país; los distintos estratos sociales , las múltiples etnias, y la centralización del poder político, económico y cultural, y como eje central, la injusticia social, que nos ha dejado como herencia, una participación marginal de la mayoría.

La fragmentación de las identidades individuales, culturales, colectivas, étnicas y religiosas, provoca profundos conflictos entre grupos sociales, que tienen que convivir en un mismo lugar, y provocan que las personas experimenten una distancia cultural, cada vez más grande entre sus vecinos, colaboradores e incluso familiares.

Los procesos de construcción de la nueva identidad cultural son opuestos a los procesos de la globalización económica, los cuales profundizan más las fracturas sociales, a nivel micro y macro.

Esta es otra de las consecuencias de la hipermundialización, y es una realidad más inquietante, en donde los Estados, las fronteras, los sistemas sociales o los sistemas educativos y las identidades culturales y políticas no tienen ya más sentido a nivel nacional, y mucho menos a nivel micro.

Las formas de transmitir los estilos de vida en una sociedad globalizada están generando contradicciones sociales que fragmentan, dividen y marginalizan a grupos sociales que a su vez, contribuyen a formar altos niveles de incertidumbre en sus identidades sociales, políticas y culturales.

La fragmentación de las identidades culturales, colectivas, étnicas, religiosas, políticas, y la falta de consciencia ciudadana, es la razón de los profundos conflictos entre los grupos sociales en las ciudades, calles y especialmente en los barrios, unidades habitacionales, conjuntos residenciales y condominios.

Estas identidades ya tocadas por los procesos de globalización, se convierten en múltiples identidades y en múltiples expresiones.

 y provocan profundos conflictos entre grupos sociales, que tienen que convivir en un mismo lugar, y provocan que las personas experimenten una distancia cultural, cada vez más grande entre sus vecinos, colaboradores e incluso familiares.

Es así, que la pérdida de una sola identidad, confronta a las personas,- especialmente si tienen que convivir cotidianamente en el mismo lugar,- a los grupos, y los incorpora en un ciclo interminable de construcción-destrucción.

CAPÍTULO 4

Diferentes tipos de vecinos

- El funcionario(a) público(a)

Este vecino tiene una versión muy equivocada de lo que es el servicio público. Considera que su puesto o posición en la administración pública, no tiene nada que ver con el servicio público a los ciudadanos y entre ellos; a sus vecinos, sino todo lo contrario. La posición que ostenta le sirve para otorgarse privilegios y para considerar a los empleados del lugar en el que reside, como empleados propios. Su actitud es de superioridad y no participa de las juntas o asambleas, sino que espera la minuta de las mismas para modificar y hasta cambiar algunos puntos de acuerdo que solo se modificarán para su beneficio propio.

Cuando pertenecen a algún partido político, -sin importar su tamaño-, hacen un despliegue de técnicas de prepotencia y autoritarismo, con el nombre del partido como parapeto de sus abusos. Cuando alguien se le opone, incluida la administración de su lugar de residencia, el funcionario público recurre a sus influencias para someter y/o vengarse de quién o quiénes se oponen.

Este vecino toxico es un claro ejemplo.

Fernando 26 años

Pertenece a un partido político de reciente creación, y por su juventud y su novatez, este vecino tóxico considera que es mérito suficiente colaborar en un partido político, aunque este, no sea un partido con reconocimiento social.
Aun así Fernando ejerce la intimidación y la violencia contra sus vecinas mujeres, - especialmente si estas viven solas.-
Una de estas vecinas cuenta su historia. Susana,- que estaciona su auto en el cajón que está junto al de Fernando, le pide cortésmente que por favor se mueva un poco hacia la derecha, pues el auto de esta vecina queda muy pegado a la pared y apenas puede salir de su auto. Fernando considera una agresión verbal esta solicitud e inicia una escalada de ofensas y agresiones, entre las que destacan, juntar todavía más su auto al de Susana, llamar una grúa para retirar el auto de Susana de la calle,- aunque no estorbaba,- y acudir a su

departamento a golpear la puerta para gritarle que él hace lo que quiere en ese edificio.

Al día siguiente, deja grandes bolsas de basura con propaganda política en el garaje, particularmente en el cajón de estos dos autos; que es área común. Cuando estas son llevadas al área de la basura, pues no está permitido dejar bultos, ni basura en las áreas comunes, este retoma la escalada de agresión y aumenta su respuesta de violencia.

Nos dice Susana; "tuve que acudir a las autoridades judiciales en busca de ayuda, pues incluso su madre se involucró en esta situación y cada vez que me la topaba en el edificio, esta soltaba a sus perros, para que me atacaran, pues los traía sin correa.

Levanté una denuncia y nos citaron a declarar días más tarde.

El día de la audiencia, Fernando negó todo y dijo que yo lo había agredido inicialmente, y que él se había visto obligado a mover su auto y ponerlo en una posición que me impedía bajar normalmente de mi auto.

Por la forma tan violenta en que Fernando se comportaba y el cómo se desarrollaron los hechos, además del nulo apoyo de la administración del edificio, interpuse dos demandas más.

> El día de esta segunda audiencia, la representante de la autoridad le pidió a Fernando reconocer sus errores y ofrecerme una disculpa por todo lo sucedido, pues esto terminaría con las denuncias de mi parte. Sin embargo y a pesar de estar viviendo las consecuencias negativas de sus actos, este se negó.
>
> Ante la imposibilidad de llegar a un acuerdo y porque el problema de la invasión de su auto en ambos cajones del estacionamiento, llamé al presidente de su partido y le expuse la situación. Gracias a esta decisión, Fernando se calmó, aunque aún persiste el problema de la falta de espacio para que yo baje de mi auto en el espacio del estacionamiento que él y yo compartimos".

- El administrador

  Este es el vecino que administra el conjunto residencial, condominio, privada, etc, sin ser administrador de profesión.

  Lo hace, por dos razones principales. La primera razón, es porque vive en el mismo condominio, privada o conjunto residencial que administra y establece su liderazgo, generalmente con el apoyo de otros vecinos que tienen más antigüedad, y que no conocen los principios de administración de una propiedad. Ni este administrador, ni los vecinos tienen un criterio adecuado respecto de los temas que administran. Lo hacen en forma totalmente improvisada.

Este tipo de administrador, reparte privilegios solo entre los vecinos que lo apoyan, y otorga poca importancia al mantenimiento correctivo, y ninguna al mantenimiento preventivo. No conoce los reglamentos de las distintas instancias que norman la actividad administrativa. Es rotativa.

La segunda razón, es económica. Solo le interesan las cuotas de mantenimiento que mensualmente se cobran, para su beneficio personal.

Existen varios subtipos de administrador:
a) El que fue electo por votación de los vecinos en un acto informal. Puede o no ser rotativa y puede o no

presentar estados de ingresos y egresos.
b) El que fue electo en una asamblea, y que por lo tanto es un administrador legítimo. Sí presenta estados de ingresos y egresos.
c) El que se autoasignó la función de administrar, pues nadie la realizaba. Puede o no presentar estados de cuenta.
d) La administración colectiva no formal. Un grupo de vecinos administran, tomando en cuenta la opinión del grupo. Es rotativa. Puede o no presentar estados de cuenta mensuales.
e) El administrador profesional que pertenece a una empresa de administración de inmuebles, que tiene un salario mensual y que fue contratado por el condominio. Conoce la normatividad administrativa y presenta estados de cuenta mensuales.

En todos los casos, es más o menos frecuente, que el administrador tenga un perfil psicopático. De ahí, las irregularidades administrativas, que dan lugar a múltiples y graves problemas que no solo no se resuelven en los condominios, sino que se agravan, porque este tipo de vecino, los crea o si ya existían, contribuye a hacerlos más graves.

- El vecino defraudador
Este tipo de vecino es de los más peligrosos. A lo largo de su vida adulta ha cometido varios fraudes como robo de identidad y apropiación ilegal de la propiedad. Utiliza básicamente dos estrategias; la primera consiste en identificar a los adultos mayores que viven solos, que están enfermos y que son sus vecinos y vecinas. Establece una relación de amistad con ellos, y obtiene información de su situación, especialmente financiera.Lo hace con la finalidad de ganarse su confianza y lograr que le firmen algún documento en el que le ceden los derechos de sus bienes inmuebles, para que una vez que estos adultos mayores fallezcan, poder apropiarse de estos.

Cuando no logra que le firmen algún documento de cesión de derechos, entonces recurre al fraude y falsifica firmas y consigue documentos apócrifos de oficinas de gobierno, en los que, al fallecer el dueño legítimo, este tipo de vecino, se apodera de la propiedad.

- El vecino saboteador
  Con el argumento de que ni las políticas de convivencia, ni las de mantenimiento correctivo pueden mejorar en el condominio, conjunto residencial o privada, este tipo de vecino sabotea todas las iniciativas de mejorar el entorno. Su finalidad es contar siempre con un argumento negativo y basándose en este, no pagar la cuota mensual de mantenimiento.

- El vecino propietario e invasivo
  Este tipo de vecino vive o vivió en el mismo edificio o condominio horizontal en el que tiene uno o más de un departamento o casa. Este espécimen considera, que por tener varios inmuebles en el mismo lugar y conocer las dinámicas del lugar en el que habita y que a su vez renta a terceros, le da derecho automático a interferir en la vida de sus inquilinos.
  Se aparece a cualquier hora de la mañana, de la tarde, de la noche e

incluso de la madrugada con algún pretexto, diciendo que pasaba por ahí y aprovechó para recordarle como hacer determinada tarea, o incluso checar que todo esté en orden en el inmueble que arrienda.

Otro ejemplo real. El de Gerardo N.

Gerardo 43 años
Insistí en vivir en ese conjunto residencial, porque ya había vivido ahí antes,- en otro edificio,- y me convenía esa colonia. Cuando me mudé, el departamento tenía muchas anomalías eléctricas, de plomería y decorativas. El propietario llevó a su electricista y a su plomero, quiénes no solucionaron el problema. Yo llevé otro electricista y otro plomero y Gerardo se negaba rotundamente a pagar los honorarios de estos y los daños que causaron dos inundaciones, porque la tubería estaba obstruida.
Además nunca me dio su número de cuenta bancaria para depositarle la renta, con la finalidad de no dejar rastro en Hacienda, pues no pagaba el impuesto correspondiente, y tampoco me daba recibo que yo necesitaba para deducir impuestos. Entonces mes con mes, me llamaba por teléfono y me pedía que le pagara la renta en efectivo y que lo hiciera en casa de su mamá, quién en dos ocasiones

me cerró la puerta en las narices, diciendo que no me conocía y otras más no abría la puerta. La respuesta de Gerardo fue, que entonces pasaría a mi departamento "a alguna hora".

En varias ocasiones lo hizo después de las once de la noche, alcoholizado, por lo que yo me negué a abrir la puerta.

Su solución fue, que yo tenía que verlo afuera de algún lugar público para pagarle. Invariablemente este llegaba con 30 minutos de retraso y no me daba ni recibo de arrendamiento, ni el pagaré que correspondía a ese mes, solicitándome que pasara a casa de su mamá a recogerlo. Entonces se repetía el ciclo en el que la señora no me abría la puerta, por lo que yo tuve que pedirle a mi hermano, quién es abogado, que le pidiera mis pagarés, que indebidamente retenía en venganza porque yo le pedí que estableciera un lugar fijo para pagarle la renta. No lo hizo y yo tomé la decisión de dejar el departamento al año, que se terminó el contrato."

- El vecino seductor
  Tiene un repertorio de halagos y frases bonitas para aquellas vecinas que le agraden. Como posee habilidades de plomería, electricidad y otros, se ofrece para reparar los desperfectos de sus vecinas, que viven solas, con la finalidad de intimar en el departamento o casa de estas. Con alguna frecuencia le hace saber al resto de los vecinos, que las vecinas "elegidas" y él, tienen algo especial, aunque esto no sea así.
- El vecino invasivo
  Este tipo de vecino es principalmente;
  a) El mecánico de autos, que ha tomado como su lugar de trabajo, las áreas comunes y estaciona los autos de sus clientes en el estacionamiento del condominio, conjunto residencial y/o viviendas de interés social y cuando estos ya no caben, entonces se extiende hasta la calle y en ocasiones obstruye la entrada al condominio. Siempre ensucia el piso de las áreas comunes con aceite y nunca realiza una limpieza después de las reparaciones.

b) El dueño de una o más bodega(s) de frutas y/o verduras en algún mercado. Este vecino considera que la planta baja de su edificio, -generalmente el hueco de la escalera,- es otra "bodeguita" en la que guarda varios costales de frutas o verduras durante la noche, para que a la mañana siguiente, se las pueda llevar, para repetir el ciclo de guardar más costales cada noche.

c) Es dueño del pequeño negocio de remodelación de casas habitación. Este vecino utiliza su auto para transportar materiales para la remodelación de casas habitación o locales comerciales. Estaciona su auto en cualquier espacio, -aunque no sea suyo,- con la finalidad de poder hacer maniobras con los materiales en las áreas comunes y dispersa estos materiales en un diámetro muy extenso, sin importarle si estorba o no el paso.

Existe una constante con los vecinos descritos en los incisos a, b y c, y es que estos pretenden, en todos los casos, que sus vecinos asuman como algo normal, las actividades irregulares que realizan en sus edificios, condominios horizontales, conjuntos residenciales o viviendas de interés social.

- El vecino negador
  Este vecino le apuesta a las soluciones espontáneas. Todo se resuelve, según él, a través de intervenciones divinas y de frases sacadas de los libros de autoayuda.

- El vecino separatista.
  Aun cuando existe un Reglamento Interno en el condominio, este vecino establece sus propias normas en forma indirecta y anónima, poniendo avisos en los pizarrones de la entrada al edificio, respecto de las acciones a seguir con los perros, la basura y las fiestas, principalmente. Nunca se identifica, pero la prevalencia de esta modalidad lo delata. Como este tiene sus propias normas, no cumple las normas establecidas.

- El vecino canino
  Sin importarle el tamaño de su departamento o casa, y si estos tienen o no, patio o jardín, este vecino posee uno o varios perros. La característica

principal de este "amante" de los animales, es que sus mascotas, en realidad no le importan para nada. Los mantiene encerrados por largos períodos de tiempo, lo que obliga a los perros a ladrar incesantemente.

- El vecino de barrio
  Este vecino tiene un gran apego por el barrio en el que nació y que ha habitado toda su vida. No es objetivo, porque su comportamiento está basado en los valores y creencias de cuando era niño y que ya han cambiado a través de los años. El sigue aferrado a lo antiguo y sus argumentos hacia lo que debe mejorar, corregirse o incluso cambiar siempre son sentimentaloides sin evaluar el factor de la plusvalía de las propiedades de sus vecinos y de la convivencia vecinal. Ejerce una superioridad,- por supuesto, falsa,- hacia el resto de los vecinos nuevos,- que puede llegar hasta la humillación,- haciéndole sentir que no pertenecen a esa comunidad y que si este vecino no quiere , no pertenecerá nunca. A quiénes tienen poco tiempo viviendo en el mismo condominio o conjunto

residencial que este, les impone su criterio e instrucciones, distintas de las de la administración, a la que intenta también imponer , su criterio.

- El vecino postergador(a)
Este vecino es miembro del Comité de Vigilancia, del Plan de Protección Vecinal y de otros programas. Su característica principal es postergar para las fechas para las asambleas o reuniones vecinales, exista o no una situación extraordinaria.

CAPÍTULO 5

VECINOS TÓXICOS Y ADICCIONES

Las drogas son de distintos tipos; las hay legales, ilegales y médicas.
Las que consumen los adolescentes, son ilegales y estos, presentan las tasas de policonsumo más altas a edades muy tempranas.
La clave para poder convivir armónicamente en un condominio, conjunto residencial o unidad habitacional, con vecinos adolescentes -adictos a las drogas y/o alcohol, es que los vecinos no adictos y la administración, aprendan a manejar situaciones difíciles en forma inteligente, porque las adicciones son un problema biopsicosocial.
El consumo no constituye, -como se cree,- un comportamiento marginal, sino que es uno de los pilares en la construcción de la identidad.

Las adicciones son una enfermedad biopsicosocial progresiva, multifactorial, primaria y crónica, que funcionan como un sustituto de la falta de comunicación y de identidad, y que se van a consumir principalmente en el grupo de pertenencia del lugar en el que viven los adolescentes. Parte de las características de las drogas que consumen los adolescentes, conlleva una manifestación de sus emociones sin responsabilidad, y la negación de sus acciones. Así, será una tarea titánica, intentar que un grupo de vecinos adolescentes, reconozcan las consecuencias de sus actos, que son contrarios a la buena convivencia, como vandalizar los autos de sus vecinos e incluso sus departamentos o casas.

En la Ciudad de México, ocho de cada 10 estudiantes de secundaria y bachillerato han consumido alcohol alguna vez en la vida, mientras uno de cada cuatro ha ingerido drogas ilegales, entre mariguana, cocaína, crack y alucinógenos, de acuerdo a la *Encuesta de Consumo de Drogas en Estudiantes de la Ciudad de México 2016.*

La Encuesta arrojó que la problemática mayor es en el consumo de drogas ilegales, en los grupos de adolescentes de las unidades habitacionales, condominios y zonas residenciales.

"Vemos que la mariguana sigue siendo la droga de principal consumo, repunta nuevamente la cocaína con un incremento importante, pero en el caso de los inhalables que muchos sabiamos que iba a crecer más se mantuvo", detalló Jorge Villatoro Velázquez, investigador en Ciencias Médicas del Instituto Nacional de Psiquiatría.

Hoy la edad de inicio en el consumo de drogas es de 12 años, por lo cual se requiere de un esfuerzo conjunto,- entre administradores de los condominios y conjuntos residenciales, y las familias, para poder prevenirlo, sobre todo cuando 11.4% de los estudiantes de nivel medio superior requieren tratamiento por consumo de sustancias, agregó Villatoro.

De acuerdo al estudio, hubo una caída en el consumo de inhalantes, de 7.5 por ciento de los alumnos de esos niveles a 5.9 por ciento, lo que en apariencia podría ser una buena noticia pero en realidad preocupa porque esos productos tienen graves consecuencias en la salud de los jóvenes, manifestó Camacho Solís.

Mientras que la cantidad de quienes consumieron mariguana se elevó en términos relativos en 48.78 por ciento.

La ciudad de México, afirmó la directora del *Instituto Nacional de Psiquiatría,* María Elena Medina-Mora, "es de alto riesgo, porque se conjugan factores para la expansión del consumo de drogas, tabaco y alcohol, por su disponibilidad, un mercado en crecimiento y una población joven que toma riesgos".

Los estudios revelan que el consumo de drogas sigue siendo más alto en hombres, aunque poco a poco se han emparejado las cifras. Actualmente, 25.7 por ciento de los jóvenes varones en secundaria y preparatoria consumen alguna droga (legal o ilegal) contra 23.1% de las mujeres.

Cifras:

53% de los jóvenes han bebido cerveza

48.1% de los jóvenes han bebido destilados (tequila, ron, vodka, etc)

39.7% de los jóvenes han bebido bebidas preparadas (Gatorade, New Mix, Sky, Kosako, bebidas deportivas de varias marcas, etc. 41% de los jóvenes ha fumado alguna vez y 14.9% de los jóvenes fuma de manera regular.

CÓMO PREVENIR LAS ADICCIONES EN UN CONDOMINIO, CONJUNTO RESIDENCIAL, etc.

Los vecinos con adolescentes deben mantener siempre y cada día, la comunicación abierta con sus hijos adolescentes e interesarse por todas y cada una de las actividades que realicen en su condominio o conjunto residencial. Antes de prohibir o permitir la relación con determinados vecinos adolescentes o jóvenes del mismo lugar en el que viven, los padres deben estar en contacto permanente con la administración, para enterarse acerca del grupo de pertenencia de sus hijos, para tener más y mejor información acerca de las negociaciones y acuerdos que estos puedan y deban cumplir.

Deben interesarse por cómo estos adolescentes ocupan el tiempo libre, y deben tener interés por conocer a sus amigos, además de intentar conocer sus actitudes frente a las drogas.

Los padres deben supervisar que sus hijos adolescentes sigan las normas de convivencia del condominio, -si las hay,- y si no, establecer un código ético familiar y tratar de razonar sin imponerlas con rigidez y manipulación.

Recomendación de algunas pautas de comportamiento para prevenir las adicciones en los entornos vecinales

- Dialogar, escuchar y razonar con ellos cuando no estén de acuerdo con las normas de convivencia de la administración del condominio.

- Supervisar y orientar las actividades de los hijos cuando estén en las áreas comunes. Pueden coordinarse con otros padres de familia y hacer rondas.

- Atender de inmediato los problemas que surjan entre los hijos de los vecinos.

- Alentarlos a compartir sus opiniones y vivencias en el entorno vecinal.

- Evitar mantener posturas excesivamente autoritarias, coaccionando su libertad de expresión.

- Evitar la crítica no constructiva hacia sus amigos

- No culpar a los hijos de los vecinos, o a la administración. de los problemas de los propios hijos, antes de analizar e investigar detenidamente.

- Ayudarles y facilitarles la relación con los demás vecinos

- Formarse como padres de sus hijos y como consejeros de los vecinos adolescentes que lo requieran.

- Evitar que tengan una dependencia casi absoluta de los vecinos.

- Ocultarles información que. –por el consumo de alcohol y drogas,- les pueda afectar en su desarrollo físico y mental.

- Es un error muy grande, pensar que la educación corresponde a la escuela u otras instituciones y que no se ejerce en el lugar donde vivimos.

- Proponer y fomentar desde la familia actividades con los vecinos de tiempo libre, deportivas, culturales, -que son un buen comienzo en la prevención de las adicciones-.

- Que la administración en turno, establezca y facilite el contacto de los adolescentes con asociaciones juveniles y ONG's

- Pensar que la experiencia, los errores, los buenos vecinos y la vida los ayudarán a resolver los problemas con las adicciones.
  Es necesaria la intervención familiar, de la administración, y profesional.

CAPÍTULO 6

El blindaje contra un vecino toxico

Caer en la provocación de un vecino tóxico, -en cualquiera de las modalidades que en este libro hemos enumerado,- es la peor de las ideas. Es primordial que no entres en sus juegos. Sigue con tus propias estrategias de convivencia. Lo que los distintos tipos de vecinos quieren de otro vecino que no se comporta de acuerdo a ninguna de las descripciones aquí expuestas es, - incluidos los psicópatas,- precisamente provocar a que los más normales, jueguen sus juegos patológicos,- entre los que destaca el conflicto y cuyas reglas él inventó, y que por lo tanto, él domina.

De esas reglas, la que le resulta más eficaz, es un mecanismo de comunicación negativo, que echa a andar simultáneamente con el inicio del conflicto y la provocación, en alguna de sus diferentes manifestaciones; verbal, escrita, corporal, y que hace que el otro interprete, que se encuentra en una situación de riesgo.

Si este es el caso, es muy importante identificar, el tipo de conflicto y si se considera funcional o disfuncional, por sus efectos y/o consecuencias.

Los conflictos funcionales son aquellos cuya intensidad puede considerarse moderada, por su naturaleza y no son amenazantes porque mantienen y mejoran el desempeño de las partes ante la toma de decisiones comunes. Ante este tipo de conflictos, no es necesaria la confrontación. Este tipo de conflicto, que puede ser constructivo, no es el que le interesa al vecino tóxico.

Los conflictos disfuncionales, si son los que le interesan, y por el contrario, sí son confrontativos y tensionan las relaciones de las personas que viven en el mismo lugar del vecino tóxico. No resolver este tipo de conflicto, puede afectar severamente la convivencia. Hay que atenderlo para evitar daños mayores.

Podemos decir que reconocer que el conflicto existe es crucial para su solución, pues de ello dependen las estrategias que se aplicarán, así como los resultados esperados.

Es de vital importancia delimitar el conflicto. Recomendamos;

a) Reconocer a los involucrados. Conocer a los involucrados nos dice cuántos y quiénes son.

En esta lógica resultan relevantes las posturas flexibles

b) Analizar la circunstancia en la que se ubica el conflicto.

Sus causas y los factores que influyen, si son internos o externos

Los conflictos, según sea el caso, requieren mecanismos diferentes para su solución, pues mientras unos ponen énfasis en la persuasión y el convencimiento, los otros implican sanciones.

c) Identificar las fuentes del conflicto. Generalmente, el clima de conflicto en un grupo crece, en relación a la cantidad de gente que lo integra.

d) Intentar la mediación de un tercero, como estrategia para la solución no violenta de conflictos.

La evasión es una solución que se presenta con mucha frecuencia entre los vecinos tóxicos, pues no reconocen que son el origen del conflicto latente, y se defienden con actitudes gandallas e indolentes perpetuando un problema que pudo haberse evitado, y niegan el diálogo como herramienta principal de cualquier desacuerdo.
Aceptarlo implica, el inicio de la solución y el fin del conflicto.
Pero eso, el vecino tóxico, no lo puede permitir.
Un conflicto confrontativo, siempre va a generar respuestas incompatibles de las partes involucradas en el mismo y nunca resuelve la situación; más bien la recrudece.
Los conflictos son en si mismos, directos, indirectos, abiertos, encubiertos, evolutivos o involutivos. La violencia que se desarrolla como

parte del conflicto, no es inherente a la vida; la violencia si lo es, aunque el vecino tóxico tratará de convencernos de que si es parte natural de la vida. Esta violencia surge, ante la imposibilidad del vecino tóxico, para enfrentar el conflicto que él mismo creó, con autocontrol, negociación, mediación, o diálogo. Asimismo, los conflictos tienen distintas características como son, manifiestas, invisibles, inexistentes, encubiertas e institucionalizadas. Independientemente de la modalidad del conflicto, el vecino tóxico va a negar que él lo inició. Cuando se le informa que sus vecinos lo señalan a él, como el autor intelectual del conflicto, este revira con toda su fuerza y responde que lo quieren perjudicar y que él tiene influencias que utilizará para perjudicar a sus vecinos.

En el contexto de los conflictos que el vecino tóxico crea, el vecino tóxico se apoya en un tipo de conflicto que le conviene mucho; el conflicto que los estudiosos del tema llaman "inexistente", y que es particularmente importante, porque el vecino agredido por el tóxico, no se da por aludido e incluso justifica al vecino tóxico, por miedo a las represalias. Por lo tanto, y ante la falta de reconocimiento del vecino agredido, de los abusos del tóxico, estas agresiones pasan a formar parte de las rutinas habituales del vecindario o condominio.
Cuando el conflicto tiene la característica de conflicto "encubierto" tampoco es fácil su solución, porque en su interior se esconden una

cadena de más conflictos menores, lesiones y agresiones sin resolver y por ello no son posibles las soluciones efectivas.

Así vemos, que hay distintas modalidades en los conflictos, que el vecino tóxico utiliza y que las características de cada modalidad,- y del propio vecino tóxico,- impiden su solución.

En este punto, y cuando han fracasado el diálogo, la mediación y/o la negociación, lo mejor es que el conflicto se presente ante las instancias judiciales formales.

Es muy posible, que el conflicto no se resuelva, sin embargo, si se aplaza, se transforma al perder intensidad y se reglamenta.

De este modo, el vecino tóxico pierde el control y la dirección del conflicto.

Ya hay una autoridad externa que lo administra quitándole a él, el protagonismo. Entonces, en la mayoría de los casos, pierde interés en continuar, no por las sanciones, sino porque éste ya no maneja el conflicto. Pero el vecino tóxico, no puede dejar de serlo.

Por lo tanto, y como en su lógica ya perdió la batalla, cambiará de estrategia, porque las personas tóxicas no pueden dejar de hacer lo que saben hacer y lo que les produce placer y sensación de poder; que es violentar a los de su entorno.

Así es que cambiará de estrategia. En vez de crear otro gran conflicto, creará muchos miniconflictos permanentemente. En este caso, lo que conviene, es evitar por completo al vecino tóxico. "Engancharse" otra vez, solo reforzara el mecanismo de este vecino tóxico, quién como parte de su patología, siempre buscará reconocimiento, incluso a sus actitudes patológicas. El usará estos miniconflictos, para readministrar su poder y recuperarlo.

Gradualmente, los miniconflictos pueden empezar a escalar, porque el escalamiento es también una estrategia de este vecino tóxico, para recuperar el poder perdido. Necesita por todos los medios, tener un rol como estratega de poder.

Es importante distinguir entre agresión y violencia, porque no son sinónimos, aunque comparten características. La agresividad es natural y forma parte de la estructura de personalidad de una persona, que en determinado momento y ante circunstancias específicas puede reaccionar agresivamente.

Entre estas características ocupa un primer lugar la incertidumbre que todos tenemos, ante nuevas reglas del juego de la economía global, ante las cuales la mayoría de las personas no podemos hacer nada y que en una comunidad, se constituyen como una amenaza y un riesgo cotidianos. En otras personas surge la agresividad frente a la búsqueda permanente de una identidad

La agresividad derivada de estas condiciones es natural, pero la violencia no. La violencia, es el común denominador de quiénes tienen un factor psicopático en algún grado.

Esta violencia se puede agravar o no, dependiendo de las normas culturales y de convivencia de cada comunidad, aunque en el caso de México hemos comprobado, que las normas reguladoras de la convivencia entre los vecinos de los conjuntos residenciales, condominios y unidades habitacionales, es generalmente mala por razones históricas en un primer momento, y después, por razones que refuerza la familia, la administración del condominio, la sociedad y hasta el Estado.

Recordemos que para un vecino psicópata no es posible eliminar del todo la violencia, pero para quienes viven en su mismo edificio o condominio, es de vital importancia reconocer si la ejerce este vecino solo, o está acompañado por terceros, si esos terceros tienen la misma condición o no, en qué proporción va a ejercer esta violencia y contra quién o quiénes.

Especial interés tenemos por la multiplicación de conductas violentas protagonizadas por niños y adolescentes tan frecuente en condominios y unidades habitacionales. Estos protagonistas realizan estos actos violentos en la mayoría de los casos, "para ver qué se siente". Debemos aprender a distinguir, si estos niños y adolescentes actúan por impulsividad y por hiperactividad, o si en esas conductas, hay elementos psicopáticos que podrían convertir a estos niños y adolescentes en los futuros vecinos psicópatas.

No debemos, ni podemos renunciar a combatir y evitar la violencia en el lugar en el que vivimos, pero como muy probablemente el diálogo y la mediación no serán suficientes con un vecino psicópata, entonces habrá que hacerlo por los medios adecuados, que son las acciones legales.

Hoy en día, las leyes penales no solo están diseñadas para los criminales; están diseñadas para la gente común y corriente y son en su mayoría leyes que intentan defender y proteger delitos contra la propiedad privada y distintos tipos de fraudes, principalmente.

CAPITULO 7

Plan de Protección Vecinal

Es indispensable formar un Comité de Protección Vecinal.
Los objetivos principales de este comité son; establecer la estrategia(s) de acción y reacción en emergencias, y discutir las acciones a seguir, especialmente en el tema de la seguridad personal, de todos los vecinos, pero principalmente de aquellos que viven contiguos a los vecinos tóxicos.

Hay que aprender a reconocer actividades,- si generan violencia o no,- las personas y vehículos sospechosos (podrían ser robados) en el condominio, conjunto residencial o unidad habitacional, con el fin de alertar a los vecinos y actuar en consecuencia.
Muchos vecinos pueden pasar por alto, alguna circunstancia o actividad que puede ser el comienzo de la comisión de delitos menores o mayores o que pueden generar emergencias en el condominio, y también pueden exagerar en el hecho de estar en riesgo solo porque su vecino está alcoholizado. Por eso es de vital importancia reconocer uno y otro caso.

Con el fin de hacer un reporte preventivo o informativo adecuado ya sea a nivel de los vecinos o una denuncia formal a las autoridades correspondientes, es importante que todos los vecinos cercanos al vecino adicto, sepan cómo hacerlo. Para ello, debería aprender como describir correctamente un evento, un vehículo o una persona, comenzando con la fecha, hora, los hechos concretos y las soluciones que los vecinos proponen.

¿Por qué crear un comité de Vigilancia Vecinal?

- La Vigilancia Vecinal lucha contra el aislamiento que crea miedo y la oportunidad para la realización de delitos y ese mismo miedo lo fomenta y acrecienta.
- Forja vínculos entre los vecinos
- Ayuda a reducir los robos y atracos sobre los bienes y las personas
- Se puede difundir internamente el Plan a todos los vecinos, incluido el o los vecinos tóxicos con el fin de que esté enterado que sus vecinos están organizados y unidos.

ANEXO

A continuación presentamos las disposiciones y ordenamientos jurídicos más importantes que norman la Ley de Propiedad en Condominio, con la finalidad de que conozca sus derechos y obligaciones.

LEY DE PROPIEDAD EN CONDOMINIO DE INMUEBLES PARA EL DISTRITO FEDERAL

TÍTULO PRIMERO

DE LA PROPIEDAD EN CONDOMINIO DE INMUEBLES

CAPÍTULO I

DISPOSICIONES GENERALES

Artículo 1. Las disposiciones de esta Ley son de orden público e interés social y tienen por objeto regular la constitución, organización, funcionamiento, administración y extinción del Régimen de Propiedad en Condominio.

Asimismo regulará las relaciones entre los condóminos y/o poseedores y entre éstos y su administración, estableciendo las bases para resolver las controversias que se susciten con motivo de tales relaciones, mediante la conciliación, el arbitraje, a través de la Procuraduría Social del Distrito Federal, sin perjuicio de la competencia que corresponda a otras autoridades judiciales o administrativas.

Artículo 2. Para efectos de esta Ley, se entiende por **ADMINISTRADOR CONDOMINO**: Es el condómino de la unidad de propiedad privativa, que no siendo administrador profesional, sea nombrado Administrador por la Asamblea General.

ADMINISTRADOR PROFESIONAL: Persona física o moral, que demuestre capacidad o conocimientos en administración de condominios que es nombrado por la Asamblea General.

AREAS Y BIENES DE USO COMÚN: Son aquellos que pertenecen en forma proindiviso a los condóminos, y su uso estará regulado por esta Ley, su Reglamento, la Escritura Constitutiva y el Reglamento Interno.

ASAMBLEA GENERAL: Es el órgano del condominio que constituye la máxima instancia en la toma de decisiones para expresar, discutir y resolver asuntos de interés propio y común, celebrada en los términos de la presente Ley, su Reglamento, Escritura Constitutiva y el Reglamento Interno.

CONDOMINIO: Inmueble cuya propiedad pertenece proindiviso a varias personas, que reúne las condiciones y características establecidas en el Código Civil para el Distrito Federal.

CONDÓMINO: Persona física o moral, propietaria de una o más unidades de propiedad privativa y, para los efectos de esta Ley y su Reglamento, a la que haya celebrado contrato en virtud del cual, de cumplirse en sus términos, llegue a ser propietario bajo el régimen de propiedad en condominios.

COMITÉ DE VIGILANCIA: Organo de control integrado por condóminos electos en la Asamblea General, cuyo cometido, entre otros, es evaluar, vigilar y dictaminar, el puntual desempeño del las tareas del administrador, así como la ejecución de los acuerdos y decisiones tomadas por la Asamblea General en torno a todos los asuntos comunes del condominio.

CONJUNTO CONDOMINAL: Toda aquella agrupación de dos o más condominios construidos en un solo predio, siempre que cada uno de dichos condominios conserve para sí, las áreas de uso exclusivo y a su vez existan áreas de uso común para todos los condóminos que integran el conjunto.

CUOTA ORDINARIA: Cantidad monetaria acordada por la Asamblea General para sufragar los gastos de administración, mantenimiento, de reserva, operación y servicios no individualizados de uso común.

CUOTA EXTRAORDINARIA: Cantidad monetaria acordada por la Asamblea General para sufragar los gastos imprevistos o extraordinarios.

DELEGACIÓN: El Órgano Político Administrativo en cada demarcación territorial.

ESCRITURA CONSTITUTIVA: Documento público mediante el cual se constituye un inmueble bajo el régimen de propiedad en condominio.

REGLAMENTO INTERNO: Instrumento que regula el uso de las áreas comunes y establece las bases de sana convivencia al interior del condominio, el cual complementa y especifica las disposiciones de esta Ley de acuerdo a las características de cada condominio.

REGLAMENTO: Es el Reglamento de la Ley de Propiedad en Condominio de Inmuebles para la CDMX.

TÍTULO SEGUNDO

DEL CONDOMINIO, DE SU UNIDAD DE PROPIEDAD PRIVATIVA Y DE LAS AREAS Y BIENES DE USO COMÚN

CAPÍTULO I
DEL CONDOMINIO Y SU UNIDAD DE PROPIEDAD PRIVATIVA

Artículo 14. Se entiende por condómino, a la persona propietaria de una o más unidades de propiedad privativa.

Se considerarán como partes integrantes del derecho de propiedad y del uso exclusivo del condómino, los elementos anexos que le correspondan, tales como estacionamiento, cuarto de servicio, jaulas de tendido, lavaderos y cualquier otro que no sea elemento de áreas y bienes de uso común y que forme parte de su unidad de propiedad privativa, según la escritura constitutiva, y éstos no podrán ser objeto de enajenación, embargo, arrendamiento o comodato en forma independiente.

Artículo 15. El derecho de copropiedad de cada condómino sobre las áreas y bienes de uso común será proporcional al indiviso de su unidad de propiedad privativa, fijada en la escritura constitutiva del condominio.

Artículo 16. Cada condómino poseedor y en general los ocupantes del condominio, tienen el derecho del uso de todos los bienes comunes incluidas las áreas verdes y gozar de los servicios e instalaciones generales, conforme a su naturaleza y destino, sin restringir o hacer más gravoso el derecho de los demás, pues en caso contrario se le aplicarán las sanciones previstas en esta ley, sin perjuicio de las responsabilidades civil o penal en que pueda incurrir. Si existiera una afectación a las áreas verdes, el administrador o condóminos poseedores, deberán dar aviso a la Procuraduría Ambiental.

Son derechos de los condóminos o poseedores:

I Contar con el respeto de los demás condóminos y poseedores sobre su unidad de propiedad privativa.

II Participar con voz y voto en las asambleas generales de condóminos, de conformidad con el artículo 31 de la presente Ley.

III Usar y disfrutar en igualdad de circunstancias y en forma ordenada, las áreas y bienes de uso común del condominio, sin restringir el derecho de los demás.

IV Formar parte de la administración del condominio en calidad de Administrador Condómino, y en su caso, con la misma retribución y responsabilidad del administrador profesional, excepto la exhibición de la fianza.

V Solicitar a la administración, información respecto del estado que guardan los fondos de mantenimiento, administración y de reserva.

VI Acudir ante la Procuraduría para solicitar su intervención, por violaciones a la presente Ley, su Reglamento, al Reglamento Interno de los condóminos, poseedores y/o autoridades al interior del condominio.

VII Denunciar ante las autoridades competentes, hechos posiblemente constitutivos de algún delito en agravio del condominio.

VIII Cada propietario podrá realizar las reparaciones y obras necesarias al interior de su unidad de propiedad privativa, quedando prohibida toda modificación o innovación que afecte la estructura, muros de carga u otros elementos esenciales del edificio o que puedan poner en peligro la estabilidad, seguridad, salubridad del mismo; de conformidad con las leyes y reglamentos correspondientes.

Artículo 17. Cada propietario o condómino, y en general los habitantes del condominio, usarán su unidad de propiedad privativa en forma ordenada y tranquila. No podrán, en consecuencia, destinarla a usos contrarios a su destino, ni hacerla servir a otros objetos que los contenidos expresados en su escritura constitutiva.

Artículo 18. Cuando un condómino no ejerza sus derechos o renuncie a usar determinadas áreas y bienes de uso común, no es causa excluyente para cumplir con las obligaciones que le impone esta Ley, su Reglamento, la escritura constitutiva, el reglamento Interno y demás disposiciones legales aplicables.

Artículo 19. El condómino puede usar, gozar y disponer de su unidad de propiedad privativa, con las limitaciones y modalidades de esta ley.

El condómino o poseedor o cualquier otro cesionario del uso, convendrán entre sí quién debe cumplir determinadas obligaciones ante los demás condóminos y en que caso el usuario tendrá la representación del condómino en las asambleas que se celebren, pero en todo momento el usuario será solidario de las obligaciones del condómino.

Ambos harán oportunamente las notificaciones correspondientes al Administrador y a la Asamblea General mediante documento firmado por ambas partes, en tiempo y forma reglamentaria, para los efectos que procedan.

Artículo 20. El derecho de preferencia respecto de la compra y venta respecto de una o varias unidades de propiedad privativa, se sujetará a lo dispuesto en el Código Civil para el Distrito Federal.

Artículo 21. Queda prohibido a los condóminos poseedores y en general a toda persona y habitantes del condominio:

I Destinarla a usos distintos al fin establecido en la escritura constitutiva.

II Realizar acto alguno que afecte la tranquilidad de los demás condóminos, que comprometa la estabilidad, seguridad, salubridad y comodidad del condominio, o incurrir en omisiones que produzcan los mismos resultados.

Efectuar todo acto en su unidad en el exterior o interior de su unidad de propiedad privativa que impida o haga ineficaz la operación de los servicios comunes e instalaciones generales, estorbe o dificulte el uso de las áreas y bienes de uso común, incluyendo las áreas verdes y que ponga en riesgo la seguridad y tranquilidad de los condóminos , así como abrir claros, puertas o ventanas, que afecten la estructura, muros de carga u otros elementos esenciales del edificio o que puedan perjudicar su estabilidad, seguridad, salubridad o comodidad.

IV En uso habitacional realizar obras y reparaciones en horario nocturno, salvo los casos de fuerza mayor. Para el caso de uso comercial o servicios, industrial o mixto, la Asamblea General de Condóminos acordará los horarios que mejor convengan al destino del condominio.

V Decorar, pintar o realizar obras que modifiquen la fachada o las paredes exteriores, desentonando con el condominio, o que contravengan lo establecido o aprobado por la Asamblea General.

Artículo VI Derribar, trasplantar, podar talar u ocasionar la muerte de uno o más árboles , cambiar el uso o naturaleza de las áreas verdes, ni aun o por acuerdo de la Asamblea General.

VII. Delimitar con cualquier tipo de material o pintar con señalamientos de exclusividad , como techar o realizar construcciones que indiquen exclusividad en el área de estacionamiento u otra área de uso común del condominio, excepto las áreas verdes ión y conservación preferentemente con vegetación arbórea, según acuerde la Asamblea General o quien estos designen; salvo los destinados para personas con discapacidad.

VIII. Hacer uso de los estacionamientos y áreas de uso común para fines distintos;

IX. Poseer animales que por su número, tamaño o naturaleza, afecten las condiciones de seguridad, salubridad o comodidad de los condóminos. En todos los casos, los condóminos poseedores serán absolutamente responsables de las acciones de los animales que introduzcan al condominio, observando lo dispuesto en la Ley de Protección de los Animales en el Distrito Federal;

X. Ocupar otro cajón de estacionamiento distinto al asignado; para el caso de las fracciones I a la X de este artículo se aplicará de manera supletoria la Ley de Cultura Cívica del DF y demás leyes aplicables.

Artículo 22. La realización de las obras que requieran los entrepisos, suelos, pavimentos u otras divisiones colindantes en los condominios, asi como su costo, serán obligatorios para los condóminos colindantes, siempre y cuando, la realización de la obra no derive de un daño causado por uno de los condóminos.

En los condominios de construcción vertical, las obras que requieran los techos en su parte exterior, y los sótanos, serán por cuenta de todos los condóminos, así como la reparación de los desperfectos ocasionados por sismos, hundimientos diferenciales o por cualquier otro fenómeno natural.

CAPITULO II
DE LAS AREAS Y BIENES DE USO COMÚN

Artículo 23. Son objeto de propiedad común:

I. El terreno, los cimientos, las estructuras, muros de carga, fachadas, techos y azoteas de uso general, los sótanos, azoteas, pórticos, galerías, puertas de entrada, vestíbulos, corredores, escaleras, elevadores, patios, áreas verdes, senderos, plazas, calles interiores, instalaciones deportivas, de recreo, los lugares destinados a áreas deportivas, reuniones sociales, asi como los lugares señalados para estacionamiento de vehículos incluidos de visitas, excepto los señalados en la escritura Constitutiva como unidad de propiedad privativa.

II. Los locales, infraestructura, mobiliario e información destinada a la administración, portería y alojamiento del portero y los vigilantes y los destinados a las instalaciones generales y servicios comunes.

III. Las obras, aparatos mecánicos, eléctricos, subestación, bombas, motores, fosas, pozos, cisternas, tinacos, cámaras y monitores, luminarias, montacargas, incineradores, hornos, canales, redes de distribución de agua, drenaje, calefacción, aire acondicionado, electricidad y gas; los locales y zonas de carga y descarga, obras de seguridad, de ornato, acopio de basura y otras semejantes, con excepción de las que sirvan a cada unidad de propiedad privativa, que asi lo estipule la Escritura Constitutiva.

IV. Los recursos, equipos, muebles e inmuebles derivados de donaciones o convenios, asi como la aplicación de programas, subsidios y otras acciones de la Administración Pública;

V. Cualesquiera otras partes del inmueble o instalaciones del condominio no mencionadas, que se resuelvan por acuerdo de la Asamblea General o que se establezcan con tal carácter en la Escritura Constitutiva y/o en el Reglamento Interno del condominio. Los condóminos vigilarán y exigirán al administrador a través del Comité de Vigilancia, Asamblea General o Sesión del Consejo, que se lleve un inventario completo y actualizado de todos los objetos, bienes muebles e inmuebles propiedad del condominio, citados en las fracciones II, II, IV y V, asi como de los que en lo sucesivo se adquieran o se den a la baja.

Los bienes de propiedad común no podrán ser objeto de posesión y/o usufructo exclusivo de condóminos, poseedores o terceros y en ningún caso podrán enajenarse a un particular ni integrar o formar parte de otro régimen condominal, a excepción de los bienes muebles que se encuentran en desuso, previa aprobación de la Asamblea General.

Artículo 24. Serán de propiedad común, sólo entre las unidades de propiedad privativa colindantes, los entrepisos, muros y demás divisiones que compartan entre sí. De tal manera, que las obras que requieran éstas, así como su costo será a cargo de los condóminos y poseedores colindantes siempre y cuando la realización de la obra no derive de un daño causado por uno de los condóminos.

Artículo 25. En los condominios verticales, horizontales y mixtos, ningún condómino, independientemente de la ubicación de su unidad de propiedad privativa, podrá tener más derecho que el resto de los condóminos en las áreas comunes.

Salvo que lo establezca la Escritura Constitutiva del Régimen de Propiedad en Condominio, los condóminos de la planta baja, no podrán hacer obras, ocupar para su uso exclusivo o preferente sobre los demás condóminos, los vestíbulos, sótanos, jardines, patios, ni otros espacios de tal planta considerada como áreas y bienes de uso común, incluidos los destinados a cubos de luz.

Asimismo, los condóminos del último piso, no podrán ocupar la azotea, ni elevar nuevas construcciones. Las mismas restricciones son aplicables a los demás condóminos del inmueble.

En el caso de que cualquier condómino haga caso omiso de los párrafos anteriores, de conformidad a lo señalado en el artículo 88 de esta Ley, el administrador o condómino deberá solicitar la intervención de la Delegación correspondiente.

El Órgano Político Administrativo emitirá en un lapso no mayor a 10 días hábiles, la orden de visita de verificación y medidas para evitar que continúe la construcción, término en el que dará respuesta a la demanda ciudadana.

Artículo 26.
    I.   Las obras necesarias para mantener el condominio en

buen estado de seguridad, estabilidad y conservación y para que los servicios funcionen normalmente se efectuarán por el Administrador, previa manifestación de construcción tipo A, B o C.

II. El propietario(s) del condominio en caso de enajenación, responderán por el saneamiento para el caso de evicción. Tratándose de construcciones nuevas, el propietario(s) original(es), del condominio serán responsables por los defectos o vicios ocultos de las construcciones, extinguiéndose las acciones correspondientes a los tres años posteriores a la entrega del área afectada.

III. Para realizar obras nuevas, excepto en áreas verdes, que no impliquen la modificación de la Escritura Constitutiva y se traduzcan en mejor aspecto o mayor comodidad, se requerirá acuerdo aprobatorio de la Asamblea General, a la que deberán asistir la mayoría simple de los condóminos, cumpliendo con lo señalado en la fracción IV, art. 32 de esta Ley.

IV. Los gastos que se originen con motivo de la operación, reparación, conservación y mantenimiento de las instalaciones y servicios generales destinadas a servir a una sección del condominio serán cubiertos por todos los condóminos de esa sección, de acuerdo a lo establecido en el art. 55 de esta Ley; y

V. Tratándose de los gastos que se originen por la prestación del servicio de energía eléctrica, agua y otros en las áreas de bienes comunes, se cubrirán de acuerdo a lo establecido en las fracciones VI y VII de este artículo. El proveedor incluirá la cantidad respectiva en la factura o recibo que individualmente se expedirán a cada condómino por el servicio en su unidad de propiedad privativa.

Artículo 27. Los Órganos Políticos Administrativos y demás autoridades de la administración pública, podrán aplicar recursos públicos para el mejoramiento de las propiedades habitacionales, mantenimiento, servicios, obras y reparaciones en áreas y bienes de uso común; así como para implementar acciones en materia de seguridad pública, procuración de justicia, salud sanitaria y protección civil en casos urgentes que pongan en peligro la vida o integridad física de los condóminos. Sin menoscabo de la propiedad o dominio de los condóminos y sin contravenir esta Ley y los ordenamientos jurídicos aplicables. Lo anterior bastará con la petición de un condómino, sin que ello impida que la misma Asamblea General contrate servicios profesionales para estos fines.

Artículo 28. Los créditos generados por las unidades de propiedad privativa, que la Asamblea General haya determinado, por concepto de cuotas de mantenimiento, administración, extraordinarias y/o fondo de reserva, intereses moratorios y demás cuotas que la Asamblea General determine y que no hayan sido cubiertas por el condómino de la unidad privativa. Por lo que al transmitirse la propiedad en cualquier forma, el nuevo condómino adquirirá la unidad de propiedad privativa con la carga de dichos créditos, y deberá constar en el instrumento mediante el cual se adquiera la propiedad, por lo que dichos créditos se cubrirán preferentemente y sus titulares gozarán del derecho que establece en su favor el artículo 2993 fracción X, del Código Civil del Distrito Federal.

TÍTULO TERCERO

DE LAS ASAMBLEAS Y TIPOS DE ORGANIZACIÓN DE LOS CONDOMINIOS

CAPÍTULO I

DE LAS FACULTADES DE LA ASAMBLEA GENERAL

Artículo 29. Esta Ley, su Reglamento, la Escritura Constitutiva y el Reglamento Interno del condominio, son los que establecen las características y condiciones para la organización y funcionamiento social del condominio.

El Órgano máximo del condominio es la Asamblea General.

Las asambleas generales por su tipo, podrán ser ordinarias y extraordinarias.

I Las asambleas generales extraordinarias se celebrarán cuando menos cada seis meses teniendo como finalidad informar el estado que guarda la administración del condominio, asi como tratar los asuntos concernientes al mismo;

II Las asambleas generales extraordinarias se celebrarán cuando haya asuntos de carácter urgente que atender y cuando se trate de los siguientes asuntos:

Cualquier modificación a la escritura constitutiva del condominio o su reglamento interno de conformidad a lo establecido por esta Ley.

Para la extinción voluntaria del régimen
Para realizar obras nuevas
Para acordar lo conducente en caso de destrucción, ruina o reconstrucción.

Artículo 30. Así también podrán celebrarse otro tipo de asambleas, siempre sujetas a la Asamblea General, su Reglamento y su Reglamento Interno.

I Las de administradores que se celebrarán en el caso de un conjunto condominal o cuando el condominio se hubiese subdividido en razón de haber adoptado una organización por secciones o grupos, para tratar los asuntos relativos a los bienes de uso común del conjunto condominal o condominio. Serán convocadas por el comité de administración del mismo:

II Las de sección o grupo que se celebrarán cuando el condominio se compone de diferentes edificios, alas, secciones, manzanas, entradas y áreas en donde se tratarán asuntos de áreas internas en común qe solo dan servicio o sirven a las mismas; serán convocadas de acuerdo a lo establecido en el Artículo 32 de esta ley y sus determinaciones en ningún caso podrán contravenir o afectar las decisiones de la Asamblea general del condominio.

TÍTULO OCTAVO
DE LAS SANCIONES

CAPÍTULO ÚNICO

Artículo 86. Las violaciones establecidas por la presente Ley, su Reglamento y demás disposiciones que de ella emanen, serán sancionadas por la Procuraduría en el ámbito de su competencia.

Lo anterior será de acuerdo a lo establecido en la presente Ley, su Reglamento, Escritura Constitutiva y Reglamento Interno.

Artículo 87. La contravención a las disposiciones de esta ley establecidas en los artículos 14, 16, 19, 21, 25, 43, 44, 49, 59 y 73:
I Por faltas que afecten la tranquilidad o la comodidad de la vida condominal, se aplicarán multas por el equivalente de diez a cien días de salario mínimo general en el DF;
II Por faltas que afecten el estado físico del inmueble sin que esto signifique poner en riesgo la seguridad de los condóminos;
III Por faltas que provoquen daño patrimonial;
IV Por incumplimiento en el pago oportuno de las cuotas de mantenimiento;
V Los administradores o Comité de Vigilancia que no hagan un buen manejo de las cuotas de los servicios;
VI Se aplicará multa de 50 a 200 días de salario mínimo general a la persona o administrador que tenga bajo su custodia el libro de actas y que no lo presente en una Asamblea General;
VII Se aplicará multa de 50 a 300 días de salario mínimo general por incumplimiento a lo dispuesto en el artículo 44 de la presente Ley, a los Administradores realicen cobros no previstos en esta Ley;

Artículo 88. Las sanciones establecidas en la presente Ley, se aplicarán independientemente de las que se impongan por la violación de otras disposiciones aplicables.

La Asamblea General podrá resolver en una reunión especial convocada para tal efecto, y de acuerdo a lo establecido en el artículo 32 de la presente Ley, para tomar las siguientes medidas:

I Iniciar las acciones civiles correspondientes para obligar al condómino que incumpla con las obligaciones de la presente Ley.

II En caso de que dicho incumplimiento sea reiterado o grave, se podrá demandar ante los Juzgados civiles, las sanciones y la enajenación del inmueble y la rescisión del contrato que le permite ser poseedor derivado.

III Solicitar a la delegación ordene la verificación administrativa cuando se estén realizando obras sin la autorización correspondiente.

Artículo 89. Para la imposición de las sanciones, la Procuraduría deberá adoptar las medidas de apremio de acuerdo a lo establecido en la Ley de la Procuraduría Social del DF.

El resto de los capítulos puedes consultarlos en la AGENDA CIVIL PARA EL DF, en el apartado de la Ley de Propiedad en Condominio de Inmuebles para el DF.

OTRAS LEYES

Cuando las leyes más inmediatas al problema, como la Ley de Propiedad en Condominio del Distrito Federal, no son suficientes para controlar el o los problemas con un vecino tóxico, y si se trata de que la persona acosada y/o violentada es una mujer, existen otras disposiciones y leyes que pueden servir como complemento para poner una denuncia.

En el caso de las mujeres, hay diversas disposiciones legales específicas en contra de la violencia contra las mujeres en todos los estados de la República Mexicana. Estas leyes son; la *Ley de Acceso a las Mujeres para una vida libre de violencia*, la *Ley de Asistencia y Prevención de violencia familiar* y la *Ley de Atención Integral para el Desarrollo de las niñas y de los niños*.

Otras leyes internacionales a favor de las mujeres, se remiten a las resoluciones de las Naciones Unidas aprobadas en la *Cumbre Internacional sobre la Mujer*, celebrada en Pekín en 1995, y en la que se considera la violencia contra las mujeres un atentado contra los derechos humanos y las libertades fundamentales y se asume que el "síndrome de la mujer maltratada", como las "agresiones sufridas por la mujer como consecuencia de las condicionantes socioculturales que actúan sobre el género masculino y femenino, y
que influye sobre los tres ámbitos de la relación de la persona; maltrato en las relaciones de pareja, acoso en la vida laboral o vecinal y agresión sexual en la vida social".

Existen además otras leyes del Distrito Federal, que se aplican a la sociedad en su conjunto y son la Ley Ambiental del DF.

Asimismo existe un Decreto de la Ley de Cultura Cívica del DF, que establece las reglas mínimas de comportamiento cívico, y la Procuraduría Social del DF, también tiene diversos ordenamientos legales para la defensa de la cultura cívica.

Para su consulta puedes visitar *www.prosoc.df.gob.mx*

¿Qué hace la Subprocuraduría de Defensa y Exigibilidad de los Derechos Ciudadanos de la PROSOC?

Determina los mecanismos necesarios para que los procedimientos de orientación, queja y conciliación administrativa se realicen de acuerdo a los principios establecidos en la Ley de la Procuraduría Social del Distrito Federal con el fin de defender los derechos ciudadanos relacionados con las funciones públicas y prestación de servicios a cargo de la Administración Pública del Distrito Federal.

Establecer las sugerencias o recomendaciones necesarias a la Administración Pública del Distrito Federal de manera cotidiana, a efecto de cumplir con lo establecido en Ley de la Procuraduría Social del Distrito Federal.

Coordinar y evaluar los servicios de orientación, queja y conciliación administrativa de manera mensual, a fin de que se haga efectiva la exigibilidad de la ciudadanía.

SUBPROCURADURÍA DE DERECHOS Y OBLIGACIONES DE PROPIEDAD EN CONDOMINIO

La Subprocuraduría de Derechos y Obligaciones de Propiedad en Condominio, tiene dentro de sus funciones, establecer las medidas necesarias a fin de asegurar una instancia accesible a los particulares y consolidar el cumplimiento a la Ley de Propiedad en Condominio de Inmuebles para el Distrito Federal.

Asimismo, le compete realizar la función de amigable composición en materia de arrendamiento de inmuebles destinados a vivienda en régimen de propiedad en condominio a fin de legitimar los derechos y obligaciones de los condóminos y sus relacionados en materia condominal. Para el desarrollo de estas funciones realiza diversas actividades como:

CONSTITUCIÓN DEL RÉGIMEN DE PROPIEDAD EN CONDOMINIO.

ORIENTACIÓN CIUDADANA.

ACREDITACIÓN DE CONVOCATORIA DE ASAMBLEA GENERAL DE CONDÓMINOS ORDINARIA Y EXTRAORDINARIA.

ASESORÍA EN ASAMBLEAS GENERALES DE CONDÓMINOS.

REGISTRO DE ADMINISTRADOR DE CONDOMINIO.

AUTORIZACIÓN DE LIBRO DE ACTAS DE ASAMBLEAS.

QUEJA CONDOMINAL.

PROCEDIMIENTO CONCILIATORIO EN MATERIA CONDOMINAL.

PROCEDIMIENTO ARBITRAL EN MATERIA CONDOMINAL.

AMIGABLE COMPOSICIÓN EN MATERIA DE ARRENDAMIENTO.

PROCEDIMIENTO ADMINISTRATIVO DE APLICACIÓN DE SANCIONES (PAAS).

CERTIFICACIÓN DE ADMINISTRADORES PROFESIONALES.

PROCURADURÍA SOCIAL DE LA CDMX

¿HAY VARIOS TIPOS DE ADMINISTRADOR(A)?
Sí. El Administrador(a) Condómino - Condómino nombrado por la Asamblea General.
También el Administrador(a) Profesional - Persona física o moral, que demuestre capacidad y conocimientos en administración de condominios que es contratado por la Asamblea General.

¿CÓMO SE ELIGE?
Por mayoría simple en Asamblea General Ordinaria legalmente convocada.

TELÉFONOS DE EMERGENCIA EN LA CDMX

- ✓ DEFENSATEL/Teléfono de Atención Ciudadana
  Tel: 5128 52 13 al 18

- ✓ ATENCIÓN CIUDADANA 911

Made in the USA
Coppell, TX
25 June 2024

33927706R00059